THINGS WE NEVER SAY

CAITLIN WEAVER

Storm
PUBLISHING

Ebook ISBN: 978-1-80508-668-0
Paperback ISBN: 978-1-80508-670-3

Cover design: Rose Cooper
Cover images: Arcangel

Published by Storm Publishing.
For further information, visit:
www.stormpublishing.co

ALSO BY CAITLIN WEAVER

Such a Good Family

To Marcus, for everything, again and again.

ONE

Anna watched the other women step out of their high-end SUVs, all smiles and carefree greetings, and tried to decide who she'd want to trade lives with. Any of them would do. They all had shiny, blown-out hair, Pilates-toned bodies, and leather totes that cost more than their nannies earned in a month. Anna ran a hand through her own limp shoulder-length hair and reached for her ancient Lululemon cross-body canvas purse, knowing deep down it wasn't the hair or the handbags she envied. It was their freedom.

A sharp rap on her car window startled her. "Are you coming?" Her husband peered in, his eyes narrowing as Anna scrambled to open the door.

"Yes, sorry," she said, getting out. The mid-August Atlanta heat hit her like a wall and she tried to match his brisk pace as they hurried toward the school's main building, an imposing red-brick structure. Inside, Anna hesitated, pointing down the hall. "I need to use the restroom."

Jerry's face soured. "Can't it wait?" he asked. "It's the first parents association meeting of the school year and you're the headmaster's wife. You should be one of the first people in the room." His British accent, so charming when they'd first met, sounded clipped and cross.

"I'll be quick, I promise."

"Fine," he said, swallowing as if to rid himself of a bad taste, his large Adam's apple bobbing in his narrow neck.

She hurried off, hoping his frustration would be forgotten before the two of them were alone again. Once locked in a bathroom stall, she took out her phone and logged into her email via a private browser. Not the account where she received Civitas Academy correspondence, messages from her daughter's lacrosse coach, violin teacher, and math tutor, but the other, secret one set up expressly for this purpose. So far, her inbox contained only five messages, all from him.

Anna reread the early message about how much he'd enjoyed their phone conversation and whether she could meet in person. Then another email immediately after their first meeting, confessing his excitement at meeting her and his hope that it was the beginning of something longer term.

Then the message she'd been waiting for, which had arrived that morning. She reread it for what felt like the hundredth time.

Dear Anna,

On behalf of Roberts, Kaplan, and Monroe LLC, I'm delighted to offer you the part-time position of Legal Consultant. I have attached the job description and the employment contract for your review. Please let me know when you are free to complete some additional paperwork and meet the team briefly. We look forward to welcoming you to the firm.

Sincerely,
Kevin Kaplan, Esq.

A job. Part-time, only twenty hours a week, but still. It felt like a beginning—though of what she wasn't yet sure.

Anna hadn't worked since Farrah was born thirteen years ago. Back then she hadn't wanted to miss a minute of motherhood, and Jerry had recently taken the job as headmaster at Civitas, one of the country's top private schools, relocating them from Chicago to Atlanta. His salary had increased significantly and he'd supported her wish to step away from the long hours at her law firm. She'd been so grateful.

If only she'd known.

Anna drafted a reply.

Dear Kevin,

Thank you for your email. I am thrilled to receive it and look forward to joining the firm.

Sincerely,
Anna

She opened the attached contract and scanned the boilerplate terminology until she came to the signature field. Her finger trembled as it hovered above the screen. It was completely reasonable to go back to work. Farrah was nearly in high school now. Besides, they could use the extra money for a nice vacation. Maybe visit her parents in California and take Farrah to Disneyland, which they hadn't done in six years because Jerry didn't want the expense.

Anna bit her lip and tried to ignore the trepidation that had lodged in her stomach like lead. She would tell Jerry tonight, after the parents association meeting. Maybe he would surprise her by being happy for her.

She stared at the signature line on the document. Then,

taking a deep breath, she scrawled her name and clicked send. Excitement fizzed in her chest.

She noticed the time, and with a jolt of dread realized the meeting had started without her. She hurried out of the stall. In the mirror above the sink she caught sight of her reflection. Her normally pale complexion looked sallow in the fluorescent light and the faint bags under her eyes seemed to have grown. Jerry liked her to wear makeup for Civitas events; he said it made her look "more put together," which Anna knew was code for "more like the other wives." But in the harsh lighting she could see she'd applied too much blush to one cheek, and penciled in one of her sparse eyebrows to be much darker than the other. She grabbed a paper towel and swooped it over her face, blotting, then dashed out of the restroom.

In the classroom, Jerry's face, which she'd once found so handsome, darkened as she entered and her stomach clenched. He wore his thick copper-colored hair short, almost military style, which made his ears stick out slightly. He smoothed it now, and continued welcoming everyone to the first parents association meeting of the school year. Anna slipped into a seat at the back, wiping her sweaty palms on her black pants. The crowd was nearly all mothers; few women who sent their kids to Civitas worked outside the home, and those who did had no time for the mandatory ten volunteer hours per year expected of each family, sometimes even sending their nannies to fulfill it. Anna knew this was viewed dimly by the moms on the PA.

"And now I'll hand the meeting over to Rhea Connelly, our esteemed parents association president," said Jerry. He stepped away from the podium and Anna noted the briefest flicker of distaste in his smile. Rhea held enormous sway over the other moms, so much so that even Jerry was often forced to run decisions by her, something he despised.

"Thanks, Jerry." Rhea tucked a lock of her dark brown,

perfectly waved hair behind her ear and offered a sunny smile. Even in her stacked-heel boots she still had to adjust the microphone downward several inches to accommodate her petite, shapely frame. She wore a sleek, sleeveless slate blue jumpsuit, making Anna feel downright dowdy in her black pants and gray sweater. "I'm going to do my best to keep things moving so we can all get home and back to Netflix," Rhea continued. All the plumped and Botoxed faces laughed as they turned toward Rhea, looking to Anna like subjects recognizing their queen.

At that moment, the door at the back of the classroom banged open. Anna jumped. A tall, dark-blond woman barreled into the room, her face glistening with sweat as she pulled her hair up into a lopsided bun and secured it with a pen. She plopped onto a chair next to Anna. "Maggie Reed," she gasped, waving to the room. "Sorry I'm late. I walked here. Google Maps said it was only twenty minutes, but"—her voice became muffled as she tugged her long-sleeved shirt over her head—"the app doesn't know I'm a middle-aged woman who hasn't exercised in over a decade." She liberated her head from the shirt, revealing a flesh-colored camisole that dug into the rolls of skin at her underarms. Anna was pretty sure it was not meant to be worn on its own.

Rhea's smile tightened in annoyance and she cleared her throat. "I'm sorry, where were we?" She pursed her lips and scanned the iPad in front of her. "Right, our first order of business is—drumroll, please—the Civitas centennial gala." An excited murmur went through the room, and Anna watched Jerry smile with satisfaction. To celebrate the school's birthday he'd planned a week of pomp and circumstance, culminating in the unveiling of the "next hundred years" Civitas strategic plan at a black-tie gala for major donors—of which there were many, given Civitas's reputation as *the* school for the children of Atlanta's "who's who."

"This gala is scheduled for mid-November, only three short months from now," Rhea continued, flashing her signature high-wattage smile. "As we prepare, we need a few volunteers to help with administrative aspects and support fundraising efforts."

Anna enjoyed the passing frown on Rhea's face as everyone suddenly busied themselves looking at their phone. No one wanted to get stuck working on "administrative aspects" of anything at Civitas.

"While not necessarily a glamorous task, it's a very important one," Rhea cajoled everyone. "Which is why I'll personally be helping out. Would anyone else care to join me?"

Anna glanced at Jerry. He'd instructed her to volunteer for the fundraising committee so he'd have eyes and ears on it, but he hadn't told her Rhea would be involved. He returned her glance with a pointed look and she quickly thrust her hand up. "I can do it," she said.

"I can help, too." Next to Anna, Maggie was waving. Her temples were still damp with sweat, and she fanned herself with a manila folder.

"Great, thank you," Rhea said, looking between them. Anna thought she saw her grit her teeth before a bright smile reappeared on her face.

After fulfilling her obligation, Anna's mind drifted to how best to tell Jerry about her new job. Her shoulders hunched and she chewed on a hangnail as she played out different scenarios, but none soothed the churning of her stomach. Maybe she should wait until she knew the role was a good fit; give it a trial period. Her shoulders dropped an inch at the thought of postponing the conversation. Looking up, she saw Rhea striding toward her. Confused, Anna glanced around, then realized she'd been so lost in thought she hadn't noticed the meeting ending.

"Hey." Rhea stopped near Anna and Maggie. Her pale skin was smooth and luminous even under the harsh classroom lighting. "Jerry's anxious for us to get started on confirming RSVPs for the gala," Rhea said, any hint of the manufactured smile she'd held at the front of the room now vanished.

Maggie wrinkled her nose. She'd put her cream-colored shirt back on over her camisole and Anna could make out a small, coffee-colored stain near her left breast. "Wait, why is it our job to confirm RSVPs?" she asked. "Isn't there an administrative assistant who can do that?"

Rhea widened her eyes and gave a slow, disingenuous blink. "Well, I'm sure Anna and I can handle it, if you'd prefer a different committee."

"It was only a question." Maggie held up her hands, her rosy skin turning even brighter red. "I mean, if it were up to me, I'd outsource this whole thing." She looked around the room. "Actually, why isn't Civitas doing that? Having professionals handle the gala seems easier than managing parent volunteers."

Rhea pressed her lips together in impatience. "Professionals are expensive," she said. Two heavy gold bracelets clinked together on her wrist as she flipped her long dark hair over her shoulder.

"Oh, Civitas could afford it," Anna said. Both Maggie and Rhea looked at her in surprise, as though suddenly discovering she could speak. "But volunteering builds community. That's why there's a ten-volunteer-hour requirement per family."

"Right," Maggie said. She removed the pen from her bun, releasing her hair, which fell in kinked, uneven waves. "Because forced labor is always so great for group morale." She laughed at her own joke.

Rhea ignored Maggie. "Anna, you'll get all the info we need from Jerry to get started?" Although phrased as a request, it was clearly an order.

"Sure." Anna nodded. She could never admit it to Jerry, but there was something about Rhea's cool efficiency she admired.

Rhea knew how to get things done and didn't seem to care what anyone else thought.

"My work schedule is tight," Maggie said, "but I'll see if I can find a time for us to meet." She flashed a clumsy thumbs up.

"Great," Rhea said, smiling through clenched teeth.

Anna raised her eyebrows. This was going to be interesting.

TWO

Rhea shut the front door behind her and stepped out of her heeled Blundstone Chelsea boots, the ones she'd bought from Nordstrom's sale rack because hardly anyone else wore a women's size 5. She didn't need to shop on the sale rack, of course. For Rhea, though, it wasn't that old habits die hard, it was that they never died at all. No matter how many zeros there were in her and Brooks's account, deep down she was still the smalltown Texas girl whose mom made chili from the dented cans of beans from the dollar store, and whose dad drove a battered pickup in which the AC conked out if it was over eighty degrees.

"Hello?" she called. Next to her boots on the rack her sons' sneakers looked comically large, like clown shoes. But her sons *were* large now; Zane had turned thirteen last month and Will was sixteen, already driving. She felt like it was only last year he'd been foot-pedaling around the driveway in his red Little Tykes car.

She padded into the living room, eager to change out of her tailored jumpsuit and into sweatpants. There she found her husband's tall, broad-shouldered frame stretched out on the couch, one eye on his laptop and the other on ESPN.

"Hey." Brooks muted the game and closed his laptop. His hair was the color of wet sand and he ran a hand through it as he sat up and opened his arms to her, his warm brown eyes crinkling with a smile.

"Hey yourself." She sank down next to him and nestled into his chest, rubbing her face against the softness of his old gray Duke's Fuqua School of Business T-shirt.

"How was the PA meeting?"

"Meh, the usual." She shrugged. It was her third year as PA president, and while she didn't particularly enjoy all the smiling and politicking the role demanded, she did like the power it afforded her.

"They don't deserve you." Brooks kissed the top of her head. "And neither do I."

Rhea smiled, basking in the warmth of his affection, then looked up as Zane loped into the room. Already five foot seven at thirteen, he was all elbows and knees as he struggled to adjust to the six inches he'd grown in the past year.

"I'm hungry," he announced. His hair was the same color as his father's, but was thicker and coarser than Brooks's. He was in need of a haircut and tonight it sprang up in all directions from where he'd neglected to comb it after dive practice.

Brooks cocked an eyebrow. "How about, 'Hi, Mom, how are you?'" he asked.

"Hey, Mom," Zane mumbled, his brown eyes darting toward her.

"Hi, sweetie," she said, beckoning to him. At thirteen Zane would still let her hug him, whereas with Will the most she got was the occasional one-armed side squeeze. Zane crossed the room and piled on top of his parents on the couch, causing Brooks to yelp.

"What have we been feeding you?"

"Not enough," he grumbled, though he was smiling. "I'm starving." Rhea breathed in his scent, the lingering smell of chlorine from his dive team practice and the deodorant she forced him to wear now that he'd hit puberty. She couldn't imagine anything better.

"I protest," Brooks said, his face smashed into the side of Rhea's head. "You and your brother each consumed an entire large pizza less than an hour ago."

"Yeah, so?" Zane asked.

Rhea's stomach growled. She'd been at Civitas for hours getting ready for the meeting and had missed dinner. "Ooh, pizza," she said. "Is there any left?"

Brooks laughed and pointed at Zane. "What do you think? These kids are going to eat us into the poorhouse."

Rhea laughed, but her jaw tensed. She didn't share Brooks's easy ability to joke about not having enough food or money, two things he'd never experienced as the son of Georgia's largest cotton producer. His father, Hugh Connelly, had parlayed his business success into a career in politics, including the last ten years spent as Georgia's senior U.S. senator.

Rhea, on the other hand, had not grown up in a spacious house with a refrigerator that was never empty. She gazed around her living room now, taking in the tasteful neutral-colored furniture that had been carefully chosen by an interior designer, and the silver-framed family photographs of ski trips and beach vacations arrayed on the bookshelves. She felt a familiar pang as she thought of how close she'd come to not having any of it, all because of one stupid decision.

She ruffled Zane's thick hair and pushed him up off the couch. "Come on," she said. "I'll make grilled cheese."

"Did someone say grilled cheese?" Will sauntered into the room, dressed in his all-season teenage boy uniform of basketball shorts and a T-shirt. He was several inches taller than Zane, but unlike his beanpole brother he'd begun to fill out, thanks to near daily weightlifting sessions with the Civitas basketball team. He had Rhea's startling green eyes and over the summer he'd let his wavy dark brown hair grow long enough to touch his collar. At sixteen he was starting to appear more man than boy. Rhea knew that with his good look and natural athletic ability, he could likely have his pick of girls. Unfortunately, though, he'd settled on dating Pen Reed, Maggie's daughter.

Rhea grinned. "Three grilled cheeses coming up," she said. She hummed as she sliced cheese and got out plates. She knew she should have the boys make their own sandwiches, but they were still used to her cooking for them. And buying their clothes, doing their laundry, and collecting the detritus of backpacks and athletic gear they trailed after them wherever they went. Part of her felt guilty for not fostering more independence in them, but another, bigger part was gratified by their dependence on her.

As she spread mayonnaise on the bread—which any good Texan knew was the secret to a good grilled cheese—she smiled at the sight of her sons on the couch with their father, arguing about the game on TV.

"Shoot the ball already!" called Zane.

"Dude." Will elbowed his brother. "They're trying to play smart and draw the foul." Only a sophomore, Will was already a starter for the Civitas varsity basketball team.

Rhea wondered how many grilled cheese sandwiches she'd prepared for her boys in her lifetime—hundreds, easily. It was one of the only things Will would eat when he was small. She smiled as a carousel of images of both boys as sticky-faced toddlers and chubby babies lazed through her mind. Then, without warning, she was back in the hospital room, sweaty and spent, her body feeling like it had been ripped apart and turned inside out.

"He's all cleaned up; do you want to see him?" the nurse had asked. Rhea had caught a glimpse of a tiny, blanket-wrapped bundle then. Tears leaking from her eyes, she'd turned away with a shake of her head.

"Honey! Honey!" Brooks's voice calling to her from the couch brought her back to the smell of smoking bread.

"The sandwiches!" Rhea gasped, and quickly flipped the sandwiches in the pan, one of which had blackened.

"Sorry," she breathed, offering a weak smile. "That one's mine."

"You OK?" Brooks gave her a concerned glance.

She forced her smile to widen. "Fine, a bit tired, that's all." When he turned back to the game she stuffed the memory deep in her brain.

In her pocket, her phone dinged with a message and she reached for it.

It's Maggie. How's Wednesday next week at 5? Or I could do Tuesday at 7am or 8pm.

Workaholic, much? Rhea thought. Maggie was a semi-renowned relationship therapist and the author of a best-selling book, *Reconnecting Between the Sheets*—which obviously Rhea hadn't read because there was nothing wrong between her sheets.

Wednesday fine for me, she replied.

Same for me, chimed in the third number, which Rhea guessed was Anna. Withholding a groan, she noted the meeting in her calendar.

"Of everyone at Civitas, I get stuck working on the gala committee with Maggie Reed and Anna Armstrong," she complained to Brooks later as they sat next to each other in bed, Rhea with a book and Brooks with his laptop. "I mean, Anna's a classic snob and Maggie... well." Rhea blew out a puff of air. "Maggie's... a *lot*."

"Have you worked with them before on anything?" Brooks asked, looking up from his spreadsheet.

"Well, no," she admitted.

Brooks raised an eyebrow. "So maybe they'll surprise you." His fingers crept under the blanket and began to stroke her leg. "Like you surprised me."

"How did I surprise you?" Rhea asked, even though she'd heard the story many times before.

A playful smile spread across Brooks's face, highlighting his square jaw and making her stomach flutter even after all these years. "Well, one day at the library this gorgeous girl sat down at the table next to me with a whole stack of books. Clearly way smarter than me. Smart and beautiful. Way out of my league." His hand crept higher on her thigh. "It took me a whole hour, but I finally got up the nerve to tap you on the shoulder, and ask to borrow a pencil. And you..." He paused for dramatic effect, widening his eyes. "You looked me straight in the eye and said—"

"I believe there's one in your hand," Rhea finished for him, and they both laughed. He leaned over and kissed her.

"I got so lucky that day," he murmured, pulling her toward him.

Rhea let herself melt into his body. She'd never let on that she already knew who he was when he approached her in the library—everyone did. Brooks was a square-jawed senior whose shaggy, dark blond hair had every girl on campus dying to run her fingers through it. He'd been accepted to an MBA program and had his own American Express card, courtesy of his father. Whereas Rhea was a freshman, living off student loans and her waitressing job. So deep down, Rhea had always known she was the lucky one.

But she also knew that if anyone ever found out her secret, her luck would run out.

THREE

Maggie escorted the couple out via the private entrance to her office, then opened the door connecting her office to the house, grateful for a short break. It had been an exhausting session. Maggie could hardly blame the wife for having an affair, which they were in therapy to discuss. The husband was as dull as a paper Dixie cup. Moments like these made her wish she could bluntly inform them their marriage wasn't going to work.

It was almost 5 p.m. and she had just enough time for a brisk walk before her next client arrived. Daily exercise was part of a long list of private pledges she'd made to jumpstart herself out of something that resembled a rut.

Slipping on sneakers in place of her Rothy's flats (today's were Kelly green—Maggie had the exact same pair in a rainbow of colors), she stepped outside. Her husband's Volvo was backing down the driveway.

"Hey," she said as he stopped and rolled down the window, still wearing his scrubs. "What happened to racquetball with Fernando?" Dan had a standing weekly gym date with his best friend from dental school.

Dan smiled, revealing the wrinkles around his blue eyes

that had showed up in the last year. "I'm grabbing my equipment—I forgot it earlier."

Maggie thought back to the early days of their relationship, when they spent every spare moment together, strolling around the University of Pennsylvania campus or watching *Grey's Anatomy* in Dan's dorm room. She shook her head, rolled up the sleeves of her cream-colored blouse—only neutral colors were allowed in her professional wardrobe (not including shoes). She of all people should know it was normal for relationships to settle into routine.

"Did you see the invitation for the Civitas homecoming fun fair?" Maggie asked, wrinkling her nose. She never would have chosen Atlanta's most elite private school for her daughter, where most of Pen's friends' families boasted net worths that surpassed the GDP of small countries. But Dan's father, Dan, and his brother had all attended, and Maggie's in-laws covered Pen's tuition, leaving her with little say in the matter.

"I got it," Dan said, pushing his hair back from his forehead. It was the color of the milky coffee he'd started letting Pen drink, much to Maggie's disapproval. "I RSVP'd and, as a romantic gesture, I left you off as my plus one."

"Thanks," Maggie said. "Oh, could you pick up Pen from tennis practice tomorrow? I had to rearrange my schedule."

"Sure thing. Did you grab the salmon for tonight?" Dan did most of the cooking, claiming he enjoyed it, but they both knew it was because Maggie was useless in the kitchen. She was, however, a very adequate grocery shopper.

"In the fridge." Maggie nodded.

Dan checked his smartwatch, on which he tracked all his physical activity. "Cool. Anything else?"

Maggie scanned the running to-do list in her brain. "Nope, that's it."

He flashed her his familiar grin, the one that had once made her heart flutter. "You know where to find me. See you later."

Maggie sipped her coffee and watched him reverse down the driveway and check his blind spot before easing into the street. There was a time when she'd taken pride in their partnership. Many of her patients, mostly women, vented about partners who shirked parental and domestic duties, but not Dan.

Twisting her hair up into a bun in preparation for her walk, Maggie then popped in her earbuds and cued up a true crime podcast.

"Hey there!"

Maggie turned to find Rhea approaching her driveway. She sported a stunning goldenrod linen shift, complemented by wedge sandals and an off-white quilted leather bag slung over her shoulder. Anna Armstrong trailed three steps behind, clad in jeans and a gray sweater, despite the warmth of the late August day.

"Hi." Maggie touched the base of her neck to hide her confusion.

"Wednesday at five?" Rhea raised an eyebrow. "We're meeting about the gala?"

Maggie attempted to conceal her disappointment as she remembered their meeting time. Joining the gala committee was the last thing she'd needed. Her schedule was already over-flowing because she hated turning away patients when they needed her, but the long hours were beginning to wear on her. Still, she needed the volunteer hours if she—and thus Pen—wanted to stay on Jerry's good side. "Right," she said. "Come on in."

Maggie watched Rhea's assessment of the kitchen, likely noting the cabinets in need of a fresh coat of paint and their aging refrigerator whose compressor sounded like a jet engine. Despite frequent discussions about renovating, neither Maggie nor Dan had the time or energy to pursue it. The shiny Viking cooktop was new, but only because their old one had finally given out.

"So," Rhea asked with a prim smile. "How's Penelope?" Maggie gritted her teeth at the forced sweetness and slight Southern twang in her voice.

"Pen is fine." Maggie nodded brusquely. Her daughter hated being called by her full name, claiming it sounded uptight. Maggie had to bite her tongue to keep from reminding her intense, exacting daughter that she wasn't exactly the definition of laid-back.

"Will's been so busy," Rhea continued with a faux pout of her well-glossed lips. "It seems like they haven't seen much of each other lately."

Pen had been dating Will Connelly for the past six months, the kind of entitled, overconfident boy Maggie had hoped her daughter would avoid. Maggie refrained from mentioning this to Pen, however. She didn't need to be a trained therapist to know that would only strengthen her daughter's commitment to the relationship with Will.

Maggie bristled. "Pen's busy too, with an online course at the Columbia School of Journalism," she said. "It was very competitive to get into."

Rhea's smile slipped and she turned to Anna. "What about you, Anna? How's Farrah these days?"

Anna shrugged and picked at a hangnail. "Farrah's good," she said. Maggie bit back a sigh. Anna's aloofness made her seem like the consummate snob.

"Farrah's in eighth grade this year, right?" Rhea gave the sickly sweet smile that drove Maggie crazy. Maggie told herself to draw on her training, to look deeper for even a shred of connection to Rhea. But the truth was, Rhea Connelly embodied everything Maggie disliked about Civitas—she was fake, overly focused on her kids, and living in a bubble of privilege.

"Why don't we get started?" Maggie interrupted. If she

couldn't connect with Rhea, she could at least keep the meeting short.

Anna nodded and reached into her Civitas-logoed tote. "Hot off Jerry's office printer," she said, placing a thick manila folder on the counter. "Here's the list of alumni to follow up with for gala RSVPs and donations." She cleared her throat. "Apparently, he thinks personal outreach from current parents might make them feel more... generous."

Maggie pressed her lips together in annoyance. Despite Civitas's substantial endowment, here she was, about to start asking people for even more money. It felt distasteful. She opened the folder and flipped through the pages, stopping on the last sheet. Instead of names, it was an email printout. The name at the top caught her eye, and she squinted to read it better. God, it really was time for reading glasses. Scanning the page, she frowned. "Wait, what's this?"

Rhea and Anna leaned forward to look. Maggie held up the email, which was addressed to Jerry, sent by Isaac Harris, the former assistant headmaster who had resigned abruptly two weeks earlier, only days after the school year had begun.

Dear Jerry,

It is with deep regret that I submit my resignation, effective immediately. Most of my ten years here at Civitas have been filled with a deep sense of pride in the difference the school has made in the lives of our students. It's been an honor to be part of an institution that, for so long, valued knowledge, hard work, and integrity. As of late, however, I no longer feel that sense of pride, nor do I feel Civitas continues to live up to its motto. I hope I will be proven wrong.

Sincerely,
Isaac Harris

Assistant Headmaster

"OK, weird." Maggie glanced at Anna. "Did Jerry mean to give this to us?"

Anna was looking at the papers and frowning, twisting a piece of her straight, limp hair around a finger. "He told me to grab what was on the printer... maybe this was for something else?" Her voice faltered.

Rhea pursed her lips. "I heard Isaac was basically fired, but no one knows what he actually did."

Maggie felt a twinge of guilt. She'd meant to reach out to Isaac when she'd heard about him leaving. They were at least friendly, if not friends—work kept her too busy for actual friends. His easygoing manner and wry asides had always made her feel less like an outsider at Civitas events. Plus, there was no denying his good looks. Once, they'd chaperoned a trip to Selma, Alabama for Pen's history class. They'd sat together and talked the whole three-hour bus ride, and a zing had gone through her body each time the bus took a sharp turn and their legs touched. She flushed now, thinking about it.

Maggie shook the page in her hand. "Anna, any idea what Isaac is talking about here?"

"Not really, no," Anna said, her expression frustratingly blank. Maggie was used to being able to read her clients' affect, but with Anna she got a whole lot of nothingness.

Rhea drummed her long, manicured fingernails on the counter. "Let's just stick to making a plan for contacting the alumni," she said.

Maggie set the printout of Isaac's email on the counter and reluctantly picked up the thick list of alumni contact information. "OK. Let's divide these up and start making calls." She separated the list into three stacks.

"Works for me," Rhea said, hopping off her stool and grabbing her portion of the list. "I love a short meeting—not usually a hallmark of the PA." She raised an eyebrow, and Maggie found herself laughing.

"I have to get ready for a client soon," Maggie said, checking her watch. "But then I'll look at my calendar and text some possible times for our next meeting."

"Would it be easier for us to book a session with you, to make sure we get slotted in?" Rhea asked with faux innocence. She gave a half-smile.

Maggie flushed at Rhea's gentle teasing. "Touché," she said with a small smile.

Anna chewed her lip, which looked dry and chapped. "I'm not a big texter," she said.

Maggie waved them out. "We'll figure it out."

Passing through the kitchen on her way to the office, she picked up Isaac's email and reread it. Strange, for sure. But probably not worth wasting time on. *Probably.*

FOUR

Anna glanced around the thickly carpeted conference room with its smooth, heavy dark wood table and ergonomic chairs. Simply riding the elevator up to the offices of Roberts, Kaplan, and Monroe, LLC, had caused her to break out in anxious sweat, making her white blouse stick to her back under her gray suit. *He doesn't know I'm here*, she reminded herself.

"Sorry for all the paperwork." Kevin Kaplan gestured to the stack of forms Anna was signing. "Donna should be in any minute," he added.

"Donna?" Anna looked up from the forms.

"The partner you'll be working for," Kevin explained. "I'm sorry; I thought I mentioned that in my email." He removed his wire-rim glasses and rubbed the bridge of his nose. "There's a lot going on—which is why we're so happy you're coming on board."

"Knock knock," called a loud voice. The door opened to reveal a tall, brightly blond woman with a wide face and sturdy build that made Anna think of a farm wife, the kind of person who could ride a horse and tie up a hog without blinking an eye

—but her expensive-looking double-breasted dark purple suit with gold buttons down the front made it clear she was no country bumpkin.

Kevin stood. "Donna Monroe, meet Anna Armstrong, the newest member of your team."

Donna's steely gray eyes fixed on Anna as she rose to her feet. She extended her arm and caught Anna's hand in a firm grip. "Great to meet you, Anna."

Kevin clapped his hands together. "Well, I'll leave the two of you to get acquainted." He whisked the forms away from Anna and smiled. "Welcome aboard."

"So." Donna plopped herself into the chair Kevin had vacated. "Northwestern Law. Then Jones Day in Chicago. Impressive." She raised her eyebrows.

Anna sat back down on the opposite side of the table and nervously rubbed her palms against her thighs. "Thank you." Her eyes dipped to her lap where her cell phone sat, assuring herself it was still turned off, her location untraceable.

"And then you took some time off." Donna looked up and Anna felt herself being appraised.

"My family—" she began, but Donna held up her hand.

"I have three kids," she said in a crisp voice. "I get it. It's not a crime to take some time to raise them. But when you come back, you have to be ready and willing to do the work." She cocked her head. "Are you ready, Anna?"

Outside the conference room Anna heard the buzz of activity, of people walking with purpose and speaking in decisive tones. She recalled all the nights she'd lain awake, dreaming of what it would feel like to have something of her own again, a part of her day when she was free from Jerry hovering and micromanaging. She sat up straighter and tucked her hair behind her ear. "I'm ready."

. . .

After leaving the office Anna found a coffee shop where she changed out of her suit and back into her jeans and sweater. Her heart rate accelerated as she powered her phone back on. It dinged with several messages. Anna hurried to read them, hoping they weren't from Jerry, wondering where she was or why her phone was off.

So far I've confirmed a dozen more RSVPs and $25k in donations! wrote Rhea, punctuating her sentence with a moneybag emoji and a bottle of champagne. *How's everyone else doing with their alumni lists?*

Good grief, it had been less than twenty-four hours since they'd met at Maggie's. How had Rhea had time for all that? Then again, she probably had a small army of household staff helping with all the cooking, cleaning, and chauffeuring that ate up Anna's time.

Haven't gotten to it yet... Maggie had replied. *But I will tonight.*

Same here, Anna typed quickly. She wished she could mention her meeting with Donna, something to justify why she hadn't even started on the alumni list yet. Explaining and justifying were second nature to Anna.

No time like the present! 😊😊😊 Rhea wrote. *I know we all want the gala to be a success. Civitas pride!* Rhea ended the text with a white heart and a dark green one, Civitas colors. Anna rolled her eyes as she read Rhea's response. Where did she get the energy to be so... peppy?

Also, Maggie wrote, *I tried reaching out to Isaac just to say hi but the number I have is disconnected. Does anyone have his new one?*

Anna tensed. There was no telling what Jerry would do if he knew she'd been discussing Isaac with Rhea and Maggie. He'd been clear that Anna must do nothing to add to the already highly active rumor mill about Isaac's departure. Anna ran her fingers over her upper thigh, where the bruises had faded but the skin was still tender. Then she swiped to delete the text chain.

She headed home, rehearsing her story about a late-afternoon dentist appointment. She'd even bought a new toothbrush and stashed it in her purse, just in case.

As soon as she entered the house, she swapped her low-heeled black boots for house slippers, something she'd been doing since she was a child. Her immigrant parents had drilled it into her, growing up—no one back in Taiwan would ever dream of wearing shoes in the house.

She padded into the kitchen to start dinner, anxiety shooting through her chest like a spear when she saw Jerry bent over in front of the refrigerator. He turned and jumped when he saw her, nearly dropping the bottle of beer he held.

"Jesus, Anna!" he said. "You scared the daylights out of me." He hadn't yet changed out of his chinos and white button-up shirt, but he'd ditched his tie and unbuttoned the shirt enough to give her a glimpse of the pasty, freckled skin of his chest.

"Sorry," she said reflexively. He grabbed the bottle opener from the counter and popped off the top. The cap hit the counter with a sharp clink, a small but piercing sound Anna knew well. It rolled a short way and settled next to two other bottle caps. "How was your day?" she asked, jumping back on script.

Jerry groaned. "Utter madness." He rubbed the skin between his hazel eyes. "Isaac couldn't have picked a worse time to show his true colors and jump ship."

Anna nodded, knowing that was what was expected of her. "I know it's been hard," she said. She moved to the refrigerator to retrieve the meatballs she'd prepared for dinner, giving him a wide berth.

"What about you?" Jerry asked. "I never got to hear about

your meeting yesterday with Rhea and Ms. Reed, Civitas's resident sex doctor." He gave the cocky half-smile Anna remembered from first meeting him, the one that had always made her feel like they were in on a joke together.

"Fine." She gave a noncommittal nod.

"What did you accomplish?" This was his headmaster voice now, the one he used with students. He leaned forward on the counter and she instinctively took a step back.

"Well, we're prioritizing the alumni follow-up, like you asked." She hugged the Tupperware container to her chest, suddenly wondering if Jerry had realized his error in leaving Isaac's email on the printer—whether he knew she'd seen it. Should she play dumb or come clean? Her thoughts spun wildly and her heart began to gallop as she tried to discern whether she was walking into a trap.

But Jerry nodded and regarded her with an expression that was almost tender. "I'm glad you're getting more involved at school, darling, like we talked about," he said. "Good girl." He paused and took a long swallow of beer.

"Mm," Anna said, relieved to have sidestepped the issue of Isaac's email. "I should check on Farrah," she said, abandoning the meatballs on the counter and edging out of the kitchen.

"Want me to plug your phone in for you?" he asked.

She hesitated. This was their evening ritual; she surrendered her phone willingly so he could avoid the awkwardness of having to ask for it. A rush of panic shot through her as she thought of the emails from Kevin, arranging today's meeting. She knew she'd looked at them in a private browser and she'd triple-checked that she'd closed out of it, but what if—

"Anna?" His impatience fired a warning signal into her thoughts.

"Sure, thank you."

Without meeting his eyes, Anna swallowed and handed over her phone, then hurried down the hall and knocked on

Farrah's closed door. It was always closed these days, despite Jerry's admonishments that she keep it open. But when it came to her dad, Farrah could get away with far more than Anna.

"Hi, sweetie." She poked her head into her daughter's room, which smelled like vanilla and the faint stink of dirty lacrosse equipment.

Farrah was stretched out on her bed in a pair of pink and white striped pajama pants and an oversized Taylor Swift T-shirt. "Hey," she said without looking up from her phone. She was freshly showered, her T-shirt damp where her long hair rested. It was a dark, rusty brown shade and far thicker than Anna's. She'd also inherited Jerry's slightly wider nose, but otherwise she had Anna's fine-boned features.

Anna waved her arms in the air and jumped around. "I said, hellooooo!"

Farrah gave a small eye-roll but smiled. "Hi, Mom. I see you."

"Phew," said Anna. "I thought maybe I'd gone invisible again." When Farrah was little, Anna had convinced her she could become invisible and watch her whenever she wanted. This was mainly to prevent Farrah from sneaking cookies out of the pantry, but then it had turned into a private joke, with Farrah pretending she couldn't see or hear her mother and Anna jumping around trying to get her attention. It had dissolved Farrah into giggles when she was small, and it could still get a smile from her now.

Anna flopped down on the bed. "How was tutoring?" she asked.

Farrah made a face. "I'm fine, thanks, how are you?"

Anna tweaked her ear. "I know how you are, I picked you up from school and dropped you off at the tutoring center, remember?" She breathed in the scent of Farrah's fruity shampoo. She knew she was lucky that at thirteen Farrah still mostly welcomed her presence.

Farrah dropped her phone on the bed. "Yeah, but a lot could have happened between now and then. Like maybe I've been struck by lightning or won the lottery or something."

Anna laughed. "I don't think you're old enough to even play the lottery, but if you do somehow win then you and I are moving to Paris immediately."

"Just us? Not Dad?"

Anna looked up to find her daughter regarding her with an expression she couldn't read. She waved her hand to cover her slip. "Of course, Dad too."

But Farrah had moved on. "Tutoring was hard. They're making me do polynomial functions." She wrinkled her face in a frown.

Anna leaned over and kissed the top of Farrah's head. "It's advanced math. It's supposed to be hard."

Farrah rolled her eyes again. "Do I really have to keep doing it? It's embarrassing to be the only eighth-grader in tenth-grade math. People think I'm a freak."

Anna smiled. "They're just jealous." She squeezed Farrah's small, smooth hand. "Dinner in fifteen minutes, OK?"

At dinner Jerry gave no indication that he'd seen anything amiss on Anna's phone. Afterwards, Anna cleaned up while Jerry retired to his recliner in the living room with his fourth beer—she was always counting. After doing the dishes, she circled back to Farrah's room, the place where she felt the safest this time of night. "Want to watch something?" she asked. "If you're done with your homework, that is."

"Yeah, I'm done." Farrah grinned. She reached for her laptop and navigated to the British detective show they'd been watching, then settled back against the headboard next to her mother. Anna knew she was free to let her guard down and disappear while Jerry "decompressed." As she lowered her guard, exhaustion descended. Her eyes drooped as the opening credits played and she wished she could stay there snuggled with her daughter all night.

But no matter how many drinks he had, Jerry would definitely notice if she didn't come to bed.

FIVE

Rhea sat at Maggie's kitchen island, grateful to take a break after the hour the three of them had spent going through the alumni lists to track down RSVPs. She sipped from the mug of coffee Maggie handed her, then spluttered and pushed it away.

"Sorry." Maggie looked sheepish. "I like my coffee strong enough to punch back."

Rhea wiped her mouth, trying to rid herself of the bitterness on her tongue, and rubbed her hands on the dark jeans she wore with a white, puff-sleeved Chloé blouse that she'd gotten on clearance. "I'm sure a good therapist could help you work through that," she said with a wry smile, wondering if she could get a rise out of Maggie.

Maggie blinked, then burst out laughing. "Ha," she said. "If only I knew one." She pushed a piece of hair that had come loose from her haphazard bun out of her face.

Rhea shook her head. "I shouldn't have caffeine this time of day, anyway." She'd been having trouble sleeping lately, waking from dreams of the faint cries of a baby she could never quite locate as she wandered the halls of an old, empty house.

"Anna?" Maggie held up a mug. "Coffee?"

A smile played around Anna's lips and she tugged on the sleeve of her shapeless black sweater. "Mm, based on Rhea's sales pitch... no thanks."

Rhea stared, trying to discern whether Anna was joking or just being her normal ice queen self. Rhea prided herself on being able to read people, but Anna was so opaque it drove her crazy.

Rhea refocused on the task list she'd created for them. "I finished my alumni follow-up," she said, peering over at Maggie's list on the counter. "Do you want me to do some of yours?"

"I've got it." Maggie crossed her arms.

Rhea fluttered her eyelids. "Suit yourself, Little Miss Over-scheduled. You know volunteering is optional, right?" She looked at Maggie, who appeared to be wearing an identical outfit to their last meeting—a cream-colored blouse over navy pants. Only her ballet flats were different: dark orange, this time, instead of green.

Maggie groaned. "Not according to the Civitas handbook." She looked at Anna. "You must have to do it all, right, since you're the headmaster's wife? Like every event and committee."

Anna bit her lip. "Well, yeah, pretty much," she admitted.

Maggie shuddered. "Oof, that's my nightmare."

Rhea narrowed her eyes. She resented Maggie's negative attitude. "Some of us like helping out and think it's a *privilege* to have our kids go to Civitas," she said. It would have been for Rhea, anyway. Sometimes she wished she could tell everyone the truth about how she'd grown up. The thrift-store clothes, the bedroom she'd shared with her three sisters, the food stamps her mother quietly applied for despite their father's near-maniacal insistence on self-reliance. Sometimes Rhea wanted people— like Maggie—to know that, unlike them, she didn't take her cushy life for granted.

Maggie looked at Rhea, clearly surprised by the force of her outburst. Her face flushed. "You're right," she said, suddenly serious. "It is a privilege. I'm sorry."

Rhea felt her anger deflate and she softened her tone. "I'm only trying to help us stay on schedule." She gestured to her task list. "There's going to be plenty to do for the gala over the next" —she checked her watch—"ten weeks. If you need help, tell us."

Anna cleared her throat. "Hey, um, sorry, but I need to get going. Parent-teacher meetings."

"Oh right," Maggie said. "Ours is tonight, too. Pen is taking it very seriously—she gave us a list of questions to cover with her teachers." She grimaced.

"Wow," Rhea said. "How... enterprising." Then without asking she slid her hand across the table, took several pages of alumni names from Maggie's stack and added it to her own.

Maggie caught her eye and gave a begrudging smile. "OK, fine," she allowed. "Thanks for your help."

Two hours later Rhea and Brooks sat across from Mr. Holladay, Will's trigonometry teacher. He looked to be in his early thirties and his prematurely gray hair clashed with his younger face. Rhea fiddled with her ring, a large square-cut diamond surrounded by a border of smaller, sparkly sapphires. Brooks had given it to her on their tenth wedding anniversary as an extravagant replacement for her original engagement ring, which had slipped off while they were snorkeling with the kids in the Bahamas. Most days Rhea missed her original, smaller ring. It had felt easier to live up to.

The classroom smelled of coffee and the cleaning solution used for the whiteboards, but it was airy and open, thanks to sparkling clean floor-to-ceiling windows. A neat row of canned seltzer and miniature bags of gluten-free cookies had been set out on a nearby table for parents.

Rhea's eyes wandered to the school crest mounted on the

wall near the door, where the school motto was spelled out in looping script: *Scientia, labore, integritas.* Knowledge, hard work, integrity.

"Will is already showing promise this term," Mr. Holladay said, his eyes fixed on the papers in front of him.

"Really?" Rhea frowned. She'd watched Will struggle with his trig homework on a near-nightly basis since school had started.

Mr. Holladay fiddled with the knot on his forest green and white plaid tie—Civitas colors—and cleared his throat. "Yes," he said. "If he keeps this up, he'll be on track to be in the top ten percent of the class again."

"That's great news," Brooks said, grinning at Rhea. He emptied one of the miniature bags of cookies into his mouth, then brushed the crumbs from the front of the gray fleece vest he wore over a blue dress shirt.

She hesitated, smoothing an errant hair back into her chignon. "What about the quiz from last week?" she asked Mr. Holladay. "He came home convinced he'd totally bombed it."

Mr. Holladay shook his head vigorously. "Oh no, not at all." He withdrew three stapled pages from a folder. On the front a large 96 was written in red ink. "I'll be passing these back tomorrow."

Rhea scanned the first page, recognizing her son's sharp, angular handwriting. "Well," she said. "He'll be pleasantly surprised."

Brooks waved his hand. "That's Will," he said. "Always underestimating himself."

Mr. Holladay gave a tight smile. "Indeed."

On the way home after they'd met with all of Will and Zane's teachers, Brooks drummed on the steering wheel as his favorite

Cars song played on the stereo. "Man, that was a long night," he sighed.

"Yes, well, they know we want bang for our buck," Rhea said, raising her eyebrows.

Brooks laughed. "And rightfully so, considering how many bucks we've given them." His tone was joking but Rhea knew he was proud to see *Brooks & Rhea Connelly* prominently displayed in the platinum donors circle in the school's entryway. Rhea had to admit she liked it, too. Having it there for everyone to see felt like proof that she'd done it; she'd made something of herself. She wished her parents could see it, and their church congregation, hell, everyone she'd gone to high school with. Everyone who'd called her trash behind her back— or to her face.

Brooks glanced over at her. "By the way, I have another work trip next week."

Rhea nodded. Since starting his company, Ironwall Cybersecurity, a few years ago, Brooks traveled nearly constantly. "D.C. again?" she asked. Thanks to his father's Senate connections, Ironwall had cornered the market on government contracts.

"Japan, actually."

"Wow." Rhea raised her eyebrows. "Fancy."

"I know." Brooks shifted in the driver's seat, his excitement palpable. He was like a little boy that way, incapable of playing it cool when he was excited about something. Rhea loved that about him. "This could be a huge new contract." His smile faded. "But it's a long trip. Two weeks."

Rhea tried not to pout. Whereas some of her Civitas mom friends claimed to love their "me time" when their husbands traveled, Rhea never felt quite right when Brooks was gone. It was like a key piece of the puzzle she'd worked so hard to put together was missing, throwing off the whole picture. "When do you have to leave?" she asked.

"Wednesday." He scrunched up his face. "I'm sorry, you know I hate being away that long." He grabbed her hand.

Rhea smiled in spite of herself. "It's fine, really, honey."

They drove in comfortable silence for a minute, her hand still in his. "You know you're the best thing that ever happened to me, right?" he said, bringing her hand to his lips.

Rhea squeezed his hand. "Me too," she said, and she meant it in more ways than one. She loved Brooks, yes, and she'd known from the minute they met in the library that they were meant to be together. But she'd also known then, like she did now, that marrying him was her best chance to leave her past behind.

SIX

Maggie checked her phone as Dan drove them home from parent-teacher conferences, the seat adjusted all the way back to accommodate his long legs. Rhea had already texted again about meeting next week. Maggie shook her head. The woman was relentless... and also maybe not as annoying as Maggie had originally thought. Maggie had been surprised at Rhea's offer to help with her part of the list, but even more surprised at herself for accepting Rhea's help. As for Anna, when she was around, Maggie always felt the need to be on her best behavior—after all, Anna was the headmaster's wife. Still, after spending some time with her, Maggie's therapist brain had clicked on, wondering if maybe Anna wasn't actually aloof but shy.

Still, Maggie thought, with a frustrated sigh as she read Rhea's text. *I'm busy, damn it. I don't need all this gala stuff taking over my life.*

Dan glanced over at her from the driver's seat. She was used to seeing him in scrubs or running gear, but in honor of parent-teacher conferences he'd donned a brown-and-white checked button-up shirt over jeans. "Everything OK?"

She shifted in her seat and tried to loosen her bun where it pulled too tight on her forehead. "Yeah, it's just this committee I'm on for the gala. Hey, remember how Isaac Harris resigned a couple of weeks ago?"

He widened his eyes slightly. The skin around them was pale compared to the deep tan on the rest of his face, a side effect of the wraparound sunglasses he wore on his morning runs. "Of course," he said. "It happened so fast. I saw him at drop-off in the morning and like an hour later I got the email that he'd resigned."

Maggie turned toward him. "Somehow a copy of his resignation letter ended up in the file of alumni info Jerry gave us for gala," she said. "In it Isaac said something about not being proud to work for Civitas anymore."

"Huh." Dan brushed his hair off his forehead and frowned. "Wait, why would Jerry give you a copy of Isaac's resignation letter?"

"By mistake, I'm pretty sure. Anna took the list straight from the printer and it was on the bottom." Maggie gave her husband's arm a gentle poke. "But don't you think that's weird? What Isaac said?"

Dan raised his eyebrows. "Apparently not as weird as you think it is." He flipped through the radio until he came to Sting crooning "Every Breath You Take." "People quit all the time for different reasons."

Maggie pressed her lips together. "I don't know. According to Rhea, he was actually fired, which I can't picture. It doesn't add up."

Dan gave her a sidelong glance.

"What?" Maggie asked.

He swallowed and tapped his long, thin fingers on the steering wheel. "Is it possible you've been listening to too many true crime podcasts?"

"Hey!" Maggie said indignantly.

He tried to hide his smile. "I'm just saying. Like, remember when you thought our dry cleaner was running a money-laundering operation?"

"They're cash only!" Maggie protested.

Dan reached over and squeezed her knee. She could see the patches of dry skin on his knuckles that came from wearing latex gloves all day with his patients. "I love your curiosity, Mags. All I'm saying is that maybe it's none of your business."

"Mm," Maggie grumbled, feeling chastened.

"What did you think about conferences?" Dan asked, changing the subject. "Seems like Pen's doing well."

Maggie tugged at her bun again, then gave up and removed the hair elastic entirely to let her hair loose. "It does. But let's not make a big deal of it with her. She's been so intense about her grades lately. I want her to relax a little."

Dan snorted and switched on his turn signal nearly a full block before their street. "As if she would. I've never met a sixteen-year-old so driven. I wonder where she gets it." He shot Maggie a teasing glance.

Maggie didn't deny it. She'd been making five-year plans since she was old enough to write, and so far she'd executed every one of them to perfection. She looked over at Dan, taking in the prominent bridge of his nose and thick eyebrows. She'd slotted him into her plans the minute they'd met at freshman orientation at UPenn.

As Dan pulled into their driveway Maggie spied the white Discovery Land Rover that belonged to Pen's friend Lainey. She frowned. "Pen knows she's not supposed to have friends over when we're not home."

Dan flashed her a guilty look. "I told her Lainey could come over to study."

Maggie made a tsking noise in her throat. "Well, at least it's not Will," she said.

Dan shook his head. "Oh come on, Mags, he's a good kid."

"And there'll be plenty of good kids for her to meet after she finishes high school. And college. And maybe grad school."

Dan gave a good-natured shake of his head. "I'm going to run and get gas," he said as she got out of the car. He didn't like to let the tank dip below half-full.

Inside, Maggie found Pen and Lainey sitting at the kitchen counter, a buffet of snacks and class notes spread before them. Her stomach rumbled at the sight of the potato chips, reminding her she'd worked through dinner.

"Hi, girls," Maggie said, dropping her bag on the counter.

"Hi, Dr. Reed." Lainey waved. Both girls wore baggy sweatpants and cropped, sleeveless tops that to Maggie looked more like sports bras than shirts.

"Hey," Pen said without looking up. Her hair, so blond it was nearly white, had a streak of turquoise dyed at the nape of her neck that only showed when she twisted it into a ponytail, as she did now. Maggie privately viewed the lone lock of color as Pen's repressed attempt at rebellion. Pen did everything by the book, and although Maggie had been much the same at her age, sometimes she wished her daughter would occasionally go off the rails or do something to shake up her otherwise highly scripted life.

Maggie fished a chip out of the bag and popped it into her mouth. "How's the studying going?"

To Maggie's surprise, Pen blushed. Lainey giggled. "We keep getting distracted," she said, pointing at her phone.

"Oh, really?" Maggie cocked her head.

Lainey stretched her hand out to reveal a video of Will standing on the sidelines of basketball practice, sweaty and shirtless. Maggie coughed and choked on her chip.

"Lainey!" Pen protested, her face reddening further.

"Honey, we've talked about this," Maggie said, brushing a chip crumb off the front of her shirt. "It's totally natural for your sex hormones to be kicking into high gear at this age, so long as you're aware of how they impact your emotions and decisions."

"Mom!" Pen looked horrified.

"What?" Maggie asked. For someone so rational, Pen certainly got worked up when Maggie brought up anything related to her work. "This stuff isn't embarrassing, it's part of life."

"Oh my God, can you please go?" Pen covered her face with her hands.

Maggie's phone buzzed and she pulled it out of her purse. It was a response from Anna to Rhea's text about a possible meeting time.

I can meet on Weds, she wrote. *But I can't text.* Three dots appeared as Anna drafted her next message. Finally she wrote, *I don't have an unlimited plan.*

Maggie frowned. Jerry's salary was published each year in the Civitas annual report, and Maggie was certain a few extra texts weren't going to break his bank. But whatever.

Pen peeked back out from her hands and Lainey giggled. "I think it's cool you and your mom can talk about sex," she said.

"We do *not* talk about sex," Pen said.

"You and Mr. Reed must have such a good relationship," Lainey gushed to Maggie.

Maggie froze. She got this comment a lot. Every time she smiled and offered some version of the same thing. "My work isn't about me." And thank God. Because if anyone knew the truth, that just might be the end of her career.

Later, Maggie was in bed reading when Dan came out of the bathroom, smelling like toothpaste and wearing boxers and a plain white T-shirt. As he climbed in next to Maggie, Lainey's comment echoed in Maggie's head. She took a deep breath and inched toward her husband.

"Hi," she said.

"Hey there," he said, patting her leg as he reached for his phone.

Drawing in a deep, nervous breath, Maggie slid her hand under his T-shirt. She placed her hand on his chest. His skin was warm and she could feel his heart beating under his narrow ribs. "Hi," she said again, in what she hoped was a breathy, sexy voice.

He placed his hand over hers through the T-shirt material and smiled. "So my mom is already planning Thanksgiving at the lake house," he said. "Can I tell them we're in?"

"Oh." Maggie stopped cold. "Um, sure."

Dan set his phone on the nightstand and leaned forward to peck her on the lips. "I'm beat. Good night, hon." Then he rolled away to turn out the light. In the dark Maggie lay still, blinking away tears as a hot wave of shame rolled over her body.

SEVEN

Anna was groggy when her alarm sounded, then vaulted upright when she realized what today was: her first day of work. A mix of anxiety and excitement swept through her. She hurried to the kitchen to make Jerry's coffee. When he came in a few minutes later, dressed for work in his customary white dress shirt and dark green tie, he handed her phone back to her. She slipped it into the pocket of her bathrobe, searching his face as usual for any signs he may have discovered something on it: the twitch of an eyebrow or tightness in his jaw. To her relief, she saw nothing.

"What's on your busy schedule today, darling?" Jerry asked, accepting the mug of coffee she offered him.

"Oh you know, errands and laundry." She waved her hand, hoping to imply it was just another day.

He paused, the mug halfway to his lips. "And you're still coming to Civitas this afternoon to help with the prospective students tour, yes?"

Anna stiffened. Maggie had hit the nail on the head when she'd guessed Anna was required to spend copious amounts of time volunteering at Civitas. According to Jerry, it signaled how invested they were in the school community and to set an example for other parents. She forced a smile. "Yes, of course, I'm looking forward to it. Oh, and I'll take your dry cleaning in today if you leave the bag out."

Jerry slurped his coffee and smiled at her. "Thank you for all you do, darling. I don't know how I'd manage without you." He gave her nose a playful tweak. "I have to run. Have a good day, Pocket." The old pet name sent a bolt of warmth through Anna. Jerry had called her that when they'd first met, referring to her petite stature. "My pocket-sized girlfriend," he'd joked, which had become "Polly Pocket" after the popular toy, and then eventually simply "Pocket." That was back in the days Anna had come to think of as Before.

Once Jerry and Farrah had departed for school, Anna raced around clearing the breakfast dishes, making the beds, trying to squeeze everything else she would normally have had the whole day to do into an hour.

After she'd showered and dried her hair more carefully than normal, she dressed in the same gray suit she'd worn to her interviews. Catching her reflection in the bedroom's full-length mirror, a tremor of nervous anticipation went through her body. It had been so long since she'd had something that was hers alone. She still couldn't quite believe she'd accepted the job. She felt like a rebellious teenager sneaking out after curfew, except it was 8:30 a.m. and she was dressed like a lawyer. Which, really, was about as far from rebellious as you could get.

Then, as her excitement crested, it receded, buried under a predictable wave of fear. She'd been dreaming of taking this first step, but now that she actually had... She shuddered, picturing the repercussions if Jerry found out. She could still back out, she realized. She could email Donna right now and explain that it wasn't going to work.

But deep down, Anna knew it had to. She knew by the steadily increasing count of the beer bottles lined up on the coffee table each night, keeping watch like tiny sentinels. She knew by the number of questions Jerry asked about how she'd spent her day, by the level of barely veiled fury in his voice when his coffee wasn't ready on time in the morning or when dinner was over-seasoned. Most of all she knew by the near-constant presence of the bruises on her upper arms or thighs—places they didn't show.

It was all getting worse.

As she walked out the door she spied Jerry's dry-cleaning bag where he'd left it for her. Shoot. The cleaner was in the opposite direction from the offices of Kaplan, Roberts, and Monroe. She'd never make it there and still get to her first day of work on time. With a hurried sigh she grabbed the orange bag to toss into the trunk of her car. She would deal with it later. She felt her jacket pocket for her phone, then remembered she'd left it under a book on her nightstand. Jerry almost never had time to call or text her during the day, but this way if he did she could claim she'd forgotten her phone while out running errands. And if he checked her location—which was more than likely—he'd find her at home.

"Good morning," Donna greeted her as she strode into the conference room. Anna pushed down a wave of nerves as she admired Donna's midnight blue suit with cropped pants over a canary-yellow blouse and a heavy gold statement necklace. She held out a Starbucks cup to Anna. "I didn't know how you took it so I guessed black, like me."

"That's perfect, thank you." Anna accepted the coffee with a confused smile. "But aren't I supposed to be getting you coffee?"

"God, no." Donna made a dismissive hand gesture. "That's what interns are for. And this is only because it's your first day, so don't get used to it. Anyway." She held up her own cup in a toast. "Cheers." While her forehead had clearly been cosmetically smoothed, the wrinkles and sun damage on her neck betrayed her age, which Anna guessed was late fifties.

"So." Donna dropped a brick-like legal file on the table. "Normally I'd start you off slow, but it's bananas around here right now. I need a brief for this case. I had a second-year associate working on it but he decided to up and quit to join a start-up—which has apparently become a rite of passage in your twenties." Donna's sour expression told Anna exactly what she thought of this particular rite. "Please tell me you have more sense than to let yourself be lured away from a solid career by foosball and free kombucha on tap."

"I hate kombucha," Anna said, trying to hide her smile.

Donna tapped the file with her index finger. "Everything you need should be here." Her lips crinkled in a frown under her dark pink lipstick. "They'll settle before we even get close to court, of course, but we've still got to do the work."

The morning flew by as Anna reviewed the file. It was a standard corporate litigation case, but the unfinished brief started by the kombucha-loving former associate was a mess. She threw the whole thing out and started from scratch. As she worked she could feel the gears in the legal part of her brain groaning for oil as they started to turn after years of neglect. But she found she sank easily back into the process of laying out an argument and knitting together precedents, and felt a refreshing sense of relief as she lost herself in the work, her brain shifting out of its normal state of vigilance.

She was so absorbed in the task that she jumped when Donna popped her head back into the room. "Knock knock," she said. "Have you even moved since I last saw you?"

Looking up, Anna saw it was after one o'clock. She was late to volunteer at Civitas, where admissions tours for prospective families had already begun despite the fact that it was only September. Admission to the school was that competitive. With a yelp she jumped to her feet and slammed her laptop shut.

Donna drew back in surprise. "Oh my, it's usually only opposing counsel who find me scary, not the people who work for me."

"I'm so sorry, I'm supposed to be at my daughter's school." Anna scrambled to stuff the documents spread out before her back into the file folder. Maybe Jerry would be too busy to check in on the tour and wouldn't know she'd been late. She began to sweat and wished she could rip off her suit jacket.

"How old is your daughter?" Donna asked, watching Anna's frenzied packing with interest.

"Thirteen." Anna shoved the company-issued laptop into her bag; she'd figure out where to stash it later.

Donna fluffed her stiff blond halo of hair. "I'm surprised she even wants you to show up at school."

"It's not that—it's my husband," Anna said, tugging on a lock of her hair. "He's the headmaster at the school and he—" She caught the frantic note in her voice and tried to steady herself. "I'm sorry, I'll finish the brief later."

"As long as it's done by the end of the week, that's fine. I know you're only part-time. For now." Donna raised an eyebrow and smiled.

In the car Anna stripped off her suit jacket and blouse and threw on a baggy black sweater. Once at Civitas, she tossed her clothes and the bag with the laptop into her trunk next to Jerry's dry cleaning and dashed up the brick path to the school. She was breathing hard when she caught up with the tour group in the library. She smiled and waved to the Civitas director of admissions, who stood at the head of the group talking about the school motto of knowledge, hard work, and integrity. Slipping into the back of the group, Anna noted with relief that Jerry was nowhere in sight. A minute later, however, the skin on the back of her neck prickled, and a hand closed around her upper arm.

"You're late," he hissed into her ear. "I've been calling you. Where have you been?" Anna's mind went to her phone, sitting on her nightstand.

"I-I'm sorry," she stammered in a whisper. "I lost track of time." He tightened his grip on her arm, his fingers digging into her muscles until she bit her lip to keep from crying out. Then he released her as the admissions director looked their way.

"We'll talk about this later," he murmured, a smile pasted on his face as he moved to the front to address the group.

Anna rubbed her arm and swallowed her tears. Later was exactly what she was worried about.

EIGHT

Rhea sat on Maggie's living room couch, wondering if this was where Will hung out with Pen when he was there. She hoped Maggie didn't let them spend time alone in Pen's room. Her eye traveled over the framed photographs on the bookshelves. There was Maggie, Dan, and a younger Pen in red slickers in front of Niagara Falls. Maggie in a wedding dress, young and smiling as Dan dipped her on the steps of a church. In each photo Maggie's face was relaxed and open, far from the harried expression she usually wore.

"Wow," Rhea said, pointing to a photo of Maggie and Dan in hiking gear, standing in front of a tent. "I didn't peg you as the, um, outdoorsy type." She gave Maggie a sidelong glance.

Maggie sighed, pulling her hair up onto her head and securing it with a ballpoint pen. Today she wore a pearl-gray version of the same blouse Rhea had seen before, and her ballet flats were a deep magenta. "I was—like, a million years ago. But I think I've officially aged out of shitting in the woods and sleeping on anything other than thousand-thread-count sheets. What about you?" She took in Rhea's black leather leggings and filmy pink Marc Jacobs top. "You don't exactly exude a crunchy granola vibe."

Rhea shook her head. "Yeah, I hate granola and I'm a huge fan of indoor plumbing."

Maggie nodded emphatically. "Yeah, fuck granola."

The doorbell sounded and Maggie rose to answer it, her blouse coming untucked in the process. She returned with Anna, dressed in a plain gray T-shirt over jeans.

"Sorry I'm late," Anna breathed. "I came from—" She cut herself off and looked at Maggie. "Could I trouble you for a glass of water?"

Maggie smiled. "I can do better than that. Be right back." She returned with a bottle of white wine and three glasses.

"To gala grunt work," Maggie said as she poured three generous glasses. Rhea watched in surprise. Was it possible Maggie Reed was loosening up?

Rhea hesitated. Whereas other people liked the social lubrication of alcohol, Rhea preferred to remain in control. Still, she didn't want to derail this new, less serious side of Maggie. She took a sip, enjoying the cold wine washing over her tongue. One glass couldn't hurt.

Maggie sipped hers, as well. Anna paused, then took a long swallow, draining half her glass.

Rhea's eyes widened. Uptight Anna was also apparently full of surprises. "Wow," she said. "Thirsty?"

Anna's cheeks flushed. She hesitated then said, "It's been quite a day."

Anna was actually pretty when it came down to it, Rhea decided, with her smooth pale skin and shiny, straight hair. She just needed an eyelash curler and some clothes that weren't from someone's grandmother's closet. Maybe they could nominate her for that makeover show, the one where five attractive gay men overhauled your life and left you wondering how you ever lived without avocado toast and a tailored blazer. Rhea giggled, then caught Maggie and Anna looking at her strangely.

She took another sip of wine and cleared her throat. "OK, so I got through my list—and yours," she said, nodding at Maggie. "I landed several big donations, for a total of fifty thousand dollars." She tried not to sound smug. No need to mention how easy it had been getting alumni to reach into their wallets once she'd identified herself as Rhea Connelly, daughter-in-law of Senator Hugh Connelly.

"Damn." Maggie saluted Rhea with her glass. "Now I don't feel so bad about letting you make my calls. You're really good at this."

Rhea tucked her hair behind her ear and tried to look modest. "Thanks," she said. "We all have our strengths."

Maggie smiled wryly. "Yeah, well, mine are more along the lines of analyzing people's relationships with their mother." She twisted her mouth into a guilty grimace. "Seriously, though, thank you. This is a crazy week at work, but I promise to be more help going forward." Rhea felt a flash of sympathy for all Maggie was clearly juggling.

"I finished, too," Anna said. She ran a finger under the collar of her T-shirt. "I got twenty thousand in donations—not nearly as impressive as you, Rhea." She dipped her chin and glanced up at Rhea.

Rhea tried to decipher Anna's tone. Was she trying to flatter her? Give her a genuine compliment? Anna was frustratingly hard to read. Was there a makeover show that could help with that?

"Wow." Maggie brightened. "That's a ton of money between the two of you. Jerry will be thrilled!" She grinned slyly. "Maybe he'll excuse us from the rest of our volunteer hours."

Rhea laughed, but Anna didn't, and Rhea caught an odd wrinkle of worry on her face.

"Actually, I'm pretty sure he was hoping for more," Anna said, her face smoothing back out. "I know he's short on his fundraising projection for the centennial." Anna clutched her hands together in her lap until they turned white. "The board really pushed him to go big this year."

Maggie lowered her pencil. "Wait, in what world is seventy thousand dollars not considered 'big'?"

Rhea held back an eye-roll. "In the Civitas world," she replied. *Welcome to the big leagues, Maggie,* she thought. "Last year's auction raised close to two hundred thousand."

Maggie's jaw dropped. "*What?* What in the world did people spend two hundred thousand dollars on at a school auction?" Rhea winced as Maggie's already naturally loud voice grew even louder.

Anna remained quiet and monotone as she ticked things off on her fingers. "The usual: spa treatments; exclusive golf outings; a private concert from Luke Bryan..."

"*Luke Bryan?*" Maggie exclaimed. "The country music megastar? Why the hell would he donate to the Civitas auction?" Her bun had grown crooked, giving her the look of a frustrated ballet teacher after a toddler class.

"His manager is best friends with one of the eighth-grade dads," Rhea said. Did she really need to explain to Maggie that every relationship at Civitas was built on some sort of quid pro quo?

Maggie blinked, processing. "Huh." She raised an eyebrow. "In that case, do you think anyone knows Harry Styles's manager? Maybe we could get him to play the next PA meeting."

Rhea drained the last of her wine. "I'll look into it," she said. She realized she felt relaxed in a way she never did in a room of her "real" friends, the other Civitas moms. She'd tried to explain it to Brooks once, how she'd never really felt a connection to them.

"But they're your friends," he'd said. "Besides, everyone loves you." Rhea didn't know how to explain that you could be loved but still desperately lonely—because love didn't count if no one really knew you.

"Anyway, we still have the silent auction to organize for the gala, so that should bring in some more money." She looked at Anna. "We need to finalize the donations. Do you have the list of businesses that have committed items or services? We can start by following up with them and then see if there are gaps to fill."

Maggie reached for the wine bottle to refill Rhea's glass and knocked her stack of documents to the floor. "Oops, shit."

Anna flinched as the papers fanned out onto the floor and jumped up to help gather them. Maggie waved her off, setting her wineglass on the coffee table, dangerously close to the edge. "I'll get them."

But Anna was already sweeping the pages up and squaring them back into a neat stack.

"Um, thanks," Maggie said, taking back the papers. Her brow wrinkled as she scanned the top page on the stack. "What's this?" she asked. Rhea noted that her bun had migrated further to the side, now resembling a strange blond tumor.

Anna leaned forward to look. "It looks like an NDA... at least part of one."

Rhea scooted over next to Anna on the couch so she could see. The document in front of them was in small type but she caught the phrases *confidential information* and *enforcement*. "How do you know what it is?" Rhea said.

"I'm a lawyer," Anna replied. Then her hand flew to the back of her neck. "I mean, I was a lawyer." She frowned at the document. "That's weird, it's signed by Rachel Burnett."

Maggie frowned. "That was Pen's favorite English teacher, but she left a couple of years ago. Pen was devastated."

"But where's the rest of it?" Rhea asked, scanning the page. "Like, the important part that says what it's about."

Maggie fanned through the rest of her pages. "I don't see it —oh, wait." She plucked another page from the stack. "Wait, this is a different one. But only the last page again. This one's signed by Robert Braun."

Rhea sat up straighter. "As in the math teacher?" She remembered Mr. Braun well. He'd also left Civitas two years earlier, but not before Will had almost failed his class.

Anna made a noise in her throat. "That man was *not* Jerry's favorite," she murmured.

Rhea caught Maggie's eye and Maggie glanced back at Anna. "Hmm, say more about that," Maggie said.

"Ah, there it is," Rhea observed, raising her now refilled wineglass. She sank back into the couch, feeling relaxed and slightly loopy.

"There what is?" Maggie asked.

"Your therapist voice."

Maggie wrinkled her nose. "My what?"

"I think it's funny how people have their real voice and their work voice," Rhea said. "Like Brooks, for example, his work voice is like half an octave lower, with lots of over-enunciation like he's a sports announcer or something." She could feel her filter slipping in front of Maggie and Anna but somehow she didn't care. She closed her eyes and giggled. "When he's working from home he walks around the house on the phone *enunciating* all the time."

Anna gave a hiccupy snort and Rhea's eyes flew open. Had she made Anna Armstrong *laugh?*

"So what does my therapist voice sound like?" Maggie pursed her lips. "Though I have a feeling I'm going to regret asking that."

Rhea considered, fanning her hair out between her fingers.

"Kind of like a cross between Matthew McConaughey and a friendly Muppet."

Maggie choked on her wine. "Matthew *McConaughey*?" she spluttered.

Anna gave another hiccup giggle. "Wait, you're more worried sounding like Matthew McConaughey than a Muppet?"

Rhea tittered. "And you," she said, pointing to Anna. "Poor thing. You must have to listen to Jerry's work voice all the time." She clapped her hands together in front of her chest and attempted a British accent. "Rightio, off to class, everyone. That's it, chaps and chapettes, put some pep in your step." She paused and assumed her normal voice. "Please tell me he doesn't sound like that home, too."

Anna's face was pink with mirth. "I mean, kind of," she managed through giggles.

"Nooo!" Rhea howled, dissolving further into laughter. Why had she been so concerned about having a glass or two of wine? She needed to do this more often.

Maggie eyed the two of them like they'd gone off the deep end. "Can we please get back to the NDAs?" she asked. "It seems weird." She turned to Anna. "Why didn't Jerry like Mr. Braun, anyway?"

Anna wiped her eyes and tried to collect herself. "Uh, I think the parents complained about him a lot."

"About what?"

Anna's eyes darted to the side. "Mostly that his classes were too hard. That he was a tough grader."

"He *was* a tough grader," Rhea said indignantly, remembering the private tutor she'd had to hire for Will.

"Jerry said it was part of cleaning house," Anna said.

"Cleaning house?" Maggie asked, her brow furrowing.

"All the teachers who left two years ago," Anna explained. "Mr. Braun was one of them. Jerry said it was part of cleaning house, starting fresh." She bit her lip and her face tensed. "I shouldn't have said anything."

The two lines between Maggie's eyebrows deepened. "OK, so we have Isaac's suspicious resignation letter and now two shady NDAs from teachers who both left Civitas at the same time."

"Suspicious?" Rhea looked at her with skepticism. "Shady? Why do I feel like you're about to tell it us was Mrs. Peacock in the library with the candlestick?"

"It's my fault," Anna said, standing and clutching the fabric at the front of her turtleneck. "I took the list from Jerry's printer. I should have double checked what I was taking... Jerry might be missing these." Her hand fluttered out to point to the NDAs.

"Even if he is... it's weird right?" Maggie said. Her bun had fully migrated to the side of her head now. "Why would teachers need to sign NDAs?"

Rhea shrugged and tried to appear unconcerned. "I'm sure there's a valid reason." But in the back of her mind a small kernel of doubt had formed.

NINE

"A B minus in French class?" Jerry held aloft Farrah's midquarter report card at the dinner table. "Really?"

Anna stiffened and set her fork down in perfect alignment with her plate.

"What's wrong with a B?" Farrah asked. She hadn't yet showered after lacrosse practice and her hair was pulled back in a headband. A faint smear of dirt was visible on one cheek.

"You mean a B *minus*?" Jerry's voice turned caustic. "A B minus won't get you into an Ivy, that's what's wrong, Farrah. These days it won't even get you into a safety school."

"But I'm not applying to college anytime soon," Farrah defended herself. "I'm only in eighth grade."

Jerry unbuttoned his sleeves and began to roll them up neatly and deliberately, a sign he was losing his patience. "You're applying to college every bloody day," he snapped. "Everything you do right now is part of your college application —lacrosse, orchestra, all the tutoring I pay for."

Anna's pulse quickened and she racked her brain for the magic words that would defuse the situation, but she felt paralyzed.

Farrah crossed her arms. "But I play lacrosse because I like it."

No, no, no, Anna tried to telegraph to her daughter. *Don't talk back.*

Jerry's smile was thin and nasty. "Trust me, you do not play lacrosse because you 'like it.'" He made exaggerated air quotes. "You play because it shows you're well-rounded and know how to be part of a team."

"But, Dad—"

Jerry slammed his palm on the table, sending his plate skidding toward Anna, who caught it and gripped it to still her trembling hands. A heavy silence followed.

"Farrah," Anna said, clutching the front of her turtleneck and forcing steadiness into her voice. "Why don't you go start your homework?"

Farrah nodded, her eyes wide and startled. She pushed her chair back. "Can I be excused?"

"You *may* be excused," Jerry corrected. "But we're not finished with this, young lady." Anna's shoulders slumped with momentary relief as she watched Farrah safely disappear down the hall.

Jerry rose and took a bottle of beer from the fridge. As he opened the freezer to retrieve his favorite glass, the one he kept chilled, Anna remembered she'd washed it the night before and forgot to put it back. Her stomach tightened.

Jerry turned to her, his mouth twitching. "Where is my glass?"

"I forgot, I'm sorry." Anna stood, intending to get a glass from the cupboard for him. But suddenly, he was in front of her again, shoving her back into the chair where she landed with a sharp jolt to her spine.

"You've been forgetting a lot of things lately," he growled. Anna glanced down the hallway toward Farrah's door. He saw her look and took a step back. "My glass, my dry cleaning."

Anna's body went rigid, picturing the bag of dry cleaning that was still in her trunk. "I'm so sorry, Jerry," she said. "I'll take it tomorrow. It slipped my mind—I've been busy and—"

"Busy?" Jerry asked. "Busy with what? Not busy making sure our daughter is maintaining her grades, that much I know." He took a long sip from the bottle.

Anna swallowed. "I'll start double-checking her homework, making sure she's on track. I can fix this."

Anna did the dishes in stiff silence while Jerry settled into his recliner to watch soccer. Once he was on his third beer she retreated to their bedroom, feeling a rush of relief as she closed the door behind her. Her eyes went to the framed pictures on their dresser. Anna picked up the one from their wedding. Jerry looked so handsome in his tuxedo with his unruly mop of hair brushed to a shine. The dimple on his chin showed as he smiled down at her. It was a cliché, but she'd felt like the luckiest woman in the world that day.

"I mean, he's British so he's practically a prince, right?" Her sister had teased her when Anna had called to tell her about the tall, handsome stranger she'd met in a bar while out with her law firm colleagues. She and Jerry had been inseparable after that, moving in together after two months (Chicago rent was expensive, so it just made sense) and getting engaged at the six-month mark (they were obviously meant for each other, so wasn't sooner better than later?)

"What's the rush?" her mother had asked. "I mean, are you sure about him?" But Anna's certainty was outweighed only by her sense of good fortune that Jerry had picked her. He was charming, handsome, ambitious, and somehow he'd chosen her. Her gratitude for this fact was so intense it sometimes felt suffocating.

"Mom?"

Anna looked up to see Farrah hovering in the doorway.

"Hi, sweetie," she said, setting the picture down and opening her arms. "What's up?"

Farrah stepped into her mother's embrace, her head resting on Anna's shoulder. "I'm sorry about my grade. I'll work harder."

The hitch in Farrah's voice made Anna squeeze her daughter tighter. "There's nothing wrong with a B," she said. She stroked Farrah's hair.

"But Dad said—"

"Dad can be a little... intense, sometimes." Anna chose her words deliberately. She'd been careful about keeping Farrah out of whatever took place between her and Jerry.

Farrah lifted her head to look at Anna. "Was he mad at you?" The concern in her daughter's large dark eyes tugged at something deep in Anna's body. Her thoughts went to her work laptop, which was hidden in the trunk of her car. She'd relished the feeling of being in an environment where people thought of her only as Anna the lawyer, not Anna the headmaster's wife. But now, looking at the worry on her daughter's face, she wondered if it was worth the risk.

"Everything's fine." She made herself smile at Farrah, then pointed to one of the photographs. "That was one of my favorite days ever," she said.

In it Anna sat on the sand in a floppy hat next to a triumphant two-year-old Farrah, whose little arms were stretched out, pointing to the huge—if slightly lopsided—sandcastle they'd built. Jerry had taken the picture on the shore of Lake Michigan, just before he'd accepted the job at Civitas and they'd moved to Atlanta. Anna had planned to go back to work after they were settled—she'd even taken the Georgia bar exam. But before she knew it, over a decade had passed and she'd never made any kind of life for herself. Their family's existence revolved around Civitas, and outside of that Anna knew virtually no one.

As she looked at the picture, something inside her unsettled, like the first pebble shifting before a rockslide. When was the last time she'd been happy in the way she had been that day at the beach? Was it possible for happiness to coexist with fear?

"We should go to the beach again sometime," Farrah said, nodding at the picture.

Anna had a flash of herself and the current thirteen-year-old Farrah at the beach, lying next to each other on matching towels. Then another of her next to Farrah as her daughter laughed and tossed her graduation cap into the air. Then another of her and Farrah, their arms encircling each other's waists, Farrah in a white dress and a flower crown. Then Farrah holding a smiling infant and offering it up to Anna to hold.

"I need to go finish my homework," Farrah said, giving her a little smile.

"OK, sweetie." Anna squeezed her arm. "Let me know if you need anything."

As Farrah padded out of the room Anna closed her eyes to resummon the comforting carousel of images she'd just conjured—and realized Jerry wasn't present in any of them.

TEN

A horn honked outside, and Pen pushed her breakfast plate away, leaving her toast half-finished. "That's Will. I gotta go." Standing, she hitched up her Civitas-issued gray pleated skirt so that it skimmed the tops of her thighs. Maggie raised her eyebrows. Pen had inherited Dan's thin, wiry frame as opposed to Maggie's rounder, broad-shouldered one, but she'd gotten Maggie's full bust, which filled out the front of her dark green polo shirt. Maggie could imagine exactly how Pen must look to Will, and she hoped he was behaving himself.

"Will?" Maggie glanced at the clock, which read 7:30 a.m., and then at Dan, who was already dressed in the mint green scrubs he favored. "What's he doing here so early? And does he no longer ring our doorbell? He summons you with a honk?"

"Honey," Dan warned.

Pen shot Maggie a dark look. "He has early basketball practice and I'm meeting Lainey to study for trig. And maybe he'd come to the door if you were, you know, less..." She waved her hands in the air and scrunched up her face.

"Less what?" Maggie asked.

Pen took a last swig of orange juice and swiped the back of

her hand across her mouth. "Gotta go," she said, grabbing her backpack.

"Less what?" Maggie called after her daughter, but the only reply was the front door slamming. She turned to Dan, hands on her hips. "Less what?" she repeated.

Dan ran his hand through his hair, long overdue for a trim. "What I think she means is that Will might be a little intimidated by you."

"Intimidated?" Maggie gave him an incredulous look. "That's ridiculous. Why would he be intimidated?"

Dan looked skyward as if the correct response might be written on the ceiling. "Pen may have mentioned that Will doesn't think you like him very much."

Ignoring the fact that Pen had confided this in her father rather than her, Maggie tilted her head in thought. "Well, that's true, so good for him. Maybe he's not as dense as I thought."

"Honey!" Dan protested. "Don't you think you might be stereotyping him the tiniest bit? Just because he's athletic doesn't mean he's not intelligent. I ran track in college, remember?"

Maggie gathered up Pen's plate and the other breakfast dishes. "Athletic, rich, popular... should I go on?" She waved a half-full juice glass, the contents of which narrowly missed splashing onto her white blouse. "Plus he's a Connelly—entitlement flows in his veins." She felt a pang of guilt. Now that she'd spent a little more time with Rhea, she actually found her funny and relatively smart. Plus she wasn't nearly as self-centered as Maggie had assumed.

Dan groaned.

"I don't want Pen to be so wrapped up in someone at this age," Maggie continued, ignoring him. "It's only high school, for God's sake. And the way she idolizes him, it's concerning. But if I say anything, she'll only double down. You know how stubborn she is."

Dan shook his head as he took the plates from her. "I can't imagine where she got her stubbornness," he said with a smile.

Maggie swatted him lightly on the arm.

"Says the man who refuses to give up racquetball even though it's obviously destroying his knees." She checked the time. "OK, I'm heading into my office for the morning."

"Have a good day, hon." Dan leaned over to kiss her cheek. "Love you."

"Love you too."

The words lingered as she stepped out of her slippers and into a pair of sunflower-colored flats and made her way to her office. She'd never doubted Dan's love, but lately it was intimacy she missed. Yes, he cooked for her, put gas in her car, massaged her feet after a long day... Maggie shook her head. If she was talking to a client she would remind them that all those things *were* acts of intimacy; that intimacy didn't need to have anything to do with sex.

Except that she wanted it to.

In her office she eyed the folder from Civitas on her desk. She took out the two NDA signature pages from Ms. Burnett and Mr. Braun. There had been a fuss two years ago when so many teachers had been replaced at once, but Maggie had been too busy to pay much attention. She noticed the countersignature line on both agreements was blank. Was Jerry meant to have signed them?

She set down the papers and focused on Isaac's resignation letter. What did he mean about Civitas not upholding its motto? And what the hell was the motto again? She pulled up the Civitas website, a tad embarrassed she didn't know. Despite not footing Pen's tuition bill, for the amount it cost to send her, Maggie should know every last damn detail about the place.

Scientia, labore, integritas. Which, according to Google, translated to "knowledge, hard work, integrity."

She scrolled through her contacts, locating Isaac's now

disconnected number. He had given it to her after their Selma trip, after they'd shared their life stories with each other on the bus ride. She revisited the handful of texts they'd exchanged since then. Recalling his Philadelphia roots, she had once sent him a link to a new Philly cheesesteak pop-up in Atlanta. His response had been #skeptical accompanied by a laughing emoji. Weeks later, he surprised her with a link to an old interview she had done with the *Today* show upon the release of her book, adding, *I didn't know you were famous!*

As Maggie's eyes flicked between their texts and his letter, she felt a subtle buzz in her chest, the same feeling she got when a client had a breakthrough. And while Anna and Rhea hadn't shown much interest in delving further, Maggie could do a little digging on her own, right? She tried Isaac's number again, getting the same computerized voice telling her the call couldn't be completed.

She pressed a finger to her lips, a plan forming. If her true crime podcast obsession had taught her anything, it was that a dead end was only the beginning. She'd blocked the morning to work on her next book. But that could wait.

An internet search for *Isaac Harris Atlanta Civitas* led Maggie to his Facebook page, but the last post dated back to 2009. The next result directed her to the First African Methodist Episcopal Church in College Park. The church website listed him as a deacon, along with his picture. Maggie was once again struck by his warm smile and square jaw. The accompanying outdated bio identified him as the Assistant Headmaster for Civitas Academy and an engaged member of the College Park Neighborhood Association.

She googled *Isaac Harris, College Park, Atlanta*, and there it was: an address.

Maggie sucked in her breath and glanced at her watch. She had time if she left now.

· · ·

Thirty minutes later, slowed by Atlanta rush-hour traffic, Maggie eased her Lexus to a stop across from a modest, two-story brick home, its garage partly obscured by a stately magnolia tree. Double-checking the address on her phone, she leaned back in her seat, her grip tightening on the steering wheel. Now what? She felt sheepish, realizing she hadn't planned beyond this point.

She sat for a minute, watching cars departing nearby driveways and children with backpacks trotting down the block. Several passersby eyed her with suspicion, and it dawned on her that her blond hair stood out in the predominantly Black neighborhood. She sighed. This was a waste of time. She was a therapist, not a detective.

At that moment the garage door across the street rumbled open. Dressed in gray sweatpants and a maroon Morehouse College T-shirt, Isaac descended the driveway, dragging a blue recycling bin along. She took him in from the safety of her car. He was shorter than Dan—likely closer to her own 5'9" stature —and his broad shoulders tapering down without a significant waistline. Tall, lanky men like Dan had always been her type, but as she watched Isaac warmth flooded her body.

As he reached the street Maggie emerged from her car. "Isaac?" she called. He shielded his eyes from the morning sun, squinting at her. "Hi," Maggie said, striding toward him. "It's Maggie Reed. From Civitas." She looked down at her therapist uniform of dress pants and a button-up shirt, for once wishing she'd worn something more interesting.

Isaac stiffened and he took a step back. "Can I help you?" he asked.

Maggie's stomach dropped. He clearly didn't remember their connection the same way she did. What had she been thinking, showing up at his house like this? She tried again. "I'm Pen Reed's mom." Silence. "We were on the Selma trip together?"

"It's not that I don't remember you, Maggie," Isaac said, his smile tight. "It's that I'm wondering why you're standing in my driveway at"—he glanced at his chunky, silver watch—"eight thirty in the morning."

Maggie flushed. "That's fair." She nodded. "I'm sorry. I tried to call but your number is disconnected." She flashed a hopeful smile.

His mouth twitched. "Maybe that's because I don't want to talk to anyone."

Maggie bit her lip. She'd really fucked this up. "How's your dad?" she ventured. "Last time we talked he was recovering from pneumonia." She felt like an idiot, realizing it had been three months since their last conversation. Why hadn't she made more effort to stay connected?

But something in Isaac's face softened. "He's doing all right, thanks." His eyes traveled over her body, and when they met her gaze again he wore a faint smile.

"And how are you?" she asked. "Since, you know, leaving Civitas?"

His smile vanished and he retreated a step. "I can't talk about that."

Maggie held up her hands. "I'm not trying to make trouble, I swear." She fumbled in her purse until she retrieved the copy of his resignation letter. "It's just, I found this and I was, um, curious about it."

While he didn't reach for it, he leaned in to examine it, closing the gap between them. Then, he took an abrupt step back, eyeing her warily. "Where did you get that?"

Maggie touched the back of her neck. "Look, I only wanted to ask if—"

"I can't talk about this." Isaac folded his arms, glanced back at the house. "For real. You should go."

The familiar buzzing in her chest grew stronger. "Does it involve the NDAs Mr. Braun and Ms. Burnett signed?"

Surprise flickered across Isaac's face. "How do you know about those?"

"What are they for?" she asked. "Why did they sign them?" She was on to something, she could feel it.

Isaac glanced down the street as though someone might be listening. "If you found all the NDAs, then you should know," he said in a low voice.

"I only have the signature pages." Maggie leaned closer. "Wait, are there more?"

Isaac edged up the driveway. "I don't need any more trouble."

"Wait," Maggie said. "Can you tell me whether this is something? Because if not, well, I'm supposed to be working on the draft of my next book that was due last month." She smiled and tried to keep her tone light in an echo of their previous rapport.

Their eyes met for a beat and Isaac's jaw loosened slightly. "It's not nothing," he said in a low voice. "That's all I'll say."

Maggie's body began to tingle. She reached into her purse, fishing out her business card and thrusting it toward him. "Thank you," she said. "And here. In case you don't have my number anymore."

His arm moved as if in slow motion, reaching for the card. His hand hovered in the air, inches from hers. Then, taking the card, their fingers brushed. A jolt went through her body. He held her gaze as though searching for something in it. Finally, tucking the card in his pocket, he turned and walked away.

ELEVEN

Rhea sat at the kitchen table just after 7 a.m., her phone displaying a miniature version of Brooks smiling up at her.

"So then I went down to the reception to tell them my key card wasn't working... and it turned out I'd been trying it at the wrong room." He slapped his palm to his forehead, making Rhea laugh.

"Maybe you should travel less," she suggested, sipping her coffee. She was still in pajama bottoms and one of Brooks's white undershirts, her face devoid of makeup. He always told her that's when he found her most beautiful.

"Or at least have a better system for remembering my room number." He shrugged and grinned. "Anyway, I miss you. Did you get the flowers?"

Rhea turned the camera toward the enormous bouquet that took up most of the table. "Oh, you mean this tiny arrangement?"

"Hey," he said in mock indignation. "I told them I wanted something large. I'm definitely asking for a refund."

She laughed and turned the phone back toward her face in time to catch him yawning. "What time is it there?" she asked.

"Seven p.m.," he said. "I should get going. They're sending a car for me soon for dinner."

"OK, Big Shot, have fun."

He gave her a look. "You know I'd rather be home with you and the boys."

"I know," she said. But she also knew he thrived on his success at work.

They had long settled into their roles, with Brooks as the provider and Rhea as the caretaker. "I make the money and you spend it," he liked to joke. But they both knew that aside from her gym membership and occasional "dermatologist" appointments, few charges on their credit card were hers alone. Brooks, having grown up with money, enjoyed spending it, while Rhea mainly liked the comfort of checking their account balances and knowing it was there.

"Speaking of the boys," she said, "I should get them moving or they'll be late for school." She was dropping them off today and had agreed to meet Maggie for coffee after.

"Hug them for me," Brooks said.

Rhea nodded. "Love you."

"Love you more."

She smiled and pressed the red button as Zane ambled into the kitchen in his Civitas uniform of gray slacks and a forest green polo shirt bearing the school crest.

"Good morning, sweetheart," she greeted him, smoothing his bedhead.

"Morning." He grabbed the plate with the breakfast sandwich she'd made him and took a huge bite.

"Any sign of your brother?"

Zane shrugged as he chewed. Rhea sighed and headed upstairs to wake Will.

. . .

Fifteen minutes later, Will sat tipped back in the front passenger seat of Rhea's Mercedes SUV, eyes closed, while Zane drummed on his knees to the song on the radio in the back. Rhea smiled—her owl and her lark, her moon and her sun.

"You're both carpooling home tonight with the Gibbs twins," she reminded them as they joined the line of cars waiting to drop off at Civitas.

"OK. Bye, Mom!" Zane bounded out of the car before she'd even come to a full stop. Will cracked one eye open, then the other, grunting as he sat up and reached for the door handle.

"Have a great day, I love you," she called after them. Zane waved, and Will gave a slight nod.

After drop-off, Rhea drove to La Bamboche, the French bakery popular with Civitas moms. The smell of hot butter and coffee made her stomach rumble. She scanned the crowd of moms in Tory Burch loafers and Burberry trench coats, looking for Maggie, but was distracted by her friend Tamara waving from the line. Tamara's tiny frame and voluminous blond hair made her look like a bobblehead as she beckoned Rhea to join her.

"Hey, you," Tamara said, giving Rhea an air-kiss on each cheek. She stepped back and surveyed her critically. "Did you get a haircut? Or a peel? Your skin looks as fresh as a baby's."

"Nope." Rhea shook her head. "Same old me."

"Huh, well, you look great, as usual." Tamara linked her arm with Rhea's as the line moved forward. Though Tamara was ostensibly her best friend, Rhea knew Tamara's affinity for her had more to do with Rhea's place at the top of the Civitas social hierarchy than any deep connection they shared. But Tamara had long ago decided they were friends, so Rhea went along with it.

"We missed you at book club," Tamara said, a hint of accusation in her voice.

"So sorry I missed it," Rhea said, hoping she sounded disappointed, "but I was wiped. Brooks is traveling again, you know the routine."

Tamara widened her deep-set eyes. "Preaching to the choir! Hugh's out of town too; I'm *drowning* at home with the twins."

Rhea smoothed the front of the sky blue Veronica Beard vest she'd thrown on over jeans that morning and resisted the urge to remind Tamara she had a nanny and a live-in housekeeper. Brooks had often suggested they hire help, too, but Rhea didn't want strangers around all the time. Her home was her refuge. Walking in the door felt like stepping out of the bright lights of being on stage and into the quiet comfort of the wings. She spent enough of her day acting the part of Rhea Connelly, Civitas PA president. At home she didn't want anyone else she had to act in front of.

"Hey, Rhea, the usual?" The young male barista smiled at her, his shoulder-length blond hair held in place by a backward baseball cap.

"Hey, Lucas," she replied. "Yes, please. Creature of habit."

He winked. "I got you. One oat milk cappuccino coming up."

"He's *so* into you," Tamara said in a loud whisper once Lucas had turned around to queue up their drinks.

Rhea ran a finger along one of her thick, well-groomed eyebrows. "Oh please, I'm old enough to be his mother."

Tamara smirked. "Only if you started young." Rhea felt her jaw tighten and she ducked her head to zip her purse while she collected herself. Tamara nodded toward a table of PA moms. "Want to join them?"

Lucas turned back toward them with her drink. "Actually I'm meeting someone." Rhea nodded toward the corner where Maggie sat scrolling through her phone. As usual, a ballpoint pen stuck out of her topknot, and several loose strands of hair hung down her back.

Tamara looked aghast. "Maggie Reed? Why?"

"Gala logistics stuff." Rhea waved to Maggie.

"Oh right, you poor thing." Tamara gave a sympathetic nod. "Well, good luck." She tossed her hair and headed off to join the other moms.

With relief, Rhea approached Maggie. "Hey," she said.

"Hey," Maggie replied as she stared after Tamara, her nose wrinkled as if she'd smelled a skunk.

Rhea glanced back at Tamara, then at Maggie. She nodded in silent agreement. Both women raised their eyebrows and smiled as they sipped their coffees. "Is Anna coming too?" Rhea asked.

Maggie shifted in her seat. "Um, I didn't actually invite her."

"Ah, OK," Rhea said, confused.

"There's some stuff I wanted to talk to you about first," Maggie went on. "Given that she's, you know... married to Jerry."

"Right, yeah." Rhea tilted her head. "Poor thing." She brought her fingers to her lips in mock horror. "Oops, did I say that out loud?"

Maggie laughed and fiddled with a yellow sugar packet, turning it over between her fingers. "So," she said. "I talked to Isaac about his resignation letter."

"What?" Rhea sat forward in her chair. "When?"

"Yesterday. At his house." Maggie reached up to squeeze her bun, as if confirming it hadn't floated away.

"His house?" Rhea's voice rose and several tables table turned their way. She coughed and leaned closer to Maggie. "I guess I didn't realize you two knew each other... like that."

Maggie flushed. "Yeah, he wasn't exactly, um, excited to see me."

Rhea eyed her with interest. "So you showed up at his house?"

"Basically." Maggie grimaced.

"Wow," Rhea said, oddly impressed by Maggie's total lack of regard for social decorum. "That's..." She trailed off. "And he talked to you?"

"Not really." Maggie frowned. "But it sounds like there are other NDAs out there, and there's definitely something fishy going on."

"Something *fishy*?" Rhea laughed. "OK, Sherlock Holmes."

Maggie raised her chin. "I'm going to take that as a compliment on my sleuthing skills."

Rhea rolled her eyes. "Sure. Go on."

Maggie shook her head. "He said he couldn't say anything else, like he was afraid of getting into trouble." She looked around and lowered her voice. "When he left, everyone assumed he'd done something, you know?" She pressed her lips together. "But talking to him... well, I got the feeling whatever happened didn't actually have anything to do with him."

Rhea chewed the inside of her cheek. If teachers were signing NDAs—the same teachers she entrusted her children to —that wasn't a good sign. Could Maggie be right? Was there really something unsavory going on at Civitas, the same school she devoted so much of her time and her—their—money to? The thought was deeply unsettling. She pressed a finger to her bottom lip. "That's... concerning," she conceded.

"We should keep looking into it, right?" Maggie said, her large blue eyes eager.

Rhea hesitated. "Yes," she said finally. "I guess we should."

On the drive home, Rhea's mind drifted to the last time she'd seen Isaac, only a couple of weeks ago at school drop-off. He'd seemed relaxed, waving to parents and high-fiving kids. When she asked through the window if he would help chaperone the homecoming dance, he gave her a thumbs up. But then, the next week, he was... gone.

Rhea was so engrossed in her thoughts that she'd nearly turned into her driveway when she saw the figure standing in her yard, peering through the side window. He was dressed in black jeans and a black T-shirt and wore a gray baseball cap. A faded army green backpack was slung over his shoulder.

Rhea's pulse quickened as she stopped short, pulled to the curb and got out. "Hey," she said sharply, striding toward the house. She squinted against the brightness of the mid-September morning sunshine. "What do you think you're doing?"

The figure jumped at her voice, the backpack slipping off his shoulder. He was young, Rhea realized, probably around Lucas's age, though shorter and more muscular. "Sorry," he called, raising his hands. "I rang the doorbell... I was only trying to see if anyone was home."

As Rhea drew closer, she could see his hair was light brown under the baseball cap. But when he looked up, it was his eyes that caused her to stumble and lose her balance. They were bright green, and as she fell toward him they widened.

TWELVE

Donna finished reading Anna's brief and nodded. "Good. I like how you included the Raycon vs. BluStar precedent." Today her suit was a bright coral color over a pale blue silk blouse. On anyone else it might have looked clown-like, but on Donna it just looked expensive.

"Thanks," Anna replied. She had enjoyed diving into the research, losing herself in the work.

Sydney, the senior associate who sat next to Anna, popped her head over the cubicle wall. "We're making a coffee run," she said, gesturing to the stocky young man in a gray suit at her elbow. "Want anything, Donna?"

Donna waved dismissively. "Not for me." She looked at Anna. "You should go along, Anna. It's time you got to know more people here, and maybe we can lure you into joining us permanently." She glanced at the young man. "Though please don't think Doug here is our top specimen."

Doug reddened and brushed his thick helmet of rust-colored hair off his forehead. "Gee, thanks."

Anna tried to hide her smile as she stood and reached for her purse. "Coffee sounds great."

In the elevator, Sydney and Doug chatted while Anna let herself sink into the pleasant hum of a conversation not centered on Civitas or her family. Yet a familiar sense of vigilance lingered. She was out of practice taking risks, even small ones, and this job—well, it was an enormous one. Every morning when she woke, she briefly considered whether it was worth it, debating whether she should quit or find a way to tell Jerry. So far, she had done neither.

"So how's it going with Donna?" Sydney asked. She was several inches taller than both Anna and Doug, and her closely shorn Afro made her eyes and cheekbones stand out.

"Fine, I think," Anna replied. "But I mean, it's only been a week or so." Her hand went to her own lackluster hair, which hung straight down between her shoulder blades. She'd always thought she would look good in a pixie cut, but Jerry liked her hair long.

"You know they had to hire you because none of the associates wanted to work for Donna anymore, right?" Doug smirked.

"You mean Donna didn't want to work with *you* anymore, Doug," Sydney said. She turned to Anna. "Or me, for that matter. She's tough."

"That's for sure," Anna agreed. So far Donna had been prickly and exacting, but also complimentary when Anna's work was up to her standards. Plus, Anna had a feeling she was far more experienced at weathering other people's difficult behavior than Sydney or Doug.

The three of them chatted steadily as they waited in line at the coffee counter in the building lobby. Anna marveled at the sea of similarly gray- and black-suited professionals around them that she was now part of. She thought of her old work friend, Kate, from Chicago. They'd been regulars at the nearby Chipotle for lunch and went to happy hour together at least twice a week. But that was before she met Jerry. He hadn't liked

Kate, complaining that Anna stayed out too late and drank too much when they were together.

Back upstairs with her Starbucks cup, Anna replied to some emails and then closed her laptop. It was a relief to finally have a desk drawer to lock it in instead of hiding it at home.

"You're not leaving, are you?"

She turned to see Donna approaching. "I was going to, yes," she said hesitantly. "It's already one thirty." After the Civitas tour incident, Anna had learned to plan for later departures from the office.

Donna frowned. "One of our top clients is coming in and I wanted you to meet them. You really can't stay?"

Anna bit her lip. "It's just, my husband—"

"Aw, surely he'd understand," Donna interrupted. "He must be proud of you, back at work after all these years."

Anna forced a smile and fingered her simple gold wedding band with its one tiny diamond. "Yes, of course. He is. But I'm so sorry, Donna, today I really can't stay."

"Fine, next time." Donna's face creased in disappointment and Anna felt a stab of regret at letting her down.

Anna rushed through the grocery store, then raced home and shoved everything into the refrigerator and pantry. She quickly moved the laundry she'd started that morning to the dryer, threw in another load, and dashed through their three bathrooms with Windex and paper towels. Jerry couldn't stand smudges on the mirrors or water marks on the counters.

She had already left to pick Farrah up from school when she realized she was still wearing her work clothes. Her mouth went dry and her stomach turned. They'd be home after Jerry and he would demand an explanation for her outfit. What if he somehow sensed the truth? Anna's nausea grew. Turning the car around, she raced back to the house and threw on jeans and a T-shirt.

She was one of the last cars in the pickup line at Civitas, which meant Farrah would be late for her piano lesson across town.

"Mo-om," Farrah complained when she got in the car. "Madame Harper always makes me do extra scales when I'm late."

"I'm sorry, sweetie," Anna said as she pulled out into traffic. "I've had a busy day."

"Of folding laundry and baking cookies?"

Anna flinched at Farrah's cutting tone. She opened her mouth to explain where she'd been, then clamped it shut. Watching her daughter pout in the rearview mirror, Anna felt anger expanding in her chest. The urge to defend herself surged like a tidal wave crashing toward shore. "You know I had a career before you were born," she said finally.

"Lots of women still work after they have kids," Farrah said with an eye-roll.

"Yes," Anna said sharply, unable to keep her resentment at bay. "And they don't pick their daughters up from school, drive them around, make them dinner, and do their laundry. Is that what you want?"

Farrah sat up straight, her eyes wide. Anna never raised her voice. "No," she said. "Sorry. But you don't have to take it so personally."

"Well, how else am I supposed to take it, huh?" Anna snapped, whipping her head around to face her daughter. Farrah had no idea what Anna put up with. No one did.

Farrah let out a cry. "Mom, watch out!"

Anna turned back around in time to hear the crunch of metal on metal.

THIRTEEN

Rhea looked up into the face of the boy holding her upright on her front lawn. He was several inches taller than her, and muscular. Up close she could see his face was smooth with the faintest hint of stubble, and his light brown hair was midway between Rhea's coffee-brown tresses and the light blond hair his father had had.

"Are you OK?" he asked, hoisting her to a standing position she wasn't confident she could maintain. Her breath was shallow, like she couldn't get enough air. The back of her neck was slick with sweat, and all the sounds around her were suddenly magnified; the chirping birds were as loud as an orchestra tuning up, and the leaf blower down the block sounded like it was right next to her ear.

She shook her head. "I need to sit." She lunged toward the house, stumbling in her heeled boots and gripping the waist-high iron lanterns along the walkway for balance, then collapsed on the bench by the front door. She grabbed her heavy mass of hair and held it away from her neck, fanning herself with her other hand.

The boy followed her silently, looking stricken. He hovered nearby as Rhea tried to catch her breath.

"Are you OK?" he asked again, his green eyes—dear God, those eyes—wide with concern.

"Who are you?" Rhea managed, making one last attempt to pretend she didn't know.

He cleared his throat and looked at the ground, then back up at her with those piercing, familiar eyes. "I... I think I'm your son."

She squeezed her eyes shut, her heart thrashing in her chest like a wild bird caged. This wasn't happening. Not like this.

She reopened her eyes and stared at him. "Why would you say that?"

The boy stepped back as if she'd slapped him. "Because your name is on my birth certificate." He reached for his backpack, struggling with the zipper, then thrust his hand inside. Rhea flinched as he pulled out a creased manila folder. Seeing her reaction, the hurt on his face deepened. "I'm not going to hurt you or anything," he added.

Rhea touched her throat where her voice was stuck. He let the backpack slide to the ground and fumbled inside the folder, extracting a pale blue rectangle of paper. "You're right here," he said, tapping the paper. "Abilene Smith."

She dropped her hair back over her shoulders and took it from him, holding it by the corner as if it might be contaminated.

Name of Child: Joshua Michael Smith
Sex: Male
Place of Birth: St. Joseph's Hospital, Odessa, TX
Name of Mother: Abilene Rhea Smith
Name of Father: Unknown

"That's not my name," Rhea said in a hoarse whisper. Her stomach churned like she might vomit. "Not anymore."

"I know." The boy's face tightened and he rocked back on his heels. "You weren't easy to track down."

She forced herself to focus on his face, noting the narrow slope of his nose, which was nothing like hers, and the square-ness of his chin, which was. The paper slipped from her fingers and fluttered to the ground. "This birth certificate was sealed. Where did you get it?"

He stooped to pick it up, his shoulders rounding in defeat under the frayed color of his worn black T-shirt. "Does it matter?"

"Yes." A rush of anger swept over her. She'd done what she was told in exchange for the promise that no one would find out.

"I did a favor for the clerk in the office of records," he mumbled.

Rhea gave a harsh laugh. "Must have been an expensive favor."

He lifted his eyes to meet hers, their likeness to hers almost too much to take in. "Believe me, it was."

She glanced around, realizing they were on the front porch and visible to anyone passing by. With a curt wave, she stood and headed toward the backyard. "Follow me."

The boy hurried after her. She punched in the code to open the pool gate, and once they were safely concealed from the street, Rhea began to pace, her palms sweaty and her thoughts racing.

"Do you want to see him?" The labor and delivery nurse's words echoed in her head. Thank God she'd said no. Because if he'd looked up at her with those green eyes shaped exactly like her own, she couldn't have let him go. Where would she be then? Probably still stuck in Texas, surviving on food stamps, at the mercy of a family and a redneck town that never forgave nor forgot anyone's sins. She shivered at the thought.

God, she'd been so naive, believing she was in love and grown-up at seventeen. He was thirty-four and worked at the car dealership where her father took his truck for repairs. He'd made her blush by calling her "ma'am." He'd started showing up outside her high school in his Corvette, and she'd felt heady with rebellion letting him drive her home—though she always got out around the corner.

He'd promised her a new life, full of the freedoms her parents never allowed. When she packed her bag and left with him in the Corvette, they didn't even come after her. They simply waited for her to return three weeks later, when her father used his belt on her. The subject had never been mentioned again. But by then it was too late.

She looked up from her pacing. "Where do you live?" she asked. His eyebrows furrowed in confusion. "Your adoptive family," she clarified. "Where do they live? Where did you... end up?"

His shoulders tightened. "My last boys' home was in Gardendale, in Texas."

A strangled gasp escaped Rhea's throat. No, that wasn't right. It couldn't be. The woman from the agency had told her they had a family all lined up, a God-fearing, childless couple who'd been praying for a baby. "No," she said, more firmly than she intended. "You were adopted."

He coughed and removed his baseball cap, swiping the beads of sweat from his brow. "My adoptive mom died when I was seven. Cancer. And my dad, well, he tried. But he couldn't do it without her." His face sagged. "So he... brought me back."

"Brought you *back*?" Shock coursed through Rhea's body.

The boy caught her expression and shrugged. "It happens more often than you think. Anyway, seven-year-old boys aren't very popular on the adoption circuit." He forced a laugh. "Most people want babies. But it's fine." He lifted his chin. "I had a few foster families, but once I was a teenager I was mostly at boys' homes."

Rhea felt her legs nearly give out for the second time and she staggered several feet to the left, sinking onto a pool lounger. Guilt stabbed at her. All these years, whenever she'd thought of Josh she'd pictured him being pushed on a swing or cuddled at bedtime by some other woman who was his mother—a better mother than her.

"It's OK." He swept his arms out and then let them hang limply at his sides. "I didn't come here to try to make you feel guilty."

Rhea hugged her arms to her body. There were faint, purplish circles of fatigue under his eyes. "Wait," she said, something dawning on her. "What did they name you?"

He gave a half-smile. "They liked Josh, so they kept it."

Relief rolled over her. For the past twenty-one years, every time she thought of him, he'd been Josh. She couldn't imagine him with another name. Then she buried her face in her hands. This couldn't be real. Any moment now, she would wake up to the sound of Brooks's alarm clock and feel his touch, waking her from the anguish of this dream. "Oh my God, oh my God," she whispered, rocking back and forth.

He took another step toward her and crouched down. "Hey, seriously, are you OK? Like should I call someone?"

Her eyes flooded with tears. She'd abandoned him, and yet here he was, asking if *she* was OK. She waved a hand in front of her face. "This is just... a lot."

He sighed and put his hat back on, his expression one of pure exhaustion. "I'm really sorry." His voice broke and she looked up to see his eyes were wet.

"Oh my God, Josh—I—Jesus, I'm sorry. Sit." She gestured to the lounger next to hers and he heaved himself onto it, wiping the back of his hand across his eyes.

"Whoa," he said with a shaky breath. "I'm sorry, I don't

know why I'm..." He ran his hand through his hair. "Just, sorry." Then he cleared his throat and squared his shoulders. "Look, I'm sorry again about surprising you like this. I figured if I'd tried to call you or something, you might not want to talk to me." He managed a smile. "But I was hoping, if you saw me, that maybe we could, I don't know, talk, or something."

Rhea nodded. "Talk. Sure." Where would they even start? Was it possible to catch up on twenty-one years? She blinked. "Where are you staying?"

He bent down and scratched his ankle. "Um, I hadn't really gotten that far," he mumbled. "I took an overnight bus from Waco to get here, didn't sleep much."

The practicalities of the situation momentarily muscled out Rhea's emotions. How was she supposed to explain this stranger in the backyard, who looked startlingly like her, to her kids? "You can't stay here," she said. The unintended cruelty of her words echoed back at her and she cringed. "Sorry, I mean, what am I supposed to tell my kids?"

"So they don't... know about me?" he asked.

Rhea had to turn away from the expression of raw hurt on his face. She was truly an awful person. But he couldn't stay and meet her kids, that was clear. Then again, if she sent him away, what if she never saw him again? The pressure of the anguish gathering in her chest made her wonder if she might be having a heart attack.

The pool house came into focus, which in reality was less of a house and more of a shed with a bathroom and a small living room with a couch. It lacked heating or air conditioning, but the early October weather was temperate. Standing, she brushed her hands against her pants. "You can stay there for tonight," she said, nodding toward the small structure. "Then we can at least... figure things out." The relief on his face made her want to cry anew.

She let him in, scooping up a pile of musty-smelling towels

that had been left by one of the kids weeks earlier. "Sorry, there's no bed."

"That's fine." He dropped his backpack on the small bistro table and sank onto the couch. Exhaustion radiated off him and his eyes drooped. "Sorry, I... do you mind if I lie down for a minute?"

"Sure." Rhea shifted on her feet. She had so many questions. "Um, feel free to rest, or whatever, and then we can talk."

He nodded, his eyes already closing as he tipped his head back on the couch.

FOURTEEN

Maggie emerged from her office to find Dan wearing his favorite apron, the one that looked like a tuxedo shirt. The sharp tang of basil and garlic made her stomach rumble, reminding her that the last thing she'd eaten was the muffin from La Bamboche when she'd met Rhea that morning.

"Yum." She wandered over to where Dan was whistling and spooning small cubes of tomato onto thick slices of bread. "This seems very fancy for a Wednesday night. Not that I'm complaining." She grabbed a piece of bread and took a large bite.

"Hey, hands off the bruschetta," Dan said. "And Fernando and Jess are coming over tonight, remember?"

"Oh, right." Maggie swallowed and felt herself deflate. She stuffed the remaining bread into her mouth and dug her finger-nails into her topknot, massaging her scalp. She had nothing against Dan's best friend, nor his wife, both of whom were lively and funny. But she'd been listening to people talk all day and right now she longed to change into sweatpants and zone out for the evening. She grabbed a second piece of bread and Dan shot her a look.

"Hon, there's not going to be enough."

"Fine," she grumbled, putting it back. Pen came in then, her backpack slung over her shoulder. "Hey, sweetie," Maggie said, then caught the dark look on her daughter's face. "What's wrong?" She glanced at Dan, who shook his head in warning.

"Oh nothing." Pen's voice was thick with sarcasm. "Only my entire future going up in flames, but no big deal." She stomped toward the front door.

"Hey, wait." Maggie followed her. "What's going on?"

Pen stopped and crossed her arms over her uniform shirt. "I got a B minus on my trig exam," she snapped.

Maggie glanced at Dan, who was trying to communicate something to her through frantic eyebrow wiggling. "OK," she said. "I mean, it's still a B, right?"

"A B *minus*." Pen's voice veered toward a shriek and her cheeks went bright pink. "Which might as well be, like, an F as far as Columbia's concerned. So now my GPA's screwed, which means I won't get into their summer program, which means I shouldn't even bother applying to college there, which means I might as well give up my dream of being a journalist and, like, become a plumber or something."

"Sweetheart," Maggie said, hoping to appeal to reason, "I hardly think one B minus—"

"God, you don't understand anything!" Pen interrupted. She started to cry and backed away from Maggie. "I'm going to Will's," she said, and slammed the front door on her way out.

Maggie turned around to find Dan with a guilty grimace on his face. "Sorry," he said. "I should have warned you. She told me earlier."

"But it's only one grade," Maggie said, pressing her shoulder blades together to stretch her back after sitting all day. "Also, if Civitas is putting that much pressure on her, maybe we should think about switching schools—"

"Mags," Dan groaned. "Can we please not do this? I get it, you hate Civitas, but not everything is the school's fault."

His comment stung. "I don't *hate* Civitas," Maggie said, though she wasn't entirely sure this was true. "I'm only saying—"

Dan waved his hands at the ingredients spread out in front of him on the counter. "Can we not do this now?" he asked. "Fernando and Jess will be here in twenty minutes."

Maggie stepped back. She'd been on the verge of telling him about her encounter with Isaac and the suspicions it had stoked; now she wasn't sure that was such a good idea.

"Sure," she said. "No problem."

"This is the best Italian food we've had since our trip to Rome, don't you think, Jess?" Fernando said. He was stocky with a broad chest made even more pronounced by all the time he spent at the gym—which, according to Dan, was a lot.

"Rome sounds amazing," Dan said, beaming at the compliment, and Maggie felt a whisper of guilt. She resolved to stop taking his cooking for granted and express more gratitude going forward.

"We love Italy," Jess said, tucking her toffee-colored chin-length hair behind an ear with several piercings. "We're going to do the Amalfi coast next summer."

"You guys should come," Fernando said.

Dan perked up. "Hey, that sounds great—right, Mags?"

"Uh, sure," she said. "But Pen's applying for that summer journalism program in New York, remember? So I guess we'll have to see." Fernando and Jess didn't have kids to account for in their vacation plans. Plus the six-week program at Columbia —the one Pen was now convinced she wasn't getting into—was expensive. If she prevailed in spite of her B minus, they likely wouldn't be vacationing anywhere for a while.

"How is Pen these days?" Jess asked. "I'm sorry we missed her."

"Oh, you know," Dan sighed. "She's a teenager."

Jess gave a sympathetic nod of her head. "The only experience I have with teenage girlhood is my own." She made a face. "And I should definitely apologize to my mother for it."

Maggie laughed. "Yup, same."

"She's gotten so intense about school lately," Dan said. "I wish she'd ease up on herself."

"Well, she definitely didn't learn that from you," Fernando said with a sly smile. "Remember the time you decided a bar crawl would be a great idea the night before final exams?"

Dan sat back and let out a short laugh. "Hey, I suggested *one* bar. All the others were your idea."

Maggie turned to Jess as the two men began to reminisce. "How's your semester going?" Jess was a professor at Emory University.

"Good," Jess replied. "Except for the fact that I got stuck teaching a freshman class this year. These kids are so young and clueless! I mean, when did eighteen-year-olds start to seem like children?"

"It's definitely not that we're getting older," Maggie said.

"No way," Jess laughed.

Maggie grinned, enjoying Jess's company and briefly envisioning a closer friendship with her. Her growing bond with Rhea and Anna had highlighted how much her life revolved around Dan. Which, lately, she had to admit felt lonely. She reminded herself that even happily married people needed friends.

"And, sadly, my freshman class also takes place at 8 a.m. tomorrow morning," Jess said. She nudged Fernando. "We should get going."

After they left, Maggie helped Dan clean up. He seemed

energized as he buzzed around the kitchen wiping down the counters, but she was spent.

"I'm going to head up to bed," Maggie said. Usually they went up together, settling next to each other in bed while Dan read and Maggie played word games on her phone before they turned out the light. But tonight Dan made no move to follow her. Instead he brushed a kiss on her lips.

"Sounds good, hon. Sleep well."

FIFTEEN

Anna watched in panic as Jerry's face turned a shade of light purple. "You didn't *see* the car coming?" he demanded.

"I'm so sorry, I—" Anna began. Time seemed to slow as she watched his anger build. She fixed her gaze on a small scratch on the dining room table.

"It was my fault, Daddy," Farrah interrupted in a high, frightened voice. She stepped forward next to Anna in the dining room. "I distracted her—" The fear in her daughter's eyes, combined with her own sense of helplessness, gave Anna the sense of being pinned down by a boulder.

"Go to your room." Jerry turned to Farrah, his eyes blazing.

"But Daddy, I—"

"Now!" Jerry's arm stretched out taut, his finger trembling as he pointed down the hall.

"Go." Anna pushed Farrah toward her bedroom, the warmth she felt at Farrah's attempt to defend her vanishing. "Now." Resisting the urge to flee and trying to control the shaking that had started up in her body, Anna planted herself between Jerry and the hallway, silently warning him to leave Farrah out of it.

She hadn't been going very fast, but the car's left side was still badly dented from where she'd run the stop sign and driven into another vehicle. For a brief second she wondered if a bad accident would have been better. If she'd ended up in the hospital. Jerry might have had some sympathy then. Or at least there would have been doctors and nurses watching over her, offering a layer of protection until his rage subsided.

"No one was hurt," Anna began, but his hand pushed up the sleeve of her gray sweater and closed around her wrist, tightening until she gave a small yelp. The sleeve of his white dress shirt was rolled at the wrist to show his embroidered monogram. "Jerry," she breathed. "Please." She looked toward the hallway and Farrah's bedroom door. Her daughter couldn't witness this. "Please."

"Stupid," he hissed. His thin eyebrows knitted together in contempt and a small ball of spittle gathered at one corner of his mouth. Anna focused on it as she tried to calm her panicked breathing. "Look what you did to the nice car I gave you. Careless and stupid," he continued, so close now she could feel his breath hot on her face. His grip shifted from her wrist to her upper arm where the bruises would be less noticeable, and he pulled her toward the door to the garage, on the other side of the house from the bedrooms.

Inside the garage she stood under the harsh light of the bare bulb and watched as he closed the door behind him. She knew from experience that fighting would only make things worse.

"Look what you did." He shoved her toward the damaged car, sending her flying onto the concrete where she landed hard on her knees. She winced and tried to stand back up, but he was already there, yanking her hair and forcing her head to turn and look at the dent. "You take me for granted, Anna. I give you everything and you appreciate none of it. You waste things. You waste my time dealing with things like this, and you waste my money fixing the messes you make." He let go of her hair and she felt a split second of relief before pain exploded in her ribs as his foot made contact with her body.

She gave a sharp cry.

"Quiet." His voice was cold.

She knew she should stay quiet, stay still. That was the quickest way to bring this to an end. But she'd stayed quiet for so long, and now it was all bubbling up inside her. She looked up at him, clutching her ribs. "I'll go to the police," she breathed. "I'll leave you."

Surprise registered on his face and then he laughed. "Oh Anna." His voice dripped with pity. "How would you ever manage that? Lawyers are expensive, as are custody battles, which don't usually favor the unemployed parent. And the police, well..." He wet his lips. "You were in a car accident; you're bound to have some minor injuries."

The flicker of resistance she'd felt burned out like the end of a sparkler, and her aching body sagged lower onto the floor. He was right. He was always right.

Jerry rolled his sleeves down and took his time buttoning the cuffs. "Take the car to the shop tomorrow," he instructed. "Drive carefully."

Anna didn't know how long she stayed in the garage lying on the cold, unforgiving concrete. Every time she breathed too deeply a burst of pain exploded in her side.

She used to cry after it happened, but she'd long run out of tears. Farrah had been a baby the first time he'd pushed her, after they'd argued about the dishes Anna had left in the sink. He'd apologized right away and her brain had been so addled with sleep deprivation that she'd forgiven him immediately.

He didn't bother to apologize anymore.

She squeezed her eyes shut in pain as she pushed herself into a seated position. She knew she didn't deserve it, of course.

But shame had long since piled on top of logic. And the longer it went on the more shame there was, and now she was trapped in a tower built of it, like some messed-up fairy tale. Because how could she ever tell anyone what she'd put up with for all these years? How could she bear that humiliation? And besides, where would she go? She couldn't leave Farrah behind. There was no way Jerry would let her leave and take their daughter.

She sat with her head in her hands for a long while, and as her body adjusted to the searing pain in her side, she thought of her first paycheck. It had just been deposited into the bank account she'd set up, at a different bank from the one she and Jerry used. She'd managed to do that much without him knowing. Maybe there was a way.

When she finally limped back inside, the house was dark. The bedroom doors were closed and behind theirs she heard Jerry snoring. The kitchen clock read 9:45 p.m.

She had fifteen minutes.

Breathing shallowly with her hand pressed to her ribs, Anna found Jerry's keys on the hook in the hall. Slipping into her sneakers, she eased open the front door. His Jeep was parked in the driveway. Anna climbed in and pulled the door closed as quietly as she could, pain roaring through her at the effort. Holding her breath, she turned on the engine, cursing the automatic headlights that lit up the side of the house like a searchlight. Her heart accelerated as she watched their bedroom window. When it remained dark, she slowly backed out into the road.

Only a handful of cars remained in the parking lot at the big box store; unsurprising, given that it closed in five minutes. Hurrying inside as best she could with her injuries, Anna made her way to the back of the store to the Electronics department.

A tall, skinny man with a receding hairline and large plugs

in his earlobes was punching away at the computer. "Excuse me." Anna waved, then winced. "I need to buy a phone."

"We're closed," he said, without looking up.

Anna checked her watch. "It's 9:56," she said.

"Yeah, and we close at ten."

"But it's not ten," Anna pleaded.

"Look, I'm already logged out of everything." He shrugged and turned away.

"It's not ten," Anna repeated, her voice gathering strength.

"Is there a problem here?"

Anna turned to see a short, wide woman with closely shaved gray hair in one of the store's signature red T-shirts. A walkie-talkie was strapped to her hip and her name tag said BEV in block letters.

"I was telling her we're closed," said the skinny man.

Anna turned to Bev. "I need a phone," she said. She checked her watch again. "And it's only 9:57."

"But I'm already logged out," repeated the man, pointing to the computer.

"So log back in, Clayton." Bev fixed him with a steely gaze and Clayton rewarded her with a heavy sigh.

"Fine," he said, glaring at Anna.

"Oh for Christ's sake," Bev barked. "Get outta here. I'll do it myself." Clayton scuttled away under her glower. "Sorry about that," she said to Anna as her fingers zipped over the keyboard, bringing the computer back to life. She shook her head. "I don't think he's going to last much longer around here. Now, what kind of phone are you looking for?"

Anna chewed her lip. "Uh, like a burner phone, I guess? Not for anything bad," she added quickly.

Bev nodded. "Pre-paid is what I believe the non-criminals call them." Anna gave a small laugh and then gasped and grabbed at her ribs. Bev eyed her. "You all right there?"

"Fine," breathed Anna. "Car accident."

Bev raised an eyebrow. "Sorry to hear it. OK, so you want calls and texts, or internet and the like, too?"

"Internet, too," Anna said. She didn't have a plan yet, exactly, but the phone would help her make one.

Bev pointed. "Then I'd go with that one. It's $69.99 on sale right now."

"Great." Looking around, Anna reached under her gray sweater into her bra and pulled out a debit card. Bev raised her eyebrows again but didn't say anything.

She paid for the phone and a reloadable data card. "Do you mind getting rid of the box for me?" Anna asked as she took the phone out and powered it on to set it up. Holding it, she felt a rush of power.

"No problem," Bev said. She smiled and reached out to pat Anna's arm. "You take care of yourself now, you hear?"

Anna grinned back at her. "Thanks. I plan to."

SIXTEEN

By mid-afternoon there had still been no signs of life from the pool house, so Rhea had loaded a turkey sandwich and a miniature bag of chips on a tray and knocked softly on the door. Pushing it open, she found Josh asleep exactly where she'd left him. She thought of all the times she'd stood over Zane and Will when they were small, watching the gentle rise and fall of their little boy chests as they slept—something she'd never had the chance to do with her firstborn.

This realization had stung her eyes with tears. She wished there was someone who knew her—really knew her—who could tell her what to do. She had a sudden urge to call Maggie. She was a therapist, after all, even if they weren't quite friends.

Josh had opened his eyes then and blinked at her standing there in the doorway. "Hey," he mumbled. "What time is it?" His sleep-creased face reminded her of Will earlier that morning, half asleep on the way to school.

"Almost two thirty," she said, setting the tray on the small table. Feeling the acute need to be comfortable, she'd changed out of jeans into her softest black leggings.

"Oh jeez, I'm sorry," he yawned. "I didn't mean to sleep all morning."

"I thought you might be hungry." She held out the tray. She imagined telling Maggie she'd offered her long-lost son a sandwich to make up for her years of abandonment. Rhea didn't need a therapist to know that was delusional.

"Would you like to stay for dinner? Meet the boys?" she blurted. It was only marginally better than a turkey sandwich, but the smile that bloomed on Josh's face made it seem like she'd told him he could fly. Rhea continued before she lost her nerve. "They have cousins from Texas who they've never met," she said. "You could be one of them."

Understanding had washed over his face then and his smile faded. "So you're not going to... tell them?"

"I can't," she whispered, hating herself as she watched his happiness evaporate. "Not yet."

"Sure." He nodded. "I get it. Dinner sounds great." The mix of disappointment and eagerness in his eyes reminded Rhea of a stray dog grateful for scraps. Josh rubbed his eyes. "Oh, uh, what should I call you?"

Rhea fingered the delicate gold chain at her throat, on which hung a W and a Z. "Rhea is fine."

"Aunt Rhea?" The tremor of hope in his voice nearly crushed her.

"Just Rhea."

Will and Zane arrived home later as she was at the stove, sautéing scallops in garlic and white wine, and drizzling olive oil over the ravioli in a bowl. A pile of asparagus sat nearby, waiting to be blanched.

"Whoa, what gives?" Zane said, surveying her dinner preparations. The odor of chlorine trailed him and he wore a hooded

Civitas Athletics sweatshirt over baggy athletic shorts. "You never cook like this when Dad's gone."

Will loped in after him. His dark hair, still damp from his shower after practice, was slicked back from his face in a way that made him look older. "Yeah," he said. "Why so fancy?"

Rhea reached up to tighten the ponytail she'd pulled her hair into while cooking. "Your cousin is staying with us tonight. My sister's son. From Texas." Her hand trailed down to her neck as she waited for the onslaught of questions.

"Cool," Will said. "Can we do banana splits for dessert?"

"Ooh, yeah," Zane chimed in. "With whipped cream?"

At that moment there was a tap on the sliding glass door that led to the backyard. From the other side, Josh raised a hand in greeting, dressed in jeans and a faded blue T-shirt with the Texas flag on it. Rhea swallowed hard and wiped her sweaty hands on her leggings, then beckoned him in.

"Boys," she said. "This is your cousin Josh." Like the boys, Josh was freshly showered, his face flushed and the neck of his T-shirt damp. There was a small nick on his throat from shaving.

Zane waved as he grabbed a plate. Will gave a slight nod as he sank onto a chair. "S'up, man," he said.

"Really?" Rhea put her hands on her hips. Suddenly it felt imperative that Josh see she had raised kind, well-mannered boys; that she'd been a good mom to her other sons despite what she'd done to him. "Surely you can do better than that."

Zane looked chastened. "Um, hey, Josh," he said, setting down the plate. "I'm Zane."

Will rolled his eyes but straightened up in his chair. "Nice to meet you, Josh. I'm Will."

Josh reddened and waved. "Nice to meet you, too." He looked at Rhea and cleared his throat. "And thank you for having me."

Flustered by the odd formality of it all, Rhea knocked into the table as she went to sit, nearly toppling her water glass. Steadying it, she tried to smile as they all sat down. She opened her mouth to speak but her mind was blank with sudden panic. What had she been thinking, introducing Josh to her children? What if he said something?

"So, what's Texas like?" Zane asked, nodding at Josh's T-shirt.

"Yeah, do they, like, issue you cowboy boots and a rifle when you're born?" Will added, pushing up the sleeves of his long-sleeved gray Henley shirt as he reached for the asparagus.

A smile played on Josh's lips. "Totally," he deadpanned. "We used to have target practice at recess."

Zane's eyes widened. "Seriously?"

Will rolled his eyes and smirked. "No, dummy, he's joking." He looked at Josh. "Right?"

"Right." Josh smiled.

Will cocked his head as he salted his scallops. "So, where'd you go to college?" Only a sophomore, he was already receiving glossy brochures from universities.

Josh cleared his throat and reached for his water glass. "Uh, Baylor."

A good school, Rhea noted with relief, still trying to make her voice work. Maybe things really had turned out all right for Josh despite... her.

Will nodded. "Cool. Good football team."

"Yeah, I played for a while."

"For Baylor?" Will's eyebrows shot up. "Dude, nice."

Josh waved his hand and he looked embarrassed. "One season as a walk-on. Then I hurt my, uh, knee."

Rhea noticed most of the food on Josh's plate was so far untouched. "Josh, is something wrong?" she asked. "Do you not like scallops?" Damnit, she should have asked him.

He looked down at his plate and shifted in his seat, rubbing the back of his neck. "Oh, no, it's not that. I'm, um, allergic to shellfish." He gave an awkward laugh. "It's pretty bad. I had to go to the emergency room once."

Rhea's mouth dropped open in horror. "Oh my God." She jumped to her feet and yanked the plate away from him like it was a snake poised to strike. They'd been reunited only a few hours and already she'd tried to kill him.

"No, it's OK." Josh looked sheepish. "I mean, I like asparagus."

"As long as it's served with a side of EpiPen," Will cracked, and Zane stifled a laugh. Neither noticed the tears in their mother's eyes.

"Let me make you a sandwich." Rhea turned away so no one could see her face. Because apparently, after twenty-one years, sandwiches were all she had to offer.

Dinner was mercifully short after that, and then Zane and Will peeled off to start on homework. Once it was her and Josh alone again, Rhea's pulse quickened. She leaned against the counter, feeling like a mannequin come to life, with no idea how to stand normally or position her limbs. Josh began to clear the table.

"You don't have to do that," Rhea said.

He gave a shy smile. "I don't mind. Thank you for dinner."

"You mean for trying to send you into anaphylactic shock?" She tried for a joke but it came out sounding as anguished as she felt.

"It was excellent grilled cheese," he said. "Truly."

They stood in silence as she bent to load the dishwasher.

"So, Baylor," she said, straightening back up and wiping her hands on her leggings. "What was your major?"

"Uh, English and business," he said, looking down and tapping his knuckles lightly on the counter.

"Wow, you were busy." Rhea smiled. "So you like to read?"

He nodded, perking up. "Yeah. My mom—my adoptive mom—read to me a lot." Then his lips curved down slightly.

Rhea felt as though a sharp splinter had entered her heart. "What was she like?" she asked softly.

He picked up the twist tie from the bread bag and began to wind it around his finger. "She was... really nice. She liked animals. She smelled good." The lines on his forehead deepened. "But I don't remember her super well, you know?" The tip of his finger turned purple and he unwound the tie.

"I'm so sorry. You were so young." The hurt in Josh's eyes bored into her, and her words hung in the air, small and inadequate like a squadron of toy ships facing a hurricane. The crack in Rhea's heart widened.

She'd always wondered how it would be if she found him. If she'd recognize him or feel an immediate connection. Now she knew. Because although the boy standing in her kitchen was a stranger, there was something primally familiar about him. She ached to touch him like she would have Will or Zane, smoothing their hair or patting their arm, reassuring herself that they were hers in perpetuity.

"It's fine," Josh said. "I'm fine." He set his jaw.

"I wasn't trying to—"

"I don't need your pity, OK?" He turned away to look out the window. "I don't need anything from you. I've been fine on my own."

Rhea felt the hot sting of rejection. She let a long moment pass before saying gently, "But, here you are."

Josh shoved his hands in his pockets and rocked back on his feet. "I needed a change of scene, you know?" He looked away. "And I guess I wanted to meet you."

Taking a deep breath, she reached out and placed a tentative hand on his shoulder, which felt stable and firm. This was the first time she'd ever touched him. Even as a baby, she'd let them take him away without holding him, without looking at him. Guilt sliced at her chest.

A loud trill startled her. She dropped her hand and stepped away from Josh to pull her phone from her pocket. Brooks's name flashed across the screen with a FaceTime notification.

"I'm sorry," she said. "I need to answer this." She swiped the screen to answer as she crossed the room, stepping through the sliding door to the backyard and pulling it closed behind her. "Hi, sweetheart," she said.

"Hey, babe," Brooks replied. His hair was sweaty and plastered to his head.

"Isn't it, like, 6 a.m. there?"

"Yup," he replied. "And I've already been to the gym. Turns out I'm a morning person in Japan." Rhea laughed without feeling it.

"God, I miss you guys," he said.

"We miss you, too," she said, glancing over at Josh inside. From the back he was broader than Will or Zane and resembled a man more than a boy.

She hadn't meant to keep Josh's existence a secret all these years. But meeting Brooks in college had felt like a fresh start. And the way he treated her back then—and still did—sending her flowers, draping his jacket over her shoulders when she was cold. He'd made her feel like a different person—someone worthy of those gestures. She liked seeing herself through his eyes so much that she kept her past to herself, until eventually it felt too late to come clean.

Now, standing only feet from Josh but unable to reveal his presence to her husband, a swell of long-buried emotions surged inside her, threatening to pull her under. The only thing she could do was keep swimming.

"I only have a minute, but I wanted to hear your voice," Brooks said. "I can't wait to be home. Just one more week."

"One more week," Rhea echoed. She wondered if he could hear her heart pounding through the phone.

"OK, sweetie, I need to run. I love you."

"Love you, too," she echoed. When she hung up she pressed the phone to her chest and looked back inside toward Josh. One more week to figure out her next move.

SEVENTEEN

Maggie handed Anna a glass of water as the women settled themselves in the living room. Anna had arrived wearing a gray turtleneck despite the late-September heat wave, and looking limp and shrunken, like a ribbon dancer outside a car dealership on a day without much wind. Maggie opened her mouth to ask if Anna was all right, but Rhea spoke first.

"Wait, is that your wedding album?" Rhea asked, reaching for the photo book on the coffee table. Feeling nostalgic, Maggie had taken it out the night before. "I love weddings," Rhea declared, opening to a picture of Maggie and Dan sitting at the head table, each brandishing a giant turkey leg. "Um, wow...?" Rhea said.

Maggie's blush stood out against her standard white blouse over gray pants. "We were really into renaissance fairs back then."

Rhea looked gleeful. "Please tell me you had a jousting match at the reception?"

"I mean, we probably would have if it wasn't cost prohibitive..." Maggie admitted.

Anna leaned over to look at the picture. "Also, last I

checked, long, sharp spears didn't mix well with an open bar," she pointed out.

Maggie laughed, relieved to see a flash of life from Anna.

Rhea giggled and flipped the page to where a younger and less tired-looking version of Maggie held a champagne flute aloft as Dan kissed her. Maggie smiled at the memory. She'd felt so beautiful that day, and so happy to have found the perfect person with whom to cross marriage off her life goals list.

Those intense feelings of passion had dulled over time, of course, but that was natural. She saw it with her clients all the time. Only last week she'd started seeing a new couple who were dismayed that their lovemaking had dwindled to once a month. Privately Maggie had had to stifle her jealousy—she would have been thrilled with once a month.

"I loved my wedding day," Rhea said dreamily, fiddling with the scalloped collar of her rust-colored eyelet blouse. "I had two different dresses and a horse-drawn carriage to take us to the reception."

Maggie raised her eyebrows. "Easy, Cinderella."

It was Rhea's turn to blush. "Yeah, I guess I did want to feel like a princess," she admitted. "I didn't have much money growing up, you know?"

"What about you, Anna?" Maggie asked. She'd often thought Anna's aloofness was a perfect match for Jerry's stick-up-his-ass demeanor. But now that she knew Anna better, Maggie wondered why she'd ever chosen Jerry.

Anna pressed her lips into a thin line. "We went to the Chicago courthouse. Jerry didn't want any fuss."

Maggie tilted her head. Anna had never struck her as a sentimental person, but in Maggie's experience—at least with her clients—most women got at least a little nostalgic about their wedding. "Was that what you wanted, too?" she probed.

Anna pulled at the neck of her turtleneck. "Oh, it was fine. It's one day, right?" She laughed haltingly, then changed the subject. "So, Mrs. Kaminski printed me the latest list of silent auction donations." Mrs. Kaminski was Jerry's long-time assistant and a fixture in the Civitas office. Anna reached to retrieve her purse, then winced and grabbed her ribs. "Oh!" she gasped.

"Are you OK?" Maggie asked, alarmed.

"Fine," Anna managed, sounding strained. "I had a minor car accident last week."

"Oh my gosh!" Rhea sat forward on the couch. "What happened?"

"I'm fine," Anna said sharply, her hand still pressed to her side. Then she looked embarrassed. "Really, I'm OK," she said in a softer voice. She reached into her Civitas tote and pulled out a thick stack of papers.

Momentarily thrown by Anna's uncharacteristic outburst, Maggie paused, then eyed the papers. "Wow," she said. "She couldn't have emailed them?"

Anna laughed, then winced again. "Nope," she said. "The woman prints everything for backup. It drives Jerry crazy."

"Hmm," Maggie said. "Then I wish we could ask her about the NDAs. Isaac said—"

"Isaac?" Anna interrupted, sitting up straighter. "When did you talk to Isaac?"

Maggie tensed, realizing her error. "Uh... I saw him the other day." She hadn't meant to bring this up in front of Anna— what if Jerry was involved in whatever Isaac had hinted at? Anna was married to him, after all. It was very likely she knew more than she was letting on. In her head, Maggie began to run through the list of possibilities that involved NDAs: some sort of sexual harassment suit? Bullying or hazing?

Anna looked like she'd stopped short at the edge of a cliff. "What did Isaac say?"

"Not much," Maggie said cautiously, trying to make sense of Anna's strong reaction. A whisper of suspicion lodged in her brain. Then she plucked out the pen that was holding her hair on top of her head and changed the subject back to safer topics. At least until she knew whose side Anna was on. "So," she said. "Let's review the final donations for the silent auction."

Anna nodded and she separated the stack of papers into three neat piles. She extended one of the piles to Maggie, wincing again. Maggie frowned. Something felt off with all of Anna's reactions today. She tried to catch Rhea's eye to see if she felt it too, but Rhea was still paging through the wedding album.

"Anna," Maggie said softly, as though Anna might spook. "Are you sure you're OK?" She pointed to Anna's hand, still clutching her ribs. "You should probably get that looked at."

Anna nodded, seemingly deflated once more. "Yeah, I probably should."

Rhea closed the album with a sharp thump. "Sorry to cut this short, but I can't stay tonight," she said. "I've got a... guest. But I'll take this and finalize it." She scooped up her portion of the silent auction list.

Anna nodded and carefully reached for her bag. "I should go, too."

"Oh," Maggie said, surprised to find she was disappointed they were leaving. She realized she'd started looking forward to their meetings. For so many years she'd been laser-focused on her career, not making time for girlfriends. Plus she'd had Dan. She still considered him her best friend, but lately she couldn't ignore the distance that had opened between them like a small crack. It had allowed loneliness to seep in, like the slow buildup of fog, imperceptible at first but now enveloping her so completely she could hardly see her hand in front of her face.

"By the way," Anna said as she rose gingerly to her feet. "I, uh, got a new phone number so you can text me now. I'll send it to both of you." She dipped her head, her fringe of dark hair making it impossible for Maggie to see her expression.

"A new phone number?" Rhea looked surprised. "Wow, that's so... early 2000s."

Anna shrugged. "Yeah, well."

As she walked them to the door, Maggie's mind cycled back through the evening. Why had Anna been so rattled at the mention of Isaac's name? Or was Maggie being paranoid? With a flash of self-doubt, she heard Dan's voice in her head, teasing her about her true crime obsession. She sighed. Maybe it was time for an actual hobby instead of dead-end amateur sleuthing. Pickleball, maybe?

Back in the living room she picked up her folder and notebook, and her phone buzzed in her pocket. She pulled it out and looked down at the screen.

Incoming call, Isaac Harris.

EIGHTEEN

After she drove home from Maggie's house, Rhea pulled into her driveway and sat for a moment before getting out of the car, overwhelmed at the thought of what waited for her inside: her sons—all three of them. Something about this thought felt so *complete.* She let that word roll around in her brain as a yearning ache began in her chest. Had it really felt incomplete before?

Memories flooded her: how Will and Zane would sneak into bed with her and Brooks when they were small, a jumble of little boy arms and legs in the middle of the night. The "restaurant" they set up for her and Brooks at ages seven and ten, each wearing one of Brooks's ties while they served them peanut butter sandwiches and Gatorade in wineglasses. Their family road trip to Maine two summers ago, the four of them hiking, roasting marshmallows, and competing to see who could use the most local slang words in a sentence.

She'd been happy in those moments. Completely happy; not happy in spite of an empty space in her heart or the constant feeling that something was missing. Now, though, having Josh here had unlocked a choppy mix of joy and regret that left her both riding the euphoric crest of a wave and afraid of drowning in it.

Exactly one week had passed since Josh's unexpected arrival, and still she was at a loss for what to say or do when Brooks returned tomorrow. He knew Josh was there, of course. Rhea had fed him a story about her college-age nephew coming to visit, just in case Will or Zane brought it up, and Brooks hadn't probed further. But if he came home tomorrow and Josh was still here, well... then he would.

Pulling herself out of her thoughts, Rhea headed inside. As she crossed the living room, voices drifted up from the basement.

"No, no, no, crap!" Zane cried.

Will laughed. "Oh man, he totally demolished you."

There was another, unfamiliar laugh—Josh's. "It was a lucky shot," he said.

Rhea realized she'd never heard Josh laugh. Her eyes brimmed with tears at the thought and she hovered near the basement stairs, listening to the lightness in his voice like it might wash away her motherly sins.

Letting Josh stay that first night had been easy; there'd been no reason for him to go. He'd settled into the guest room, keeping it so tidy it almost looked unlived in. His gratitude was palpable, evidenced by the way he tidied the kitchen while she took the boys to school, and helped with dinner. But each silent act of thanks only added to Rhea's guilt.

Now, though, with Brooks due home in less than twenty-four hours, the sickening mix of emotions in Rhea's stomach intensified. All week she'd felt buoyed by the immense gratitude and relief that Josh was there with her, that he wanted to be with her despite the awful thing she'd done. Yet, she'd also been paralyzed, floundering in the face of an impossible decision—and she was nearly out of time.

She closed her eyes, wishing they could remain in the beautiful bubble of the past week indefinitely. Zane had taught Josh to play Fortnite, and two nights ago she'd found Josh sprawled on Will's bedroom floor, helping him with his trigonometry. Could she really tell Josh their time was up now, that he had to leave to ensure her husband and her illegitimate son never crossed paths?

The thunder of footsteps on the basement stairs jolted her back into the moment and Rhea's eyes flew open.

"Oh, sorry," Josh said, slowing. "I didn't realize you were home." He wore a worn-out gray hooded sweatshirt over the same T-shirt with the Texas flag from the first night. His green eyes crinkled as he smiled, causing Rhea's heart to leap in her chest.

"I just got back," she said, returning his smile. Almost instinctively, she moved closer, yearning to touch him, to wrap her arms around him and promise she'd never leave him again. Instead, she hugged her arms to her sides.

"Will and Zane are hungry so I was going to put in some frozen pizzas—is that OK?"

Rhea laughed. The way he took charge of the two younger boys reminded her of an overeager camp counselor. "Of course."

Josh tilted his head, the permanent worry line on his brow deepening. "What's funny?"

"You know you don't have to babysit them when I'm not here, right?"

His face darkened. "I wasn't... I mean, I actually like hanging out with them," he said, his tone short.

Regret surged. "I'm sorry, I didn't mean—" she began, pausing to gather her thoughts. Every word between them felt so important. "What I mean is," she continued, "I can tell you would have been a great big brother." She caught herself, shaking her head. "That you are a great big brother. Damn it," she swore softly, her mask of decorum slipping, and brought her palm to her forehead. "I'm sorry. This is... hard."

Josh nodded and gave a small smile. "It's fine, I get it. Thank you."

The boys trooped upstairs for pizza a short while later. Rhea sat with them but her mind was elsewhere as they chattered.

"Right, Mom?" Zane asked. A smear of pizza sauce streaked across his cheek.

"Hmm?" Rhea snapped back to attention. "I'm sorry, what's that, honey?"

"Josh should come to my dive meet, this weekend, right?" Zane repeated.

Rhea's heartbeat quickened as she scrambled for a response. She knew Josh had to go before the weekend, but the idea of him leaving, of not being with her every day, felt unbearable.

Zane turned to Josh. "And after my meets we always go to El Pollo Loco for tacos—that means 'the crazy chicken' in Spanish."

"Dude, he knows that," Will interjected, popping a stray piece of pepperoni into his mouth and wiping his hands on his dark green Civitas sweatshirt. "P.S., you eat like a toddler." He pointed at Zane's face.

Zane narrowed his eyes and swiped at his cheek with a napkin. "*Maybe* Josh doesn't speak Spanish."

Will smirked. "Bro, *you* don't speak Spanish."

Zane glared. "Do too!"

Will rolled his eyes and addressed Josh. "He spent a week with a host family in Costa Rica last summer and now he thinks he's fluent." He turned to Zane. "Say something in Spanish."

Zane scrunched up his face in concentration. "Um, yo puedo comer siete tacos. There." He stuck his tongue out at Will and turned back to Josh. "That means, 'I can eat seven tacos.' But I bet you can eat way more. So, are you gonna come this weekend?"

Josh glanced at Rhea and cleared his throat. "If I can make it, I'll definitely come."

Later that night Rhea found herself walking toward the guest room. "Hey," she said, standing at the half-open door. She'd already washed off her makeup and twisted her hair into a haphazard bun.

"Hey." Josh looked up from where he was reading, his compact, muscular frame stretched out on the bed.

"The boys used to love that movie," Rhea said, pointing to his battered copy of *The Jungle Book*.

"I never saw it," he said. "I'm not much of movie person." He gave a half-smile. "The TV room was always where the fights broke out at group homes."

Rhea swallowed, once again overwhelmed by how much of his life she'd missed. She stepped further into the room. "How many were you in?" she asked.

Josh set the book face down on his stomach and folded his hands behind his head. "Three. Four, if you count the one I only stayed at for a week, but I don't."

His words were like a punch she hadn't braced for. "Why so many?"

He shrugged. "Reorganizations, quotas, budgets, who knows. I learned to stop asking and always be ready to go."

A nauseating mixture of guilt and self-loathing rose in her throat and she buried her face in her hands.

"Hey." Josh lowered his arms and sat up. "I'm not trying to guilt-trip you here."

She lifted her eyes to his, her anguish amplified by his earnest expression. "You have to understand," she said, recalling her father's stark ultimatum. "Keeping you wasn't an option. I couldn't have taken care of you if..." She balled her hands into fists, trying to imagine walking out of the hospital with a baby and nowhere to go.

"I know," he said. He swung his legs over the side of the bed and sat there, his face taut with emotion.

Rhea took another step forward and sank down next to him. "I'm sorry," she said, gesturing to her tear-streaked face. "I should be the one comforting you. After all, I'm your..." She trailed off, then looked at him and whispered the word she'd been desperate to say. "*Mother.*" Taking a deep breath, she put out her hand. He hesitated, then took it, his fingers warm and rough against her own.

The only sound was the ticking of the clock on the bedside table, and Rhea would have given anything to grab it and turn back time and erase the way she'd failed her son, husband, even herself. But she didn't know what she was supposed to have done differently.

She squeezed Josh's hand and managed a teary smile. "I'm glad you're here."

He squeezed back, his voice thick. "Me too."

Their shoulders touched, and as she felt his breath rise and fall so close to her, something primal took over. "Will you stay a bit longer?" she asked.

Releasing those words felt like loosening an iron corset from around her ribs. Her chest expanded at the possibility of Josh's continued presence. Yes, it meant piling more lies on top of the one that already existed between her and Brooks. Yes, it meant altering the precious ecosystem of her family. Yes, it meant rethinking her entire identity. But also, it was her one chance to make things right.

And anyway, there was no going back now.

NINETEEN

Anna struggled to concentrate on the legal document displayed on her computer screen, but her thoughts kept returning to Maggie's living room the previous day. While part of her admired Maggie's in courage tracking down Isaac, it had also stirred up a fresh wave of worries.

Anna was surprised at how much she liked being on the committee with Maggie and Rhea. Though it had only been a month, she'd begun to relax around them, no longer feeling like she was treading on eggshells as she did around anyone associated with Jerry and Civitas. She'd felt at ease enough that for a split second yesterday she'd even considered telling Maggie exactly what she knew about Isaac's resignation—which, she realized now, would have been a huge mistake.

Maggie could never understand how it felt for Anna to finally be making progress on her plan. Landing this job had been a huge step, but its success hinged on placating Jerry. Stirring up things at Civitas, especially regarding Isaac's contentious departure, would only provoke Jerry and further complicate Anna's life.

Anna glimpsed Donna approaching and shook her head to

refocus. She compared her own gray suit to Donna's attire—a yellow blazer layered over a peacock-patterned dress—and wondered what it would feel like to dress to stand out instead of blend in.

"Good morning." Donna saluted Anna with her ever-present Starbucks cup.

"Good morning," Anna replied cautiously. She'd learned that the better Donna's mood, the more work she was about to give Anna.

"I've been thinking," Donna said.

"Famous last words," Sydney muttered as she walked by and flashed Anna a sympathetic smile.

"I've got a new case I think you're perfect for." Donna dropped a file on Anna's desk. "Pro bono. A friend of a friend kind of thing."

"What's the issue?" Anna eyed the folder. Already she was barely keeping up with the work she had.

"Domestic violence. The husband's a real piece of work." Donna pinched her lips together. "The wife's pressing charges, trying to get a protective order, emergency custody situation, the works."

Anna's body went rigid, her heart jumping like it had been snapped by a rubber band. "But we do litigation," she stammered. "Not family law."

Donna put a hand on her hip. "Surely you can figure out how to file one measly order of protection." Then she lowered her voice. "Look, I know it's not our usual thing, but it's a friend of my niece's. I said I'd help."

Anna glanced at the multiple documents open on her screen that demanded her attention, then back at the file folder. She sighed. "Fine."

"That's the spirit." Donna waved her coffee like a flag.

"When does it—"

"Yesterday."

Once Donna had retreated, Anna opened the folder and paged through it, finding a handful of police reports, the first from five years earlier.

The defendant, Bryce Martin, and the victim, Kayla Martin, have been married one year and have no children in common. The victim called 911 to report a domestic altercation. Deputy Harold Wilson 6745 responded and upon meeting the victim, she was visibly shaking and sobbing uncontrollably. She advised that the defendant had accused her of flirting with another man and had pushed her up against a wall and struck her on the left side of her face, leaving a visible mark. No charges filed.

Another from three years ago:

The victim and the defendant have one child in common, age 11 months... the victim reported being held down on the sofa by the defendant and punched in the stomach. The victim claims to be pregnant. No charges filed.

The latest one was from a week ago.

The victim, Kayla Martin, reported being slammed against the wall and strangled while the defendant reported he was going to get a gun and kill her. Charges filed: Aggravated Battery— Domestic Violence; Commit/Attempt Specified Felony Could Cause Death.

Anna's hands trembled as she dropped the reports, shivering as if someone had cranked the air conditioning. She flashed back to being curled on the garage floor, the explosion of pain in her ribs, the pungent smell of her own panicked sweat.

She'd called the police once when Farrah was eight. She'd fought back that time, leaving a scratch on Jerry's cheek, the only visible evidence when the officers arrived. Not the finger-shaped bruises that would form later or the sharp pain in her skull from being shaken so hard she thought her neck would snap. Overwhelmed and hysterical, she'd unleashed years of pent-up conflict to the officers, while Jerry remained composed and apologetic, minimizing the incident. When given the opportunity to press charges, Anna wilted under Jerry's warning glare. Later, lying on the floor in Farrah's room, listening to her daughter breathe, Anna finally grasped the futility of her situation.

"Hey." Sydney's voice yanked Anna back from the dark corners of her memory. "You OK there?"

"What?" Anna shook her head and forced a laugh. "I'm fine. Just tired."

"Coffee run?" Sydney suggested, consulting her watch. "I've got ten minutes before my next call and I'm going to need it." She mimed trying to keep her eyes open.

Anna looked down at the police reports on her desk and the cache of photos documenting Kayla's injuries. She had a set of pictures like that somewhere, photos she'd snapped in a rare moment when her denial had temporarily lifted. "Sorry," she said, looking up at Sydney. "This is urgent."

TWENTY

When Brooks landed the next morning he went straight to the office. "I'm sorry," he groaned over FaceTime from the car en route from Atlanta airport to the Ironwall offices. "All I want is to come home and see you—all of you." He raised his eyebrows suggestively.

Rhea laughed. "I missed you, too."

"I won't be late, I promise," he continued, rubbing the stubble on his chin after his long-haul flight.

"Great," she said. Then, trying to keep the tremor out of her voice, she added, "Also, my nephew is still here."

Brooks sighed. "Still?" He spent a lot of time traveling, and Rhea knew he liked things to be a certain way when he was home. Calm. Predictable. Routine. Having a sudden, open-ended house guest was none of these. He frowned. "It's weird, I've never once heard you mention this kid. Also, how does your sister already have a kid in college? Isn't she only a year older than you?" He smirked. "Is this one of those teen mom situations?"

Shame bloomed in Rhea's chest and she forced a smile.

"Sweetheart, I've got to run or I'll be late for Pilates," she lied, eager to get off the phone before her emotions betrayed her.

"Fine," Brooks said. Any hint of his earlier smile was gone. "I'll see you at home later."

With Josh occupied at the public library polishing his résumé and the boys off at school, Rhea found herself alone the rest of the day. Anxiety buzzed within her chest and she busied herself making her famous pulled pork recipe—the one good thing she'd gotten from her mother. It was Brooks's favorite, and she hoped it would smooth over his irritation at Josh's presence.

After the meal prep, she indulged in a long shower, then carefully did her makeup and blow-dried her hair instead of bundling it into a ponytail as she had been all week. She knew Brooks wouldn't care whether she was in sweatpants or couture, but full hair and makeup felt like necessary armor, along with her favorite black Reformation sweater dress. No one knew her better than her husband, but now she feared that knowledge meant he'd take one look at Josh and guess the truth.

The boys all arrived home around the same time and drifted down into the basement with a tray of snacks. With nothing left to do, Rhea began to pace from the kitchen to the living room, struggling to keep her anxiety at bay.

Lost in thought, she jumped at the sound of the garage door going up as Brooks walked through the door. His eyes were red and tired looking and his light blue dress shirt was wrinkled and rolled at the sleeves. But the smile spreading across his face felt like a life raft.

"Hey," she said. In her chest, the gratitude that he was home battled with the worry about what came next. He bent to kiss her, his lips lingering on hers. Then he pressed his forehead against hers.

"Mm, it's good to be home," he said. He drew back and squeezed her hand.

"Where are the boys?"

"Downstairs." She hesitated and tried to sound casual. "With Josh." She crossed to the basement stairs, where voices and laughter could be heard. "Dinner!" she called down.

"Is Dad home?" came Zane's voice.

"You bet he is!" bellowed Brooks, and a cheer went up from downstairs.

Footsteps rocketed up the stairway and Zane barreled through the door, tackling his father in a hug.

"Hey, buddy," Brooks said, mussing Zane's hair. "God, it's good to see you." He stepped back and held Zane at arm's length. "And how did you get taller? I wasn't gone that long, was I?"

The collar of Zane's dark green Civitas polo shirt was turned up on one side and his face glowed with excitement. "Guess what, Dad? I got to start working on a reverse pike dive!"

Brooks put his arm around Zane again. "Awesome, I can't wait to see."

Will emerged next, also still clad in his Civitas uniform of gray dress pants and polo shirt. His eager smile melted Rhea's heart. "Hey, Dad," he said, brushing a wave of hair off his forehead and letting himself be folded into a bear hug.

As Will and Brooks broke apart, Josh emerged from the stairway. Rhea's pulse quickened. Even after only a week together, she could tell he was nervous by the tightness of his smile and the way he held his broad shoulders squared. Normally he dressed in a T-shirt and his threadbare hoodie, but today he'd donned a striped rugby shirt with a collar.

"Sweetheart," Rhea said, putting a gentle hand on Brooks's arm, "this is my nephew, Josh."

Josh stepped forward like a solider in formation. "It's nice to meet you, sir," he said, putting out his hand.

Brooks shook hands and gave the briefest of nods. "Nice to meet you, too," he said, then turned back to Will and Zane. Rhea thought she saw the slightest shadow of longing flit across Josh's face as the other two boys settled onto the couch with their father.

She clapped her hands, eager to bring them all back together. "Dinner's ready," she said. "We'll eat in the dining room."

The five of them filed in, with Will and Zane talking nonstop over one another and jockeying to sit next to Brooks.

"Something smells amazing," Josh said, glancing around the chairs. Rhea touched his shoulder and directed him to the one next to her.

"Well, it's definitely not Zane," Will said.

"Hey!" Zane punched his brother in the shoulder.

"Huh?" Will said, feigning confusion. "Did a tiny, weak little fly just punch me?"

Zane snorted and slid into his seat. "At least I don't stink as much as you do at Fortnite."

"Oh please," Will said, flopping onto a chair. "Josh beat you like a million times in a row and it didn't even look like he was trying that hard, right?" He looked to Josh for backup.

Josh put up his hands, looking more relaxed now that they'd all sat down. "I'm Switzerland, remember? Totally neutral." Will and Zane both laughed, but Brooks looked unamused as he gazed at Josh with his jaw set. Rhea's heart thudded in her ears as she tried to catch his eye. Had he somehow guessed?

"Dad," Zane said once Rhea had served them all a plate of steaming pork, cornbread, and green beans. "Did you know Josh played football in high school?"

Rhea shook her head. Zane desperately wanted to play football but both she and Brooks were against it, given the high rate of head injuries.

"Mm," Brooks said, sounding uninterested.

"And there's nothing wrong with his brain." Zane gave Rhea a pointed look, then turned back to Brooks. "He even played for Baylor for a while."

"Baylor?" Brooks looked up from his plate, perking up for the first time since walking through the door. "Good school. And good football team."

"I was a walk-on," Josh said hastily, fiddling with the button at his collar. "For, like, half a season before I hurt my knee."

"See, he hurt himself," Rhea said to Zane, who pouted.

"What was your major, Josh?" Brooks asked. Rhea's shoulders sagged in relief, seeing the spark of curiosity in her husband's eyes. He simply needed to realize what a good kid Josh was, how well he fit into their family. Then maybe she could finally tell him the truth.

"I studied English and business, sir."

"You don't have to call him sir," Zane said. He stuffed nearly a whole piece of cornbread into his mouth and made a show of saluting his father.

"Yeah," echoed Will, making a slashing motion in front of his throat. "You're making us look bad."

Brooks raised his eyebrows. "Then maybe you guys should step it up," he said firmly, and Josh blushed. "Will, you should talk to Josh about college," Brooks continued, then looked back at Josh. "Will's thinking about studying business."

"Nice." Josh nodded.

"As long as he can keep his grades up," Rhea reminded Will.

"I am!" Will protested, sitting up out of a slouch. "Look how good I did on my trig midterm."

"How well," Brooks corrected.

"Will, how's Pen?" Rhea asked, sensing the need for a

change of subject. She also realized she hadn't seen Pen at the house all week, when normally it felt like she was underfoot all the time. She'd even had the audacity to add her favorite brand of yogurt to the grocery list Rhea kept taped to the fridge. "I haven't seen her lately."

Will shrugged and sank back down in his chair. "Fine," he mumbled. "We've both been kind of busy."

The three boys kept up a steady stream of banter for the rest of dinner, but Brooks was mostly quiet.

"You OK?" Rhea asked lightly when she managed to catch his eye, still trying to gauge whether he'd guessed.

"Yeah, only tired, sorry. It was a long trip."

She nodded and patted his hand, relieved when he smiled in return.

When they finished eating, Josh got up to clear the table. "Please," Rhea protested. "I'll do it."

"Will, help your mother," Brooks instructed.

"But it's Zane's turn," Will complained, tossing his napkin on his plate.

"Nah-uh, I did it last night." Zane edged out of his chair.

"Here's an idea," Josh said, flexing his bicep. "Whoever can beat me at arm wrestling doesn't have to help with the dishes."

"Bro, no thanks," Will said, nodding at Josh's muscular arm. "I can't get involved with that."

"I bet I can beat you, no problem." Zane puffed out his chest.

"All right then, give me your best shot." Josh bent over and planted his elbow on the table. Zane walked over to him, and after a brief struggle in which Josh let Zane almost win, the older boy prevailed.

"Aw man," Zane said. "I almost had you. Rematch!"

"Later," Josh promised with a smile.

Later, when Rhea got ready for bed, she opted for a slinky silk nightgown instead of her usual oversized T-shirt; she and

Brooks usually had sex the night he got home from a trip. When he came out of the bathroom wearing only his boxers, a zing went through her at the sight of his broad chest. Climbing into bed, he stroked her hair and leaned in to kiss her, slow and deep, his fingers tracing a circle on her thigh as they inched her nightgown up.

Finding their rhythm took longer than usual, but once they did, they efficiently satisfied each other. Usually Rhea slept well after they made love, but tonight she tossed and turned, unable to settle into a comfortable position. Her whole family was home and safe. Dinner had gone well. So why was she still lying awake, wondering if she'd made a huge mistake?

TWENTY-ONE

In the four days since filing Kayla Martin's protection order, Anna's thoughts had been consumed by it. The paperwork had included a move-out order, mandating that Bryce Martin vacate their home while legal proceedings unfolded. Kayla also gained temporary custody of their young daughter and son. As Anna had completed the paperwork, she'd wondered whether Bryce really did have access to a gun. They were easy enough to get in Georgia. Jerry had even once discussed getting one for "protection," a notion that sent shivers through Anna.

She had been so preoccupied thinking about Kayla that twice Donna had caught her with her mind elsewhere during meetings. Now, driving home, she was nearly in her driveway before she noticed Jerry's Jeep parked out front. Adrenaline surged as she accelerated past the house, taking the first turn off their street and running a stop sign in the process. *No, no, no,* she thought, making three more turns before feeling safe enough to pull over. It was the middle of the day—what was he doing home? And more importantly, had he seen her?

Her heart pounded in her chest and she gripped the steering wheel. She couldn't go inside like this, in her work clothes. Looking around, she got out of the car and opened the trunk, retrieving a plastic bag with her regular clothes from under the spare tire. In the back seat, she shimmied out of her suit and into leggings and a T-shirt, praying no one would pass by while she was half-naked. She rolled up her suit, stuffed it back in the plastic bag, and returned it to the trunk.

Back at home she parked in the garage, and with a shaky breath she let herself into the house. "Hello?" she called, trying to keep the fear out of her voice. Dropping her purse by the door, she continued warily through the house, as though Jerry might pop out like a mechanical ghost in a haunted house. Finally she reached their bedroom, where Jerry was huddled under the covers.

"Darling," he groaned. "Don't come too close."

She stopped in the doorway, her heart still hammering. "What on earth is wrong?"

"Something I ate..." he rasped. His face looked pale and clammy. "Or maybe a stomach bug."

The relief that flooded her body was so powerful she grabbed the door jamb to steady herself. "I'm so sorry," she said. "Let me see if we have any Gatorade."

He grunted and rolled onto his side. "I doubt I'll keep it down." Then he frowned. "Where were you? I tried calling."

Anna gripped the doorway tighter, her palms suddenly slippery with sweat. "I forgot my phone," she said, backing away toward the kitchen. The suspicion on Jerry's face vanished, replaced by a look of nausea as he let his head fall back onto the pillow. "I'll be right back," Anna said.

That evening, with Jerry still in bed, Anna treated herself and Farrah to takeout from their favorite sushi place. Jerry hated sushi. "All that rice and seaweed," he complained. They ate off trays in the living room, watching old episodes of *The Great British Baking Show*.

"Why have we never gone to England?" Farrah asked as on the screen a plump, nervous woman watched the judges bite into one of her scones. Farrah's hair was parted neatly in the middle and pulled into space buns, and she wore nylon shorts so short they disappeared under her enormous Civitas lacrosse T-shirt.

"England?" Anna frowned.

"Yeah, I mean, Dad's from there." Farrah squeezed an edamame shell and popped the small green beans into her mouth.

"Well, yes, but his parents—"

"Yeah, I know they died a long time ago, like before you met. But doesn't he have, like, cousins or something? Why wouldn't he want to visit?"

"He was an only child, like you." Anna scooped up a healthy dollop of wasabi and mixed it into her soy sauce.

Farrah sucked the salt off her edamame shell. "We never go see Ama and Pop Pop anymore, either," she said, her tone almost petulant. "And they don't come here."

Anna's chest tightened with guilt as she thought of her parents out in California. They were getting older, but Jerry complained tickets to the West Coast were too expensive. And whenever her mother suggested visiting them in Atlanta, Jerry had shot it down, claiming work was too stressful for him to endure visitors. Eventually her mother had stopped bringing it up.

"Plane tickets are expensive," Anna said to Farrah. "And anyway, when would we go? Between lacrosse and school, you hardly even have time to sleep."

"But don't you want to go?" Farrah persisted, waving a chopstick in the air.

"Well, of course, but—"

"Then you should go," Farrah said sharply.

Anna froze, startled.

"You should go if you want to go," Farrah repeated. She stabbed a piece of sushi with her chopstick. "Just like you should cut your hair if that's what you want to do, and work if you want to work." She paused, her chin jutting forward. "But he won't let you do any of that, will he?"

Anna swallowed hard and tried to speak. "Farrah, I—"

"I hear everything, you know," Farrah said quietly, looking down at her plate.

Anna struggled to take in a breath, feeling like the oxygen had suddenly gone out of the room. "What do you mean?" she managed.

Farrah threw down her chopsticks and crossed her arms. "I mean, I hear the way he talks to you when you both think I'm not around. He says... mean stuff." She coughed and blinked back tears, her shoulders sagging. "How can you let him be so *mean* to you?"

"Oh, sweetheart." Anna wrapped her arm around Farrah's shoulder and tried to corral her galloping thoughts into something she could share with her thirteen-year-old daughter. "I'm so sorry you have to hear us argue," she said carefully. "And yes, Daddy can be, well, rude sometimes. But he's under a lot of stress and—"

Farrah wiggled out of Anna's embrace. "I knew you'd say that," she said flatly, swinging her legs onto the floor. She stood up and faced Anna, her hands on her hips. "I knew you'd just act like it was OK."

"Farrah," Anna pleaded. "Relationships can be complicated. You'll understand when you're older." But her words rang hollow even to her own ears. As Farrah turned away and headed down the hall to her room, Anna felt a wave of desperation crash over her. She'd let things go on for too long, and she'd been stupid enough to think she could keep it from impacting her daughter.

But in the midst of her despair she felt something else, too. As she thought of her job and the independence it could provide, she felt the unfamiliar stirrings of hope, like a tiny seedling uncurling in the sunlight.

She only hoped it wasn't too late.

TWENTY-TWO

Maggie walked into the diner, surprised to find it crowded at ten thirty on a Monday morning. Isaac had been hard to pin down, but when he'd finally agreed to meet she'd canceled her patients, a rarity for her, but this meeting felt critical.

There was no traffic on the way to College Park, so she arrived early. Isaac was already there, however, settled at a table in the back. He caught her eye and raised a hand in greeting, standing up as she approached. He wore dark jeans and a black T-shirt with ATL in white block letters on the front. Maggie glanced down at her own outfit—standard gray dress pants and a boring white button-up shirt—wishing she'd worn something more stylish. Even her ballet flats were gray today. She dressed to blend in, ensuring her patients could concentrate on their shared inner work rather than on her fashion choices. Pen joked that this usually made her look like the manager of an Olive Garden, and in this moment, Maggie didn't disagree.

She approached Isaac and without thinking she leaned in to kiss him on the cheek as if he were an old friend, and felt his stubble graze her face. She caught a whiff of something woodsy and clean-smelling and felt her pulse speed up.

"Oh," he said, stepping back. "So we're doing *that* now?"

Maggie flushed. "Sorry," she said. "I got caught up in the ambiance of this place." She gestured at the Formica tables and metal chairs that looked prison-issued.

"Make fun all you want," Isaac said as they sat, "but this place has the best biscuits in the city. Plus they serve breakfast all day."

"Breakfast? You know it's almost eleven, right?" Maggie raised her eyebrows.

"So?" he scoffed. "There's never a wrong time to eat French toast. Plus, I'm unemployed, remember?"

The hint of a smile on his lips sent a fresh wave of dizziness over Maggie. She pressed her palms onto the cool tabletop, trying to regain her composure. She felt like one of the silly, hormonal teenage girls constantly crowding into her house.

"Here you go, sugar." A smiling, round-shouldered older woman with a white pouf of hair appeared at their table, holding a heavy-looking white plate with a tall stack of French toast. The intoxicating aroma of butter and molasses wafted toward Maggie.

"Thanks, Hazel." Isaac smiled. "Sorry." He looked toward Maggie. "I was early—and hungry—so I went ahead and ordered."

Hazel looked Maggie up and down and her smile vanished. She pulled a little white notepad from her apron pocket. "For you?" she asked.

"Um, coffee for me, thanks. With oat milk if you have it," Maggie said.

Hazel snapped her notepad shut without writing anything down and walked away, leaving Maggie unsure as to whether the woman had actually taken her order.

"So how's Pen these days?" Isaac asked as he doused his plate with maple syrup. "Still wielding an iron fist over at the

Recorder?" He grinned. "I swear the *Washington Post* has lower journalistic standards than she does."

Maggie laughed. Pen took her duties as editor of the school newspaper, the *Civitas Recorder*, very seriously. "I forgot you were the faculty advisor for the school paper," she said.

He shrugged. "Yeah, when Ms. Burnett was fir—" He caught himself. "When Ms. Burnett left, no one else wanted that one so I got stuck with it," he said.

Maggie cocked her head. "So she *was* fired. Is that why she had to sign an NDA?"

Isaac pressed his lips together with a guilty look. "You didn't hear that from me."

Maggie frowned. "She was Pen's favorite. She's the one who inspired her to seriously consider studying journalism in college."

Isaac shifted in his seat and cleared his throat. "She was a lot of people's favorite."

Maggie started to speak, but Isaac interrupted. "Speaking of favorites," he said, pushing his plate toward her. "You have to try this. It's my standard order."

Maggie raised an eyebrow, accepting his change of subject— at least for the moment. "After the way you looked at me in your driveway when I showed up, I'm surprised you wanted to meet, much less share your breakfast," she said.

He set his fork down. "Forgive me for saying this, but in my neighborhood, when a crazy white lady shows up in your driveway at eight thirty in the morning, it's not usually a good thing."

Maggie grimaced, embarrassed. "Sorry about that."

He cut a bite of pancake, speared it with a spare fork and handed it to her. "It's OK. I mean, don't do it again, but we're cool."

She took the fork from him and put it in her mouth, trying not to think about the fact that his fingers had touched it. The tang of molasses sent a ripple of pleasure over her tongue. "Oh, wow," she said, covering her mouth as she chewed. "You're not kidding."

"Have as much as you want," he said, patting his stomach. "My waistline will thank you."

Hazel came back and set a mug of coffee and a tiny pitcher of milk in front of Maggie without a word.

Maggie watched her go. "Was it something I said?" she asked wryly.

Isaac laughed. "Naw," he said. "She gets jealous. I'm usually in here alone."

Maggie felt a zing in her chest. Did that mean he didn't have a girlfriend? She knew he wasn't married from their previous conversations—*No, stop it*. She interrupted her own thought. *Get a grip.*

She cleared her throat. "So, you wanted to talk."

Isaac's fingers tensed around the fork and his smile faded. "I did."

"Why?"

He frowned. "What do you mean why?"

"Before, you said you didn't want to talk," Maggie replied. "So why now?"

He pushed the plate toward her. "Let's just say I got to thinking about what you said and, well..." His lips twisted, as if recalling something.

"I won't tell anyone we talked, I promise." Maggie tried to keep the eagerness out of her voice, sensing she was close to uncovering something.

Isaac leaned back, waving his fork. "Look, I like you, Maggie." Her blush deepened. "But I don't totally trust you. Not yet, anyway. I think you mean well. I think you truly want to get to the bottom of things, and I believe it's for the right reasons. But I'm not about to screw myself by violating my NDA. I'd be in a heap of trouble if it was traced back to me."

Maggie raised her eyebrows. "So you *do* have an NDA?"

He paused and pressed his lips together again as if to prevent more words from escaping. "See, this is why I shouldn't be talking to you."

Maggie felt her excitement building. Finally, someone who could tell her what was behind the NDAs. Her money was on some kind of harassment scandal, though she couldn't imagine Isaac being involved in anything like that. "I won't tell anyone you were my source," she said, putting her hand on her heart.

Isaac laughed. "Your source? What are you, like, Shaft?"

Maggie's cheeks burned. Being in Isaac's presence felt like one long perma-blush. "You know what I mean," she said. "Please."

He looked over his shoulder, then lowered his voice. "Look, Jerry and I didn't part on the best of terms. But I can't say much more. I can, however, point you in the right direction. That is, if you want to be pointed."

Their eyes met and this time Maggie felt certain the sparks she felt were not solely on her end.

"Yes, I do," she said. "I would very much like to be pointed."

Fueled both by Isaac's revelations and the surge of endorphins she'd felt being near him, Maggie was distracted the rest of the day. An energy for which she had no outlet surged in her, like a Formula One car stuck in traffic. She took the wrong exit driving home and was late for one of her appointments, then later forgot to pick up Pen's asthma medication from the pharmacy, and during her nightly shower she caught herself seconds before she lathered up her hair with the shaving cream she'd meant for her legs.

Her skin was damp and rosy when she stepped out of the shower. Catching sight of her naked body in the mirror, she was generally pleased with what she saw. Her breasts, while lower than they'd been a decade ago, were still round and mostly firm. And yes, she had some extra flesh on her hips and around her middle, but overall her body was still lean despite her lack of regular physical activity. She wondered what Isaac would think of her.

She ignored the pulse of guilt that thought sent through her body and began smoothing lotion onto her arms. She closed her eyes and imagined it was Isaac's hands doing so. They ran up across her shoulders and continued to massage her skin as they inched downward toward her breasts. Then slowly one of them continued its path down across her stomach toward—

The bedroom door opened in the next room and Maggie jumped. She heard Dan turn on his bedside lamp and then the familiar creak as he climbed into bed. Her body hummed with a feeling she hadn't felt in a long time. Fuck it. It was time.

Unlocking the bathroom door, she walked naked into the bedroom and climbed straight onto the bed.

"Whoa, hello there." Dan's eyebrows shot up and he tried to sit up as she crawled on top of him and began to kiss the side of his neck. She placed his hand on her breast, then slipped her fingers under the covers, rooting around until she found the elastic of his boxers.

"I thought we might..." she breathed, pushing up his shirt. She began to trace her tongue down his chest, across his belly until—

"Easy there," he said with a nervous laugh. He grabbed her head and guided it back up. "Wow, Mags, I appreciate your enthusiasm."

Maggie felt the air rush out of the room like a balloon going slack. She sat back on her knees to face Dan, her arms crossed to cover her nakedness.

"But what?" she asked, her tone petulant.

"I have a patient coming for jaw surgery at 6 a.m. tomorrow," he said, his face creased in apology.

A fire of embarrassment ripped through Maggie. What was wrong with her that her own husband didn't want her? She spent her days preaching the importance of physical intimacy in a relationship to her patients, but it had been over three years since she'd slept with her own husband.

"Sure," she said, scrambling out of the bed. "I understand." Then she fled to the bathroom where she ran the water to cover the sound as she cried hot tears of frustration.

TWENTY-THREE

Rhea sank into Maggie's couch with her wine, surprised at how happy she was to be there. It was a welcome change from her earlier lunch with Tamara Gibbs and the other Civitas PA moms. With them it was a constant effort to balance being outgoing but contained, confident but modest, attractive but demure. She often felt like she was being scrutinized, playing a part that didn't entirely suit her anymore.

Tonight, though, Rhea hadn't even looked in the mirror before leaving, instead throwing on a sweatshirt over her Pilates gear and brushing a kiss across Brooks's lips as she left. "See you later," she said.

He'd kissed her back, then traced his finger along the side of her breast and down her waist, setting off a small explosion of longing in her body. "Looking forward to it."

Their relationship seemed to be back on more solid footing. Brooks and Josh had been under the same roof for nearly a week now and thankfully most of the tension from that first night had eased. Each day it felt a little more normal for the five of them to eat dinner together, and for the three boys to shoot baskets together in the driveway after. One night Brooks had even joined the three of them for a game of two-on-two, after which they'd all trooped back inside together, sweaty and high-fiving.

Now, though, Rhea was eager to hear how Maggie's meet-up with Isaac had gone. She leaned forward. "So, what did he say?" she asked.

Maggie also looked more casual than normal, in jeans and a blue V-neck sweater. It was nice to see her in something other than her scrupulously neutral color palette. "Well," Maggie said, "Isaac confirmed he also signed an NDA." She tossed a cautious glance in Anna's direction. "And that he and Jerry had a falling out."

Anna twisted her wineglass back and forth at the stem and cleared her throat. "That's true," she said. She was in her familiar gray turtleneck, Rhea noted, but at least this time it matched the cooler early October weather.

Maggie's eyebrows shot up. "What do you mean?"

Anna hesitated, then looked around as if someone might be listening. "Jerry and Isaac had an argument, right before Isaac resigned." She looked down into her wineglass, letting her shiny hair form a shield around her face. "It was late and I was picking Jerry up because I'd used his car that day. No one else was around, and when I got there they were in his office with the door closed. But they were practically yelling so I could hear everything." Anna's knuckles turned white as she gripped the stem of her wineglass.

"What were they talking about?" Maggie shifted in her seat, clearly excited.

Anna kept her gaze averted. "I don't know, exactly. But Isaac said something about refusing to continue, that it had to stop somewhere. And Jerry said that was impossible, but that if Isaac..." Her eyes flickered up to Maggie and Rhea, then away. "That if Isaac didn't have the balls for it anymore he knew where the door was."

A jolt of surprise went through Rhea. Who would have

expected that Anna would have the inside scoop? Quiet, aloof Anna, who, it turned out, maybe wasn't so quiet after all. She leaned forward to make sure she didn't miss a word. "Did they say anything else?

Anna raised her head to look at them, tucking her hair behind her ear. "No. Isaac came out of the office then, and when he saw me standing there he kind of... froze."

"What about Jerry?" Maggie asked. One of her legs jiggled wildly.

Anna's expression darkened. "He didn't see me. I got out of there as soon as Isaac left and came back ten minutes later so Jerry wouldn't know I'd overheard anything."

Rhea tried to make sense of what she'd heard. Anna made it sound like her husband had threatened Isaac, but why—

"Why are you telling us this?" Maggie interrupted, reading Rhea's mind. "And why didn't you say anything before?"

"It's not easy being the headmaster's wife." Anna's voice dropped, and Rhea felt a rush of sympathy for her. She knew what it was like to be forced into a role you'd tired of playing. "I hear things sometimes, but, well, Jerry likes to keep work and home separate." She hesitated. "But with this... Isaac was—is—a good guy. Whatever happened, I have a feeling it wasn't his fault." She turned to Maggie, biting her lip. "What else did he say when you saw him?"

"Well, first, that it's not some kind of sex scandal, which was my guess," Maggie replied, lightly snapping the elastic hair band on her wrist. "It's financial, somehow. Some kind of fraud, maybe? And Mrs. Kaminski has the files we want in the records room behind her desk," Maggie replied. "That's a direct quote."

Rhea tried to process the conversation. If it involved financial fraud, was Jerry at the center? What did that mean for Anna, then? "What files?" she asked Maggie, her eyes on Anna. "Because there are, like, a million file cabinets in that room. Mrs. Kaminski keeps everything."

"Did Isaac say anything more specific?" Anna asked, fiddling with the collar of her turtleneck sweater.

"Yeah." Maggie nodded. "He said what we're looking for is probably in with the Civitas Fund documents." She frowned. "But I don't know what that is."

Rhea rubbed a finger over her lips. The name sounded familiar.

"That's a donor fund for a handful of the school's major contributors," Anna explained. "Like, really big money. I remember when Jerry set it up a few years ago. The board was practically salivating."

"That's right," Rhea said, snapping her fingers. "I've seen the Civitas Fund listed on some of our bank statements." Questions swirled in her mind. Was the fund part of some kind of financial fraud? Should she mention this to Brooks?

"And that would explain why I've never heard of it. Dan and I are not exactly in the 'big money' category," Maggie snorted.

Rhea tapped a fingernail on the side of her glass. This felt like dangerous territory. As the Civitas PA president, she didn't want to get caught poking around in the school's financials. It felt unsavory, somehow. Plus, she had bigger problems at the moment—like the fact that at some point she needed to come clean with Brooks about who Josh really was... didn't she? "Look, maybe we should let this go," she said. "Especially if we've hit a dead end."

"I don't know..." Maggie said. "I have this feeling Isaac got blamed for something he didn't do." She pressed her lips together. "It doesn't seem fair."

Rhea considered this. She'd always liked Isaac, but even with Anna's new information, meddling in this felt risky. In the past, she'd learned the hard way about the consequences of breaking the rules. Since then, she'd made a point of never straying outside the lines, and it had served her well. She cleared her throat and pointed to her task list for the gala. "I think we've got enough to do for the gala, without getting involved in... whatever this is."

"I guess," Maggie said, sounding unconvinced. She leaned back, allowing her eyelids to flutter shut for a moment before peering at Rhea. "Hey, did Will happen to mention anything about an argument with Pen?"

Rhea cocked her head. "No, why?"

"She'd kill me if she knew I was telling you this," Maggie said, chewing her lip, "but apparently she's got some beef with your... nephew, is it?"

"Josh, yes." Rhea's pulse quickened.

"Apparently Will's struck up quite the friendship with him and I think Pen's feeling a tad jealous."

"Jealous?" Rhea frowned.

"I guess so," Maggie replied. "Seems like Will's been spending quite a bit of time with Josh. Time Pen thinks should be hers." She raised an eyebrow.

"You forget Rhea doesn't know anything about teenage girl drama," Anna quipped. "Lucky her."

Maggie let out a snort. "For real."

Rhea glanced at Maggie. "Will hasn't mentioned anything about Pen. Should I ask him?"

Maggie gave a vehement shake of her head. "Absolutely not! She'd kill me." She continued with a pained expression. "It's just—God, you can't breathe a word of this to her, but she's head over heels for Will, and, well, he's great and all, obviously, but I'm afraid she'll end up hurt."

"Mm." Rhea nodded, relieved to learn Maggie also didn't want the teenage relationship getting too intense. "Yeah, sorry, that's hard."

Maggie sighed wearily. "Yeah."

"Is Josh staying long?" Anna interjected, shifting the conversation.

"I hope so," Rhea replied, a slow smile spreading over her face. "We don't really, um, know each other that well. So, it's been nice having him here." She paused, and for a split second she considered telling them everything, starting from the moment she first slid into that Corvette at seventeen.

Being on the front lines of the Civitas social scene meant Rhea constantly had her guard up against the subtle judgment of her so-called friends. She'd seen firsthand how a misstep could jeopardize your status—look at Camilla Knowles, a former Civitas mom who'd been so ostracized after rumors of her coziness with her tennis pro got around that she'd been forced to enroll her kids in the lesser Bennington Academy the next year. Yet, with Maggie and Anna, Rhea sensed a difference —a refuge from judgment. Perhaps she'd finally found someone beyond her family with whom she could truly relax and be herself.

"He might stick around for a bit," Rhea continued, her thoughts drifting to Josh, who'd hinted that he was looking for jobs in Atlanta.

"That's nice," Maggie said. Then she hesitated. "And about the Isaac situation... I understand if you two want to let it slide. But I'm going to keep digging. I feel like I owe it to him."

Seeing the earnest look on Maggie's face, something in Rhea shifted. Maggie was clearly passionate about righting this potential wrong. With a twinge, Rhea realized exactly how much she could relate to that—though she wondered how she could ever begin to make up for her own transgressions with Josh. She bit her lip, hoping she wouldn't regret what she was about to do. "OK," she relented. "Let's make a plan."

TWENTY-FOUR

Anna's hands felt light and tingly on the steering wheel as she drove home from Maggie's, like they might float up to the ceiling of the car and take the rest of her with them. She couldn't believe she'd told Maggie and Rhea about the argument she'd overheard between Jerry and Isaac. Replaying the conversation, she waited for the familiar stab of dread that came whenever she stepped out of line, but all she felt was... excitement.

And now they had a plan.

Anna knew she should head straight home to tackle the dinner dishes and check over Farrah's homework. Instead, she drove out of her way to an address she knew by heart from the paperwork she'd filed. The one-story brick house was among the older ones on a street in northern Atlanta, and stood out amidst the mostly new McMansions that surrounded it, all with elaborate inflatable Halloween decorations in the front yard. But it looked well-cared for with its bright white paint and a front porch lined with large potted ferns and the grass had recently been trimmed. The windows were dark, which made sense. According to Donna, Kayla and the kids were staying with Donna's niece for a while, just in case.

By now Anna had Kayla's case file memorized: *Laceration, upper left cheek. Evidence of strangulation. Grade 2 concussion. Contusion, right lower ribcage.*

Anna had felt an exhilarating rush of power when she finished filing the restraining order, almost like the emotional high she'd had after giving birth. *Take that, Bryce Martin.* She pictured the sheriff pulling up to serve him the papers and waiting while Bryce packed his bags. But as quickly as the euphoria came, it faded; she was powerless again. There was nothing more she could do.

Sitting in front of Kayla's house, though, Anna felt a flicker of that power again. She'd felt it tonight when she'd told Maggie and Rhea what she knew about Isaac's resignation, the same as when she'd filed Kayla's paperwork.

Anna realized she trusted Maggie and Rhea. Maybe not enough to spill all her secrets yet, but enough to risk sharing what she'd overheard in Jerry's office. Being with them felt like cracking a window in a stuffy, stale house; she could breathe in enough fresh air to remind her it existed, and to make her wonder what was on the other side. And now, with her paychecks being deposited into an account bearing only her name, she was that much closer to finding out.

Over the years, Anna had carefully woven a comforting narrative: Jerry wasn't a bad person. He was under a lot of stress, that's all. She thought of the early days, when the two of them had laughed easily and fallen asleep in each other's arms. Those memories were like shards of stained glass, beautiful but capable of cutting deep. These days she clung to tiny gestures of kindness, weaving them into fragile proof that he wasn't a monster. After all, what monster remembers to buy his wife's favorite ice cream on the way home, or surprise her with flowers?

Now, though, she realized the flowers and ice cream didn't mean anything. Farrah had known that all along; that much was clear from their recent conversation. The fact that Anna had allowed herself to be placated by a simple gesture made her cheeks burn with shame.

She shifted in her seat and rolled her window down, breathing in the crisp air. The quiet street was empty of cars except for her own, but she couldn't shake the prickling sensation along her spine. Taking one last look at Kayla's house, Anna eased her car into gear and drove off.

She sang along to the radio on the way home, trying to dispel the unease. Then, turning onto her street, she silenced the music. The light, tingly feeling from earlier had vanished, replaced by a knot of anxiety.

Regret washed over her. Had she been naive, entrusting Maggie and Rhea with her knowledge? What if Jerry somehow traced it back to her? What if he had done something awful or illegal? The last thing Anna needed was to rock the boat, not when she'd begun charting a new course for herself—and Farrah—toward freedom. Pulling into the driveway, she resolved to stay out of it going forward. Maggie and Rhea could keep investigating if they chose, but Anna needed to focus on self-preservation.

Inside, Jerry was in his recliner, and from where she was standing she could see four or five empty beer bottles on the kitchen counter.

"Hello, sweetheart," he said, muting the television. "You're later than I thought you'd be."

The muscles across Anna's back tightened. "There's so much to do for the gala," she said, forcing a smile. "But we're making good progress." Her senses were on high alert, waiting for any sign of what might come next. Fortunately, Jerry smiled —a real smile that emanated from his eyes.

"I'm glad," he said. "I know you understand how important the gala is, so it really puts me at ease to know you're helping make it a success."

"Of course." Anna shifted on her feet, the tension coiling in her stomach.

"Come, sit with me." Jerry rose and moved toward the couch, gesturing for her to join him. "We can watch an episode of that dreadful baking show you and Farrah are always on about."

The relief that flooded Anna's body was so intense it was almost painful. She exhaled loudly and walked over to sit next to him as he flipped through the channels. When Jerry put his arm around her, she let herself lean into him, like a normal couple would do.

Except they were anything but.

TWENTY-FIVE

Rhea's head spun slightly as she drove home from Maggie's, partly from the wine but also from the plan they'd devised to get to the bottom of Isaac's resignation and the NDAs. She felt a twinge of hesitation; *I mean, the president of the Civitas PA taking on the headmaster?* That was risky. But especially after what Anna had revealed, Rhea was increasingly certain Jerry was hiding something. Rhea had been shocked when Anna spoke up, but pleased she was finally coming around, shedding her icy exterior and participating more fully in their trio.

At home Rhea walked into the pleasantly surprising tableau of her whole family gathered together in the living room, watching the Atlanta Hawks game. Normally the boys were off in their rooms on their own devices. Tonight, though, Pen sat between Will and Josh on the couch, her arms crossed. Brooks lounged in the recliner with his feet up on the coffee table, while Zane sprawled sideways in the club chair, his legs dangling over the side.

"Hey honey, come watch." Brooks opened his arms to her. Smiling, Rhea lowered herself onto his lap.

"Gross," Zane muttered, shaking his head at them.

"Oh, you want to see gross?" Brooks teased, pulling Rhea in for a long kiss.

"Oh my God, stop!" Zane looked horrified.

"Dad, eew!" Will threw a popcorn kernel at his parents and Pen snickered.

"Hey!" Rhea protested, though she was far from angry.

"Hell yeah!" Will cheered at the TV, and pumped his fist at an alley-oop dunk. He high-fived Josh over Pen's head. Her petulant expression deepened. "We gotta practice that one later," Will said.

"Absolutely, man," Josh said. "But first I'll have to give you some lessons on dunking."

Zane hooted with laughter.

"You wanna see me dunk, huh?" Will said, jumping to his feet.

"Sit down, babe, I can't see," Pen said, trying to pull him back down next to her.

Ignoring her, Will shadow-boxed closer to Josh. "I'll show you a dunk!" He grabbed a throw pillow and tackled Josh with it. Pen shrieked and leaped off the couch as the boys tumbled sideways, wrestling and laughing.

"Ambush!" cried Josh, fending him off.

Rhea watched as Pen stood on the sidelines, glaring at Josh before looking to Rhea for help. Rhea felt for her, but she was too accustomed to these random wrestling matches to intervene.

Later in bed, Rhea snuggled into Brooks's side with her book as he scrolled through the news headlines. "Will and Josh seem to have hit it off," she said.

"They sure have," he replied, setting down his phone. He gave her a sheepish look. "He seems like a good kid. I'm sorry I was, well, less than welcoming at first."

Rhea warmed at the unexpected apology. "It's OK," she

said, smiling. "I understand." She moved closer and traced her fingers over the soft fabric of his white T-shirt.

"He's really working hard to land a job," Brooks said.

Rhea blinked, surprised to find he'd discussed Josh's plans with him. "Oh?"

Brooks nodded, cupping his hand over hers on his chest. "Yeah, I gave him some feedback on his résumé. The problem is he's short on work experience, unless you count construction jobs during the summers."

"Mm," Rhea said, still processing the fact that Brooks and Josh seemed to have struck up their own rapport. It was a good thing, she told herself, ignoring the flicker of anxiety that surfaced.

"I was thinking," Brooks continued. "Do you think he'd want to work for Ironwall? Short-term, to bolster his résumé."

"Ironwall?" Rhea withdrew her hand from Brooks's and straightened up. "What, like with you?" Her mind went into overdrive. The way Josh had fit into their family seemed almost too good to be true, and Brooks's offer would only solidify that. But while she loved having Josh with them—with her—there was so much they still needed to talk through. Plus, how much longer could she keep the truth from Brooks?

Brooks rubbed his chin. "Well, probably not with me, directly. But the investor relations group is looking for someone." He shrugged. "Like I said, Josh seems like a good kid. He went to a good school. But he needs a break."

Rhea smiled to conceal her roller coaster of emotions. "I mean, are you sure?" she asked, still trying to convince herself this was a good thing. She should want Brooks and Josh to have a relationship. She *did* want them to—just not one based on her lies.

Brooks nodded. "I have a good instinct when it comes to people." Then with a slow smile he plucked the book from her hands. "You're done with this, right?" he said in a husky voice.

Rhea raised an eyebrow. "Should I be?"

"Yes," he said, rolling on top of her and pulling off her T-shirt. "You definitely should be."

But as they kissed, her worries grew. How long could she keep this up? And, more pressing, how long could she expect Josh to?

TWENTY-SIX

"Busy?" Donna asked Anna.

Anna quickly minimized her browser window where she'd pulled up Zillow. "Sorry, no, I mean, yes, I—"

Donna waved her hand, Anna's cue to stop talking. They'd been working together for a month now and Anna had a full mental catalogue of Donna's mannerisms. The way she clenched and unclenched her jaw when she liked what she was hearing from you. The half-smile she gave when she was about to verbally eviscerate someone. The mostly empty Starbucks coffee cup she carried around like a security blanket. "Did you finish the motion for the Lancaster case?" Donna asked. Today she sported a periwinkle pantsuit with an elaborate gold chain-link belt built into the jacket.

Anna nodded. "In your inbox."

"And the discovery for Mobicon Inc.?"

Anna gestured to a fat file on her desk. "I'm about to dive in."

"Good. We need to go fast on that one and there's a lot there, so ask Doug for a hand if you need it."

Anna looked up sharply. "Doug? But he's—"

"About as useful as a hill of beans? I know," Donna sighed. "But everyone else is slammed so he'll have to do."

Anna smiled. "No, I was going to say that he's a second-year associate and I'm only part-time. I can't ask him to—"

"Of course you can." Donna waved her coffee cup. "You're twice the attorney he is. Tell him I said so if it makes you feel better."

Anna's cheeks turned red at Donna's praise. "Thank you," she mumbled, fidgeting with the button on her suit jacket.

Donna rolled her eyes. "Now don't go getting all flustered over one little compliment. I'm sure I'll find something to roast you over this afternoon." She tapped the top of Anna's cubicle and walked off.

When she left work Anna ran through her mental to-do list for the rest of the day. She needed to go to the grocery store, then stop at home to prep dinner and throw in some laundry before picking Farrah up from lacrosse practice. Instead, however, she found herself navigating back to Kayla's house.

After her first drive-by she'd told herself that was it, that she'd needed to see for herself that everything was fine and then she would stay away. But here she was again, parked outside the tidy white house.

There was no car in the driveway and no movement inside. Satisfied that all was well, Anna was about to leave when a white SUV turned onto the block. It slowed to a crawl as it approached the house. The hair on Anna's arms prickled and she kept her face turned away, pretending to look for something in her glove compartment. When she finally peeked over she saw a man in an orange baseball cap looking toward the house. He turned his head to catch her looking at him, and Anna gasped. She recognized his cool blue eyes and his University of

Tennessee hat from the picture of him she'd found online. It was Bryce Martin.

Anna pulled away from the curb, her eyes darting to the rearview mirror until Bryce drove off in the opposite direction. Then she dialed Donna's cell number.

"Donna Monroe." Donna answered immediately, her voice coming through Anna's car speakers.

"Donna it's Anna. I'm at Kayla Martin's house and I saw—"

"You're *where*?" Donna asked.

Anna signaled and pulled into the left lane. If traffic wasn't bad she had should still make it to the sports fields to pick Farrah up on time. "At Kayla Martin's address. I wanted to check things out—"

"And why would you do that?" Donna's voice was calm but had an edge to it.

Anna hunted for words. "Um, I thought I'd swing by and—"

"Anna," Donna interrupted again. "Are you a trained police officer?"

"Well, no."

"And did anyone order or otherwise request you to perform a security check at the Martin residence?"

In one crushing moment Anna realized the stupidity of her actions. "No."

"Then what the hell are you doing?" Donna's voice rose and Anna groped for the volume button in the car to turn her down. "For Christ's sake, you're a lawyer, not a goddamn Navy Seal. Get out of there and leave the policing to the police."

"Bryce was there." On the other end of the line Donna went quiet, a rarity for her. "Bryce Martin," Anna prompted. "Kayla's husband?"

"I know who he is," Donna snapped. "Well, shit on shingle." She sighed. "OK, call it in. But Anna..." She paused. "After this, stay out of it."

"Yeah," Anna said. But she stopped short of promising.

After notifying the police, who promised to send an officer around, Anna raced through her errands and then headed home. She was sweating when she finally pulled into the sports complex to pick Farrah up with five minutes to spare. Taking out her new phone she pulled up the Zillow website and filtered for two-bedroom apartments in her price range and desired neighborhoods. *No results found.* Anna frowned and increased her maximum monthly rent by two hundred dollars. There were three results, all of which were so small and depressing they looked like they might double as prison film sets. She upped her maximum another three hundred dollars. Thirty-two listings, including a few in nice-looking buildings near Piedmont Park or the Beltline. She could work with this.

She switched over to her bank account and studied the two paychecks she'd deposited so far. She needed enough for three months' rent plus a security deposit, which would take at least two more pay cycles.

She was so thankful for her law degree and the fact that she'd taken the Georgia bar exam when they moved, despite Jerry's protests. What did people do otherwise? People like Kayla, who, according to Anna's online sleuthing, had never finished college. Anna shivered, picturing the cold blue eyes staring back at her out of the white SUV.

A knock on the car window startled her. She yelped and looked up to see Farrah making a piggy nose and sticking out her tongue at the passenger-side window.

"Jeez, Mom," Farrah said as she climbed in. "Jumpy much?"

Anna inhaled the smell of her daughter's sweaty hair and baby powder deodorant, willing her pulse to slow. "Sorry, too much coffee," she said, leaning over to kiss Farrah on the cheek. "How was practice?"

"Good." Farrah eyed the phone sitting on Anna's lap. "Did you get a new phone?"

Anna slapped her hand over the phone and pushed it back

THINGS WE NEVER SAY   157

into her purse. "Um, yeah," she said, trying for nonchalance. "My, uh, screen cracked on the old one." She paused, wondering if she should ask Farrah not to say anything about it to Jerry, or if that would only make it into a bigger deal.

"Jelly!" whined Farrah, who'd been asking for a new phone for months.

Anna took a deep breath and decided to let it go and cross her fingers that Farrah wouldn't think to mention it.

That night Jerry was in good spirits, smiling and whistling as he walked around the house and even ordering pizza so she didn't have to cook. "How about a family game night?" he proposed, setting the pizza boxes on the table.

Farrah shook her head. "I have homework." Anna tensed at Farrah's flippant dismissal of Jerry and waited for the storm clouds to gather on his face. Instead, he turned to Farrah with an exaggerated pout.

"Pretty please?" he asked.

Farrah rolled her eyes and giggled. "OK, fine. But I get to pick the game."

She chose charades and Jerry picked first, blanching when he unfolded the piece of paper and read it. "Ahem," he said, holding up two fingers and then one.

"Two words, first word," Anna confirmed.

Jerry nodded and began moving his hand in a tight up-and-down motion.

"Patting? Waving?" Farrah said. He shook his head and pressed his thumb and forefinger together as part of the motion.

"Sewing?" Anna suggested. Jerry flapped his arms with excitement.

"Stitching!" yelled Farrah. "Knitting?"

He snorted with laughter, made a motion for them to stop and help up two fingers again.

"Second word," Farrah said. Then Jerry mimed running in place, his arms pumping furiously. "Running? Racing? The Olympics?"

"Being chased," Anna tried. Jerry shook his head and brought his hand to his forehead in mock frustration as the timer sounded.

"Taylor Swift, obviously," he cried, holding out his arms.

"But why were you sewing—ohhhhh," Anna said.

"OMG, *tailor!*" Farrah burst out laughing. "Actually that was pretty good, Dad."

"Well, not good enough, clearly." Jerry smiled and caught Anna's eye. Her heart did the tiniest of flips. This was the charming, goofy Jerry who had captured her heart in the first place. Then he cleared his throat. "I have some good news," he said.

"Ooh, you're finally getting me an iPad?" Farrah asked, clapping.

Jerry smoothed the front of his shirt. "Ha. No, this is good news for all of us." He turned to Anna, a self-important grin spreading across his face. "I'm a finalist to be the next headmaster for Pembroke Preparatory."

The pen Anna was holding slipped from her fingers as the breath left her lungs. She'd let her guard down in the glow of their evening of family fun, and this was a sharp kick to the stomach she hadn't been braced for.

Farrah frowned. "What's Pembroke Preparatory?"

Jerry puffed out his chest. "It's only the number one private school in the nation," he said.

"In New Hampshire," Anna managed.

"New Hampshire?" Farrah's face fell. "But I don't want to live in New Hampshire!"

Jerry's smile faded and Anna grabbed her daughter's knee and gave it a sharp squeeze. "That's, um, big news," Anna said, squeezing her hands into fists beside her. "When did this happen?"

Jerry touched the hair at his temple. "The recruiter updated me today. I've been in their search process the past couple of months but didn't want to say anything unless it panned out. But now that I'm one of the final two candidates, they want to fly me up for interviews." He took Anna's hand and she forced herself not to recoil. "And you too, darling, eventually." He nodded toward Farrah. "And you, Farrah. They want to meet the whole family, have the chance to show us around campus, to see our new potential home. I hear the headmaster's house is quite posh."

"The headmaster's house?" The pizza Anna had eaten churned in her stomach.

"Yes, the faculty all live on campus." A bit of tomato sauce had stuck to the corner of Jerry's mouth and Anna focused on the red speck to keep from passing out. She pictured herself trapped in a cold, drafty house in rural New Hampshire with nowhere to slip away to. No job, no friends, only total isolation.

"Well, it's a lot to think about," Anna managed, and then caught Jerry's warning look and quickly corrected herself. "Congratulations, sweetheart."

TWENTY-SEVEN

"I wish she was, you know, more available," the man said. He sat on one end of the low-backed gray couch in Maggie's office.

At the other end of the couch his wife rolled her eyes. "Maybe I'd be more *available* if I wasn't so tired from doing *everything* around the house. How am I supposed to feel sexy when I'm exhausted?" She heaved a sigh.

Maggie suppressed a sigh of her own and stole a glance at the clock. Seven minutes to go in the session. Her mind wandered to the Halloween candy she needed to buy for next week—how was it possible it was already almost the end of October? Refocusing, she leaned toward the wife. "Hayley," she said, "let's talk about what *does* make you feel sexy."

Listening to the woman's response, Maggie's mind drifted to her own failed attempt to initiate sex with Dan. A fresh wave of embarrassment swept over her. How could she spend her working life talking about communication and yet be so painfully unable to broach the subject with her own husband?

After the couple left, Maggie's phone buzzed with a text. A pleasant tingle ran through her body as she recognized the number.

Hey

She replied immediately:

Hey yourself.

Any luck with what we talked about?

Not yet. Haven't had the chance to look. Mrs. Kaminski is on vacation until tomorrow.

The records room had been inaccessible while the Civitas office manager was away, but now that she was back, Rhea had a plan.

Too bad.

Maggie gripped her phone. She didn't want that to be the end of the conversation. *What are you up to?* she wrote, immediately regretting her choice of such an inane question. But a second later a picture came through. A familiar-looking plate piled with French toast. *Creature of habit!* she wrote, smiling.

What can I say? Isaac replied. Then, *We should have break-fast again. Hazel misses you.*

Maggie laughed out loud. *I doubt that*, she typed.

Aw, give the woman a break. She's not used to having to share me with an attractive blond.

Maggie felt a warmth rush through her chest. Unlike her husband, Isaac thought she was attractive. *Tell Hazel I hope to see her soon*, she replied.

Smiling, she pressed the phone to her chest.

Later that day, sitting in her car in the Civitas parking lot, Maggie reread their text exchange. A wave of heat rose through her body. Isaac had called her attractive. He wanted to see her again. He'd been flirting with her... hadn't he? Her instincts were rusty. It had been so long since anyone had noticed her like that. During her last three years of involuntary celibacy, it was as if she'd packed her sex drive away in a dusty attic. She knew this was common for women, who often don't feel desire until after foreplay begins—"responsive arousal" was the technical term she used with her clients. She also knew that lack of intimacy breeds less desire, which leads to even less intimacy. But honestly, she was always busy with work and tired, and she hadn't missed it much... until now.

But with the sparks she'd felt with Isaac, desire had come roaring back.

A text from Rhea popped up on her screen:

Where are you?? I'm starting to feel like a stalker lurking in the hallway.

Coming, Maggie replied, dropping her phone in her purse and scrambling out of her car. Though it was already the third week of October the weather was sunny and warm as she hurried up the brick path to the main Civitas building, unbuttoning her olive green quilted jacket.

Inside, class was in session and the halls were quiet. Looking around, Maggie made her way down the hallway toward the main office. She rounded a corner and yelped as Rhea stepped out from the stairwell, dressed in black ankle boots and a navy blue sweater dress belted at her narrow waist.

"Over here," Rhea hissed. She held a white bakery box and several others were piled at her feet.

"Shit, you scared me," Maggie scolded, her hand over her pounding heart. "I'm already nervous, I don't need you jumping out at me from the shadows!"

Rhea pulled her into the stairwell, where four white shopping bags from La Bamboche sat on the ground. "You're the one who's supposed to be in the shadows, remember?" she said, then looked skyward like she was summoning her strength. "I can't believe I let you talk me into this." She gestured toward the bags. "It's not too late to call it off. Instead we could go sit in my car and eat several dozen pastries."

"No way." Maggie shook her head. "We know something is going on—that Jerry's cooking the books or something—Isaac said so. We have to get into those file cabinets."

Rhea sighed. "Fine, but no more Veronica Mars stuff after this, OK? Only normal things, like drinking wine and complaining about our husbands or whatever." She checked her watch. "You ready? Class lets out in two minutes, so you'll blend in with the crowd."

"Make sure she doesn't lock her desk," Maggie reminded her.

"Don't worry, I've got it covered." Rhea pointed to the bakery box. "They're her favorite. Ready?"

Maggie nodded and wiped her sweaty palms on her pants. Her skin felt hot and itchy. Maybe she wasn't cut out for detective work, after all.

"OK, let's go." Rhea picked up the shopping bags, balancing them with the bakery box. Maggie reached to help, but Rhea batted her hand away. "No, I need to look like I'm struggling."

The bell rang as they stepped out, and the hallway swelled with students. Maggie followed Rhea toward the main office. "It might be a few minutes," Rhea muttered. "Mrs. K loves a gossip sesh." She nodded at Maggie and went inside.

Feigning nonchalance, Maggie leaned against the wall a few feet from the office. Five minutes ticked by, then ten. What the hell was Rhea doing in there? How much Civitas gossip could there be?

The warning bell for the next class sounded and the crowd in the hallway began to thin. Then the door of the office opened and Maggie jumped back around the corner.

"Thank you so much for helping me with these," Rhea gushed as she exited carrying two of the shopping bags. "The PA wanted to show our appreciation for all the hard work the faculty and staff have been doing to get ready for the centennial."

"You're too good to us, Rhea," Mrs. Kaminski said. She carried the other two bags and in the fluorescent light of the hallway, Maggie caught the sheen of white, sugary powder around her mouth.

"Well, the treats are from the whole PA," Rhea said modestly.

"Say what you want, dear, but I know you do most of the work," Mrs. Kaminski replied. Her voice trailed off as they continued down the hall away from Maggie. Glancing around, Maggie slipped inside.

The waiting area had a row of stiffly upholstered chairs and an end table with Civitas brochures and a droopy, overwatered plant. An imposing wood desk sat across from the chairs, holding a large computer monitor and a row of framed pictures of small children. A white mug labeled "World's Best Nana" held highlighters and pens next to the keyboard.

The doors that led to Jerry's office, and next to it what had been Isaac's office, were closed. Isaac. Maggie's chest fluttered just thinking about him. *Focus*, she reminded herself sharply. The remaining door, her target, was directly behind Mrs. Kaminski's. It was also closed.

"She keeps the keys to the file cabinets in her top-left desk drawer," Rhea had said, and sure enough, as Maggie slipped behind the desk and opened the unlocked drawer, there they were. Glancing over her shoulder, she opened the door to the records room and stepped inside.

"Shit," Maggie murmured. One whole wall of the narrow room was lined with file cabinets. She'd never make it through all of them in the time she had. "Civitas Fund," she reminded herself. Each drawer was labeled, but none mentioned the fund. Rattled, Maggie began flinging drawers open at random, beads of sweat collecting on her upper lip. "Shit, shit, shit," she muttered, scanning old annual budgets, attendance lists, and personnel files of teachers who'd retired a decade ago. There was even a drawer full of copies of the school paper from the early 2000s, before they'd gone digital.

"Iris?" A door opened and Jerry's voice called on the other side of the door. Maggie froze. "Iris, are you out here?" The voice got closer and Jerry's footsteps approached. Frantically she searched for a hiding spot, but there was none. "Blast," Jerry muttered, his voice right outside the door. "Where has that woman got to now?" His footsteps receded, and Maggie heard a door close. Slumping against a file cabinet, she let out a long breath. Her phone buzzed with a text from Rhea.

> 5 more min, max.

Maggie pressed her palms to her cheeks and forced herself to slow her breathing. She scanned the file drawer labels again, more slowly this time. There it was, "Civitas Fund," written on one of the labels in faint pencil, like an afterthought.

Yanking open the drawer, Maggie pulled out the lone unlabeled file. She flipped it open to find a list of student names, each followed by one, two, or three Civitas course names scribbled in pencil over the typed list.

- *Roundhouse, Brian – A.P. Lit, Trig*
- *Starkey, Franklin – Trig, Econ, French*
- *Takata, Caroline – Euro Hist.*

Maggie paged through, finding more lists, some of which dated back two years. The one on top, though, was recent enough that she recognized some names as she scanned through it.

- *Abbot, Mary Grace – A.P. History*
- *Banks, Lucas – Spanish, A.P. Bio*
- *Connelly, William – Trig*

She stopped reading when she got to Will's name. Why was Rhea's son listed? What was this?

Her phone buzzed again.

Time's up

Under the lists were some other printouts Maggie didn't have time to read. Instead she stuffed the whole folder in her tote and darted out of the room, dropping the keys back into Mrs. Kaminski's desk drawer on her way.

TWENTY-EIGHT

Rhea sipped her spiked kombucha and massaged her sore muscles. She and fifteen other women in high-end fitness gear had just finished a private ballet barre class that doubled as a fundraiser for the Atlanta Food Bank, where Tamara's husband was a board member. Yet despite the punishing series of pliés and lunges, Rhea hadn't been able to stop thinking about Josh. True to his word, Brooks had hooked him up with an internship at Ironwall. And while it warmed Rhea's heart to see the two of them walk out the door together in the mornings, it also felt like the ultimate double-edged sword—Josh was now not only firmly cemented in her life, but in Brooks's, too. One slipup from him could destroy it all.

"Oh my God," Tamara said, grabbing Rhea's arm. She was clad in an eye-wateringly neon pink leotard and leggings. "I'm going to be so sore tomorrow. That was so good."

"So good," Rhea agreed, trying to project enthusiasm.

Tamara lowered her voice. "But can you believe Erica showed up?" She nodded toward a petite blond woman standing on her own in a corner. "I mean, I'm not sure I'd be ready to show my face."

"What do you mean? What's going on with Erica?" asked another woman who'd drifted toward them. Rhea recognized her from Civitas—Thea, or maybe it was Lea.

Tamara glanced around. "Well, you didn't hear it from me, but apparently she's been drinking lately—like, a lot." She raised her eyebrows and dropped her voice to a scandalized whisper. "Apparently she was *drunk* while she was chaperoning the homecoming dance."

Thea-maybe-Lea wet her lips in appreciation of the gossip and both women looked to Rhea for her reaction. Rhea closed her eyes for a brief second, wishing she was home on the couch with Brooks. But when she opened them, she was still there, dressed in over five hundred dollars of athletic clothing in a room full of people who, more and more, she had little patience for. She sipped her mouth-puckeringly sour drink—at least it was strong—and gave Tamara her most pitying smile. "Oh Tam," she said. "We're not so bored with our own lives that we're making stuff up about other people's now, are we?"

Tamara flushed, her mouth agape. Thea-maybe-Lea tittered. But as much as Rhea wanted to enjoy putting Tamara in her place, her victory was overshadowed by the fear of what Tamara would say if she ever discovered Rhea's own secret. For years, Rhea had carefully curated her image as the unflappable queen bee, relishing the control and influence it brought. But she could feel the cracks forming in her facade, and it was only a matter of time until Tamara and the others noticed them too.

Rhea had seen it happen before: one misstep, one rumor, and a person's reputation would crumble, leaving them ostracized. These social casualties were a haunting reminder of the price of vulnerability. Yet increasingly she felt weighed down by her lies and mistruths. She wondered what it would feel like to be real in a world that demanded perfection.

. . .

When Rhea pulled into her driveway, she bypassed the front door and headed straight for the back patio to stretch and calm her racing thoughts. She considered the list Maggie had shown her with Will's name on it.

"I mean, we still don't really know what it means," Maggie had said, not meeting Rhea's eyes.

"Right," Rhea agreed. "It could be nothing." Will's sudden turnaround in trigonometry had nagged at Rhea for weeks, especially considering his ongoing struggles with the homework. It didn't add up. Was he cheating? She sucked in her breath at the possibility. It couldn't be. They'd taught him better than that.

She stepped onto the back patio and bent down in a hamstring stretch. It was dusk, and though the day had been warm, the air was cooling. All at once she heard the sound of rocks crunching and whipped her head around. Josh sat back on his knees in front of a hydrangea bush. "Oh my God, you startled me," she said, placing her hand over her heart.

"Sorry," he said.

She looked closer and saw he held a pair of garden shears. "What are you doing?"

"Cutting back some of the old growth now that they're going dormant," he said, gesturing to a pile of brown-green stems next to him. "You'll get better blooms that way."

Rhea smiled. "You know we have a gardener for that, right? Plus it's dark. And getting cold." She pulled her puffer vest closed.

He stood up and brushed the dirt from his jeans, wiping his hands on his gray hoodie. "Trying to be useful," he said, and the grin he gave her caused a twinge in her chest. "I worked for a lawn-care company for a while and I always liked doing the flower beds."

"You know," she said, trying to keep her tone light, "no one expects you to earn your keep." She shifted and adjusted her ponytail. She'd done everything she could to make him feel at home, making him breakfast along with the boys, asking about his day, leaving copies of books she thought he might like on his nightstand. Yet things between them remained vaguely formal, like they were circling each other at a distance. It made her feel like a failure somehow, the fact that she still didn't know how to mother him after all these years—or even if he wanted her to.

Josh's smile faltered as he stood and thrust his hands into the pockets of his sweatpants. She'd noticed he did laundry every three days because that was about how many clothes he had. She should take him shopping. Not to assuage her guilt— well, at least not only to assuage her guilt. But because she was his mother and she wanted to give him everything he needed. "I don't know," he said. "I mean, I did, like, show up on your doorstep like a stray dog." He kicked at a rock on the grass in front of him. "That had to have been... a lot."

"You're not a stray dog," she said quietly. "You're my son." The word lingered in the air between them like the bubbles she used to blow with the boys out here in the yard, precious and fragile. She wanted to reach out and cup the word in her hand, to hand it to him as an offering to make up for everything else she'd failed to give him.

She sank onto the couch and nodded toward the seat next to her. "You want to sit?"

"Sure."

The couch dipped as he settled in beside her. Rhea ran a hand through her hair. "So, I guess we have to talk about it at some point," she said.

"Talk about what?" Josh asked, though she knew he knew. This was the delicate game they played.

"Why I abandoned you," Rhea said. She slipped out of her shoes and pulled her knees into her chest as emotion surged in her, threatening to choke her. She pushed it back down. She needed to say this. "How I couldn't even look at you when you were born because I knew if I did I'd never let them take you away. Then how I got the hell out of Texas as soon as I could and never looked back." Tears brimmed in her eyes. God, she was a terrible person. She'd abandoned her child, her perfect, beautiful child. Because she'd known he would be perfect and beautiful; that's why she hadn't looked.

"Look, I'm sure you had your reasons," Josh said. His face was creased with emotion but bore no hint of the judgment she knew she deserved.

"I can't even say I wish I'd fought harder to keep you," Rhea said, her voice choked. "Because then I wouldn't have had Will and Zane, and I'd never give them up." She turned to Josh, hoping he understood what she was trying to say, though it was coming out all wrong. "But I gave *you* up. You should hate me."

He looked down, examining his fingers. "I did hate you, believe me. For a long time. But I also always wondered what you were like, if I had your eyes or your smile. And now"—he gestured at the house and Rhea—"everything, all this. Your family... it's more than I ever—I mean..." He sighed and his eyes flickered up to her face. "I think I'm afraid of breaking the spell of whatever this is."

Rhea closed her eyes and inhaled the musky fall scent of dirt and dead leaves. "Me too."

They sat in silence as the crickets tuned up around them. Josh cleared his throat. "Do you think you'll ever tell them?"

Rhea opened her eyes to meet his, which were full of questions she couldn't answer. "I have to someday," she said, her chest tightening with a familiar guilt. "But not yet. I can't. I'm sorry." He nodded and looked away, and anguish flared through her body. "Josh," she said, taking his hand. Startled, he looked back at her, then down at her fingers gripping his. "I want you here, that much I know." She squeezed his hand in a silent plea.

Gently he dropped her hand and stood up. "I get it, I think.

I just..." He scratched his head. "I'm part of it now too, you know? The lie."

The word hit her like the BB pellets her father used to fire at the squirrels in her mother's garden. Her mouth went dry. "I promise I'll tell them," she pleaded. "But I need more time."

He nodded, then turned and walked inside.

Rhea sat for a few more minutes in the quiet darkness of the yard. She knew Josh was right to ask when she was going to tell her family the truth. It was something she spent an increasing amount of time trying not to think about. Because this couldn't go on forever... could it? The night air had grown cooler and she shivered and stood. It was late. She needed a shower and her pajamas.

Back inside she paused at the basement door and walked down the first few stairs, expecting to see Pen on the couch with Will. Lately she felt like the girl was trying to move in, which she supposed made sense if what Maggie said was true and Pen really was feeling jealous of the time Will spent with Josh. Instead, she found Will stretched out alone, scrolling through his phone. "Is Pen still here?" Rhea asked.

"Naw." Will glanced up from his screen. "She left."

"OK. I'm heading to bed soon and so should you, sweetheart."

"Yeah, all right." Will yawned. "Night, Mom."

"Love you," she said.

"Yeah, you too." He waved without lifting his eyes from the video he was watching but Rhea would take it.

As Rhea walked through the living room she heard raised voices coming from outside in the driveway. She moved to the window and saw Pen standing with her hands on her hips, her face stormy. With her was Josh, who stood with his back to Rhea, his body looking taut and coiled like a spring. His voice was low and terse in response to Pen's raised one. Then he turned abruptly and headed back up the driveway.

Rhea darted toward the couch, where she began smoothing the throw pillows.

"Oh," Josh said, startled, as he came through the front door. In an instant his dark expression was replaced by a smile. "Hey."

"Everything OK?" Rhea asked evenly.

"Yeah, fine." He ran a hand through his hair and shifted on his feet.

She paused, debating whether to press further, but he offered no encouragement. "Was that Pen outside? Is she upset about something?" she asked. She wondered whether she should text Maggie to let her know what she'd seen.

Josh's smile didn't reach his eyes. "She's fine. It's all good."

Rhea hesitated again. "Well, OK then," she said. She'd let it go with Maggie, she decided. No one needed her playing the meddling mom. "I'm headed to bed."

"Yeah, me too. Good night." He waved, and Rhea watched him walk down the hall to the guest room, suddenly aware of how much she didn't know about him.

TWENTY-NINE

Anna looked around the steak house, which was crowded on a Saturday night, taking in the low murmur of conversation and the clink of silverware on plates. Farrah was at a sleepover, so Jerry had proposed they go out to dinner. "What, I can't take my lovely wife out to dinner?" he'd said when Anna had looked surprised. They'd given up the pretense of date night long ago. "Wear something nice," he added.

Anna struggled to find anything in her closet beyond her usual jeans and sweaters or the gray suit hidden in the back that she reserved for work. She settled for the pale pink silk dress she'd worn to the Civitas graduation last year. It clashed with the crisp fall weather, but it would have to do.

Now, sitting across from each other, Jerry scanned the menu. "We'll each have a glass of champagne to start," he informed their bouncy, blond server, winking at Anna. "We're celebrating."

"How nice." The young woman smiled. "What's the occasion?" Anna thought of how Jerry must appear to her: a passably handsome man with a charming smile, oozing confidence in his expensive suit and tie.

Jerry grinned back at the server. "A new job." He reached across the table and took Anna's hand. "And a fresh start."

"Does that mean you got the job?" Anna asked in a low voice once the server had retreated. She felt her palm begin to sweat in Jerry's and hoped he wouldn't notice.

Jerry wet his lips and puffed out his chest. "No, but I had a call today with the search firm Pembroke is using and they let slip that I'm the strongest candidate."

"That's wonderful." She pulled her hand away and reached for her water glass to hide her panicked expression.

"I was thinking we could fly up to have a look around the week after the gala."

Anna choked on her water. "That's only a little over a month away," she sputtered.

Jerry gave a self-satisfied chuckle. "They want to move fast. I thought we'd leave on a Wednesday and stay through the weekend so we can really get to know the area. Farrah too, of course."

Anna's stomach dropped as she thought of her cases at work. How was she going to explain a sudden absence to Donna?

Their champagne arrived and Jerry raised his glass. "Chin-chin," he said. Anna watched as he took a large swallow. Then he turned his gaze to her, his eyes suddenly tender. "A change of scene will be good for us, don't you think, darling?"

Anna nodded, understanding the role she was supposed to play. Then Jerry's expression turned serious. "Things have been tough lately, haven't they?" he said slowly. Anna's smile faltered; this wasn't part of the script. "I realize I haven't been the best husband," he murmured. "I've been under so much pressure from the board and their relentless fundraising demands." He found her knee under the table and squeezed gently. "And you've been an angel through it all. I don't know where I'd be without you, Pocket." His voice caught on the last word.

Anna stared at her husband. Were those tears in his eyes? She'd only ever seen Jerry cry twice before, once when Farrah was born and once when Leicester City, his soccer team, won the Premier League championship.

He withdrew his hand from her knee and wiped his eyes, then reached out to take her hand again, stroking the top of it with his thumb. "I'd like to start fresh, darling. I know I have my shortcomings, but I want to do better. I want us to be happy. I think there's a real chance for that in New Hampshire."

A cautious trickle of hope began to flow through Anna's body, like a rusty faucet turning back on after years of disuse. It was the first time she'd ever heard Jerry acknowledge anything that took place between them.

"I'd like that," she said, surprised to find that she was also choked up. "I'd like for us to be happy." And for that moment, she let herself imagine it was possible.

They lingered over dinner, reminiscing about their early days in Chicago and about Farrah's baby years, laughing over how she used to say "bobbers" for blueberries and "upslide-down." Anna had a second glass of wine, and enjoyed the unusual experience of feeling relaxed in Jerry's company. For dessert, he joined her side of the booth, his hand grazing her leg as they shared a crème brûlée, Anna's favorite.

They were still laughing when they got home, and when she went to brush her teeth, her reflection in the mirror glowed with the pleasure of the evening. She slipped into bed next to Jerry and squeezed his hand. "That was fun," she murmured, feeling sleepy and content.

"It was," he said, squeezing back. Then he bent to kiss her. "Good night, darling."

But his lips lingered, and Anna found she welcomed the sensation. Slowly his mouth made its way down her neck to the hollow of her throat and her breath caught. He brought his hand to her breast and cupped it, tentatively at first, then more firmly as he bent to catch her nipple in his mouth. She gave a surprised gasp of pleasure and melted under him as he brought his mouth back up to hers and slid his hand up her leg.

It hadn't been this way with him for so long, and the waves she rode as their bodies came together crested over and over. Afterwards, she lay with her head on his chest, listening to his heart rate slowly return to normal. *A fresh start*, she thought as she drifted into a heavy, sated sleep. Maybe it was possible? Maybe that was all they needed.

THIRTY

Dan whistled as he dropped his toiletries kit into the open suitcase he'd mostly packed the night before. From her side of the bed Maggie caught sight of his swimsuit.

"Is there a beach in Denver?" she asked, yawning. Dan was already up and fully dressed for travel in jeans and a navy blue three-quarter-zip sweater with a rolled neck. He was catching an early flight to Denver for a dentistry convention.

"No, but the hotel has a pool," he said, zipping the suitcase closed. "I thought I might swim some laps since I won't get to play racquetball this week."

"Mm," Maggie said. "Sorry you have to go. I know you hate those things."

Dan gave a good-natured eye-roll. "I mean, being trapped in a convention center with hundreds of other dentists, what's not to like?" Maggie gave an exaggerated shudder and he laughed. "There's leftover risotto in the fridge for you and Pen tonight, and there's chili in the freezer for tomorrow. Thursday you can have leftovers and Friday night I figured you could order something."

Maggie struggled to sit up in the bed. "I assure you I am

fully capable of feeding myself and our daughter while you're gone."

Dan eyed her with skepticism. "I actually wouldn't bet on that."

"Hey!" Maggie tossed a pillow at him. He caught it and dropped it back on the bed.

"Promise me you won't only eat cereal for dinner like last time?"

Maggie crossed her arms. "I happen to like cereal." She still hadn't found the right moment to tell him what she'd discovered about Civitas—mainly because that would mean telling him she'd met up with Isaac. Not that she was doing anything wrong, of course. But now was not the time. It could wait until he returned.

He leaned forward to kiss her. "I'll see you Saturday. Love you."

"Love you, too," Maggie said.

Maggie watched the clock more than usual during her sessions that day, willing time to pass faster. When she finally wrapped up with her last patient she went upstairs to change. She donned a navy blue silk shirt over a tweed wrap skirt that skimmed her thighs, then added knee-high leather boots with a two-inch block heel and stood back to study herself. The look she wanted was, "I wore this to work today and thus did not change my outfit to impress you." *Not bad*, she thought. Her shirt accentuated her blue eyes and her legs looked shapely in the tall boots.

She gave herself a last-minute spritz of the perfume she hardly ever wore, then popped her head into Pen's room, where her daughter was lying on the bed with her phone. "I'm heading out," Maggie said. "But I won't be gone long. No friends over, OK?"

Pen rolled her eyes and then they flickered over Maggie. "Why are you so dressed up?"

"Just meeting a friend for a drink. Dad left dinner in the fridge," she said, not meeting Pen's eyes. She glanced around her daughter's room. It was the only one in the house that contained any plants: a hanging basket and a large fern that Pen tended to with more love than she usually showed Maggie. The walls were covered with prints of Matisse's art, along with a framed poster of Walt Whitman's "Song of Myself." Maggie found it all rather sophisticated for a sixteen-year-old. At that age her bedroom walls had been covered with magazine cutouts of Luke Perry and Leonardo DiCaprio.

Pen shrugged. "I'm going over to Will's anyway."

Maggie pursed her lips. Lately Pen had been spending even more time than usual at the Connellys'. "You were at Will's last night," she said.

"And?" Pen lowered her phone, a look of challenge on her face.

"Don't wear out your welcome, OK?" Maggie raised her eyebrows.

"Whatever," Pen snorted. "I'm not the one who should be worrying about that."

Maggie tilted her head. "What do you mean?"

"That Josh is the one mooching off them, not me." Pen's eyes narrowed. "Will's, like, obsessed with him. It's so dumb."

"Well, Josh is family; you're not."

"Whatever," Pen said, waving her hand. "There's something off about him."

Maggie glanced at her watch. She needed to leave or she'd be late. "Look, I have to go, but I won't be late. And you be home by nine, OK?" Pen went back to her phone without replying.

. . .

Maggie had arranged to meet Isaac at a wine bar in Grant Park, which was closer to her house but still far enough away that she wouldn't run into anyone she knew. She'd asked him to meet so she could tell him about what she'd found in the Civitas file cabinets and he'd agreed immediately.

When she arrived, the hostess showed her to a cozy wraparound booth that faced out into the restaurant. Above it hung a chandelier that sparkled dimly in the low lighting. The ambiance was several notches more romantic than Maggie had intended.

"Hey." Isaac's rich, warm voice caught her off guard.

"Oh, hey!" She scrambled to her feet to greet him, catching her foot on the edge of the booth and toppling toward him. He laughed and grabbed her arm to steady her.

"Wow, uh, that's quite the greeting," he said, not letting go of her arm. He wore dark jeans and a slim-fit light gray button-up shirt open at the throat. This time he was the one to extend his face toward hers to brush her cheek with a kiss. Her center turned to liquid.

He released her arm and she grabbed for the glass of ice water on the table as she sat back down. As he slid into the booth, its semi-circular shape caused him to end up next to her instead of across.

"Thanks for meeting me," she said. "I hope I'm not taking you away from your family or anything."

He shrugged. "My dad's pretty good with the microwave, so he'll be fine. And my five kids are already in bed." Her surprise must have registered on her face because he laughed. "I'm kidding. No kids."

"Only you and your dad then?" she asked, trying to seem nonchalant. "No wife? Or girlfriend?"

He gave her an amused, knowing smile and she flushed at her transparency. "Just me and my dad."

Their server appeared and they each ordered a glass of red wine. "Do you want to make it a bottle?" the server asked.

"No," Maggie said quickly. A bottle of wine would only deepen the quicksand she knew she was already in. The server nodded and left, and an awkward silence descended.

Isaac cleared his throat and straightened the silverware in front of him. "So," he said. "You wanted to talk about what you found."

"I did, yes." Relieved, Maggie remembered why they were there. "The lists, they go back the last two years."

"To when the Civitas Fund was established," Isaac said. "Which I know you already figured out. So, I'm not giving you any new information that I wouldn't be prohibited from talking about... right?" He raised his eyebrows.

"Right." Maggie nodded, confirming she understood what he was getting at.

"What else was in the file?"

"Only the lists," she said. "And as far as I can tell, the students on them don't have much in common."

"Don't they?" Isaac cocked an eyebrow. Maggie pulled the file from her purse and opened it on the table. Isaac blanched, his eyes darting around the restaurant.

"Sorry." She whisked the papers off the table and onto the bench between them.

"It's fine," he said, rubbing his neck. "I'm paranoid. Civitas can afford much better lawyers than I can." He gave a strained laugh. Then the smile returned to his face as he pointed down at the various highlighter colors she'd used on the pages to try to find patterns. "Anyway, I see you've been hard at work, Shaft."

Maggie blushed. "I have some theories," she said.

"Go on," Isaac prompted.

She cleared her throat. "Well, like, is this a cheating thing? Or some kind of preferential treatment? At first I thought maybe it was the athletes, because Will Connelly is on the list. But not all the students on the lists are athletes."

Isaac glanced around again. "Stop looking at the students," he said in a low voice. "Start looking at their families." He'd moved closer to her as they looked at the lists, or maybe she'd moved closer to him. In any case, their thighs brushed up against one another under the table. Maggie grabbed her glass and took another long swig of ice water.

"Two glasses of the Sangiovese." The server arrived with their wine. "Can I get you anything else right now?"

A cold shower? Maggie thought, hyper-aware of the few inches of her body that were touching Isaac.

"We're fine, thanks," Isaac said.

Abbot, Banks, Connelly, Gibbs, Joon... Maggie scanned the most recent list again. In large part she recognized the names because most of it read like a who's who of monied Atlanta. "Lots of pretty wealthy families," she said.

"Bingo." Isaac raised his glass. "Cheers."

Maggie clinked her glass against his and frowned. "OK, but so what does that mean? That the wealthiest families in the school are the ones donating to the Civitas Fund?"

"Not all of them," Isaac said. "Just *these* families. Families who are very concerned about the welfare of their kids." He took a long sip of wine. "Specifically, their *academic* welfare."

A small itch developed in the back of Maggie's mind, but she couldn't quite reach it. Her frown deepened and she raised her wineglass as she tried to line up the puzzle pieces bouncing around in her head. Then, as the rich, earthy wine hit the back of her throat, so did the truth. "They're paying," she spluttered, setting her glass down with such force that wine sloshed over the side, staining the white tablecloth. "Oh my God, they're fucking paying for grades. In the classes on the lists." Isaac looked away, then turned back with a pained expression.

"Wait," she gasped, "you *knew*? Oh my God, were you *involved*? Is that why they had you sign an NDA?"

"No!" he said. "God, no." He held his hands up in a gesture of innocence. "I found *out*, which Jerry wasn't happy about. About six months before I was—before I resigned."

Maggie leaned back. The puzzle pieces were snapping into place at a dizzying rate. "But how? How did they get the teachers to change the grades? I mean, they wouldn't do that."

Isaac's face was grim. "You'd be surprised. I mean, Civitas pays well for a private school but not *that* well."

"But the other NDAs... Mr. Braun and Ms. Burnett."

Isaac shook his head. "I don't know anything about those. But if I was a betting man"—he gave her a sidelong glance— "which, for the record, I'm not, so we're not having this conversation—I'd wager every teacher who was fired two years ago was someone who refused to sign on to inflate student grades." He made a sour face. "And I bet they all got generous severance packages in exchange for signing, like me."

Maggie's head was spinning. She signaled for the server and tapped her wineglass. "I'm going to need another one."

When they stepped out onto the street hours later the cool air hit Maggie, contrasting with the warm buzz throughout her body after three glasses of wine.

"Why don't I drive you home." Isaac took her arm. "You can get your car tomorrow."

She didn't protest as he led her to his car, a newer model, gray-blue Ford Bronco.

"Nice car," she said as he walked her to the passenger side and opened her door.

"Thanks," he said with a wry smile. "It was my severance present to myself."

When he started the car a local jazz station played softly.

Maggie studied his strong hands gripping the steering wheel, aware of how much the car smelled like him: a mix of shea butter and the leathery tang of what she guessed to be his cologne. She tried not to ignore the tingles his proximity caused.

When he pulled up in front of her house, he put the car in park and looked over at her. "What now, Shaft?" he asked.

Sweat pooled between her breasts. Oh my God. Did he want to come inside? Did she want him to?

"I'm married," she blurted.

He drew his head back, blinking. "I meant with everything we talked about," he said. "The Civitas Fund."

Maggie felt the flush creep up her neck to her face, wishing she could disappear. "Right," she said. "Wow, I'm sorry, I thought..." She closed her eyes and reached for the door handle.

"Wait," he said. "Don't go." She opened her eyes and the intensity of his gaze paralyzed her. "I know you're married. I also know I'm super attracted to you. But I'd never..." He hesitated. "Not unless it was something you wanted to..." He shook his head and groaned. "OK, that makes me sound like a sleazeball."

"No, it doesn't," she said. "And I'm married but I'm not..." She searched for the right words. "It's—I don't really know what's going on with that right now. So..." She held his gaze and smiled. "I don't think it makes you sound like a sleazeball at all."

He blew out a sigh of relief and gave a small smile. "Phew."

"And with the Civitas Fund," she continued, "I don't know. I need to think about what to do about it. But whatever it is, it won't be traced back to you, I promise."

"I'd appreciate that."

Instinctively, she reached over to touch his arm. "You can trust me."

"I know," he said. "Thanks." He placed his hand on top of hers. "You need help getting inside or are you good?"

"I'm *fine*," Maggie said defensively.

"Whatever." He rolled his eyes, not removing his hand from over hers. "Lightweight."

Her gaze caught his and almost imperceptibly she felt them moving toward each other.

Suddenly the motion-activated light in the driveway came on, flooding the car with its bright, white beam. *Shit, Pen!* Maggie thought, snatching her hand away from Isaac's. She whipped her head around to peer out the window.

A raccoon stood frozen in the driveway, its eyes glinting out at them.

"I should go," Maggie said, keeping her eyes down as she climbed out of the car before she could do something stupid.

THIRTY-ONE

Rhea stood at the stove, tending to a pan of scrambled eggs. Next to her sat four English muffins, ready to be transformed into breakfast sandwiches. Though she usually only had coffee and a banana in the morning, there was something about making her boys a warm breakfast that made her feel like a good mom.

She heard footsteps and was surprised to see Will enter the kitchen, already in his Civitas polo shirt and gray pants. His dark hair was matted down on one side where he'd slept on it. "Hey, you're up early," she said, surprised.

He yawned and rubbed a crust of sleep from his eye. "Pen has an early meeting for the school paper and wanted me to drive her."

Rhea struggled to keep the annoyance off her face, unhappy about the idea of Will sacrificing his precious sleep when Pen could have easily gotten to school herself. "That's nice of you," she said, turning off the burner and scooping eggs onto the English muffins. "Speaking of Pen," she said, striving for a casual tone, "how are things between you two these days?" Ever since Maggie had mentioned Pen's jealousy of Josh, Rhea had been searching for a way to broach the subject with Will.

Will yawned again. "Uh, fine, I think." He shrugged. "She's been kind of a lot lately, but yeah, fine."

"Oh?" Rhea cleared her throat. "Well, you know I think she's a very nice girl, but—"

"I know, I know," Will interrupted, rolling his eyes. "We're young, it's only high school, whatever. I get it. You remind me all the time."

Rhea wrinkled her nose, feeling chastened. "I do?" She sighed. "I'm sorry, honey. I'll lay off... it's your life. And I do like her. Truly." She attempted to sound upbeat as she handed Will one of the sandwiches.

"I mean, you don't like her that much," he said with a begrudging smile.

Rhea offered a sheepish smile of her own. "I only want what's best for you. It's a mom thing."

"I know," he said, grabbing his car keys off the counter. "'K, I gotta go."

"Have a good day, sweetie," Rhea called after him.

"... the thing is, the interconnected nature of the supply chain can introduce a lot of risk, especially with third-party vendors." Brooks and Josh walked into the kitchen as Will left.

"You mean like attackers targeting vendors to gain access to systems or sensitive data?" Josh asked.

"Exactly." Brooks snapped his fingers. Both he and Josh were dressed in navy dress pants, button-down shirts, and quilted vests. Rhea smiled at their coordinated attire and handed Brooks a plate. "The kid's catching on quick," he said, grinning at Josh.

Josh smiled modestly, and Rhea's heart momentarily swelled, seeing the pride in his eyes. But the feeling was immediately replaced by the familiar pang of fear at seeing them together. It was one thing to ask Josh to live with her lie at home, but now he had to conceal it from Brooks all day at work, too.

Brooks and Josh settled at the table with their breakfast sandwiches and coffee, still engrossed in work. Rhea left them to go wake Zane and then shower. She'd finished and opened the bathroom door when Brooks walked into the bedroom to retrieve his phone from the nightstand. He stopped short, taking in her naked body, her skin pink from the steam.

"Whoa, how am I supposed to leave for work now?" he asked, approaching.

Rhea laughed and swatted him away as she grabbed her robe. "You're like a teenager," she said.

"Are you complaining?" He leaned in to kiss her.

"Never." She kissed him back, then pulled away. "I can't be late to drop Zane off."

Brooks sighed. "Go ahead, break my heart." He picked up his phone. "Oh, I'm thinking of taking Josh to happy hour tonight so he can do some networking. I'll let you know if we're going to miss dinner."

Rhea paused, searching for the right question. *Have you seen his eyes?* she wanted to say. *How they look exactly like mine?* "So things are going well for him at work?" she asked.

"So far so good," Brooks said, running his hand through his hair. "Everyone has great things to say about him. He asks good questions and really seems to want to learn, which is more than I can say for some of the interns we've had—usually the ones with a dad or an uncle on our board." He gave a wry smile. "God, some of these kids are so entitled."

"Kind of like our kids?" Rhea said. She meant it as a joke but Brooks didn't laugh.

"Not at all like our kids," he said, frowning. "Will and Zane work hard. Which, these days, isn't even enough."

Rhea tilted her head. "What do you mean?"

He sighed and tugged at his ear. "Being smart and working

hard isn't enough anymore. You have to be outstanding. To the point where no one can question that you deserve that spot at a top college, or that job, or that promotion. And I get it, there's maybe some correction that needs to happen in the world. I only wish it wasn't happening right as our sons were going out into the world."

"Mm." Rhea considered his words.

"Anyway, I've got to run." He leaned in for one last kiss, his lips warm and reassuring on hers. But all Rhea could think about was the list she'd seen with Will's name on it.

THIRTY-TWO

Anna turned onto the now familiar street, slowing as she neared the white house. This time there was a light on. Kayla was back home.

She knew Donna was right—she should stay out of it. But that didn't stop her from driving by a couple of times a week. Sometimes she saw a police car idling up the block, which comforted her. She hadn't seen Bryce again after the first time. Until today, the house had remained dark. She hoped Kayla's return was a good sign, an indication that she felt safe. Anna wondered what that felt like.

Her phone chirped—her Jerry phone, as she now thought of it—and she answered on speaker as she drove away from Kayla's house. She noticed her pulse didn't quicken as it usually did when his name appeared. Since their night out, he'd remained tender and solicitous, making her coffee one morning and even suggesting a trip to see her parents if he had time off between jobs. She found herself increasingly lulled into the idea that maybe New Hampshire was exactly what she needed.

"Hi, honey," she answered.

"Hello, Pocket. What are you up to?" It was his roundabout way of asking where she was.

"I just pulled up to Maggie's. We're meeting about the gala stuff," she said. The lie made her stomach lurch, despite the new precautions she'd taken.

Using her new phone, she'd discovered an app that could fake her location on her old one, which was easier than hiding it at home when she went to work. Today, she set her blue dot at Maggie's address. Despite their recent détente, she wasn't ready to tell Jerry about her job, especially if she'd have to quit for a cross-country move soon anyway.

"Ah OK," he said. "Well, I'll see you at home a bit later then."

"Sounds good."

"Kiss kiss," he said, then disconnected.

When Anna pulled up to Maggie's house fifteen minutes later, a sense of relief washed over her. She could relax here. There was no need to walk on eggshells or look over her shoulder.

As she walked to Maggie's front door, it hit Anna how much she looked forward to seeing the other two women every week. Sure, they worked on drafting silent auction descriptions and uploading everything to the event website, but they also swapped funny stories about their kids, talked about screen time and school shootings, or sometimes watched silly TikToks together.

Their conversations made Anna feel part of something. The only drawback was that the relaxing, easy time she spent with Maggie and Rhea emphasized the stark loneliness of the rest of her life. Every time she left Maggie's, it felt like going from living in full color to grainy black and white.

Maggie answered the door and handed Anna a glass of wine. "You're going to need it if we're going to finish all the auction descriptions today," she warned. She'd changed out of her work clothes and into leggings and an oversized UPenn sweatshirt.

"Hey." Rhea's face brightened and she stood to embrace Anna when she walked into the living room. "How are you?" She was also dressed casually, though her natural elegance managed to make her gray cashmere sweatsuit and ponytail look like it was straight out of fashion week. Anna looked down at her own thin black sweater, noting that she'd probably need some warmer clothes for New Hampshire.

"I'm a little stressed," Anna admitted as she sat on her usual end of the L-shaped couch. Her mind ping-ponged back to Kayla.

"What's up?" Rhea frowned in concern.

"Oh, work stuff," Anna said, waving her hand. She couldn't stop wondering whether it was actually safe for Kayla and the kids to be back home.

"Wait, work stuff?" Maggie stopped and stared at Anna. "Since when do you have a job?"

Anna snapped to attention, realizing her slip.

"Oh wow, big news," Rhea said, clapping her hands. "Tell us all about it!"

Panic shot through her, but as Anna looked at their smiling, encouraging faces, it faded. Screw it, she thought. They were her friends now, weren't they? They had no reason to tell Jerry —and maybe it wouldn't matter soon, anyway, if New Hampshire became a reality.

Anna took a deep breath and chased it with a long sip of wine. "I'm a lawyer," she said. "I mean, I was a lawyer, back in Chicago. A long time ago. But I decided it was time to go back to work." She shook her head. "It's only part-time, not a big deal. Really."

"Actually, it's huge deal," Maggie said, her face serious. "For women, going back to work after time away is fraught with all kinds of emotions. I see it all the time with my clients."

"Easy with the therapy voice," Rhea said, raising her eyebrows in Maggie's direction. She turned to Anna and smiled. "What Maggie means to say is, congratulations!" She set down her wine and pulled Anna into a hug. "We're so proud of you."

Anna's cheeks flushed with pride, but her buzz quickly vanished. What was she thinking? What if they mentioned something to Jerry? "Thanks," she said. "But it's kind of a sore spot with Jerry, so if you see him, maybe don't—you know?" Maggie frowned in confusion. "He's still adjusting to me being busy and having less time for family stuff," Anna added hastily, rolling her eyes in what she hoped was a nonchalant gesture.

"Um, sure," Rhea said, her expression a mix of curiosity and concern. Then she smiled and she raised her glass. "Cheers to you!"

"Cheers!" Maggie echoed. Then her face darkened. "OK, not to break the mood, but I need to tell you both something." She twirled her wineglass nervously in her hands.

Anna felt a tug of anxiety in her stomach. Maggie was never nervous.

Maggie took a deep breath. "OK, here goes. So I had a drink with Isaac and—"

"A drink?" Rhea sat up straighter. "With Isaac? Wait, do you have a crush on him?" Maggie's face turned tomato red and Rhea squealed. "Oh my God, I knew it," she said, then paused, considering. "I mean, I can see it, I guess. He's attractive in a kind of Jamie Foxx meets Jimmy Fallon kind of way."

Maggie shook her head, her moment derailed. "I'm sorry, *what*? Jimmy Fallon?"

"I happen to think Jimmy Fallon is hot." Rhea shrugged.

"OK, that's weird," Maggie said.

Rhea rolled her eyes. "Anna, you agree, right? I know you do."

Anna laughed. "I mean, he's funny, but I wouldn't put him on the cover of a romance novel or anything." She paused, suddenly viewing the moment from the outside and wishing she could freeze time to savor it: laughing and drinking wine with her friends on a random Wednesday night. It was everything she'd ever wanted. Would she be able to find this again in New Hampshire?

"Whatever, never mind," Rhea said. "Let's get back to your date with Isaac."

Maggie's face remained splotchy red. "Shh, Pen is home," she whispered. "And it was strictly business. *Not* a date."

"Sorry," Rhea mouthed, putting her finger to her lips. Anna tried to hold in her giggles but ended up snorting, which set Rhea off again.

Maggie glared at them, waiting until they'd collected themselves. "OK," she said, biting her lip. "I talked to Isaac and... God, I don't know how to say this. Because it's bad."

Anna tensed and her laughter dissolved. Had Maggie discovered something about Jerry? She thought of her plan—she still needed more time. She couldn't risk him being provoked by something.

Rhea's eyes widened. "What do you mean?"

Maggie scrunched her eyes closed. "Please don't shoot the messenger, OK?"

Anna tried to speak but only a high, nervous laugh came out.

Maggie cleared her throat, then began talking fast, her words tripping over one another. "The student lists I found are all families who've donated to the Civitas Fund. It turns out it was set up for wealthier families to give in a more, um... anonymous way."

Rhea squinted. "And that's bad... because why?"

Maggie's gaze lowered to her wineglass as her voice grew quieter than Anna had ever heard it. "The money in the Civitas Fund is from families who paid to have their kids' grades, um, elevated. Part of it goes to the teachers and part stays with the school." Her eyes flickered to Anna.

The room fell silent as Anna tried to process Maggie's words. "I don't get it," she said. "Why would they do that? I mean, every kid on that list was already on the Dean's List... oh." Suddenly, it hit her. Her mind went momentarily quiet, as if her brain had flatlined, then all her thoughts rushed back like a whirlwind. This didn't make sense. Or did it? Jerry always complained about board pressure to fundraise, and she knew his compensation was tied to hitting targets. She knew from listening to Jerry complain each year that the board kept setting more ambitious goals, which he somehow always met. A sudden, sour feeling twisted Anna's stomach.

"Which teachers?" Rhea asked, interrupting Anna's whirling thoughts. "All of them?"

Maggie grimaced. "I don't know for sure, but... probably."

Anna's breath was shallow and her heart thudded at an alarming rate. "But how could they?" she asked. This was far worse than she'd imagined.

"I don't think they were given much choice." Maggie pursed her lips. "Remember the faculty shake-up two years ago?"

"Do I ever," Anna said grimly. The faculty changes hadn't gone unnoticed, and Jerry had come under attack for quietly replacing over half the Civitas staff during the summer break. The board even briefly considered ousting him. Anna had borne the brunt of his stress. That summer, she and Farrah had bought matching swimsuits to wear to the nearby community pool. But Anna never wore hers, instead watching her daughter splash around from under an umbrella in a long-sleeved shirt.

"Well," Maggie continued. "It sounds like the new teachers were hired under a certain... understanding." Her eyes went to Rhea. "And the ones who left got generous severance packages in exchange for going quietly."

Maggie's words hit Anna like a nuclear bomb, the shock

waves reverberating through her body. Her husband was the mastermind behind it all. He'd corrupted one of the oldest, most prestigious schools in the country for his own gain.

Even when she hated him, Anna had always admired Jerry's principles when it came to Civitas and the way he held students to high standards and talked about instilling them with the "Civitas character." Now, she realized bitterly, he was a fraud through and through. A fraud who'd been planning to run away to New Hampshire, and to take her with him.

There was a crash and Anna turned to see Rhea's glass shattered on the wood floor, wine spreading in a pool until it reached the rug and began to darken the fabric. Then Anna remembered.

Will was on the list. Someone had paid for his grades, and from the look of shock on Rhea's face, Anna was certain it hadn't been her.

"Fuck," Rhea said quietly. Then louder, "Fuck, fuck, FUCK!"

"Shh!" Maggie warned, looking stricken and glancing over her shoulder toward the kitchen.

Rhea buried her face in her hands. When she raised her head again her hands shook and her eyes blazed. "I'll kill him," she said. "I'll fucking kill him."

THIRTY-THREE

Maggie stared after Rhea, who had walked out without a word. Shit. This wasn't how things were supposed to go. Maggie sprang up. "Rhea!" she called. But by the time she reached the front door, Rhea was already backing down the driveway.

Damn it. Regret surged through Maggie. Of course Rhea would react that way. Maggie had been so nervous about sharing what she'd learned that she'd considered keeping it to herself. She should have been more careful in how she communicated it instead of being her usual blunt self. Was there a good way to tell someone their husband was at the center of a major school scandal?

Maggie closed the door and pressed her hands against her forehead, cursing. *Stupid, stupid!* Rhea was probably on her way to confront Brooks, who would call Jerry, giving him time to sweep everything under the rug because Maggie had no proof. Yet. And Anna, she was probably on the phone with Jerry, demanding answers and blowing the whole thing up.

Berating herself, Maggie hurried back into the living room. She was surprised to find Anna on the floor, calmly picking up the shards of Rhea's wineglass.

"Please, leave it," Maggie said, reaching for her own glass.

Anna ignored her and continued to place pieces of glass in a neat pile on the end table. When she finished she stood and turned to Maggie. "So," she said. "What now?"

Maggie gulped her wine, unsettled by Anna's cool, blank expression. After all, she'd just told her that her husband had corrupted one of the nation's top private schools with a pay-for-grades scheme Anna should have been the one storming out.

"Are you OK?" Maggie asked with concern.

Anna's mask slipped and she gave a short, bitter laugh. "Does it matter?"

"Yes," Maggie said quietly. "It does." Her stomach twisted into knots as she thought of the past few weeks with Rhea and Anna. It was the most time she'd spent with anyone outside of her family or patients in ages. At some point she'd decided she was too busy for friends. But during their hours together, she'd noticed the dull ache of loneliness she'd gotten so good at ignoring was gone. And now she'd fucked it all up.

She squeezed the bridge of her nose. "Look, I shouldn't have blurted everything out like that. I mean, I don't even have any actual proof yet—"

"But you will." The wrenching despair in Anna's voice sent a chill through Maggie; she had never seen Anna this emotional before.

"What makes you so sure?" Maggie asked.

"Because it makes sense. Jerry's only ever out for himself."

Maggie sucked in a breath. What a thing to say about your own husband.

Anna made a harsh noise in the back of her throat. "Don't look so surprised," she said. "I'm not." Her voice quavered and she looked on the verge of collapse.

"Anna." Maggie reached out to steady her. "God, I'm so sorry. This is all so fucked up." Anna gripped her arm like Maggie was pulling her into a life raft.

"I've been so stupid for so long," she whispered.

"You couldn't have known," Maggie soothed.

Anna's shoulders slumped forward. "You don't understand," she said, her voice breaking. "He's... he's an awful person. I've known that for so long but I've never been able to—I should have..."

The desperation in her voice unsettled Maggie. "Anna, what's going on?" she asked. "If there's anything I can do—"

"No." Anna released her grip on Maggie's hand and stepped back so quickly she had to grab hold of the couch to steady herself. "There's nothing anyone can do. Not now."

Once Anna left, Maggie threw away the broken glass and poured herself the last of the wine. "What a fucking day," she muttered. In the last hour she'd alienated her only two friends and ruined her chance to expose the fraud. By now Jerry had probably spoken to Brooks and begun covering his tracks.

Maggie paused, staring at the framed school photo of Pen on the bookshelf. Her mind went to Pen's B minus in trig and the angst it had caused her. Maggie knew the class was graded on a curve, so that meant... She let out a sharp breath. Someone else's falsified A grade—someone like Will—meant Pen had suffered.

She realized she hadn't seen Pen since she'd gotten home earlier. Pen had gone straight up to her room without stopping for her usual snack of a mini bagel with cream cheese and a side of chocolate chips.

Padding up the stairs, Maggie clicked on the food delivery app on her phone. Even defrosting the chili Dan had left them felt like too much work right now. "Pen?" She knocked on her daughter's bedroom door. "Honey, I'm ordering pizza for dinner, what do you want?" When there was no answer, she knocked again, then cracked the door open.

Pen sat huddled in the corner of her bed, her arms wrapped around her knees in a tight ball. Her eyes were red and swollen, and what looked like an entire box of used tissues lay scattered around her.

"Oh my God, honey, what's wrong?" Maggie rushed to her daughter, wrapping her in a tight embrace. Pen collapsed into her arms, letting out deep, gasping sobs. "Are you hurt?" Maggie's mind raced. "What's wrong?" Her mind darted through a series of disasters: bullying, an assault on the way home, nude pictures gone viral.

Pen gasped for air. "Will," she managed to say, "broke up with me."

Maggie processed this for a beat, then sighed with relief. She could deal with a teenage breakup.

"Oh no, I'm sorry." She rocked Pen and kissed the top of her head. "Do you want to talk about it?"

"He called me *jealous*." Pen pulled back from Maggie and spat the word.

Maggie gave Pen's shoulder a sympathetic squeeze. "I'm sure he gets a lot of attention from other girls."

Pen's face twisted with disdain. "Not from other girls," she retorted. "From Josh." She wriggled out of Maggie's embrace and flopped backward onto the bed.

"Josh?" Maggie's brow furrowed. "His cousin?"

Pen sat back up abruptly, fists clenched. "Who's probably not even his cousin."

"I'm confused," Maggie said. What the hell was Pen talking about?

There was a beat of silence before Pen's face crumpled again, and she let out a guttural wail. "How could he?" she sobbed, burying her head in Maggie's lap.

"I'm so sorry, honey," Maggie said, stroking her daughter's hair. "I'm so sorry."

. . .

Close to midnight, long past Maggie's usual bedtime, Dan finally returned her call. But tonight, between what she'd learned about Civitas and Pen's emotional breakdown, she'd been lying in the dark while her mind whirred at top speed.

"Hey," she greeted him on the first ring, her voice tinged with reproach. "I've been trying to call you."

"Sorry, hon," he replied. "It's been a busy day. Everything OK?"

Maggie cradled the phone against her cheek and shook her head. "No."

"Talk to me, Mags," Dan said, hearing the stress in her voice.

She filled him in on everything to do with Civitas and Pen, with the exception of her meeting—*not* a date—with Isaac.

"Oh, poor Pen," Dan said, and the concern in his voice quelled Maggie's resentment at not being able to reach him earlier. "Do you need me to come home?"

"No," Maggie sighed, exhaustion setting him. "It's only a teenage breakup. I'm sure she'll be fine." She smoothed her hand over Dan's empty side of the bed. "Honestly it's the other stuff I'm more worried about."

"Understandable," Dan said. "I mean, if what you're saying is true, well, that's really messed up." There were muffled noises in the background.

"What do you mean 'if it's true'?" Maggie asked, defensive. "And where are you? It's late."

He sighed. "At this stupid networking thing. And it's two hours earlier here, remember? But I'm beat, I'm about to head back to the hotel. Can I call you in the morning?"

"Sure." Maggie nodded. Everything would look better in the morning.

THIRTY-FOUR

Rhea drove home from Maggie's on autopilot, her brain consumed with what she'd learned. Brooks had flown out that morning for another trip. Lucky for him, because she wasn't sure she could have kept from punching him if they were face to face. Her brain was so overloaded with anger and shock she couldn't even remember where he'd gone—Seattle, maybe? San Francisco?

Rhea stepped out of the car and walked in circles, unable to face going inside yet. She paced in the driveway, fists tight and then loose, adrenaline coursing through her, ringing in her ears, and leaving a sour taste in her mouth.

Brooks, the son of Senator Hugh Connelly, known for his campaign slogan "Truth and honor," had been paying for Will's grades. This revelation shook Rhea to her core. The same Brooks who championed meritocracy at work, and who always returned it if he was given too much change. Her handsome, funny, loving husband who always took the moral high ground —except when it came to buying his own son's success.

As she paced, Rhea berated herself for her blindness. She'd seen Will's struggling with trigonometry. She should've known his miraculous A grade wasn't earned. But did Will know? Or had Brooks done all this behind their son's back, too?

The sound of a car startled her and she turned to see Will maneuvering his RAV4 up the driveway. While many of his friends drove BMWs or Range Rovers, Brooks had been against anything fancy for Will's first car. "He's only going to bang it up," he'd said. So expensive cars were out, but expensive grades were fine.

"Hey, Mom." Will unfolded his long body from the driver's seat, clad in a Civitas sweatshirt over his basketball uniform. His backpack was slung over one shoulder and he cradled a basketball under the other arm. Tears welled in Rhea's eyes at the sight of her tall, handsome boy, with his beautiful green eyes and lazy smile. She'd do anything to protect him. But while Brooks might have felt the same, his actions spoke otherwise.

"You good?" Will asked, eyeing her with concern.

Rhea wiped her eyes and smiled. "Yeah, fine, just my allergies kicking in. Pollen and stuff." She waved her hand in the air. "How was practice?"

"Good." He dropped his backpack on the ground, dribbled over to her and launched a shot. It swished through the net.

She turned toward the house to hide her teary face. "I'm going to start dinner. Is Pen coming over tonight?"

Will shot again and the ball clanged off the rim. "Nah," he said. "Actually we, um, kinda broke up."

Rhea stopped mid-stride and turned back. "Oh, sweetie," she said. "I'm sorry."

"S'OK." Will gave her a half-smile and bounced the ball between his legs. "Like I said, things were getting, like, intense. And she had this crazy jealousy thing going on with Josh. I decided I couldn't deal with it anymore."

Rhea's mind flashed back to seeing Pen and Josh outside, arguing. "What does Josh have to do with it?" she asked, frowning.

"Honestly?" Will said, still dribbling. "Beats me. She got all salty all of a sudden and kept saying how she thought Josh was sus, or whatever." He frowned. "It was low-key messed up." Then he dribbled several feet down the driveway, turned and fired a shot that swished through the net.

"Oh." A loud ringing started up in Rhea's head. "But you like having Josh around, right?"

Will looked at her, surprised. "I mean, yeah, dude's cool."

Rhea felt like a vise was tightening around her chest. "OK. But if you ever, you know, feel like it's time for him to go, for it to be the four of us again, you can tell me."

Will looked confused. "Why would I want him to go?"

"No reason." Rhea massaged her temples. "No reason." She checked her watch. "Dinner in thirty, OK?"

Will nodded as another shot swished through the net.

Inside, she slipped into autopilot mode, boiling water for pasta and sautéing onions and ground beef. But when she tried to open the jar of marinara sauce, it wouldn't budge. She tried her usual trick of running it under cold water, but it remained stubbornly stuck. Hearing the front door open and close, she called out, "Will? Sweetie, could you open this for me?"

"It's me." Josh waved as he entered the kitchen. He wore a blue button-down shirt that made his green eyes stand out. Rhea's heart seized with pride at how handsome he looked.

"Hey," she said.

"Do you want me to...?" He gestured at the jar in her hand.

She blinked. "Oh, yeah, thanks."

"That smells delicious," he said. "Can I help with anything?" Normally she found his presence calming, but today she felt on edge standing next to him.

"No, I've got it," she said. "Thanks."

He grinned and grabbed an apple from the bowl on the counter. "Then I better go change so I can beat Will in a HORSE before dinner."

Rhea tried to smile, then she bit her lip. "Hey, that argument you had with Pen the other night—did it have to do with her and Will breaking up?"

Josh stopped, his shoulders rising. "I didn't know they broke up," he said. "Is Will OK?" Concern creased his face. "And no, nothing to do with that," he added.

Rhea smiled, trying to gauge whether he was telling the truth. "OK." She nodded.

After dinner Will and Zane had settled in to start their homework when the doorbell rang. "I'll get it." Zane eagerly dropped his textbook and jumped up from the couch.

Rhea waved him off. "I'm sure it's only UPS or something."

But when it rang again she checked her Ring camera app to find Tamara on the doorstep. "Huh," she murmured. "That's weird."

"Hey!" Tamara held a bottle of wine in her hand and leaned forward to hug Rhea when she opened the door. "Sorry, I know I'm a little bit early."

Rhea gave her a blank stare. Tamara's eyes traveled over the living room where Zane's schoolwork and snacks were spread across the coffee table, and then over to Rhea, still dressed in her joggers.

Tamara gave an astonished laugh. "Wait, did you forget you were hosting book club tonight?"

"Oh my God," Rhea breathed, remembering. She ran an embarrassed hand through her hair and her face flushed. "Um, yeah, I guess I did."

"Wow, who are you and what have you done with my hyper-organized best friend?" Tamara giggled. Usually when Rhea hosted she put together an elaborate charcuterie board and a tower of mini cupcakes frosted in colors to match the cover of whatever book they were reading.

"It's been a busy day," Rhea said curtly. She turned to Zane. "Can you finish upstairs?" He sighed and made a big show of collecting his stuff as Rhea headed for the kitchen.

Tamara watched silently as Rhea assembled a tray of gold-fish crackers, Brie cheese, and assorted granola bars for the living room. By the time the doorbell chimed again, Rhea had added a bowl of potato chips, some Sour Patch Kids, and a bottle of Pinot Noir, ignoring the judgment on Tamara's face.

"Hellllo!" trilled Amy Finch, another of the PA moms, as she gave Rhea air-kisses upon entering. Then she took in Rhea's last-minute buffet on the coffee table and exchanged a look with Tamara.

"She *forgot* she was hosting," Tamara said, widening her eyes for effect.

"I've been really busy with the gala plans," Rhea said, which was partly true. "And Brooks has been traveling."

"Mm." Amy nodded. "That's why I usually have our chef put something together."

Rhea forced a smile. "Well, our chef would be me."

Amy's voice dripped with faux sympathy. "Oh honey, that's your problem right there—you're understaffed."

The rest of the group arrived and they had all settled in with their wine when Josh breezed into the room dressed in running shorts and sneakers. He stopped short as the women turned to stare at him. "Oh, sorry," he said, glancing at Rhea. "I didn't realize..."

"It's fine," she said, forcing a smile, realizing she hadn't mentioned Josh's presence at her house to Tamara or any of her other friends. She hadn't been hiding it, exactly, but the more people she lied to about his true identity, the more significant the transgression seemed. If it was only her immediate family— and Anna and Maggie—then it wasn't such a big deal, right? But now Josh was on full display for the Civitas PA moms. "Every-one," Rhea introduced, "this is my, um, nephew, Josh. He's staying with us for a while and working for Brooks." She laughed nervously and turned to Josh, who offered a tight smile. "Josh, meet... everyone."

"Nice to meet you all." Josh waved, flashing his charming smile. "I'm headed out for a run."

"See you later." Rhea nodded.

"Wow," Amy exclaimed after he'd left. "He looks so much like you. So handsome!"

Tamara cocked her head, a hurt expression crossing her face. "I didn't know you had a nephew," she said.

"Yup," Rhea said. Her face felt strained from smiling. "My sister's son. Back in Odessa." She twisted a cocktail napkin in her lap and gave a nervous laugh.

Tamara's frown deepened. "You're from Odessa? I thought you grew up in Dallas."

"Oh, Odessa's the town from *Friday Night Lights*, right?" Amy asked. "So redneck." She giggled.

Rhea swallowed. They were straying into dangerous territory. "So," she said, groping for a change of subject. "Who actually read the book this time?"

THIRTY-FIVE

Anna had been distracted and on edge the last forty-eight hours since Maggie's revelation. She burned dinner one night, forgot to wash Farrah's lacrosse uniform, so she'd had to practice in a dirty one, and then this morning she'd made coffee without setting the glass carafe under the dispenser, only realizing her mistake when she'd returned to the kitchen to find Farrah frantically mopping up the brown flood on the floor with paper towels.

"I didn't want Dad to get mad," Farrah said, looking up at Anna with large, frightened eyes that caused a seismic crack in Anna's heart.

She'd been off her game at work, too, mixing up dates on two of her motions. "Get with the program," Donna had snapped. But still Anna struggled to focus, her mind consumed by Maggie's revelation. And while there wasn't any proof yet, Anna had no doubt it existed. The faculty shake-up, Jerry's shortened fuse, his argument with Isaac, and the students who had no place on the Dean's List—the pieces all fit.

Had she been that easily swayed by a fancy dinner, a good lay, and a week of Jerry's charm? Shame washed over her as she realized how easily she had taken to fantasizing about herself, Jerry, and Farrah dressed in tweed, tramping through brightly colored leaves in New Hampshire, the picture of a happy family. She was so desperate for her happy ending that she'd let herself believe that, even after everything, he could grant it.

Now, though, her path was crystal clear: escape was the only option left, and it had to happen fast. A scandal like this would ruin Jerry, but would it take her and Farrah down along with him? Cost her her job? A lawyer married to a criminal was hardly an easy sell. And if she couldn't work, she couldn't support Farrah. The only choice was to leave as soon as she could, and to get as far away as possible from Jerry before everything exploded in her face.

The week before their romantic dinner date, Anna had prepared her own restraining order paperwork. Safely tucked in her desk at work, it sat alongside printed photographs documenting her injuries over the years. She'd begun documenting them while mostly still in denial, printing them out and hiding them after deleting the images from her phone, lest Jerry find them. Because deep down, despite her dogged refusal to accept what her life had become, she'd known.

All that remained was to sign and file the paperwork. Yet, unlike Kayla, Anna knew she couldn't have Jerry removed from their home; her name wasn't even on the deed. Back when they'd bought it, it had been somehow easier to leave her off the paperwork—something about a credit check, details Anna couldn't recall clearly—and Jerry had promised they'd add her later. They never had. So if Jerry wasn't leaving, it meant Anna and Farrah would have to.

Anna met with the rental manager that afternoon, still dressed in her suit in order to look like a model (i.e., employed) tenant. She'd scrolled through the online pictures so many times that the actual tour felt almost unnecessary. The apartment was a corner unit on the twelfth floor, boasting southern exposure and floor-to-ceiling windows on one wall.

"You'll get great sunsets," the manager said. His teeth were the same unnatural shade of white as the mints Donna kept in a bowl on her desk, and his biceps strained against the material of his bright pink button-up shirt.

Anna opened the door to the small patio, and the city noise filtered up to her ears. When she stepped back inside, the door closed with a satisfying *thwunk*. The noise immediately ceased, as though the apartment was hermetically sealed—exactly what she wanted.

She walked briskly through the open kitchen, living area, and the two bedrooms, each with an ensuite bathroom, as the manager ran through the amenities—gym, party room, coworking space—peppering his speech with phrases like "best-in-class" and "top of the line."

"OK," she said, turning so quickly he nearly crashed into her, his cologne overpowering. "Where do I sign?"

The manager flashed a surprised, too-white grin. "Decisive," he said. "I like it." He rifled through the glossy folder he'd been carrying and pulled out several pieces of paper. "We'll have you do the lease application really quick, and then sign here and here to authorize a credit check." He pointed. "I'll need copies of your last three pay stubs."

Anna blanched. "I've only been working for a couple of months."

"No problem-o," he said. "You'll need to submit a copy of your most recent bank statement showing you have enough savings—typically it's at least six months of rent."

Anna stared at him, panic beginning to creep over her. Jerry didn't allow her access to their bank accounts, and her own account was too new, her funds too meager. "I don't have a bank statement yet," she said. "I only opened the account a month ago. And I don't have six months of savings." The manager's face fell. "But I have enough for the security deposit and first and last month's rent," Anna assured him hastily. "So that's fine, right?" Her voice pitched high and desperate.

He shook his head. "Won't work, sorry."

"Please." Tears pricked at the corners of Anna's eyes. "I really need this apartment."

She felt unsteady, as if the ground beneath her was shifting, and leaned against the wall for support. Anger flared momentarily—why weren't these requirements clearer on the website? But it swiftly gave way to a familiar sense of self-loathing. How had she been stupid enough to believe she could manage to pull this off?

The manager sighed and straightened the paperwork in his hand, then put it back in the folder. "I'm sorry," he said again. "I don't make the rules."

THIRTY-SIX

Dan was due home Saturday afternoon, so Maggie had asked Isaac to meet up Saturday morning. Maggie had gone to get Pen's favorite breakfast sandwich from La Bamboche and left it under a glass bowl, ready for when her daughter woke up. *Love you*, Maggie had written on a sticky note next to it.

Pen was struggling with the breakup, evident from her red, swollen eyes each morning and her quick retreat to her room after school. Maggie felt a pang; she'd do anything to take away Pen's pain. But right now, as she prepared to meet Isaac, a conflicting wave of excitement crowded out her concern for Pen.

The late October day was warm and sunny, and Isaac had suggested a hike in Sweetwater Creek State Park. It was a few miles west of the city, and Maggie was relieved to be assured of not running into anyone she knew. Plus, she thought with a pang of guilt, it didn't involve wine, dim lighting and cozy booths.

She'd texted Isaac after the fiasco with Rhea.

I shouldn't have told her. I don't even have any proof yet.

Let's talk.

Maggie headed out dressed in running shoes and her favorite leggings, the ones that propped up her butt up like she was twenty-five again. She'd opted for minimal makeup, a touch of mascara and lip gloss, determined to look as she normally would on a low-key Saturday morning—or maybe the tiniest bit better.

Isaac's Bronco was already in the parking lot when she pulled in, and when he got out he sported a maroon Morehouse baseball cap, a black three-quarter fleece zip-up and dark gray joggers that clung just enough to show off the muscles in his legs.

"Hey there," he said, walking toward her. As he leaned in to kiss her cheek, Maggie felt a rush of dizziness.

She looked around. "I've never actually been here."

"Yeah, I'm not surprised," he replied, looking her up and down. "You don't strike me as the outdoorsy type."

"I'm not," she admitted with a laugh.

He made a wide sweeping motion with his arm. "Welcome to the great outdoors, Maggie Reed."

"Looks nice," she joked. "Do they have Wi-Fi?"

He laughed and they began walking. They left the parking lot and veered onto the trail, joining a handful of other early-morning hikers and a couple of dogs sniffing eagerly around. "So, how you been, Shaft?" he asked.

Her heart stuttered at his use of his nickname for her. *Stay focused, damnit*, she reminded herself.

"Honestly, not great," she said. She filled him in on Rhea's silent treatment and her newfound understanding of how Pen had been penalized in the whole mess. "It's not fair that Pen's being punished for someone else's crime," she said, the passion in her voice growing.

Isaac's mouth twitched. "You know this isn't, like, only

personal for you, right? I mean, Pen's probably the least likely to actually be impacted by this."

"What do you mean?" Maggie asked. "She's—"

Isaac held up his hand. "So she got one bad grade, big deal. She's a white girl at a good school who's going to go to a good college, no question. And she has you. A safety net." He shook his head, his face growing dark. "But the scholarship kids who get bussed in from my neck of the woods and other neighborhoods?" He glanced at Maggie. "Yeah, there's more of them than you'd think, thanks to the generous alumni community." He rolled his eyes. "But *those* kids—if they start slipping in their grades, they lose their scholarships. Then bam, back to underperforming public schools and probably no college." He looked at her and raised his eyebrows. "You get me?"

Maggie flushed at her insensitivity. Isaac was right, plus he'd lost his career over this—not just one stupid grade, like Pen. Feeling warm with embarrassment, she stopped to take off her sweatshirt and caught Isaac glancing over her body. Her flush deepened, but this time it wasn't unpleasant.

"I don't think there's anything I can do without some kind of proof," she said. "Unless you think any of the teachers who were fired would talk to me? Maybe come forward?"

"No," he said. He stayed close to her as they started to walk again, their arms brushing from time to time. "No one's talking. It would ruin their life—the NDAs made sure of that."

Frustrated, Maggie threw her hands up in the air. "OK, so what then? I'm supposed to forget about it?"

Isaac stopped walking. "That is the one thing you can *not* do. This has to come out, Maggie."

She let out an exasperated sigh. "So help me, then!"

A dog rushed past, throwing her off balance. She caught hold of Isaac to steady herself, and a tingling sensation washed over her body. He took her hand and gave it a gentle tug, leading her down a wooded path branching off from the main trail.

"Let's go this way," he said, without letting go.

They walked in silence for a minute or two. Goosebumps rose on Maggie's arms, whether from the deep shade of the path or her hand in Isaac's, she wasn't sure. When they'd gone far enough that the main path was no longer visible, he stopped. "There are emails," he said in a low voice. "I've seen them. I mean, these rich families are cocky, so sure nothing can ever happen to them. The shit they put in black and white." He shook his head. "You've got to find a way to get them."

Maggie tried to process what he was saying. "But how?"

The intensity of his gaze liquefied her insides. "You're smart. You'll find a way."

They started walking again and Maggie shook her head, thinking of her full schedule of clients, plus all the work she was doing for the gala. "I wish I had more time," she said, frustrated by the feeling of helplessness. "I'm stuck helping with the stupid centennial gala—which now feels like such a farce."

Isaac let out a low whistle. "Can you imagine if everything came out before then?"

Maggie gave a wry smile. "That would definitely put a damper on things." She stopped short, a thought crystalizing.

Isaac stopped beside her. "What?" he asked.

Her mind was racing, a plan coming together in her mind. *No way*, she thought, shaking her head. *That would be insane.*

"I might have an idea," she said.

He took off his baseball cap and ran his hand over his head. "I'm not dragging you into something you don't want to be part of, am I? I realize I can get passionate about this."

They turned to face each other, and Maggie shook her head. "I want to make things right. I reached out to you, remember?"

"Yeah," he murmured. "I remember."

Maggie struggled to steady her breath as he leaned closer,

his finger slowly tracing her jawline until it stopped lightly on her lips. Maggie tilted her head toward his, then jumped back, startled as her phone rang. She snatched it from her pocket. Dan's name flashed across the screen and she felt a pang of guilt.

Silencing the call, Maggie shoved the phone back into her pocket, but not before Isaac had seen Dan's name.

He stepped away from her. "Maybe we should get back."

Maggie nodded, and wordlessly they turned around, her heart racing with what she'd almost done.

THIRTY-SEVEN

After Maggie's revelation, Rhea decided to wait until Brooks was back from his trip to confront him. It meant putting her anger on hold, but it felt worth it to wait until he was back and do it face to face. She needed to see his body language, to watch his face for signs of what else he might be keeping from her.

"I miss you guys," he'd told her the night before over Face-Time. "I can't wait to be home tomorrow."

"Don't worry, we're fine," Rhea told him. She'd tried to keep their nightly FaceTime calls short, claiming she was tired.

"I know you're fine." Brooks smiled. "But I want you to be great. I want you to be so great that when I get home, the first thing I'm going to do to you is..."

She tuned him out as he ran through the list of everything he wanted to do to her. She was in no mood for phone sex.

"I'm sorry, honey, I'm really beat," she interrupted with her sweetest smile. "Can we put a pin in this until I see you tomorrow?"

"Oh," Brooks said, sounding deflated. "Sure. Love you and see you Thursday."

The word had hung in the air after Rhea disconnected and

tied her stomach into knots. Brooks would be home then, and she'd be left with no choice but to confront him. The ticking timer on the bomb she'd been carrying around all week would finally go off.

Now, she changed into pajama pants and one of Brooks's T-shirts, then padded toward the kitchen to see if some chamomile tea might settle her nerves. Walking in, she was met by the mouthwatering scent of frying butter and melting cheese. Josh was at the stove, his back to her, still in his work clothes.

"I didn't know you were home," she said.

He jumped at the sound of her voice and dropped the spatula. "Sorry," he said, retrieving it.

He'd seemed on edge lately, Rhea noted. She peered over his shoulder. "What are you making?"

"Grilled cheese." He ran a hand through his hair, which had grown shaggy in the nearly two months he'd been with them. "I worked late. Want one?"

Rhea considered the offer. "Maybe," she said. Her stomach growled in agreement.

Josh grinned. "I think that's a yes."

He grabbed a plate from the cabinet and plucked a napkin from the drawer. By now he knew where everything in the kitchen was—more so than Will or Zane. Stepping back to the stove, he flipped the sandwich, browning it evenly, set it on a plate on the counter and neatly arranged the napkin beside it.

"Thanks," Rhea said, sitting.

"Not so fast," Josh said. He disappeared into the pantry and came back with a bag of potato chips and shook a handful onto her plate. "The final touch."

"Wow." Rhea smiled. "Full service." She popped a chip into her mouth.

Josh gave her a lopsided grin. "Nothing like dinner at 11 p.m." He went back to slicing cheese for another sandwich. "So, what's keeping you up?" he asked.

Rhea shook her head. "Some stuff with the boys' school."

Josh nodded. "It sounds like a pretty intense place, according to Will."

Rhea swallowed the bite she'd been chewing. "Oh really? Like, what does he say?"

Josh shrugged, sliding the second sandwich into the pan. "It sounds like a lot of pressure, you know? And I think he feels like he needs to be perfect. Never let anyone down, or whatever."

Rhea laughed. "Will? No way, he's like the opposite of stressed. He doesn't even know what day it is half the time."

Josh glanced over at her from the stove. "I think you're one of the people he's worried about letting down."

Rhea opened her mouth to protest but then stayed silent. Had she put too much pressure on Will? Was this her fault?

"He wants to make you proud," Josh continued. "Like any son would."

They were silent for a moment as she chewed. "Were you happy?" she asked finally.

Josh flipped the sandwich, his mouth twisting in thought. "Happy is relative. I mean, I didn't have all this"—he gestured around at the large kitchen with its shiny appliances—"but it didn't bother me because I never thought I could. It would have been like being mad I didn't have a Lamborghini or a million dollars or something. It was unattainable, you know?" He frowned. "So I guess it was more like I was happy within this box." He drew a square in the air. "Like, you get to hope for this and no more; that way you're not disappointed." His eyes flickered toward her. "I did always wonder about you and my dad, though." Rhea's shoulders tightened at the mention of Josh's father. "Is it OK if I ask about him?" Josh said.

Rhea pulled her hands onto her lap, wiping her palms on her pajama pants. "I figured you would at some point," she said, pushing her plate away. Her appetite was gone.

Josh took the pan off the burner and glanced at her. "Was he... I mean, did he know about me?"

Rhea shook her head. "No."

"Did you ever want him to?"

"No," she said again, breathing deeply as her chest clenched. She could get through this.

Josh frowned. "He didn't... did he?"

"God no," Rhea said quickly. "Nothing like that. He... he was a lot older. I was a stupid teenager."

"Do you regret it?"

Rhea brought her hands to her cheeks and they came away wet with tears. "No," she whispered.

How could she regret Josh, especially now that she'd been given a second chance—a chance she didn't deserve. She was a selfish monster who'd chosen her own happiness over her child's for twenty-one years. Once her body healed from giving birth, once she'd met Brooks and been swept into the Connelly orbit, she'd started to go days without thinking about her baby. Then weeks, then months. She'd erased that part of her life entirely and had been glad to do so. What kind of mother did that?

She had a lot of making up to do.

The next morning she checked her email as she waited in the car for the boys to come out, refreshing it as a new one came in. *Student Achievement Award* read the subject. The sender was Jerry Armstrong.

Congratulations! I'm pleased to announce that William has been nominated for the Virtus Award. Given once per term, this prestigious award recognizes students who excel both in and out of the classroom and embody the Civitas character. The award will be presented at the upcoming centennial gala. Please accept my sincere congratulations on William's well-deserved honor.

With all best wishes,
Jerry Armstrong

Rhea froze. The Virtus Award wasn't one of the most prestigious awards, it was *the* most prestigious. Only two were given out per year and they were usually reserved for seniors.

Had Brooks paid for this, too? The white-hot anger Rhea had felt at Maggie's house rolled back over her. She'd wanted Will to be prepared for the real world with all its challenges and heartaches. Instead, she'd let his path be groomed, all obstacles to success removed. And the worst part about the smooth, wide-open highway of Will's life was that he thought he'd earned it. Rhea's fingers trembled with anger. When had she become so clueless about her own family?

To her surprise, Will came out first, opening the car door and climbing into the front seat, his long legs stretching out in front of him. Rhea glanced over at him and tried to smile. "I got the email about the Virtus Award."

Will's ears turned pink as pride battled with feigned nonchalance. "Yeah, they told me yesterday."

"Congratulations." Rhea's voice was flat and devoid of enthusiasm.

Hurt and surprise flashed over his face. "Aren't you happy? It's kind of, like, a big deal or whatever." He looked away and chewed a hangnail.

Rhea gripped the steering wheel, searching for something to say that wasn't a lie. "It is a big deal," she said. "But you know I'd love you the same no matter what, right?"

Will shrugged. "Yeah, of course." But he didn't sound convinced.

THIRTY-EIGHT

Maggie opened her latest text from Isaac and reread it.

How are you? Can I see you again?

He'd sent it Monday, a full two days ago. But despite the warmth she felt in her body—and between her legs—every time she reread his message, she hadn't responded. What was there to say? She was no closer to figuring out how to access the emails Isaac had referenced. Plus, she didn't need to be a marriage therapist to know the way she couldn't stop thinking about him was trouble.

Her hand in his. His finger tracing her jaw. His lips—*Stop*, she commanded herself.

She'd almost crossed a line. *But I didn't*, she reminded herself.

Now the clock was ticking. In less than two weeks, Civitas would celebrate "One hundred years of excellence." *Excellence, my ass*, thought Maggie. Because while the Civitas Fund had been established only two years ago, who knew how long before that the corruption had started. Jerry had been at the school for eleven fucking years. That was a long time to have your finger on the scale in favor of the already ultra-privileged.

Maggie gathered up the laundry, her mind drifting to Anna. Unlike Rhea, who had stormed out in anger after Maggie's revelation about the Civitas Fund, Anna had seemed to deflate. Maggie shuddered, imagining how awful it would be to find out your husband had done something so corrupt. That was a lot to deal with. Yet, Maggie couldn't shake the feeling that Anna wasn't entirely surprised. Feeling guilty that she hadn't done it earlier, Maggie resolved to check in on Anna after she got the laundry started.

Maggie grabbed Pen's dirty clothes from her room and recalled her daughter's outburst over the trigonometry grade. Thinking of the tears Pen had shed, all the while thinking she hadn't worked hard enough—when really it was all rigged—sent a hot spike of rage through Maggie's chest. Pen had been penalized because Maggie and Dan played by the rules. Because they hadn't been part of the elite club that ran by a different moral code. With a resounding thud, Maggie dropped the laundry basket to the ground, her frustration boiling over. She wanted to scream and hit something, but she settled for hurling large handfuls of clothes into the washer with as much force as she could manage.

As she stuffed in a pair of Dan's jeans, something clattered against the metal interior of the machine. Rooting around, Maggie fished out a small hotel key-card holder. On the front was an abstract drawing of a palm tree and the words HOTEL JUNE MALIBU.

Her stomach dropped.

Over her career, Maggie had listened to countless clients describe this exact moment. The one where their fundamental understanding of their marriage exploded in their face like a land mine.

Snatching the jeans from the washer, the ones Dan had

packed for his trip, Maggie retrieved her phone from her pocket. A quick Google search confirmed her suspicions: Hotel June Malibu wasn't a convention hotel in Denver but a luxury spot in Malibu, California.

Fucking California.

Maggie's hand searched for the wall's support, then she slid down to the floor, stunned. He'd called her every day, complaining about the boxed tuna sandwich lunches and the windowless convention rooms. He'd told her how much he missed her and Pen. And only yesterday, he'd sent her a list of Paris hotels for their upcoming twentieth-anniversary trip in April. There had to be a mistake. Why would he do any of that if he was—

Maggie closed her eyes, clenching the key card in her fist. In an instant, her marriage, once a solid structure, had been revealed as a facade. How could she, a marriage therapist, have missed the cracks in her own foundation?

The doorbell chimed and her eyes flew open. Dropping the key card, she winced at the deep groove it had left in her palm. What was she supposed to do now? Drive to Dan's office to confront him? Pack up his belongings? Pack hers? The options swirled, overwhelming her.

The doorbell sounded again and at the same time her phone buzzed with a text from Rhea.

We're here.

Maggie checked her watch. It was their usual weekly meeting time, but she hadn't expected Rhea and Anna to show up after the dead air between them since last week.

She answered the door in a daze and the air hung heavy between the three women as they followed Maggie to the living room and took their usual seats.

Anna sat in the armchair, legs tucked beneath her, arms

crossed tightly, dressed all in black as if for a funeral. Rhea perched on the edge of the couch, swathed in a giant sweatshirt over leggings. Her normally carefully styled waves were limp and her skin appeared pallid. Maggie slumped at the other end of the couch, her blouse untucked and wrinkled, wishing she could disappear into the cushions.

"Will got the Virtus Award," Rhea blurted.

"Mm," Maggie said. She tried to raise her head but it felt like it was made of concrete.

"Congratulations," Anna offered.

Rhea's voice turned sharp and she stabbed a finger in the air to emphasize her words. "Not congratulations, *no*. Because it's *fake*. It's all *fake*. For all I know, Brooks was simply the highest bidder."

Anna's head snapped up from where she'd been staring at her lap. "Wait, you haven't talked to Brooks yet?"

"No." Rhea's words were muffled as she rubbed her face. "He's been away. And I have no idea what the hell to say to him when he's back tomorrow. Or Will," she added. "Am I supposed to tell my son he doesn't deserve the award? That it turns out he's not exceptional? That his own parents didn't believe he could succeed on his own so they bought his achievements?" Her voice was raw with fury. "I can't let him accept the award. I can't make him more of a fraud than he already is."

Maggie pressed her palms against her eyes, trying to relieve the tight band of pain gripping her skull. "You tell Will the truth," she muttered. "Everyone deserves to know the truth."

"Easy for you to say," Rhea snapped. "You're the only one whose family isn't completely fucked."

Maggie leaned forward and put her elbows on her knees, burying her face in her hands. "Dan is having an affair."

The room went so silent Maggie could hear the hum of the refrigerator in the next room.

"Dan?" Rhea said. Maggie looked up to see her shocked expression.

Anna shook her head so vigorously, her hair swished from side to side. "No," she said. "That can't be right. You and Dan are happy."

"Like, annoyingly happy," Rhea insisted.

Maggie sighed. "We haven't had sex in three years," she said dully.

"Ohhh," Rhea said, the word coming out like a train slowing down as it pulled into the station.

Anna frowned. "But—you're a sex therapist."

"I'm aware." Maggie clenched her teeth to try to keep from crying.

Rhea whistled. "And to think I was finally about to buy your book."

"Rhea!" Anna said.

"I'm sorry, I'm sorry." Rhea rocked back and forth and rubbed her palms together. "Bad joke. Terrible joke. Oh my God. Maggie, I don't know what to say. Honey, I'm so sorry."

Maggie looked into the faces of the two women, their expressions brimming with tenderness and concern, and something inside her broke. Tears streamed down her face as she let out a gut-wrenching sob. Her whole life, everything she'd worked for and believed in, was crumbling, all because of one stupid hotel key card. And then there was her stupid, humiliating flirtation with Isaac. Had she really craved attention so desperately that she'd deluded herself into thinking there was something real between them?

Rhea and Anna were by her side in an instant. Anna squeezed her hand while Rhea rubbed gentle circles on Maggie's back as it convulsed with sobs. She couldn't recall the last time she'd cried like this, with angry wails and loud, sniffling gasps. Neither Rhea nor Anna tried to get her to stop crying, and neither told her it was going to be OK. They were long past that now.

As Maggie's sobs subsided into wet, raspy breaths, Rhea's voice cut through the heavy silence. "Fuck them," she said. "We bend over backwards to do everything right, and what do we get? Lies. Fucking lies." She rose to her feet and turned to face Anna and Maggie. "I'm done with it. Let them have their lies, their affairs, their petty games. But I'm through." Her eyes gleamed with determination. "If they can change the rules, then so can we."

THIRTY-NINE

Anna removed the lid from her cappuccino and blew on the white foam. She slid into the chair across from Sydney, whose short, close-cropped hair had been replaced by a cascade of tiny, tight braids down her back. Donna was out of the office that morning so Anna and Sydney had decided to linger at one of the tables in the lobby coffee shop instead of heading back to the elevator.

In the weeks they'd worked together, Anna had grown fond of Sydney, who alternated between being a hard-nosed junior lawyer with a take-no-prisoners attitude and a giggly twenty-something who kept Anna up to date on all the celebrity gossip.

"What?" Sydney asked, eyeing Anna. "Why are you looking at me like that?"

"You mean, like, smiling at you?" Anna asked.

"Yeah, but in a creepy, nostalgic way, like you're going to tell me I'm your long-lost daughter or you're dying and I'm the only one with a kidney that's a match or something."

Anna rolled her eyes. "You watch too much TV, Syd."

"Incorrect," Sydney said, sipping her drink. "I don't watch

enough TV. I work all the time and I'm way behind on my shows."

Anna laughed, grateful she wouldn't have to say goodbye to Sydney any time soon. Then she shivered, thinking about how she'd almost agreed to move to New Hampshire, like a pathetic mouse marching into a lion's den. Thank God for Maggie's revelation about the Civitas Fund. Finding out the extent of Jerry's involvement was exactly what Anna needed to remind her exactly who she was married to. Now there was no chance she'd let herself get pulled back in by Jerry's charm; not when she was so close. She just needed a couple more months to save the money for an apartment. She could pretend for a little while longer, couldn't she?

Sydney stared over Anna's shoulder at the large television that played the news on a loop in the lobby. "God, did you hear about this?" she asked, shaking her head.

"About what?"

"This poor woman." Sydney widened her eyes. "She was stabbed by her husband. In front of her four-year-old daughter! I mean what kind of sicko does that? Awful."

The breath rushed out of Anna's lungs. "Was she OK?" she managed.

Sydney shook her head. "No, he killed her."

Anna turned around, feeling like she was in slow motion. There on the screen was a picture of Kayla Martin.

The contents of Anna's stomach rose into her throat and she shot to her feet. Sydney yelped as Anna nearly upended their table, narrowly making it to the nearest trash receptacle, where she emptied her stomach. When Anna finished, she stood for a minute, breathing hard. She wiped her mouth with the back of her hand and she turned to see Sydney standing a few feet away, looking stricken. "Whoa, are you OK?"

Anna forced a nod. "Something I ate, probably," she mumbled.

"I hope it's not the flu," said Sydney, stepping back. "I cannot afford to get sick right now with the Brewster case looking like it's going to trial."

In the elevator back upstairs Sydney stood as far away from Anna as possible but wore a sympathetic look. "Do you need anything?" she asked as they stepped off onto their floor.

Anna shook her head. "I'll be fine." She smiled weakly.

Back in her cubicle, she collapsed on her chair and googled Kayla's name. Her hands were shaking so badly she could hardly type and the search results on the screen swam before her eyes.

... estranged husband... domestic dispute... restraining order had been filed...

Closing the browser, she yanked open her top desk drawer, retrieving her own yet-to-be-filed restraining order. Tracing her finger over her name on the form, the same spot where Kayla's had been, she felt a fresh wave of nausea.

How stupid she'd been to think one piece of paper could make any difference, for Kayla or for herself. It was just words on a page, and words were useless in the face of men like Bryce and Jerry. Men who never changed.

Swiveling her chair around, Anna held the form above the document shredder that sat on her desk. As she watched the paper disappear into the slot and catch in the sharp teeth of the machine, everything came into sharp focus.

It was up to her. No one else was coming to save her.

FORTY

Brooks flew in on the red-eye and went straight to the office. All day Rhea steeled herself to confront him about the Civitas Fund and Will's award, and when she heard his car in the driveway that evening, the spike of dread went through her chest.

"I know you get it," came Brooks's voice as he walked in. His shirt was wrinkled from hours of wear but there was a jauntiness in his step. "We need to keep the investment dollars flowing to stay on top of our network infrastructure and keep our incident response teams nimble."

"Totally," agreed Josh, trailing behind him, nodding emphatically. "Did you get a chance to look at the list of potential investment partners I put together?"

"You bet," he said. "There are some promising ideas in there. I'm passing it along to the finance guys to look at." He caught sight of Rhea and broke into a broad grin. "Well, there's a sight for sore eyes." He opened his arms and, out of habit, she went to him and let herself be embraced.

As she breathed in his familiar scent of cinnamon gum and musk, a wave of unease washed over her. Normally the warmth of his embrace should have been comforting, but today it only heightened her anxiety. She pulled back, forcing a smile. "How was your trip?"

"Productive," he said, squeezing her shoulder. "Josh really stepped up when I needed some data at the last minute. I think he's got a good future with us."

Rhea watched Josh smile as he disappeared down the hall to what she now thought of as his room. She tamped down a familiar, queasy feeling thinking about her own lie and when she'd have to come clean. She brushed away the thought and refocused on what she needed to do.

Brooks walked toward the kitchen and she followed, her heart pounding. She watched as he poured himself a glass of water, the moment stretching unbearably. The wall clock ticked like a grim countdown.

"Brooks," she began, her voice trembling despite her efforts to keep it steady. "We need to talk." She wrapped her arms around her midsection, rubbing the soft material of her white mohair sweater between her fingers to calm herself.

Concern flickered in his eyes. "What's wrong?"

The pressure of the words she needed to say grew in her throat. "I know about Will," she blurted.

Brooks looked alarmed. "What about Will? Did something happen?"

Rhea steadied herself against the cool, smooth marble of the counter. "I know about the Civitas Fund."

A peculiar expression crossed her husband's face. "You mean our donations?" he ventured, his tone casual.

For an instant, a kernel of hope bloomed in Rhea. Perhaps she was wrong. Maybe Brooks had only lent his support to Civitas as a proud parent. Then a flicker of guilt crossed his face, crushing her last shred of hope under the mounting weight of her anger.

"Enough," Rhea said, crossing her arms. "I know, OK? The

bigger question is, does Will? Does our son know you've been buying his grades?"

Brooks paled, placing his glass on the counter before leaning against the fridge. His eyes lingered on the window for a moment before hardening as he looked back to Rhea. "No," he replied flatly. "Of course Will doesn't know."

The truth hung in the air like smoke, permeating everything. "Why?" she demanded, biting back her tears of betrayal.

"Seriously?" Brooks said, incredulous. "Please tell me you're not that naive, Rhea."

She recoiled from his sharp tone. "But Will doesn't need your help," she said. "He's doing his best. Plus"—she raised her chin—"he's a Connelly." She felt a twist of guilt as she admitted out loud what they'd always left unsaid: that Will would probably always benefit from his family's name.

"Well, his best isn't cutting it," Brooks snapped, rubbing his tired eyes. "Look, it's not a great time to be a white guy. Yeah, maybe five or ten years ago Will could have coasted on the Connelly name. But now?" He gave a short, mirthless laugh. "Now, any success he achieves will be under a microscope and questioned because of his so-called privilege. So, no, he can't just 'do his best.'" Rhea flinched as he threw her words back at her. "He has to be perfect," Brooks continued. "Unassailable. He has to be bullet-proof." He locked eyes with her. "That's what this is about. Making sure my son is bullet-proof."

Rhea felt knocked sideways by Brooks's utter lack of remorse. She tightened her hands into fists. "But he didn't ask you to," she protested. Her anger boiled dangerously close to the surface. "And neither did I! You lied to me."

Brooks clenched his jaw. "I did what needed to be done."

"We have to tell Will." Rhea's voice stretched tight with outrage. "He deserves to know."

"Absolutely not," Brooks countered, crossing his arms.

Rhea gripped the edge of the countertop to keep from

lunging at Brooks. She wanted to do something—anything—to make him feel the same pain that his betrayal had caused her. "How can you stand by and let Will accept the Virtus Award at the gala, knowing it's all fake—that he's a fraud?" she challenged, her gaze narrowing. "Or did you buy the award for him, too?"

"I didn't buy the award," Brooks retorted, his gaze flickering downward. "Jerry threw it in as a kind of bonus for all the donations I—we—made."

Rhea recoiled. "Jesus, Brooks." Then she squared her shoulders. "Tell him. Or I will."

His head jerked back up. "You can't. It would destroy him."

"Well, you should have thought about that," she shot back. "You should have thought about all of us."

"Damn it, all I ever do is think about you!" Brooks slammed his palm onto the counter with such force that Rhea jumped. "All three of you! Why do you think I do all this?" He jabbed his finger toward the laptop bag he'd dropped by the door. "The travel, the long hours?"

"Do *not* put this on me." Rhea grabbed an apple from the bowl on the counter and squeezed it as hard as she could, resisting the urge to hurl it at him. "This was your choice. I wasn't consulted, remember?" she snapped.

Their eyes met in a tense standoff, the room filled with ragged breathing. Gradually, Rhea let out a long exhale and gently placed the apple back down. "The gala is at the end of next week," she said. "Tell him before then, or I will."

FORTY-ONE

Anna sat in her cubicle, her mind racing. Normally the white noise of murmured conversations and the click of keyboards provided the perfect backdrop for her to focus on her work, but today her thoughts were a tangled web of the news about Kayla. Bryce had been apprehended right away; there was no question of his guilt. But no judge or jury could undo what had happened.

"Anna."

She looked up to see Donna standing by her desk, hands on her hips. Today she wore a hot-pink blazer with an asymmetrical zipper up the front.

"There you are." Donna snapped her fingers. "I don't know what planet you were on."

Anna flushed. "Sorry."

Donna nodded at Anna's computer monitor. "How's the motion going?" She checked her watch. "I need it in an hour."

"I'm giving it one last review and then I'll send it to you."

Donna nodded. "When you finish, stop by my office."

Anna's heart sank. Was she in trouble? Donna had been especially critical of her work lately, slashing through her briefs with comments like "Weak argument" and "Get to the point." A sick feeling churned in her stomach. Was she about to be fired? Her contract was only temporary, after all. She thought of her bank account, which she checked several times a day to relish the fleeting sense of freedom the balance gave her. She had plans for that money. She needed every penny before Jerry either dragged her to New Hampshire or was exposed for his role in Civitas's academic fraud.

Anna tried to smile to cover the anxiety that was expanding in her chest. "Sure, I'll come by in a few minutes."

After she read the motion a final time, triple-checking every comma and footnote, she pushed her chair back and walked down the hall toward Donna's office.

"Come in," Donna called when Anna knocked on the half-open door.

Anna cleared her throat. "You wanted to see me?"

Donna's expansive office had a wall of windows overlooking downtown Atlanta, and behind her large desk, built-in shelves held rows of law books and sculptures of smooth, colored glass that glowed in the sunlight. Anna wondered what it must be like to have so much space to herself.

"Sit." Donna pointed to the chair opposite her desk.

Oh my God, she *was* being fired.

Anna sank into the chair, grateful for it because she was afraid her legs would no longer hold her.

"You've been off your game the last few days."

"I'm sorry," Anna began, her palms suddenly clammy. She couldn't lose her job, not now. "I'll do better, I promise. I—"

But Donna shushed her. "I assume you heard about Kayla Martin?"

"I saw the news, yes." Anna's voice was barely above a whisper and she blinked rapidly in an attempt to keep the tears at bay. *Please don't let me cry in front of my boss*, she thought.

Donna swiveled her chair to look out the window, her face

grim. "It's an awful thing. My niece is beside herself, as you can imagine." She turned back to Anna. "But the truth is, the odds weren't in Kayla's favor. No amount of lawyers or protective orders could have prevented what was probably inevitable from the day she met that man."

Anna swallowed and looked down at her hands. The tiny diamond on her wedding band caught a shaft of light, but instead of sparkling the stone looked hard and cold. What would Donna think about her situation? Would she think Anna was stupid and weak for staying all these years? A warm rush of shame mixed with her despair.

"Anyway." Donna clapped her hands. "That's not what I called you in here to talk about." You've been with us two months now, yes?" She glanced down at a file on her desk.

Anna stiffened. "Yes."

"You're still rusty," Donna said. "And you need to speak up more in meetings because you're usually one of the smartest people in the room." She smiled. "After me, of course."

Anna tilted her head, trying to gauge where this was going.

"So enough of this part-time bullshit," Donna continued. "I'd like for you to join us full-time, and the other partners agree. If you're interested, of course. It would mean more hours, but we can offer some flexibility." She folded her hands on her desk and looked at Anna.

Stunned, Anna leaned forward. "You want me to... I thought I was... Full-time?" Her voice shot up an octave. She paused to collect herself, then tried again. "I mean, thank you."

Donna pushed a piece of paper across the desk toward Anna. "The details of the offer are all here. There's not much room for negotiation, but I think you'll find it's generous."

Anna took the document and scanned it, trying to keep her eyes from widening at the annual salary that was listed. It was nearly double what she'd made the last time she'd worked, thirteen years ago.

"Look it over and let me know as soon as you can," Donna said.

"I will." Anna stood, clutching the paper and feeling the unfamiliar stirrings of both relief and hope. "Thank you so much."

Donna made a shooing motion with her hand. "Now get back to work."

Later, Anna left the office, heady with possibility. A full-time job meant she could apply for an apartment sooner than expected, get her own credit card, her own car. She'd be dependent on no one. And most importantly, she wouldn't have to move to New Hampshire. Hope fluttered deep in her chest as she turned out of the parking garage and headed home. Now there was only the question of Farrah. Jerry would fight her, she knew he would, so she needed to be prepared.

She would need insurance.

She didn't take the turnoff that led to her street. Instead, she kept going, winding her way through an adjacent neighborhood until she pulled into the Civitas parking lot. Taking off her suit jacket, she pulled on a sweater, then checked her watch and hurried inside. She should have just enough time.

"Hi, Mrs. Kaminski, is he in?" Anna pasted on a bright smile as she entered the school office.

The older woman removed her glasses from the bridge of her nose and smiled. "Anna, dear, nice to see you. But no, I'm afraid he's in the weekly faculty meeting."

"Oh, of course. It's Thursday. I forgot." Her pulse accelerated at the lie. Anna had endured many of Jerry's dinnertime rants about his 3 p.m. Thursday faculty meetings that never ended on time. She nodded at Jerry's closed office door. "I thought I'd surprise him. Do you mind if I wait?"

"Of course not, dear, go on in." Mrs. Kaminski nodded. "Let

me know if you need anything." She slid her glasses down her
nose and turned back to her computer.

Trying to steady her breathing, Anna walked into Jerry's
office and closed the door. Her heart pounded so loudly it
seemed impossible that Mrs. Kaminski couldn't hear it from the
next room. She felt like a futuristic robot in a sci-fi movie, her
brain running a complex algorithm as she methodically scanned
the room for what she needed.

The top of Jerry's desk was neat and nearly bare. She
opened the top drawer, finding only a Post-it and a pack of mint
gum. The other drawers were equally unhelpful, holding a
shoeshine kit, the tea sampler she'd given him for Christmas last
year, and a bottle of Scotch. A wave of spite surged through her.
She didn't even like Scotch, but she grabbed the bottle and
thrust it into her purse. In doing so, she bumped the mouse on
his desk, and the computer monitor sprang to life, asking for a
password.

A bolt of adrenaline shot through her as she remembered
the yellow Post-it she'd glimpsed in the top desk drawer. Sure
enough, there it was when she reopened the drawer, scrawled
with Jerry's handwriting:

Passwords -
~~*LeicesterCity0205 2016#*~~
~~*LeicesterCity0205 2016$*~~
LeicesterCity0205 2016!

Of course. His stupid soccer team. She tried the last one
listed, and the screen unlocked with a loud chime. She snatched
her hand back from the keyboard as though burned, knocking
an empty coffee mug with the Civitas crest off the desk. It hit
the carpeted floor with a loud thud.

"Anna?" Mrs. Kaminski called. "Are you all right?"

"All good," Anna called back brightly. Keeping an eye on the half-open door, she unminimized the email program and typed "*Civitas Fund*" into the search bar. A flood of emails appeared, mostly annual fundraising updates to the broader Civitas community. But the screen kept populating, and soon there was one from Hugh Gibbs. Anna's breath caught; Hugh's son Beau had been on the list. Then another from Roland Finch. Then Brooks Connelly. And other familiar names from the list Maggie had shown them.

Without stopping to read them, Anna selected the individual emails to print. The printer next to Jerry's desk beeped and whirred to life and began spitting out pages. Anna grabbed the first one and scanned it. It was from Jerry to Brooks Connelly:

Confirming the following for Will:

Trigonometry w/Holladay - $50k

Brooks's reply was succinct:

Confirmed. Payment has been wired.

"Back already?" said Mrs. Kaminski in the other room.

"Shocking, I know," Jerry replied. "The first faculty meeting in the history of the world to ever end early." Anna froze, her heart galloping as the printer continued to whir. "Say," Jerry said, "I've been meaning to ask about that grandson of yours. Did they ever figure out what he was allergic to?"

"Sesame," Mrs. Kaminski replied. "And who knew how many things have sesame in them?"

"Well, I'm sure it's a relief to his parents to know," Jerry said. "What a fright they had with the little chap. Oh, if you have a minute, would you mind brewing a fresh pot of coffee?"

"Of course," Mrs. Kaminski said. "And Anna dropped by. She's waiting in your office."

"Oh." The surprise in Jerry's voice sent ice through Anna's veins. "Thank you."

Anna closed the emails on the screen, snatched the final page off the printer and stuffed it in her purse as the machine quieted.

"Darling," Jerry said, stepping into the room. "To what do I owe this lovely surprise?" He looked crisp and official in his white shirt and Civitas green tie.

Anna assumed what she hoped was an innocent expression and clutched her purse to her body. "I was on my way home from the store and I just thought I'd say hi." She walked over to him and put her arms around his neck. "I missed you, that's all." She kissed him, slipping her tongue between his parted lips.

"Oh!" He cleared his throat, glanced behind him and pushed the door mostly closed with his foot. "Well, that's a very nice greeting." He glanced at his watch. "I'm afraid, though, we'll have to save the rest of it for later. I have a student meeting in ten minutes."

She slid her hand down his chest and allowed her lips to linger on his cheek. "I'll see you at home in a bit," she whispered.

If he was surprised by her uncharacteristic display of affection, he didn't show it. "I look forward to it," he said, patting her bottom as she edged toward the door.

Anna held her breath on the way to the car, resisting the urge to look over her shoulder to see if he'd come after her, her elation increasing with each block as she drove away.

When she arrived home, Anna read the pages with shaking hands. There were a dozen emails between Jerry and other families from the list, some even more explicit than the one from Brooks. She couldn't believe it. This was what she needed.

Then a thought emerged from the recesses of her mind.

What about Rhea? Now there was proof that Brooks had been intimately involved—what did that mean for her?

Her mind spun as she went inside. She stashed the folder in the laundry room, in a high cabinet behind the spare bottle of detergent. It would be safe here; she couldn't remember the last time Jerry had set foot in the laundry room. Then she pulled out her phone and fired off a text to Rhea and Maggie.

> You won't believe what I found. Meet tomorrow, 4pm?

FORTY-TWO

Dan hummed as he tossed a rainbow of vegetables into the wok Maggie had gifted him for his birthday three months ago. They'd joked that it was really a present for her, given how much she loved his Szechuan stir fry. Now, all Maggie could think about was how much she wanted to return to that night when he blew out the candles on his ice cream cake with her and Pen, before she discovered there was another woman.

"So the Civitas stuff, I guess you need to talk to a lawyer? Or the police?" Dan said, wiping his hands on his apron, which said *Yes, Chef* on the front.

"I guess," Maggie replied. She undid and then refastened the top button of the white blouse she hadn't yet swapped for her evening uniform of a T-shirt and sweatpants. Exposing Jerry was suddenly the furthest thing from her mind.

"And what about Pen, how do you think she's coping?" Dan moved the vegetables around with a wooden spoon, his back to her.

"Well, she seems to be eating something other than frozen yogurt again," Maggie sighed. "So that's a good sign."

"I mean, they hadn't even been dating that long, had

they?" Dan turned, scrunching his face as he tried to remember, an expression Maggie had always found endearing. Now, though, it brought a sob to her throat. She struggled to hold it back.

"Six months," she said. "Which I think is, like, an eternity in high school."

"And you've talked to her, right?"

Any other time, Maggie would have been touched by Dan's confidence in her ability to get through to Pen. But right now, she was struggling to hold herself together. "I tried," she said.

"Should we do something for her, like take her on a trip or something?" Dan mused.

"Like to Malibu?"

Dan froze at the stovetop. For a long moment, the only sound was the whir of the kitchen fan. Then, as if in slow motion, he removed the pan from the burner and turned it off. When Maggie finally dared look up, he wore a stricken expression.

"I don't know what to say," he said, his voice cracking.

Maggie let out a strangled laugh, still in disbelief that they'd ended up here. "Who is she?" she demanded.

Dan's face went from pale to flushed. "Honey, there's something you should—"

Maggie slammed her palm on the countertop, wincing as the impact shot up her arm. "Tell me who she fucking is," she said. She was crying, the last thing she'd wanted to do in front of him. Despite her anger and humiliation, she still wanted him. She wanted to have dinner with him, share her day with him, hear him whistle in the shower, and have him surprise her with grocery store flowers. She wanted the life they'd built together. They made each other laugh. She loosened him up; he kept her grounded. They *worked*. Until now.

Dan lowered his eyes to the floor. "It's Fernando," he said.

Maggie staggered backward, as if caught in a burning building's backdraft. Losing her balance, she began to fall, but Dan caught her wrist, holding her steady.

"Honey," he said. "Maggie..." His eyes were pleading.

They stood barely inches apart. "Fernando?" she whispered. "Your *friend* Fernando?" She shook her head, trying to comprehend. "But he's married—to a woman." The irony of her words struck her as soon as she spoke. Shaking off Dan's hand, she began to pace, gasping for air. What the fuck was happening? *Fernando* was the other woman? Fernando with his dorky crew cut and novelty socks? She halted, looking at Dan. "So, you're... gay?"

He cleared his throat. "I mean, I think so, yes."

"What do you mean you *think* so?" She folded her arms.

He flushed again. "Well, Fernando is the only... I mean, before him I'd never..."

"Fucked a dude," Maggie finished for him.

Hurt flooded Dan's face. "Made love to a man," he said.

Maggie placed her hands on her burning cheeks. "Love? Oh my God." She started pacing again. "You love him?" She whirled to face Dan. "You love him."

Dan gave a tortured nod. "It wasn't like we meant to—it just happened, OK?"

"I almost kissed someone," Maggie said, the memory of the moment in Isaac's car flooding back. Her voice grew louder. "I felt so guilty about it, and here you've been sleeping with someone else for—" She stopped. "How long?"

Dan closed his eyes like he was facing a firing squad. "Three years."

"Three years?" Maggie's voice rose. "Three fucking years?"

"I'm sorry," Dan whispered, his eyes filling with tears. "I never wanted to hurt you. I love you so much, Mags."

"Oh my God." She buried her face in her hands, then looked up. "So that explains why we haven't slept together. All your excuses."

Dan looked more miserable than the time he'd gotten food poisoning on the thirteen-hour flight home from their honeymoon in Bali. She thought of how oddly happy she'd been then, tending to him on the plane, knowing he was her person, that they'd always take care of each other. And now this.

Dan started to reach for her, then drew back. "It felt wrong to be with him and then come home and be with you. I didn't want to act."

"But you have been acting," she said, her voice a low rumble of anger. "You've been acting for three fucking years."

"No, I haven't," he said, desperation on his face. "This—" He spread his arms out and looked around the room. "This isn't an act. Our life together? Not an act. I wanted to be with you, too, only in a different way than I wanted to be with him." His voice broke. "Honey, you and Pen are my whole life. And I didn't want to give you up. I was being selfish and I'm sorry."

Maggie pursed her lips. "Clearly we're not your *whole* life."

Dan untied his apron and set it on the counter. He hung his head. "Do you want me to go?" he asked quietly. "If you want me to, I will."

Maggie imagined the house without Dan. In an instant, the anger fled her body. "No," she said, her lip quivering. "At least, not yet."

Maggie retreated to her office for the evening, where she lay on the floor, alternating between crying and staring numbly at the ceiling. Eventually, she peeled herself off the rug and went upstairs. After washing her tear-stained face and brushing her teeth, she climbed into the empty bed and attempted to read.

After a while there was a soft knock on the door and Dan came in. "Just getting my toothbrush," he said, the puffiness of his eyes mirroring hers. "I'll sleep in the guest room tonight."

"Please don't," Maggie said, her voice a hoarse whisper. She knew it was pathetic, but she didn't want to be apart.

A few minutes later he came to bed, smelling like mouthwash and wearing a T-shirt and the ratty flannel pajama bottoms she kept trying to get him to throw out. They turned out the lights and lay there in silence for a moment. Then Maggie rolled toward Dan to find him already reaching for her. Both their faces were wet with tears as their arms found each other in a tight embrace. They fell asleep that way, with their heads touching and Maggie's heart shattered.

FORTY-THREE

That night, after her confrontation with Brooks, Rhea tossed and turned in bed, watching the hours tick by. He'd retreated to his study after a stilted family dinner, and when she found herself still awake at 2 a.m., he still hadn't come to bed. Eventually her exhaustion won out and she fell into a dreamless sleep, waking only when the sliver of sunlight that crept around the edge of their curtains made its way onto the bed.

The angle of the light told her it was late. Confused, she sat up and rubbed sleep from her eyes. Was it the weekend? She squinted at the clock: eight thirty. Then, the events of last night came flooding back, flattening her back onto the bed like a tsunami. Her stomach churned as she replayed the conversation with Brooks.

A muted chime sounded repeatedly. It took her a moment to realize it was her phone alarm on the bedside table. She had slept through it—for the last two hours. The realization jolted her upright. They were going to be late. But as she dashed into the kitchen, she was met with silence.

Instead of her family, she found the room littered with empty cereal bowls, toast crusts, and a carton of orange juice sweating on the counter. She put it back in the fridge. They had all come and gone. No one had needed her.

She moved through the day on autopilot, going to the grocery store, the dry cleaners, and even Pilates with Tamara, who seemed to have moved past the disastrous book club meeting. Rhea managed to nod and smile through Tamara's ceaseless chatter about the new cleanse she was doing and her outfit plans for the upcoming gala.

Rhea's phone pinged periodically with texts from the PA moms' group chat, and each time she checked her phone she hoped it might be Brooks. They usually exchanged messages throughout the day—funny memes, quick "I love you"s. But today, he was silent.

Finally, a little before 4 p.m., she texted Maggie and Anna: *On my way*. She was curious to know what Anna had discovered that was so urgent, but mostly she was grateful for the distraction.

At Maggie's house, she had to ring the doorbell twice before there was any sign of life. The door finally cracked open, and Maggie peered out. She wore sweatpants and an oversized sweatshirt. Her eyes were puffy and red, her skin dull, and her hair was pulled back in a lopsided bun.

"Please tell me you're not seeing patients looking like this," Rhea said, stepping inside.

Maggie shook her head.

"Oh, honey," Rhea said, pulling her into a hug. "I'm so sorry," she murmured, rubbing Maggie's back. "They're such shitheads, aren't they?"

The doorbell rang again. Rhea opened it with one hand, keeping the other around Maggie. Anna stepped inside, exchanging a look of concern with Rhea when she saw Maggie. "Looks like it's a good thing I brought this," she said, holding up a bottle of Scotch.

Rhea raised her eyebrows in surprise. "Impressive." She tilted her head. "I didn't peg you as a lover of the hard stuff."

Anna smiled darkly. "I'm full of surprises." She took Maggie's arm and propelled her gently forward toward the living room. "Come on. Let's start drinking."

Once they were settled Maggie took a sip of the amber liquid, immediately gagging. She flapped a hand in front of her face. "Gah! How do people enjoy this?"

"Take small sips until your tongue goes numb," Rhea advised. Back when the boys were smaller and ran her ragged, she'd treated herself to the occasional 3 p.m. glass of Brooks's whiskey.

Anna looked at Maggie with concern. "So," she said, "how is... everything?"

"Well, for starters I was wrong, there's not another woman." Maggie pinched her nose and took another large swallow of Scotch. "It's another man."

Rhea spit out the sip she'd taken and began to cough.

Anna's mouth fell open. "What?"

Maggie gave a miserable nod. "Fernando, his best friend from dental school. And before you ask, it's been going on for three years, so no, it's not a phase."

Rhea sat back on the couch. "Wow, OK," she said, the Scotch burning in her stomach. She sat back up. "So what do you want to do?"

"Honestly?" Maggie's lip quivered. "I want to think about something else for a while."

Rhea and Anna exchanged glances and a beat of silence filled the room.

"I talked to Brooks," Rhea offered.

Maggie's eyebrows shot up. "And?"

"And it did not go well." Rhea bit the inside of her cheek. "I kind of gave him an ultimatum."

"Like what?" Anna's eyes widened.

"That he had to tell Will by the gala. Or I would."

"That had to have been hard," Maggie said quietly.

Rhea nodded and blinked back tears, overcome that, in the depths of her own despair, Maggie would think to comfort her.

"Would he go to Jerry?" Maggie asked.

Anna leaned in, excitement gleaming in her eyes. "Forget about that. Wait until you see what I have." She reached into her purse and pulled out a handful of printouts. Then, her gaze flickered toward Rhea. "Rhea, you might want to—"

"It's fine," Rhea said stiffly, moving closer to read over Anna's shoulder. "I already know what I'm up against."

Maggie's eyes widened as she scanned the documents. "Holy shit," she murmured, glancing up at Anna. "The emails. Isaac was right. It's all here." She sucked in her breath, eyes glued to the pages. "Where did you get this?"

"From Jerry's office." There was a note of triumph in Anna's voice.

Rhea breathed in sharply as she read. Then her eyes caught on something and she snatched the page from Anna, her face turning ashen.

"Hey," Anna said. "Are you OK?"

But Rhea remained silent and frozen, her grip loosening on the page as it fluttered to the floor.

"Rhea?" Maggie prompted. "Rhea, talk to us."

"Fifty thousand dollars," Rhea whispered. "That's what he paid." Then, as if a jolt of electricity had surged through her, she scooped up the paper and waved it furiously in the air.

"Fifty thousand dollars," she repeated, her voice sharp with bitterness. "And that's only for this year." She snatched the folder from Maggie, dumping its contents onto the floor, and sank to her knees, pawing through them like a starving animal. Fifty thousand dollars could have changed her life all those years ago. But for Brooks it was the negligible cost of bribing their son's school. "Here," she said, grabbing another page. "And this? Fifty thousand for last year, too." She crumpled the page in her hand, shaking with anger.

"Rhea, honey," Maggie said, her voice cautious as though trying to soothe a wild animal.

Rhea sat back on her knees. She'd never felt so powerless, like everything in her life had been turned upside down and shaken around. "Brooks is in serious trouble," she said grimly. Then she closed her eyes, reality sinking in. "Which means I am, too." Everything she'd worked so hard for, her perfect, unimpeachable life—all of it would vaporize the instant this got out.

Anna bit her lip. "Maybe we could leave the emails from Brooks out," she said hastily. "I mean, there's more than enough proof without it."

Rhea opened her eyes and smiled weakly. "No," she said. "It doesn't matter. It'll come out eventually. Everything does." She shuddered at the thought.

"Are you sure?" Maggie asked. "I mean, maybe there's a way to expose this without implicating Brooks." She turned to Anna. "And Jerry."

Rhea pushed her palms into her eye sockets, exhausted by all the lies. "I'm sure," she murmured.

"Anna?" Maggie asked. "What about you?"

Anna fell into silence, her gaze fixed on her intertwined hands in her lap. When she eventually looked up, weariness and resignation marked her expression. "It's fine," she said softly. "I'm done. I was done a long time ago."

Maggie sucked in a breath. "I'm sorry," she said in a low tone. She cleared her throat. "So do we go to the police? What's the move here?"

Anna shook her head. "Not the police—not first. Civitas has an army of lawyers. They'd crush this so fast."

They were quiet for a moment, and then Maggie spoke. "What about the gala?"

"The gala?" Rhea's eyebrows knit together. What did the gala have to do with this mess?

Maggie raked a hand through her hair, her fingers snagging in her bun. "We go public at the gala," she proposed. "Lots of powerful alumni will be there, politicians, the works." Her voice gained strength and she lifted her chin. "We stand up and tell everyone exactly what's been happening. Names, amounts of payoffs, the whole truth."

Rhea raised up on her knees. "But the gala... Brooks will be there—and Will—" Her voice cracked.

"Then you can't let them go," Anna said firmly. "And you warn Brooks—" She bit her lip and glanced at Rhea. "That is, if you want to."

Did she? Rhea's thoughts blurred, a sickening mix of emotions rising in her throat. A hot bubble of anger swelled and burst in her chest, spreading through her body. She rose to her feet, squaring her shoulders.

"All right." She nodded, then looked at Maggie. "But you have to do it. I can't..."

"Understood." Maggie rose to stand next to her, taking Rhea's hand. Rhea clung to her as if seeking high ground during a tsunami. Because that's what they were about to cause.

"Jerry will try to bury this," Anna warned.

Rhea gripped Maggie's hand. While she feared the tidal wave that was coming, her anger was now far vaster than her fear. Brooks had made his choice; without telling her he'd swum so far out to sea that she couldn't have saved him if she wanted to. And she wasn't sure she wanted it. She clenched her jaw. "After the gala we turn everything over to the police and post it to social media. Let's see them try to bury it then."

Rhea felt high with adrenaline as she drove home. For the first time in a long time she was taking action, making something happen. She glanced at her watch as she closed the door behind her and dropped her keys in the bowl near the door. She'd stayed longer than she'd meant to at Maggie's and was behind on getting dinner started. Screw it, she'd just order pizza.

A movement out of the corner of her eye startled her. She turned toward the living room and there was Pen, sitting rigidly upright on a chair, a grim expression on her face.

"Pen!" Rhea yelped. "Jesus, you scared me." She placed her hand on her chest. "Will isn't here, he has practice tonight." Then she narrowed her eyes. "Wait, how did you get in?"

Pen shrugged. "I know your garage door code." She consulted her watch. "And don't worry, Will's going to be home any minute." She gave a strange smile. "I have something important to tell him."

FORTY-FOUR

Anna felt lighter than she had in years as she stood over the sink, scrubbing the pan in which she'd browned beef for the stroganoff they'd had for dinner. To Anna it was the ultimate comfort food, but she'd stopped making it years ago because Jerry didn't like it.

He'd given her a look of disapproval when he'd come home and smelled the sauce simmering on the stove. While the old Anna would have flinched and backed down, the new Anna no longer cared. She was on the brink of making her escape, not to mention leaking documents that would destroy Jerry's career and possibly land him in jail.

So, when Jerry pushed his plate away untouched and opened a third beer, she refused to let fear overtake her. Maybe he'd hit her later, maybe he wouldn't. It no longer mattered. She was so close to freedom she could taste it.

"You're awfully chipper tonight," he observed sourly.

"I had a good day." Anna smiled, thinking of the plan they'd hatched at Maggie's. When Maggie stepped up to the podium at the gala, Anna would post the documents to the school's public Facebook group, then forward them to the police.

"Me too," Farrah chirped. "Coach told me I'm in the starting lineup for our next home game."

"That's great, sweetheart." Anna smiled, but Jerry's face remained stormy.

Farrah looked from her mother to her father, sensing the tension. "You'll both come, right?"

"Of course," Anna said, squeezing Farrah's arm. "We wouldn't miss it."

Farrah's game was the day after the gala, just over a week away. If everything went according to plan, Jerry had a better chance of being in police custody than at the lacrosse field. Anna smiled at the thought. Then the Monday after, Anna was scheduled to start her full-time position. She'd confirmed she could submit the offer letter as her proof of income for her rental application, and had an appointment next week to sign the lease on a two-bedroom townhome in a quiet cul-de-sac in a nearby neighborhood. It had large windows, high ceilings, and a small, leafy back patio perfect for a café table and two chairs. She could picture herself and Farrah having breakfast there.

As Farrah took a second helping of stroganoff, Anna gazed around the dining room. She'd always wanted to repaint the dark wood trim and add some livelier art to the walls to replace the moody watercolors chosen by Jerry. In her new home she pictured streamlined, Scandinavian furniture with soft blankets and bright throw pillows, and large, bold canvases on the walls. She'd even bookmarked the bedroom set she wanted—a blond wood four-poster canopy bed with extravagantly soft sheets.

Anna's eyes continued their path around the dining room. Would she miss anything about this house? It was, after all, where Farrah had taken her first steps, learned to ride a bike in the driveway, and helped plant a vegetable garden in the back-yard, only to dig up the seeds later to "check on them." Despite all the bad, many good things had happened here too.

Anna shook her head, determined to avoid getting lost in

nostalgia. There were plenty more memories to be made—somewhere else.

She pushed her chair back and moved to clear Jerry's untouched plate. "Dessert, anyone?" she asked. "I made butterscotch bars." Another of Jerry's least favorites.

"I'll pass," he said with a scowl, dropping his napkin on his plate and reaching for his beer.

That night, Anna treated herself to a long, hot bath. She used the unopened bath salts Farrah had given her for Christmas, dumping the whole container into the steaming water. As she soaked, her mind spun out into the future. Maybe next year she and Farrah could go to Paris for spring break. She wouldn't be able to afford private school anymore, but the townhome was zoned for a decent public school. They'd be fine financially, at least for now.

When she emerged from the bath her skin was pink and wrinkly, and she took her time smoothing lotion on it. Donning her bathrobe, she walked into the bedroom, then froze.

On the edge of the bed sat Jerry, holding her new phone.

"I see you got a new toy," he said. Anna's heart galloped in her chest as she felt behind her for the bathroom doorknob. But locking herself in had never stopped him before, and the bathroom had no other exit. "Anna, Anna, Anna," Jerry whispered in a chilling voice. His upper lip curled. "You should learn to hide things better—or did you think I was stupid?"

Goosebumps rose on her arms as panic swept over her. Normally when she got home she slipped the phone into a tear in the lining of her purse. Tonight she'd forgotten and left it in her jacket pocket.

He held the phone out to her. "You've gotten several texts," he said, raising his eyebrows expectantly. "I'd love to see why you're so popular."

Anna took the phone from him, her hands shaking so badly she nearly dropped it. On the screen she saw eleven new text indications in her group with Maggie and Rhea. "Go ahead," Jerry urged, as though she was a toddler about to try a new food. "Unlock it."

It took Anna three fumbling tries before she put her passcode in correctly. Without a word she passed the phone back to Jerry.

His thin-lipped smile sent a shiver through her. "Now, let's see what you've been up to."

FORTY-FIVE

Rhea stared at Pen, who looked far too comfortable in Brooks's recliner. The hair on the back of her neck rose. "Pen, sweetie," she said, trying for a calm tone. "What's going on?"

Pen crossed her arms. "That's between me and Will."

Will and Zane barged through the front door at that moment. Will had his brother in a headlock, while Zane swiped at him with little effect. "Ow, dude, knock it off!"

"Dude, I'll knock it off once you—" Will stopped short once he saw Pen, releasing Zane so quickly his brother tumbled to the floor.

"Hey!" Zane cried, scrambling to his feet. Then he, too, noticed Pen, and fell silent.

"Hey, Will." Pen smiled and gave a small wave. She wore jeans and a snug top and her blond hair was brushed to a shine. Rhea looked closer—was she wearing lipstick?

"Uh, hey." Will shot Rhea a puzzled look, and she responded with a curt shake of her head to indicate this wasn't her doing.

"Whoa, did you guys, like, hook back up?" Zane elbowed his brother and kicked off his Adidas slides.

"No," Will said flatly, and Rhea saw hurt flicker across Pen's face.

The sound of the garage door opening rumbled through the room. Rhea glanced out the window to see Brooks's Porsche gliding up the driveway.

"What's going on?" Will asked, frowning at Pen. He crossed his arms over his white Nike sweatshirt. "Are you, like, OK?"

"Am I *OK*?" Pen asked, incredulous. "You dumped me over text. So no, I'm not, like, OK."

"By text?" Rhea looked at her son. "Will, seriously?"

Will looked at the ground. "It seemed easier," he mumbled.

"Idiot," Rhea muttered. Her fingers flew over her phone as she sent a text to Maggie.

> Pen is here. Seems really upset.

Maggie's reply was immediate.

> Omw.

"Hey, everyone," Brooks said as the door opened. "Uh, hi, Pen." He frowned, casting a questioning glance at Rhea. She held back an eye-roll. Since when was she responsible for everyone else's drama?

"Perfect timing," Pen said; her gaze flicked to Josh, who entered behind Brooks.

Josh's face tightened at the sight of Pen, and Rhea's heart sank. She knew instantly this wasn't going to end well.

Rhea took a step forward, suddenly desperate to head off whatever was about to happen. "Pen, look, I know you're upset—"

"No," Pen interrupted, holding up her hand, and turned to Will. "I thought you should know the truth about your new bestie. He's not your cousin, he's actually your brother." Her words flew through the air like poison darts seeking their target.

Will's brow furrowed and he looked at Josh, whose face had gone pale.

A ringing started up in Rhea's head, like a distant siren growing closer, and her breath quickened.

"Wait, what?" Zane said.

"Well, half-brother." Pen crossed her arms and laughed like she'd shared a funny TikTok video. "I know, it's crazy, right?"

The ground tilted away from Rhea and she stumbled back, gripping the arm of the couch to keep from toppling over.

Will looked from Rhea to Brooks. "That's not true, right?"

Pen pulled a piece of paper from her pocket and waved it in the air. "Oh, it definitely is. It says so right here on his birth certificate." She held the paper in front of her. "Joshua Michael Smith, born to Abilene Rhea Smith." She nodded at Rhea. "That's you."

Zane looked confused. "But her name's not Abilene."

Rhea glanced at Josh, who appeared to have stopped breathing, then over at Zane. "It was, honey," she whispered. "A long time ago." She turned to Brooks. His normally warm brown eyes looked cold, and the tendons in his neck were pulled tight, jutting out like a mountain ridge. If only she could read his thoughts. She'd been so angry with him lately, but now the idea that she may have hurt him as deeply as he'd wounded her made her feel sick.

"Where did you get that?" Josh's voice pierced through the stunned silence of the room. "Did you steal it from me?"

"Rhea?" Brooks looked at her, his face stony.

Rhea struggled to speak over the lump in her throat. "Pen, I really think it's time for you go," she croaked.

"Wait," interjected Will, his voice rising an octave higher than usual. "So it's true?" He jerked his head from Rhea to Josh. "He's my *brother*?"

The room swam before Rhea's eyes, like asphalt shimmering in the distance on a hot day. Josh sprang to his feet, taking a step toward Pen. "Did you go through my things?" Pen, seeing his broad shoulders and angry expression, raised her hands in defense.

"Josh," Brooks warned sharply.

"She had no right!" he countered.

Pen spun to face him, hands on her hips. "Just like you had no right to tell everyone you graduated from Baylor! You never even went to college." Josh froze, his face draining of color. "That's right," Pen pressed on. "I called the records office, and guess what? They've never heard of you." Her gaze toward Josh was pure venom. "So what else did you lie about, huh?" Then she turned to Will, her expression softening. "I only wanted you to see what a liar he is."

Rhea glanced at Josh in time to see his face crumple before he turned and walked out. "Josh," she called, but her voice was too weak to carry across the room, let alone down the hall.

"Pen," Brooks said firmly. "You should go now."

The doorbell sounded three times in quick succession and Maggie burst in. "What's happening?" she said, looking at Pen. "Are you OK?"

Pen began to cry and Maggie wrapped her arms around her daughter. Across the room Rhea caught Brooks's gaze, which was icy and distant.

"Take your daughter home," he commanded Maggie.

Maggie bristled. "Not until someone tells me what happened."

"Maggie." Rhea's voice was pleading. "Please." The women exchanged a long look and Maggie relented.

"Let's go, sweetie," she said to Pen, who slumped against her mother and kept her eyes on the floor as Maggie led her to the door.

When they were gone, Brooks turned to Will and Zane. "Boys," he said, "I need to talk to your mother."

FORTY-SIX

Once they were safely in the car, Maggie turned to her daughter. "Are you OK? What the hell happened back there?" She ran her fingers along the length of her daughter's arm as if searching for a wound that needed staunching.

"Ow." Pen tried to pull away. "Stop poking me!"

"I'm trying to make sure you're all right," Maggie said, clinging harder.

"I'm *fine!*" Pen yanked her arm free and crossed her arms over her chest. "How did you even know I was here?"

"Why did Brooks tell you to leave? What did Will do?" Maggie's voice escalated into a yell as she felt herself spinning out of control.

Pen shrank into herself, her demeanor suddenly sullen. "He didn't *do* anything, OK?" she muttered. "I mean, other than break up with me like a total asshole." She looked down, avoiding Maggie's gaze. "I was trying to do him a favor by telling him the truth about Josh."

Maggie's frown deepened. "What do you mean? What are you talking about?"

Pen finally looked up, wearing a sneer. "You mean you

didn't know Mrs. Connelly was a secret teen mom? I thought you guys were, like, BFFs."

Maggie's stomach twisted in confusion. She balled her hands into frustrated fists. "Seriously, Pen, what are you talking about?"

"That Josh is Will's half-brother, not his cousin. Which Will deserves to know, don't you think? I mean, he basically worships Josh," Pen said, her eyes narrowing. "And all the while Josh—and his own mom—have been lying to him."

Maggie exhaled sharply and grabbed the steering wheel as if to shake it. "*Jesus*, Pen. None of this is any of your fucking business."

"How is it none of my business?" Pen protested. "Will dumped me because he thought I was jealous, when really I was the only one looking out for him." She paused, her eyes lapsing into a dreamy, unfocused gaze. "And now that he knows that, maybe we'll, like, you know..." She trailed off and shrugged.

Maggie's laughter bordered on hysterical. Some relationship expert she was. Her own marriage was crumbling because she hadn't noticed her closeted husband's multi-year affair. And now her teenage daughter had tried to win back her boyfriend by exposing a secret with the potential to destroy a family— Rhea's family, for God's sake, Maggie's first real friend since God knows when. Maggie fought the urge to rush back into the house to check on Rhea and try to salvage things. Instead, she refocused on her daughter.

"Pen, that's insane," she said. "Not to mention incredibly immature."

Pen bristled. "You do *not* get to tell me—"

Maggie slammed her fist onto the steering wheel. "No, actually, I do. Insane is kind of my area of expertise. I have years of training in it. I have a fucking PhD in it." She gestured toward Rhea's house. "God, Pen, what were you thinking?"

Pen's eyes turned watery. "I wanted to make him love me again," she whispered, and she started to sob.

Maggie felt as if her heart had vaporized, like one minute it was there, and then *poof!* it had exploded into a million tiny particles drifting around in her body. "Oh honey," she said, squeezing Pen's hand as tears welled in her own eyes. "You can't make anyone love you."

Maggie pulled into their driveway on the heels of Dan.

"Hey," he said, stepping out of the car. They were still treading carefully around each other, speaking cautiously and avoiding too much eye contact.

"Hi," Maggie said curtly. Dan caught sight of Pen, red-eyed and sniffling as she ran inside the house.

"What happened?" he asked. The concern etched on his face would have shattered Maggie's heart if it hadn't already been in pieces.

Maggie gave a long exhale. "We have a situation."

Dan's jaw dropped as Maggie relayed what she'd pieced together from Pen's confession. "The Connellys have a secret kid?" he exclaimed.

Maggie shook her head wearily. "Only one of them does, and it seems the other just discovered it. Anyway, that's not the point. The issue is our daughter thought it was OK to meddle in someone else's private family affairs." Her mind went to Rhea again. God, how must she be feeling right now? What were they all saying to each other? She felt a sting that Rhea hadn't confided in her about Josh. She thought they'd grown close over the last few months.

Dan cleared his throat. "OK, I'm going to go out on a limb here and point out that Pen's not the only one who likes to, um, meddle." He cast a sidelong glance at Maggie and she realized he was trying not to smile.

"Hey!" She crossed her arms. "I resent that. I am not meddling, I'm on the verge of exposing major fraudulent activity happening in the halls of one of the country's most hallowed academic institutions."

Dan nodded, his teasing evident now. "That's good. It should be in the intro to your podcast."

Normally Maggie would have laughed, but her hurt and anger were too fresh. She wasn't ready for normal yet. "Seriously," she said. "This is bad. I need to talk to Rhea and find out what exactly happened."

Dan wiped the smile off his face. "OK. I'll go try to get the story out of Pen."

They nodded at each other, eyes locking for a second longer than necessary. Then Maggie turned away and reached for her phone. As she dialed Rhea's number, a terrifying thought crossed her mind—what if Rhea blamed her for what Pen had done? What if this meant the end of their friendship? Maggie tightened her grip on the phone as it rang until Rhea's voicemail clicked on.

FORTY-SEVEN

Rhea watched Will and Zane exit the room, wearing identical expressions of shock and hurt. Her legs weak, she staggered toward the couch, deliberately avoiding the recliner where Pen had been sitting.

"Is it true?" Brooks asked, his face hard.

Rhea nodded and slouched forward, burying her face in her hands. "I was seventeen," she said softly. "I didn't know what else to do." She felt adrift, like a ship tossed by the waves in a storm, searching for a lighthouse where she knew there was none.

Brooks's voice was icy as he began to pace the room. "And you never once thought to tell me?"

Rhea had never heard such coldness in his voice. She lifted her head to look at him, noticing the silver strands that were now threaded through the hair at his temples. Twenty years was a long time to keep a secret from the person you loved the most. "I always thought I would at some point," she said, managing a faint smile. "But I never found the right moment. And then he showed up one day. Out of nowhere." She felt turned inside out, like her heart and all her raw nerve-endings were on the outside of her skin. And yet there was also a strange sense of relief. The worst had happened. Now all that was left was to move forward.

"And you didn't think that maybe *that* was the right moment to tell me? The moment you invited your secret son to live with us?" Brooks's tone was curt, his face twisted with anger as Rhea dared to meet his gaze.

Rhea's voice wavered, but she told the truth. "I didn't want you to think less of me."

The anger on Brooks's face dissolved into a wounded expression. "Jesus, Rhea. Do you really think so little of me?" he asked. "To assume I'd judge you like that?"

A heavy sadness welled up in Rhea like someone had filled her with wet concrete, and she sagged further into the couch. When she spoke, her voice was barely above a whisper. "It seems like maybe we don't know each other that well, after all."

Brooks's face hardened again and his voice turned gruff. "This has nothing to do with what I did for Will," he said.

"No? Then why keep that from me?" Rhea flexed her hands in a sudden surge of anger. She wasn't the only one who'd kept secrets. "Or maybe you were afraid I might judge *you*?"

"It's not the same—"

"Because you *knew* it was wrong," Rhea interjected. "Like I knew it was wrong not to tell you about Josh."

"You let me give him a job!" Brooks's voice rose. "A kid, it turns out, you knew nothing about. Who lied to all of us. I mean, are you sure he's really even your son, or just some opportunist scammer who came across an old birth certificate?" He ran his hand through his hair, which had grown wild in his anger, gesturing toward the guest bedroom. "I mean, who even is this kid?"

"He's my son," Rhea shot back, her voice like a loaded gun. "Of course he is. Don't you think I'd know?"

Brooks shook his head. "I don't know anything anymore." He set his jaw and locked eyes with Rhea. "Except that he needs to go. Immediately. Whatever's happening, we will figure it out as a family, without him around."

"Josh is my family, too." Rhea's voice broke. She couldn't ask Josh to leave any more than she could cut her own heart out of her body and still survive.

"He needs to leave. Now."

A resolute calm came over her and she stood, smoothing the front of her shirt. She was done keeping up the perfect facade. It was exhausting. "Then I'll leave too," she said.

Brooks tilted his head, weighing the credibility of her threat. "Fine," he said after a beat. "Do what you need to do." With that, he retraced his steps toward the garage. Rhea heard the creak of the garage door reopening and the Porsche's engine roaring to life. Tears welled in her eyes. Was he really going to let her go? And was she really going to walk away from her whole life?

She collapsed onto the couch, pounding the pillow with her fists, first one, then the other, until her arms became a blur as she pummeled it, *left right left right left right.* Then, out of breath, exhausted and sore, she clutched the pillow to her face, unleashing a long, guttural howl of anger and frustration.

She dropped the pillow and allowed her head to flop back against the couch. Had Josh lied to her, as Pen claimed? And if he had—so what? He was still her son, still the baby she'd left behind to save herself. She thought of him playing basketball with Will and Zane, of the family dinners where it felt like he'd always been there, of Brooks's pleasure as the two of them talked shop—none of that had been a lie.

She pushed her hair out of her face and stood up. Striding down the hall she gave a sharp rap on the guest room door, then pushed it open. Inside, the bed was neatly made up and the nightstand had been cleared of Josh's books and phone charger.

Her stomach dropped as she walked to the dresser and pulled open the drawers. Empty. The same with the closet.

He was gone.

FORTY-EIGHT

Jerry kept a close eye on Anna all weekend, ensuring she didn't leave the bedroom. From under the covers, Anna heard him telling Farrah she was sick, and she squeezed her eyes shut against the tears that welled up at the sound of her sweet daughter's concerned reply.

On Monday morning, before Jerry left with Farrah for school, she heard him turn on the security alarm to the same setting they used overnight, which meant she could move around the house freely but couldn't open any doors or windows without triggering the alarm.

"You'll find the disarm code has been changed," he'd told her while she lay curled in bed facing the wall, still in her bathrobe from the night before. Even if she hadn't been too sore to look over at him, she wouldn't have. His presence made her want to vomit.

"How will Farrah get to lacrosse?" Anna mumbled.

"I've made arrangements. People were very willing to help, given that you're under the weather."

Anna gave a bitter laugh and winced from the sharp pain in

her ribcage. She didn't need a doctor to tell her something was broken.

"Bye, Mom, feel better!" Farrah called from the hallway.

Tears stung the raw skin at the corners of Anna's eyes. "Thanks, sweetie, love you," she croaked.

"Love you too!"

After Jerry had left, Anna peeled herself off the bed and struggled to the bathroom. Bracing herself against the counter, she looked in the mirror and pressed lightly on the large, raised bump on the back of her head from where she'd hit the concrete garage floor. The throbbing pain made her reflection blur before her eyes. There was an angry gash on her right cheekbone from where her face had caught the corner of the metal garage shelving unit as she fell, but otherwise her face looked decent. Her neck, however, had a row of purple, fingerprint-sized bruises on either side of it from where he'd squeezed until she'd blacked out.

She shrugged her robe off one shoulder, and turned around to get a view in the mirror. Her pale skin bore a mass of dark blue bruises from where he'd kicked her as she lay curled, shielding her head.

There had been a brief moment when she'd thought maybe it wouldn't come to that. That they could talk rationally; she could share with him the enjoyment she'd found at work and he'd come around, particularly when he heard how much money Donna had offered her to join full-time.

She'd sat in panicked silence for ten excruciating minutes while he'd gone through her phone, looking at every text and email she'd sent or received and every website she'd visited. Thankfully none of the texts from Maggie or Rhea exposed their plan for the gala, but there were plenty of other things to worry about.

"A job?" His eyes narrowed and he looked up at her. "You've been working all this time."

"Only part-time," Anna whispered, as if that would absolve her. "I thought it would be a nice surprise that I could contribute, you know, financially."

Jerry's lips stretched into a thin, dangerous line. "You think I need you to contribute? You don't feel I'm taking care of your every need and more? Keeping a roof over your head, paying for a nice car for you to drive, nice clothes, anything you could want?" The color in his face deepened. "And instead of being grateful you insult me by going behind my back to get a job?"

"I am grateful," Anna managed. "Very."

"But you wanted to *contribute*," Jerry continued. "Which is why you're keeping the money from this job in a bank account I know nothing about." He jabbed the phone toward her. "And spending it on things I know nothing about."

"I'm sorry," she whimpered, hating herself for being weak enough to say those words.

"You're looking at apartments," he hissed. "Furniture. Were you planning to leave me, Anna?"

Desperation gripped her. "No, I—"

"I will not be lied to, Anna." He stood and walked toward her, cracking his knuckles.

FORTY-NINE

Maggie left another voicemail for Rhea, her fourth in the last seventy-two hours. So far all of her texts had gone unanswered, too. She tapped on her message icon to double-check that she hadn't missed a reply and reread the last one she'd sent.

> I understand if you're angry and don't want to talk. But please know I'm here for you. I hope we can talk at some point.

At this rate, though, it seemed like some point might be never.

"Give her some time," Dan advised, placing a mug of coffee before her. Already dressed in his scrubs, he joined her at the kitchen counter and gave her a sidelong glance. "But whatever happens, I'm glad you made a friend."

Maggie shot him a look. "I have *friends*," she said.

Dan raised an eyebrow. "Mags, come on. Outside of work and your family, you have people you're forced to interact with."

She sighed in exasperation. "OK, fine. But I didn't need any friends, I have—" She caught herself. "Had you."

Dan looked pained. "Hey, you still have me." Tentatively he reached out and laced his fingers through hers. She didn't pull away. "I'm here, aren't I?"

It had been nearly a week since she'd confronted Dan, and since then her anger had evolved from a raging inferno to a large, controlled burn; still potent, but not blazing through everything in its path. And Dan *was* here. Despite everything now being out in the open, he remained by her side. He still climbed into bed with her at night, held her as she cried or raged, and made her morning coffee.

"Yes, you're still here," Maggie said dully. "But it's not the same. It will never be the same."

Dan ran his finger around the rim of his coffee mug. "I know," he said quietly, his eyes shiny with tears.

Maggie's phone dinged and she grabbed for it, her stomach doing a small flip when she saw Isaac's name.

Can I see you again?

Her fingers still intertwined with Dan's, she flushed at the memory of her almost-kiss with Isaac. God, what was wrong with her? Her world was falling apart, and here she was, feeling giddy over a silly text.

"Is it Rhea?" Dan asked.

Maggie silenced her phone and tucked it into her bathrobe pocket. With so much uncertainty swirling around, she didn't have the energy to respond to Isaac. She had to sort things out with Dan first, whatever that meant. She needed to know if Rhea was OK, and Anna. Plus there was the matter of whether they were still proceeding with the plan to expose the Civitas Fund at the gala that weekend.

Anna hadn't been answering Maggie's calls either; her phone seemed to be completely switched off and had been for days. Maggie worried that Anna might be backing out of the plan, especially since she was the one who had the emails that proved everything.

On the other side of the counter Dan's phone chimed with an incoming text. He sighed as he read the message. "It's Pen," he said. "She forgot her English folder and it's an emergency."

Maggie sipped her coffee. "What level of emergency are we talking?"

Dan held up his phone so she could see the screen. "Five exclamation points." He looked apologetic. "I'd go drop it off for her but my first appointment is in thirty minutes, which means I should have left ten minutes ago."

"I'll do it," Maggie said. "My first patient isn't until ten."

"Thank you." He squeezed her hand and stood to go. "Have a good day, love you," he said, then froze. He turned around and bit the side of his cheek. "Sorry," he said. "Habit... I... is it still OK to say that?"

"It's fine." Maggie smiled through the tears in her eyes. "Love you too."

Maggie arrived at Civitas as students were changing classes, and she fought through the crowd to the office. "I'm dropping this off for Penelope Reed," she said to Mrs. Kaminski, waving the folder.

"I'll make sure she gets it," Mrs. Kaminski assured, extending her hand. Maggie's gaze flickered to the records room behind the desk, the one she had recently broken into.

"Thank you," Maggie said, averting her eyes in case Mrs. Kaminski could see her guilt. She hurried out of the room.

Exiting the office, Maggie collided with a girl with long, dark hair. "Farrah!" Maggie exclaimed, grabbing the girl's arm to steady herself. "Sorry about that."

"It's OK," Farrah replied, giving Maggie a strange look. Maggie realized the girl had no idea who she was.

"I'm a friend of your mom's," Maggie explained.

"Oh." Farrah nodded.

"Actually, I've been trying to call your mom," Maggie said. "School stuff. But I think maybe she accidentally left her phone off?" It was worth a shot, she figured, to see if Farrah knew what the hell was going on.

"Yeah, she's sick," Farrah said, tucking her shiny hair behind one ear in a gesture that perfectly mimicked Anna's.

"Oh no." Maggie furrowed her eyebrows. "Is she OK? I've been trying to reach her for a few days now."

"She has COVID," Farrah said.

"Oh God, I'm so sorry," Maggie said. "It must be bad."

Farrah shrugged. "No, I think she's fine, I think she's just, like, isolating, you know? So I don't get it before my lacrosse game."

"Oh." Maggie's shoulders slumped. If Anna wasn't really that sick then there was no excuse for her silence—unless she was deliberately avoiding Maggie. "Well, would you tell her to call me when she feels better? It's important." She tried to mask the desperation in her tone.

"Sure." Farrah smiled and waved, then dove back into the throng of kids.

Maggie stood in the middle of the hallway as the sea of kids parted around her, wondering which ones had benefited from having their spots on the Dean's List bought for them. Wondering which ones were going to undeservedly come out ahead of her daughter. She gritted her teeth. Fuck this. One way or another she was going to bring shit down.

FIFTY

Rhea found a spot in a downtown parking lot with no meters or signs, watched over by a guy near a booth asking for twenty dollars cash and giving no receipt. She handed over the money and hoped her car would still be there when she returned.

She'd started with the hospitals, not knowing where else to look. But none of them reported admitting a green-eyed boy in his early twenties. She'd moved on to youth hostels, of which there were a handful in Atlanta but had similarly struck out. So, she'd moved on to shelters. Josh had only been working for Brooks for a few weeks in an internship that likely didn't pay much, so she reasoned he wouldn't have money to spend on a hotel or an Airbnb. And he didn't seem to have any friends yet, other than Will and Zane.

There was a chill in the mid-November air as she walked the three blocks to one of the addresses and she thrust her hands into the pockets of her navy blue wool trench coat, shaking her head in disbelief. Visiting homeless shelters to find the son she'd welcomed back into her life only a couple of months ago felt like a twisted Lifetime movie—but without the guarantee of a happy ending.

Outside the nondescript brown brick building, a group of men sat on the stoop playing cards. They nodded and moved aside as she approached. Inside, a wall of plexiglass separated her from a man with long salt-and-pepper dreadlocks. His raised eyebrows as she approached confirmed they both knew she was out of place there.

"Hi," she said. "I'm looking for someone and was hoping you could help. My son, Josh." The man nodded for her to continue. "He's twenty-one, about six feet, light brown hair, green eyes. He looks like he works out." She managed a shaky smile, and the man's face softened.

"Do you have a picture?" he asked.

Rhea flushed, shaking her head. Each place she'd visited had asked for a photo, and the shame hit her every time. What kind of mother didn't have a picture of her son? "No, I'm sorry," she said. She glanced around as if Josh might be nearby, but all she found was an empty room with a brown couch, a few chairs, and a television tuned to a local news channel.

"I haven't seen anyone like that," the man said. "I'm sorry."

"Can I leave my number?" Rhea asked.

He nodded and she scribbled it, along with the description of Josh, onto a piece of paper. "You might try Covenant House over on the Westside," he said as she handed it through a small slot in the plexiglass. "It's a youth shelter."

"Thank you," Rhea said, fighting back tears. "I will."

Back outside the card game moved aside once more. "You have yourself a nice day, ma'am," one of the men said.

"You too," Rhea said, nodding at him.

Rhea found her car still parked in the lot, decorated with a red-and-white ticket for unauthorized parking. The attendant was nowhere to be seen. Tears welled in her eyes. It wasn't the fine itself, but the way she felt so close to breaking down completely that even the tiniest thing threatened to crack her into a million pieces.

Back home, she went to the guest room, where she'd slept, and retrieved her laptop. She'd made a spreadsheet of shelters to call or visit, and now she added the number the man had given her to the list. It was one of the last possibilities.

Setting the laptop aside, she collapsed onto the bed, burying her face in the pillow. The scent of Josh lingered faintly—a blend of shea butter soap and woodsy pine deodorant. Tears stung her already red, raw eyes.

"Mom?"

She looked up to find Zane hovering in the doorway in his plaid pajama pants and Minecraft T-shirt.

She sat up and swiped her hand across her eyes. "Hi, sweetheart."

"Are you OK?"

Rhea nodded and patted the bed next to her. "Come sit for a minute?" He joined her on the bed and she wrapped her arms around him and buried her face in his hair. "I'm so sorry for all of this," she said.

He leaned into the hug and gave her hand an awkward pat. "It's OK."

She drew back, gripping his shoulders firmly. "No," she said. "This is not OK. I need you to know that. This is not how families are supposed to operate. We're supposed to be honest and open with each other. We're not supposed to keep big secrets from each other, like I did, and your dad."

Zane's brows furrowed in confusion. "Hold on, what did Dad do?" His worried gaze roamed around the room, taking in her glasses on the nightstand and pajamas draped over the chair. "I mean, it must be bad if you're sleeping in here."

"Oh, sweetie," she said, feeling a stab of guilt at involving him in any of this. "It's nothing you need to worry about. Sometimes grown-ups need a little space when they have big feelings."

Zane rolled his eyes. "Mom, I'm not three."

Rhea's own laughter caught her off guard. It had only been four days since her life had fallen apart, but laughter already seemed like a distant memory.

She sighed, squeezing Zane's hand. "Sorry, I know you're not. And obviously you can see your dad and I are taking some space right now. But it's going to be OK." She blinked back the tears that had started again. So many goddamn tears. "I'm really sad Josh left. I mean, I'd just found him again, you know?"

"I'm sorry, Mom," Zane said earnestly. "That really sucks. I hope you find him."

"You do?"

He shrugged. "Of course. He's a way cooler big brother than Will." Then he reddened. "Don't, like, tell Will I said that. I mean, he's OK sometimes too, or whatever."

Rhea smiled through her tears. "I won't." She hesitated. "Is he mad?"

"Will?"

"Yes."

Zane considered. "I don't know. Maybe more... surprised?" He looked down. "And we're both wondering why you didn't tell us, you know—or why Josh didn't. And also who Josh's dad is, and all that stuff." He glanced back up at her.

"Those are good questions," Rhea said, wiping her eyes again. "And I want to answer all of them, I really do. But I need some time. Is that OK?"

"Yeah, sure." Zane nodded. He glanced toward the door. "Can I play PlayStation?"

Rhea raised an eyebrow. "Did you finish your homework?"

Zane heaved a sigh. "Fine," he said, slouching to his feet.

"Finish up and then come talk to me," Rhea said.

As Zane headed back down the hall, the doorbell rang. Rhea ignored it, then it rang again. Annoyed, she swung her leg over the side of the bed and headed down the hall. The picture on the security camera showed a familiar blond bun with a pen stuck in it on the doorstep.

"Hey," said Maggie in surprise as Rhea opened the door. "You're alive."

Rhea blinked, recalling missed calls and texts from Maggie. "Yeah, sorry, I meant to call you back but..." She trailed off, too exhausted to explain the blur of the past few days she'd spent either in tears or pleading with a God she barely believed in to bring back her son.

Maggie charged across the threshold without waiting to be invited. "Oh thank God," she said. "So you don't hate me?"

Rhea frowned. "Hate you? Uh, no." She hesitated, wondering how to explain that for the last few days she'd been unable to think about anything but finding Josh.

"I can't believe Pen would... I mean I had no idea she..." Now it was Maggie who was on the verge of tears. "I'm so sorry."

"It's not her fault," Rhea said, rubbing her aching eyes. She knew it was true. It was solely Rhea's own choices that had led her to this moment. Pen was simply kindling for the match Rhea had lit twenty-one years ago when she'd decided the baby she gave away would be her secret. She looked at Maggie, suddenly overcome with relief at her presence. She couldn't do this by herself anymore.

Maggie pulled her into a ferocious hug. "I've been so worried about you."

Rhea surrendered to Maggie's embrace, grateful to finally have something solid propping her up. "He's gone," she whispered as she clung to Maggie, her voice raw from all the tears she'd already shed. "Josh is gone."

"I'm so sorry," Maggie murmured, rocking Rhea back and forth. In the arms of her friend, Rhea let herself go and began to sob.

FIFTY-ONE

Anna lay on the bed in her dirty bathrobe, focusing on the shadows on the ceiling. If she concentrated, she could almost imagine she was outside, gazing up at the clouds with Farrah like they used to do, lying on a blanket in the backyard and pointing out the ones that looked like hearts or ponies.

It was Wednesday, five days since Jerry had found her phone, and now her third day of not showing up for work. She wondered what Donna thought, if she'd tried to call, or if Jerry had even bothered to contact her with an excuse. And what about Sydney—was she wondering where Anna was? A deep sadness gripped Anna at the thought that that was all finished now; she could never go back.

"Hey, Mom?" Farrah called from the hallway. Anna scrambled to put on her N95 mask, a ruse invented by Jerry to conveniently cover the bandage on her cheekbone and the now greenish-yellow bruise. Jerry had been careful not to leave Anna and Farrah alone long enough to have a meaningful conversation—not that Anna could imagine explaining things to Farrah anyway—so Anna assumed he wasn't far away.

"Come on in," she called, wincing from the pain that still shot through her ribcage when she moved too quickly.

Farrah entered, dressed for lacrosse practice, a surgical mask hanging on her wrist. "I'll stay six feet away," she promised. "Have you seen my green headband? I put it in the laundry and now I can't find it." Farrah had been superstitious since she was little, refusing to step on sidewalk cracks or pet their neighbor's black cat. She'd won her first lacrosse game last year while wearing a neon green headband, and now she was convinced she couldn't play well without it.

Anna gave her a weak smile. "I haven't done much laundry lately," she said. Jerry had been limiting her time out of their bedroom. "Did you ask Dad?"

Farrah nodded. "Yeah, he hasn't seen it."

"Did you check your equipment bag?" Anna suggested.

"Yeah," Farrah replied in a halting tone, which Anna knew meant she hadn't. "But I guess I could, like, check again." She paused. "Are you feeling any better?"

"Much better," Anna said, trying not to grimace as she sat up straighter. "I'll be back on my feet in no time." *You can't keep me in here forever, Jerry*, she thought.

Farrah twisted the elastic of her mask around one finger. "I'm glad," she said.

Anna's chest tightened at her daughter's forlorn expression. "Come here," she said, patting the bed next to her.

Farrah looked wary. "But Dad said—"

"Please," Anna said, keeping her voice down. "I only want to give you a quick hug. You're not going to catch anything, I promise." It had been nearly a week since Anna had touched her daughter. The need to feel Farrah's silky hair against her cheek consumed her.

Farrah glanced over her shoulder, then put on her mask and walked over to Anna. Anna's body relaxed as she felt her daughter lean against her, her brain happily drowning in the feel of Farrah's skin against hers and the scent of her citrus shampoo. They stayed that way for a moment before Farrah sat up and wrinkled her nose. "No offense, Mom, but you stink."

Anna tried to remember the last time she'd showered. "Yeah," she said, laughing sheepishly. "I probably do." She tweaked Farrah's nose. "I love you."

"Love you, too." She gave an excited smile. "So Dad says I get to go to the gala with him this weekend since you're sick. He said I can get a fancy dress for it and everything."

Anna's smile froze. "Wow," she said, struggling to corral her thoughts. She'd nearly forgotten about the gala amid her self-pity. She bit her lip in frustration, thinking of the plan with Maggie and Rhea to go public at the event. Why hadn't she left the emails with Maggie? They were carefully hidden, and she prayed Jerry wouldn't find them. But without them, Maggie and Rhea had nothing.

"Mom?" Farrah looked at her quizzically.

Anna shook her head and refocused. She squeezed Farrah's hand. "That's exciting, sweetheart. Though between you and me, those kind of fancy events are usually pretty boring."

"Farrah?" came Jerry's voice from the kitchen. "Darling, we need to leave if you don't want to be late."

Farrah jumped off the bed and scampered to the door. "Bye," she mouthed to Anna, blowing a kiss.

Anna pretended to catch it and press it to her cheek, and held her hand up in a wave.

After Anna heard the front door slam and the security alarm beep to life, she went to the kitchen to make a cup of tea. Waiting for the water to boil, she smiled bitterly at her distorted reflection in the stainless steel kettle. Her eyes wandered around the small kitchen. Was this her life now? This room, this twenty-five hundred square foot house, and then maybe another house like it in New Hampshire? She shook her head. How stupid she'd been to think she could pull it off—a job, an apartment, all behind Jerry's back. She should have known better.

The water boiled, and Anna poured it into her waiting mug. As the tea brewed, she walked to the laundry room, pulled out the stool, and opened the top cabinet. Maybe there was a way to still get the emails to Maggie. But as she reached for the stack of printouts she'd hidden, her hand found only bare wood.

"Looking for this?" came a voice from behind her.

Anna spun around, smacking her head on the open cabinet door and letting out a yelp of pain. There stood Jerry, wearing a cold smile and brandishing a stack of paper. A loud whoosh of static sounded in Anna's ears, and every muscle in her body tensed as she hobbled down from the stool.

"What are you doing home?" she asked, breathing so fast she could hardly take in air. "Did Farrah forget something?"

"I dropped her off and then came back to talk with you."

Anna shivered at the familiar, menacing tenor of his voice. Doing her best to avoid looking at the papers in his hand, she gestured toward the cabinet. "I was looking for Farrah's green headband," she said.

The vein in the middle of Jerry's forehead pulsed. "How ironic," he said, his tone icy. "So was I... when I found these." He shook the papers, and Anna flinched. "You're a thief," he hissed, advancing toward her. "And a liar."

The small of Anna's back pressed against the counter; she was literally backed into a corner. Then, like lightning shattering the surface of a frozen lake, something cracked open inside her. "I'm the thief and the liar?" Her fists clenched, and she stepped forward. "Look who's talking." Surprise flickered across Jerry's face, and he took a step back. "I know what you did," she pressed on, surprised by the strength in her voice. "What you've been doing." She laughed bitterly. "You really have everyone fooled, don't you? Thinking you're actually good at your job. A big shot. Worthy of all the awards, the bonuses, the job offers." She scoffed. "But the truth's going to come out sooner or later."

He grabbed her wrist and thrust the papers in her face. "Who else has seen these?" Anna tried to wriggle away, but he twisted her arm until she let out a cry of pain. "Who else?" he repeated, louder.

As quickly as her fiery outburst had begun, it fizzled under a blanket of fear. "Only me," she gasped, tears of pain flooding her eyes. "I swear." The least she could do was protect her friends.

Jerry dropped her arm and Anna crumpled to the ground, rubbing her wrist. "If I find out you're lying," he growled, "very bad things can happen."

Anna nodded, her last shred of resistance fading like invisible ink.

FIFTY-TWO

Maggie stared at the last several texts she'd sent Anna.

> Hey! Left you a msg, call me when you can.

> Hi! Are we still a go for the gala?

> Haven't heard from you, all good?

> Just checking in. We're running out of time if we're going through with this.

> Are you OK?

She tossed her phone onto the bed in frustration. Of all the times for Anna to go silent. It didn't add up. While it had taken Anna a while to warm up in their meetings, recently she'd shown so much spark. She'd been cracking Maggie and Rhea up with her sarcastic humor and spilling insider Civitas gossip, like the fact that Mr. Holladay and Ms. Ferrara, the German teacher, were hooking up. And while Anna probably had the most to lose if they went public about the Civitas Fund—her husband had broken multiple laws—she'd been the most adamant about their plan for the gala. And now, poof. She seemed to have vanished.

Something Anna had said nagged at Maggie—something about having been done with her marriage a long time ago. Maggie wondered what in the world had happened in Anna's relationship to make her so eager to end it.

Maggie's alarm went off for the third time, and she rolled over to silence it. If she didn't get up now, she'd be late for her first patient. The smell of coffee wafted up from downstairs. She hugged a pillow to her chest, trying to quell the dull ache. There would come a day when Dan wasn't downstairs making her coffee and scrambling eggs that Pen would refuse to eat. They were existing in a kind of limbo. Twice Maggie had over-heard Dan talking on the phone in a soft, murmuring voice. Once, she'd heard him end the call with "I love you, too." She'd nearly collapsed from the pain of hearing her husband say those words to someone else. Still, he continued to fall asleep next to her at night, refusing to abandon her. The pain from that was almost worse.

She forced herself out of bed and shifted into autopilot as she washed her face, brushed her hair. Then she opened her closet and stared at the row of white and gray button-up shirts hanging neatly. They seemed to be taunting her with their blandness. *No wonder Dan isn't interested in me*, she thought, then immediately squashed the notion. The therapist part of her understood it was much more complicated than that. The messy human part of her, however, wanted somewhere to assign blame, and Ann Taylor seemed like as good a target as any.

Downstairs, Dan had finished a run and stood at the counter in shorts over running tights and a long-sleeve zip-up. Pen sat nearby in a gray skirt, dark green Civitas polo shirt and gray cardigan, sipping from Maggie's favorite turquoise vintage Fiestaware mug.

"Is that coffee?" Maggie asked Pen.

She turned to Dan, who gave her a guilty look.

Pen rolled her eyes. "Mom, chill. It's coffee, not cocaine."

Maggie crossed her arms. "You're too young for coffee. And, for the record, also cocaine."

Pen's mouth turned down in a sour expression. "Seriously? You guys are breaking up, and you're worried about me drinking *coffee*?"

Maggie shot Dan an alarmed look. So far they hadn't said anything to Pen. They'd agreed it didn't make sense to worry her until they knew what was going to happen. "Sweetheart," Maggie said, "what makes you say that?"

Pen treated her to another eye-roll. "Save your therapy voice for your patients, Mom. I'm not stupid."

"Though you did get that B minus in trigonometry," Dan deadpanned. Pen shot him a murderous glare. He glanced at Maggie. "Too soon?"

Maggie pursed her lips. "Way too soon."

Pen stood up and threw her napkin down. "Like, enough already." She turned to Dan. "I know you cheated on Mom." Then she shifted her dagger eyes to Maggie. "You and your new BFFs aren't exactly quiet when they come over." Maggie's heart raced. If Pen had overheard her talking to Anna and Rhea about Dan, what else had she heard?

"Pen, honey," Dan said, moving toward her.

"Don't touch me," Pen snapped, stepping away and sniffling, her eyes red. Maggie dug her nails into her palm, fighting back her own tears.

From the beginning, Dan had been better at braiding Pen's hair, reading bedtime stories, and coaxing her to try new foods. He'd always been her biggest supporter, and now Maggie could see the hurt in his eyes at being rebuffed by his daughter.

Maggie took a deep breath to keep from screaming in frustration. It was so confusing to be furious at someone while also loving them as much as she still loved Dan. "Pen," she said, "your father has something to talk to you about. But before he does, I want you to know that I support him one hundred percent, and that while we have a lot to figure out as a family, it's going to be OK." She glanced at Dan, who nodded his thanks. Then, so they couldn't see her cry, she picked up her coffee mug and headed for her office.

Despite the hollow feeling in her chest, Maggie made it through her morning of patients. Wondering how Dan's conversation with Pen had gone, she started to call him before remembering he had back-to-back root canals that day. The thought made her want to cry all over again—would there come a time when she didn't know his schedule by heart?

In the late afternoon Maggie had a break between patients, and she drove to Whole Foods and stocked up on artisan soups and fresh-pressed juice. It was time to figure out what the hell was going on with Anna.

She parked on the street and rang the Armstrongs' doorbell once, then again when no one answered. Then she heard the beeping of an alarm keypad—strange, since they were home—and the sound of the lock turning. To her surprise, Jerry answered, wearing a starched white shirt and his omnipresent green tie.

"Maggie," Jerry said, his eyebrows shooting up. A flicker of displeasure crossed his face so quickly Maggie almost missed it. Glancing back into the house, he stepped outside and closed the door behind him. "What a surprise. I just got home."

Maggie gave a tight smile. She'd been hoping to catch Anna alone. "Hi," she said. "I wanted to see how Anna was doing."

Jerry cleared his throat. "Um, how do you mean?"

"Farrah said she's sick."

"Ah yes, that," Jerry said with an odd look of relief. "She is indeed, I'm afraid." He rubbed his hands together. "COVID. Quite a bad case."

"I'm sorry to hear it, poor thing." Maggie set down the grocery bag and fished around in her purse. "Well, I've had my booster vaccine." She pulled a surgical mask out of her purse and waved it. "So I don't mind if you don't."

Jerry placed a protective hand on the doorknob behind him. "Oh, I'm afraid that's out of the question," he said. "She's quite ill."

Maggie frowned. "Farrah said she was fine, only isolating to be safe."

"She's up and down," Jerry said. His eyes darted behind him at the closed door.

"She's not answering her phone," Maggie said, her frown deepening. Something felt off. "And I really need to talk to her about some of the stuff for the gala—final logistics and stuff." She tried to channel Rhea and give her most charming smile. "We want it to be perfect, you know?"

Jerry's smile grew chilly. With slow, deliberate movements he straightened his tie. "I wouldn't want to worry her with any of that," he said.

"Oh." Maggie stepped back, feeling a ripple of unease as she remembered this was the man who had orchestrated what was essentially a school-wide bribery ring. A man Anna had admitted to being eager to be free of. But he wasn't actually dangerous, was he?

She retrieved the brown paper shopping bag and thrust it toward him. "I brought some soup for her. And can you ask her to call me?"

"Of course." Jerry took the bag from her, his face reset into pleasant neutrality. "How kind."

Maggie took another step back and caught herself right before she stumbled off the porch. Turning around, she walked as fast as she could toward the car. Glancing back, she saw Jerry standing on the porch, watching her go.

FIFTY-THREE

The first time the doorbell rang, Anna ignored it. It was probably a delivery of some kind; no one ever came to their house unannounced. But when it rang again, she hurried to the bedroom door, her bruised body protesting every step, and listened as Jerry deactivated the alarm and opened the door.

"Maggie," she heard him say in a sour voice. Adrenaline shot through Anna's body. Maggie was here; everything was going to be all right. Relief washed over her and she started to laugh, until a sharp pain in her side cut her off. Gripping the wall for support, she limped down the hall. But before she could reach the entryway, Jerry was already heading back, a shopping bag in hand.

"Was that Maggie?" Anna asked. She walked to the window in time to see Maggie's car turning out of the driveway and down the street.

Jerry held up the bag. "She brought soup, wasn't that thoughtful?" He smiled sardonically. "Too bad she couldn't stay."

Anna trailed him into the kitchen. "It can't be like this forever," she said. Part of her wanted to laugh at the absurdity of the situation, but another part threatened to cry and scream and pound her fists on the wall. "You can't keep me inside forever," a note of defiance creeping into her voice.

Jerry's frown deepened. "You're free to leave whenever you want," he declared. Anna eyed the door warily, sensing a trap. "Seriously," he insisted, with a dismissive click of his tongue. "If you're intent on leaving, by all means, please do." He set the grocery bag on the counter, wearing a derisive smirk. "But you're a lawyer, I'm sure you understand the implications," he continued, his face darkening. "A nasty custody battle, legal expenses. And good luck finding a judge who'd fault me for seeking a better life for our daughter in idyllic rural New Hampshire to attend one of the best schools in the country." Anna's breath hitched as his words sank in. "It wouldn't be difficult for me to ensure you never saw her again," he warned, his voice dropping to a menacing whisper. "Except for the occasional holiday, if I'm feeling generous. But, by all means, challenge me."

Anna struggled to take a deep breath, to force oxygen to her brain. He couldn't really—could he? Tears of desperation pricked in her eyes.

"So I'll ask you again, Anna." His voice had a sinister calm to it and the sound of her name on his tongue made her want to retch. "Do you want to leave me?"

Squaring her shoulders, she blinked back her tears. "No," she said in a flat tone.

Jerry gave a short, harsh laugh. "I thought as much."

Anna's stomach churned with his threat as she turned back toward the bedroom. Once there, she leaned on the dresser and buried her face in her arms, muffling a sob. Pushing herself upright, something caught her eye. There, from beneath Jerry's clothes, peeked the email printouts.

Anna glanced at the pages, then scanned the room, suspicion creasing her brow. Why would he leave them out like that?

A sickening realization followed. It didn't matter; trapped and isolated, there was nothing she could do with the emails now, anyway.

With trepidation, Anna nudged the printouts from under the clothes, half-expecting them to explode or trigger an alarm. But they were just papers. Papers that once held the key to her future, now useless.

She could leave anytime, it was true. She pictured herself packing a bag, walking out the front door without a backward glance, the alarm blaring in her wake. The notion was both exhilarating and terrifying. She could pack a bag for Farrah, too, but where would they go? To the police? To Maggie's? Could she bear to leave Farrah behind, even temporarily? Surely there had to be a way to make a judge see how unfit Jerry was.

Deep down, though, Anna knew what it would be like to go up against Jerry for custody. Jerry with his smooth British accent and excellent job, not to mention his connections to influential Atlanta families, all of whom owed him favors. Anna shuddered. There was no way she could risk losing Farrah.

Later, Anna resumed folding laundry, a task Jerry had decided she'd recovered enough to start doing again. With Farrah occupied in the shower, Anna carried a stack of clothes into her room. As she set them down among the clutter on Farrah's dresser, her fingers brushed against her daughter's phone. Anna froze. Then, glancing over her shoulder, Anna quickly pocketed the device, her heart racing. Ensuring Jerry was still in the living room, she hurried back to their bedroom.

Shutting the door quietly behind her, Anna retrieved the email printouts from beneath Jerry's clothes. Quickly, she used Farrah's phone to snap a picture of each page. Then she opened up a fresh text message and attached them.

As Anna's fingers paused over the "To" field, the sound of

the shower in Farrah's bathroom ceased. Panic surged within her. She didn't have Maggie or Rhea's phone numbers memorized—they were stored in her phone. "No, no, no," she muttered under her breath. She opened an email instead, racking her brain. What was Maggie's email? MaggieReed-PhD@bettertimestherapy.com? Or was it DrMaggieReedPhD? Were there dots separating her names? And was it Better Times Therapy or Better in Time Therapy?

She heard the creak of Jerry's chair in the living room as he got up. Her fingers trembling she typed out a hurried message, remembering Maggie's email as best she could.

Undeliverable.

She wanted to punch the wall, or herself, for her own inability to remember a simple phone number or email address.

"Mom?" Farrah called from her room. "Have you seen my phone?"

"Be right there," Anna called. Sweat trickled down the back of her neck, and her hands grew clammy. God, she'd make a terrible spy. In desperation she moved the photos from Farrah's "Recent Photos" to an album she labeled "Stuff," praying it sounded innocuous enough to escape Jerry's notice if he checked Farrah's phone.

Then, her eyes trained on the living room for any sign of Jerry, Anna slipped back into Farrah's room. Her daughter stood wrapped in a fuzzy pink bathrobe, her damp hair spilling down her back.

"Oh, hey," Farrah said.

Anna held out the phone. "Sweetie," she said. "I need you to do me a favor."

FIFTY-FOUR

Rhea woke to the gentle touch of fingers brushing her cheek. Sleepily she reached up and grabbed the hand, pressing it against her face. Her eyes snapped open. "Josh?"

Brooks gazed down at her, disappointment in his eyes. "It's me," he said softly.

"Oh," Rhea said. His hand felt dry and rough under hers and she quickly drew her arm back, an echo of the distance between them in recent days. Their exchanges had been clipped, reduced to the bare minimum they needed to function in their roles as parents. *"Are you driving Zane this morning?" "Yes." "Seen Will's sneakers?" "No."*

She wasn't sure, then, what it meant that Brooks was sitting on the bed—closer to her than he'd been in days—or how she should react.

It had been a week since Josh's disappearance, and her hope of finding him was waning. She was still sleeping in the guest bedroom, unable to leave the space he'd last occupied. Her calls to shelters and hospitals now felt more like a penitence ritual than a pursuit of hope. He was gone, along with any hope she'd had of stitching together her past and her future.

"What time is it?" Rhea asked, eyes adjusting to the darkness.

"Late," Brooks said. "Sorry, I didn't mean to wake you." He was still dressed in his work clothes, his shirt wrinkled and rolled at the elbows, and he smelled like cinnamon gum and a hint of whiskey.

"Then why are you in here?" Her anger rekindled and she rolled away from him.

Hurt flashed in his eyes. "I wanted to check on you," he said. "That you were, you know, breathing." He gave a sad smile and her mind went to the nightly ritual they'd had of tiptoeing into each of the boys' rooms after they'd fallen asleep, tucking in blankets and switching off lamps left on to fend off imaginary monsters.

They sat there for a minute, their faces barely visible to each other in the dark. The bed sagged as Brooks shifted. "I'm sorry I lied to you," he whispered. "I thought I was doing the right thing."

His words hung in the air like the incense from her childhood church: a holy offering she wasn't sure she was ready to accept. A lump lodged in her throat.

After another moment of silence, Rhea spoke. "I thought I was doing the right thing, too," she said. "But somewhere along the way it became wrong."

"Same." His voice was tight with emotion.

Pushing herself up to lean against the headboard, she crossed her arms. "Well, technically yours was wrong from the beginning."

He stiffened. "Are you saying lying to me about who Josh was wasn't wrong from the beginning?"

"No." Rhea shook her head. "I'm saying that's where it became wrong."

"What about the fact that you never told me about him to begin with, back when we met? When we were falling in love."

His voice broke on the last word.

Rhea rubbed her eyes and sighed. She felt wrung out and exhausted from the emotions of the last few days; from the last couple of months, really, starting the day Josh showed up. She'd been walking on eggshells since that moment, trying to find the right thing to say to him, to Brooks, and to the boys, to shield them from the truth. Now, though, with everything laid bare, she felt a strange sense of relief amidst the wreckage of her shattered life, unburdened by the need to make everything look perfect. "I didn't tell you then because you would have judged me," she said.

"But—"

"Don't argue," she interjected, halting his protests with a raised hand. "You know it's true. You were the great Brooks Connelly, with big plans that didn't involve a former teen mom as your wife. You may have loved me, but it would have been less. And that would have spelled the end for us." Tears formed as she spoke the painful truth out loud.

He hung his head, but didn't protest. "You're right," he admitted, lifting his gaze. "Back then I would have loved you less for what you did."

Rhea thought of the time their family had gone whitewater rafting and what it had been like to bump and jolt through the frothy waves. Her heart felt like that now, but without the safety of a raft and life vest. Instead it was being tossed around in the angry, foaming water, crashing against rock after rock.

Brooks reached for her hand. "But that was then. Now I know I could never love you less. Rhea, please."

The pain in his voice sliced through her. She gripped his hand and forced the words out before she lost her nerve. "The problem is," she said, "I might love *you* less." In the dark she heard the sharp intake of his breath.

Slowly he released her hand and stood, looking down at her

with a tender, anguished gaze. "I'll let you get some sleep," he said.

The next morning Rhea moved through her routine on autopilot, brewing coffee and waking the boys for school. Right after she'd dropped the boys off, a text came in from Maggie.

> Anna's been radio silent. I'm worried. No idea what's going on. Has Jerry ever given you like a creepy vibe? Also without the emails we have fucking nothing to go on for the gala. There's no point.

Time had become fluid, but now Rhea remembered the gala was the next day. Her dark pink strapless dress, the one she'd chosen with such care a few weeks ago, hung in the closet alongside Brooks's tuxedo. She'd been trying to find the right moment to tell Brooks that he and Will shouldn't attend—and why—but hadn't been able to bring herself to do it. At least now she wouldn't have to.

So then we have nothing, she replied.

Clutching the phone to her chest, Rhea was taken aback by the unexpected sense of relief washing over her. She tried to picture standing in the crowded ballroom, ready to expose everyone involved, including her husband. A few days ago she'd welcomed the thought. But her anger at Brooks for what he'd done felt muted now in the face of what she'd already lost.

See you tomorrow then, Maggie wrote. *For a long night of nothing.*

When she returned home after dropping off the boys, Rhea paused in the quiet of the house. Each time she opened the front door she held out a glimmer of hope that Josh might be there, on the couch with a book or in the kitchen preparing a snack, as if he'd never left. Yet, the house remained still. The only signs of recent life were Zane's abandoned hoodie on the floor near the door and the cereal bowls in the sink.

Sighing, she walked to the counter to load the dishwasher. Then she saw it: a piece of paper on the counter. It was a printout of a Google map with an address on it circled. In Brooks's handwriting it read, *I think I found him.*

FIFTY-FIVE

As Maggie drove, Pen remained silent, her gray cardigan pulled tight around her and her forehead resting on the passenger-side window. Pen had said little since Dan had told her about Fernando, and Maggie couldn't blame her. She had only a few days' lead time on Pen and was barely coping herself, her emotions a confusing roller coaster of rage, shame, and even the odd, quiet moment of acceptance.

"Do you want to talk about it?" Maggie ventured. Pen responded with a curt grunt. "So, that's a no?" Maggie persisted. Pen shot her a glare that could have melted steel.

As they approached Civitas, Maggie maneuvered to the curb, expecting Pen to bolt from the car as usual. Instead she turned to Maggie. "How could you not know?" she said, her face reproachful. "Back when you and Dad met? Then none of this would be happening."

Maggie suppressed a resentful sigh. Of course Pen blamed her. It was always the mother's fault. "Known that your father was gay, you mean?" she asked evenly. Pen nodded angrily. "Well, sweetheart, I'm pretty sure he didn't even know until fairly recently."

"But you guys have always hung out with Fernando and his wife!" Pen huffed, crossing her arms.

"We did," Maggie said. "And I can see why your dad—" She groped for words. "I can see why he likes Fernando." *Loves* Fernando, was what Dan had said. But Maggie needed more time before she could say that out loud, especially to her daughter.

"And why are you so, like, OK with it? It's *weird*," Pen said, now near tears.

"Oh sweetheart," Maggie said, gripping the steering wheel even though they were parked. "I'm so not OK with it." She laughed because she didn't know what else to do. "Actually, I'm really fucking angry. Not at your dad—well, OK, kind of at your dad, but mostly angry that it's happening at all—to me, to you, to our family." She blinked back tears, trying to keep the bitterness from her voice. "Mostly, I'm angry at myself for ignoring my feelings for so long." Her heart raced; her knuckles whitened around the steering wheel. She loosened her grip, taking a deep breath as she ran a hand through her unwashed hair. "I'm sorry, sweetheart," she said. "It's not your job to listen to me vent."

Pen wore a look somewhere between shock and approval. "Actually," she said, considering, "I think needed to hear that. In a weird way it helps to know that you're pissed off, too."

Maggie laughed and took a deep breath. "Fair enough." Then to her surprise, Pen leaned over and pecked her on the cheek.

"Bye, Mom." And then she was gone, leaving Maggie on her own in a stew of emotions.

Maggie leaned back and closed her eyes, the emotional exhaustion of the week washing over her. All she wanted was to go home, crawl into bed, and stay there for the rest of the day, the week, or maybe the year. Her instinct was to turn to Dan, to seek comfort from him, but she knew she had to learn to live without him as her only emotional support. So, instead, she dialed Rhea's number.

Rhea picked up on the first ring, sounding like she was in the car. "Hey. How are you?"

Maggie started to answer, but a strangled sob came out instead of words.

"Oh, honey," Rhea said, her voice low and soothing. "I know, I know. Everything sucks right now."

"I'm sorry," Maggie said after a minute, sniffling.

"Don't be. We get to have feelings, too, even while we're taking care of everyone else's."

Maggie almost laughed. "Now you sound like the therapist."

"Yeah, well, maybe you're rubbing off on me."

"Anyway," Maggie said, smoothing her hair, "how are you?"

There was a beat of silence, then Rhea spoke, her voice thick. "I think I found Josh."

Maggie sat up straight. "Where?"

"I mean, Brooks did, or at least he thinks he did. But I have an address and I'm headed there right now."

"Do you need me to come?"

"Thank you." Rhea's voice cracked. "Seriously, you don't know how much that means. But I need to do this on my own."

"Understood. But keep me posted, OK?" Maggie said. "I'm here if you need me."

"Thank you," Rhea said. "Truly."

After hanging up, Maggie went to put the car in gear and noticed Pen's phone on the passenger seat. Any other day, she would have taken it home and gifted her daughter the character-building experience of surviving the day without it. Today, though, after Pen's uncharacteristic display of affection, Maggie felt a burst of benevolence and turned into the Civitas parking lot instead of heading home.

By the time she found a parking spot and made her way

inside, the halls were quiet as the last students filtered into their classrooms. Banners in forest green adorned the walls for the centennial, and a large screen in the main hallway cycled through photos and bios of prominent alumni. Maggie recognized some names as VIP gala guests: *Richard Hoberman, CEO of Polygen Chemicals; Lorelei Wells, Anchor for Good Morning Atlanta; Trevor Park, Deputy Secretary of State under George W. Bush.* In frustration, Maggie balled her hands into fists and thrust them into the pockets of her long camel-colored trench coat. Tomorrow was supposed to have been a day of justice. Instead, it would be a celebration of fraud and deceit.

Holding Pen's phone, she headed to the office, where the ever-present Mrs. Kaminski greeted her. Maggie left instructions for the phone to be passed along to Pen and felt a pang at the sight of the locked records room door. After all the trouble they'd gone to, now nothing would come of it.

Turning to leave, her eye caught the brass nameplate next to Jerry's door: *Jerry H. Armstrong, Headmaster.* Seeing it made Maggie's blood pressure rise. It infuriated her that Jerry—and everyone else involved—should get away with this. But especially Jerry. All while people like Isaac and her own daughter paid the price for his gains.

"Are you all right, Ms. Reed?" Mrs. Kaminski was staring at her.

Maggie smoothed the scowl from her face. "I'm fine," she said curtly. "And it's Dr. Reed."

Feeling flushed and sweaty from rage, Maggie made a sharp left into the girls' restroom after leaving the office. She splashed cold water on her face and, at the sound of footsteps, quickly straightened up and grabbed a paper towel.

"Oh, hi," Farrah said, halting in the doorway. She was dressed identically to how Pen had been that morning, in a gray skirt and cardigan over a green polo. She looked at Maggie's dripping face and the wet paper towel. "Um, are you OK?"

Maggie was touched that the girl even noticed. A note of nostalgia reverberated in her heart, like a single guitar string plucked. Pen had been that way when she was younger, exquisitely tuned to her mother's emotions. Then she grew older and got lost in her own teenage swirl. But maybe they were finding their way back to each other. Their conversation in the car felt like progress.

"I'm fine." Maggie managed a smile.

Farrah shrugged. "OK." She continued past Maggie into one of the stalls, then stopped and turned around. "Hey, I can give them to you, right?"

"Give what to me?" Maggie asked, confused.

"The pictures. From my mom? She told me to text them to Pen because I could get her number from the student directory, and then to tell her to send them to you," Farrah said. "But if you're right here then I don't need to send them to Pen and everything, right?"

Maggie stared. "The pictures?"

Farrah pulled out her phone and unlocked it. "Here." She scrolled for a minute and then held it out to Maggie.

Maggie squinted and then zoomed in on the photo of a printout on the screen. "Holy shit." Recognition sweeping over her, she nearly dropped the phone. She looked at Farrah. "Do you have all of them?"

Farrah bit her lip with confusion. "Uh, maybe? I don't really know what they are, but she said it was important." She looked down. "And not to tell my dad."

Scrolling, Maggie saw that every document Anna had shown them was there. She lowered the phone to look at Farrah. "Wait, why couldn't your mom send these to me herself?" The convoluted communication made no sense.

Farrah shrugged and traced a circle on the ground with her toe. "I don't really know, I'm sorry." She looked at her watch.

"Anyway, I need to pee and I should get back to class before I get in trouble. So, um, do you want them?"

Maggie nodded so hard her neck cracked. "Yes," she said. "I definitely want them."

FIFTY-SIX

The GPS in Rhea's car was set to an address in south-west Atlanta, not far from the airport. When she'd seen the note from Brooks, she hadn't stopped to think. She'd simply turned around, walked back to her car, and punched in the address. Merging onto the freeway, she realized she wasn't sure if she'd locked the front door—or even closed it.

She was still in the flannel pajama pants and Atlanta United T-shirt she'd slept in. Normally, she'd at least put on leggings and a cute sweatshirt for school drop-off—not to mention a bra—but this morning she hadn't even swapped her fuzzy pink Ugg slippers for real shoes. They were still on her feet as she weaved around moving vans and eighteen-wheelers.

She'd called Brooks the minute she was in the car. "How did you find him?" she asked before he could even say hello.

"I had someone at work look into it based on cell phone pings and financial records," he said. Then he lowered his voice. "Which is against about a dozen laws."

"Thank you," she said, accelerating to overtake a minivan. "I mean it." The driver of the minivan laid on his horn as she cut in front of him.

"Where are you?" Brooks asked, a note of concern in his voice.

"On my way." The traffic in front of her slowed suddenly and she hit the brakes. "Crap."

"To the motel?"

The GPS beeped and began to recalculate. Rhea watched the "time to destination" click up. "Yeah, but I've hit traffic." She pounded the steering wheel in frustration. "Shit, shit, shit!" Not now, not when she was only a few miles away. What if she somehow missed him?

"Hey," Brooks said, his voice laced with worry. "Deep breaths. Do you want me to... maybe I should—"

"I'm *fine*," Rhea interrupted. "I just need to get there."

"OK," Brooks said. "But will you call me when you do? It doesn't look like the greatest neighborhood."

"Sure." Rhea began inching her way over into the right lane, setting off a chorus of honks from the cars next to her.

"I love—" he began.

She hit the disconnect button.

The dramatic reunion scene she'd been picturing, where Josh fell into her arms, was quickly fading from her mind. "This is not how things go in the movies," she muttered, inching forward. Then, with no rhyme or reason, traffic picked up again, along with her heart rate.

A few minutes later she was exiting the freeway as directed by the maddeningly calm GPS voice. "A little urgency, please?" Rhea glared at the screen on her dashboard. As she rolled through the streets she saw several boarded-up buildings. The only businesses seemed to be gas stations and check-cashing storefronts. Most of the houses had peeling paint and were surrounded by sturdy, chain-link fences.

Your destination is on the right, proclaimed the zen-like GPS lady. Rhea turned into the parking lot of the Skyway Budget Motel. Spikes of grass grew through huge cracks in the asphalt. The only other cars in the parking lot were a Chevy Cavalier that looked like it had once been red but had faded to a pinky maroon and a dented Nissan pickup truck covered in a layer of dust so thick it was clear this was long-term parking. Rhea let her eyes travel over the two-story stucco building with identical rows of wooden doors. Which one was Josh behind?

She locked her car and walked her fuzzy slippers across the parking lot to the door with a sign that said *Office*. Inside, it smelled like stale cigarettes and Fritos. "Hello?" she called. Somewhere a toilet flushed, and then a short man nearly as broad as he was tall walked in through the door behind the desk, still tucking his shirt in. He had a smooth, plump face and receding hairline, making him look like he could have been sixteen or sixty.

"Yeah?" he said.

"Hi," Rhea began. "So, ah, my son is staying here but I forgot his room number. I was hoping you could look it up for me." She smiled and shuffled forward, hoping her slippers were out of his view.

The clerk looked unimpressed. "Why don't you trying calling him?"

Rhea laughed and fluttered one hand in the air. "Oh, I tried, but his phone is off."

The man blinked. "Sounds like he doesn't want to see you then." Rhea's fake smile faltered. The man nodded outside to the parking lot at her shiny white Mercedes. "That you?" Rhea nodded, unable to trust her voice over the lump that had formed in her throat. The man looked her up and down. "Sorry, can't help you. Unless..." He raised his eyebrows.

"Unless...?" Rhea asked, then it hit her. "Oh!" This *was* how things happened in the movies. "Sure, um, see, the thing is I left my wallet at home. I was in such a hurry." She lifted up one leg and pointed to her slipper as evidence. "But I might have, like, a Starbucks card in the car." Her desperation was growing.

The clerk snorted and shook his head. "Sorry."

Rhea felt the tears start. "Please," she said. "It's really important."

"So is the privacy of our guests." Then he heaved himself down onto the stool and picked up a worn copy of *Guns & Ammo* magazine. "Now if you'll excuse me."

Rhea's frustration ratcheted up to anger and she had to keep herself from reaching over the desk and ripping the magazine out of his hands. Instead, she hurried back outside, her mind racing to come up with Plan B. On the way she stumbled in her slippers, stubbing her toe on a piece of buckled asphalt.

"Ow!" she yelped, bending over to clutch her foot.

"Rhea?"

She straightened up. There he was, on the walkway of the second floor, dressed in jeans and his old gray hoodie, his backpack slung over one shoulder. He shielded his eyes in the morning sunlight as he looked down at her.

"Josh!" she cried. Relief crashed over her with such force it took her breath away. He was here. He was safe. She tried to stand up but her legs wouldn't work. Instead she sank onto the asphalt where she was and the world went blurry with tears.

In seconds he was next to her, wrapping his arm around her shoulders. "Are you OK?"

She shook her head. She hadn't been OK in so long. And now what she wanted more than anything was to stop pretending that she was. "You left," she said. It came out more accusing than she meant it to.

Josh stiffened and pulled away, his hair flattened in the back where he'd slept on it. Though it had only been a week since she'd seen him, he looked older, his face tired and drawn. "What else was I supposed to do?" He stood up and jammed his hands in his pockets.

Rhea scrambled to her feet. "Stay, obviously!" Her voice cracked. "We would have figured it out. We can still figure it out."

Josh gave a harsh laugh. "Right, so I'm supposed to stay even though you left." In the sun his green eyes nearly glowed with emotion.

Rhea felt like a grenade had denotated in her chest. She stepped back. "You said you didn't blame me anymore."

Josh kicked at a loose piece of pavement. "Yeah, well, it turns out maybe I still do—at least a little bit."

The ache in her chest was so sharp Rhea looked down to make sure she hadn't been shot. "Come home," she begged. "Please. We can talk about it, with everything out in the open."

The piece of pavement broke free and Josh kicked to the side. "It's not my home," he said. "That's where I messed up. I got comfortable."

Rhea wanted to grab him, both to hug him and shake him. *That was the point!* she wanted to yell. She'd tried so hard to make him comfortable, to make a place for him in her family's life, but all she'd done was screw it up.

"Please," Rhea pleaded. "Please, let's start over."

Josh looked at her. "Pen's right," he said. "I'm not who you think I am. I lied about college, like she said. I lied about a lot of things." He glanced up at the sky, blinking rapidly. "I was worried you'd think—"

"I don't care," Rhea interrupted. "I don't care about any of that. I care about having you in my life." She wished she could make him understand that there wasn't anything he could tell her that would make her love him less. She knew now that while things may ebb and flow with Brooks, her love for her boys was constant and unconditional, whether she'd looked into their eyes the minute they were born or twenty-one years later.

"Does Brooks want me there? Or Will? Zane?" Josh asked.

Rhea's stomach dropped. "Look, clearly we all have a lot to talk about—"

Josh looked away, but not before Rhea saw his forehead creased in hurt. "Yeah, I thought so." He hitched his backpack up on his shoulder. "Look, maybe once I get on my feet we can be in touch or something. But I don't want any more charity." His face turned grim. "It's not worth it."

"Charity?" Rhea said, shaking her head as desperate tears leaked down her cheeks. "Josh, it's called family."

"Family, huh?" he said, like he'd never heard the word. Then he sighed. "Look, I'm heading out for a bit, I'd appreciate it if you'd leave in the meantime." Then he turned and began to walk away.

"Josh!" she called after him. "Josh!" She kept yelling, but he didn't stop.

Rhea tried to go after him but her sobs racked her insides and she couldn't breathe. She doubled over and cupped her hands around her nose and mouth, trying to choke back her cries. She finally made it as far as her car, leaning against it for support before mechanically opening the door and sliding into the driver's seat.

Let him walk away if that's what he needed to do, but she would never leave him again. She would be right here when he got back. She would sit in this parking lot the rest of her life if she had to. She buried her face in her hands.

After what could have been a minute or an hour, a knock on her window made her jump. She raised her head to find Brooks staring back at her. He opened the door and she fell forward into his arms, still sobbing.

"He won't—he doesn't want to—he told me to leave," she managed, gasping for breath and wiping her nose on Brooks's quilted vest and dress shirt.

"Shh," he said, pressing her face into his chest and rubbing her back. "Shh. It's going to be OK."

"What are you even doing here?" Rhea asked, her breath already slowing now that his arms were around her.

"I left work right after I talked to you," he murmured. "I know you said you'd be fine, but I wanted to be here if you needed me." He looked around. "Where is he?"

Rhea pointed down the street where Josh had disappeared. Brooks kissed the top of her head. "Stay here," he instructed, then climbed into his car and roared out of the parking lot. Rhea watched him round the corner and disappear.

She leaned back in her seat, her head throbbing. How had she ended up in the parking lot of a cheap airport motel with a son who didn't even want to see her?

Rhea wasn't sure how long she sat there, but her eyelids grew heavy and she let them fall closed. Then, as though through a long tunnel, she heard the sound of an engine. Opening her eyes she saw Brooks's car pulling slowly back into the parking lot. *Please, please, please.*

With the glare of the sun, she couldn't see in the window as he parked. The driver's side door opened and Brooks climbed out. *Please, please, please.* Then the passenger door swung open and there was her son.

Brooks stood next to the car as Josh crossed the parking lot and walked up the stairs. He continued down the breezeway to one of the doors and disappeared inside. It was all Rhea could do not to bolt out of the car and pound on the door, but she forced herself to sit. *Please, please, please.*

Finally, the door opened. Her heart leaped into her throat as Josh came out with a large duffel bag slung over one shoulder. He walked to the parking lot, toward Brooks's car, and tossed the bag in the trunk. Rhea rolled her window down as Brooks approached. He wore a tired but triumphant smile.

"We'll meet you at home," he said.

FIFTY-SEVEN

Anna set down the makeup brush and gazed at Farrah in the mirror. Her hair was curled into loose waves and Anna had applied a hint of blush to her cheeks and one coat of mascara to her already long lashes. Between the makeup and Farrah's glow of excitement at getting to dress up and attend a grown-up party, she looked stunning. Beautiful, but still thirteen, which is what Anna had been going for. She wasn't ready for Farrah to grow up yet.

"Can we do a tiny bit of eyeshadow?" Farrah whined. "Please?"

Anna shook her head. "Your father would kill me." As soon as the words were out she wanted to snatch them back. Anna shivered as they hung in the air. Farrah, though, remained unfazed, rooting through Anna's makeup bag. "Maybe a little of this?" She held up Anna's eyeliner pen.

Anna placed her hands on Farrah's shoulders and leaned her face close to her daughter's. Jerry could no longer pretend she needed to quarantine and a simple Band-Aid now covered the cut and bruise on her cheek. Farrah hadn't even mentioned it.

"You look beautiful exactly as you are," Anna said. Then she straightened up and opened a drawer. "But we can finish you off with this." She held up a square, pale pink bottle of perfume. "Close your eyes," she instructed, then spritzed in Farrah's direction.

"Mm." Farrah inhaled and opened her eyes. "Why don't you ever use any of this stuff?" She gestured to the perfume bottle and the makeup.

Anna gave a dismissive laugh and looked away. "I never go anywhere," she said, gesturing to her sweatpants and old black T-shirt. She dumped everything back in her makeup bag and zipped it shut. "By the way," she said, trying to sound casual. "Did you ever send those pictures to Pen?"

"Actually I gave them to her mom," Farrah said, turning to admire her profile in the mirror.

"To Dr. Reed?" Anna tried to keep the excitement out of her voice. "How?"

"I saw her at school." Farrah paused. "Was that OK?"

"Of course," Anna said, struggling to keep a triumphant smile from spreading across her face. Her plan had worked; Maggie had the emails. "Did, uh, Dr. Reed say anything about them?" Anna asked.

Farrah bit her lip. "You won't get mad?"

Anna's heart hammered. "Of course not," she breathed.

"She said, 'holy shit,'" Farrah reported.

Anna laughed with shaky relief. "Yup, that sounds like Maggie," she said. Then she squeezed Farrah's shoulder. "Come on, I can't wait to see you in your dress."

Jerry had taken Farrah shopping at one of the upscale department stores and the price tag attached to the dress they'd brought home had made Anna gasp. She thought wistfully of her bank account and the joy she'd gotten from seeing the number tick up, knowing she could spend it however she pleased. But that was gone now, along with everything else she'd worked for.

As Farrah stepped out of her shorts and tank top, Anna noted how her body was shedding the sharp angles of girlhood. She had yet to get her period, though in the last six months she'd graduated from her training bra to an A cup. She thought of Farrah growing into a woman under Jerry's watchful eye and her stomach lurched.

"What do you think?"

Anna looked up to see Farrah doing a slow twirl. She'd chosen a forest green sleeveless dress—a nod to Civitas colors—with a high neckline. A pattern of rhinestones glittered from the fitted top, and layers of tulle extended from the waist down to her knees to create a full, airy-looking skirt.

"Oh, honey," Anna said, her eyes filling with tears. "You look gorgeous."

"She does indeed." Anna and Farrah both turned to see Jerry standing in the doorway with a broad smile on his face. And though he looked handsome in his tuxedo with his copper-colored hair brushed to a shine, Anna wanted to recoil. "And to mark the occasion, I have a little something for you, Farrah." He pulled a small velvet box out of his pocket and presented it to her.

Farrah's eyes lit up as she flipped open the box, revealing a thin gold chain on which was nestled a single small diamond. Farrah gasped and she looked up at Jerry in excitement.

"I wanted the first diamond you ever got to be from your father," he said, taking the box from her and removing the necklace. Anna tried to swallow the bile rising into her throat. She had a diamond necklace too, buried deep in her jewelry box, but she'd received hers for an entirely different reason.

Jerry fastened the delicate chain around her neck and Farrah admired it in the mirror.

"Oh, Daddy, I love it," she said, flinging her arms around him. "Thank you!"

"You're welcome, darling," he said, patting her on the shoulder. "And now we'd best be off." He offered her his arm with a flourish. She giggled and took it, then looked at Anna, her smile fading.

"I wish you were coming, too, Mom."

Anna glanced at Jerry, trying to mask her hatred. "I'm better off resting, honey," she said. "You can tell me all about it when you get home."

As they hurried out the door, Anna felt a deep twinge of guilt, wishing she could pull Farrah back. Now that Maggie had the emails... well, Anna hadn't counted on her daughter being present to witness the takedown of her own father. Did this make her a terrible mother? Would Farrah be scarred for life? Yes, Anna decided with a stab of remorse, on both counts. She only hoped she'd be able to make it up to Farrah somehow. Before Jerry had found Anna's phone, she had pictured the happy years she and Farrah had ahead, just the two of them, with plenty of time to help her daughter understand why Anna had done what she'd done. Now, though, all of Anna's hopes were pinned on this one night in order to set them free.

But it had to be done. And there was no other way.

FIFTY-EIGHT

Wearing the fanciest dress she owned—a plain, calf-length black wrap number—Maggie examined herself in the full-length bathroom mirror.

"Didn't you wear that to my uncle's funeral?" Dan asked, passing behind her with a load of clean towels. He was dressed in joggers and a long-sleeve T-shirt from his most recent 10k race.

Maggie shrugged. "Probably." She dabbed at a small stain in her thigh region with a wet washcloth. For the millionth time, Maggie wished Dan was going with her to the gala. It would have been comforting to look for his face in the crowd when she commandeered the podium to make her announcement. As a mere volunteer, though, she didn't merit a plus one.

It was probably better he wasn't there, she reasoned. Given the awkwardness between them, she hadn't bothered to tell him her plan. Gazing at him in the mirror now, she thought about mentioning it, but stopped. It was time for her to start forging some independence outside their life as a couple.

"You look gorgeous," Dan said, smiling.

Maggie tilted her head and tried to smile back. "But not gorgeous *enough*."

His smile faded. "Mags, you know this has nothing to do with you."

She looked away and blinked back tears. "I know."

As Maggie entered the hotel ballroom for the gala, she felt a sharp thrill of anticipation, like being strapped into a roller coaster clicking upward. Surveying the sumptuous setting and well-heeled crowd, she waited for the usual anxiety of being out of place at Civitas events to come over her. To her surprise, it didn't. Because this time, she had a purpose.

She gazed around the ornate ballroom, with its sparkling chandeliers and floor-to-ceiling windows wrapped in gold curtains. Round tables topped with white tablecloths and flower arrangements in Civitas colors of white and forest green were scattered around the room. Tasteful jazz flowed from hidden speakers, mingling with the low rumble of conversation. At the front center stood a podium draped in white. Off to the side was a large projection screen, ready to be wheeled over when the official program started. That was when she'd need to be ready.

She spotted Rhea several yards away in a stunning rasp-berry-colored strapless dress, her bangs swept to the side and the rest of her hair twisted up onto her head. She stood with Tamara Gibbs and some other PA moms. As Maggie made her way over she noted how the group resembled a flock of brightly colored tropical birds, shimmering and strutting in their finery. She didn't even bother to try to slip into the conversation the group was having, but instead grabbed Rhea's elbow, pulling her away toward a quiet corner of the room. "We need to talk," she muttered.

Rhea let herself be steered away. "Thank God," she said,

downing what was left of her drink. "I swear Tamara thinks she's Joan Rivers, giving red carpet commentary."

"Did you find Josh?" Maggie asked in a low voice, once they were out of earshot.

A smile bloomed across Rhea's face. "Yes. Brooks found him. And he convinced him to come home"—her voice hitched on the word—"while we... figure things out."

"Oh honey, that's amazing." Maggie squeezed Rhea's shoulder. "I'm so happy for you." Then her face turned serious and she looked around. She clutched Rhea's arm and lowered her voice. "Rhea, I have them." She slipped her hand into her purse and pulled out a USB drive.

"Have what?" Rhea's brow creased in confusion.

"The files. Anna got them to Farrah, who—" Maggie shook her head. "Never mind. The important thing is I have them. *We* have them. The plan is back on." She narrowed her eyes with determination.

Rhea's complexion drained of color. "But I thought..." She shook off Maggie's grasp, trying to process her words. "No," she said sharply. "I can't. Not now. Not after..." She raised her eyes skyward in despair, then looked back at Maggie. "Brooks found Josh for me. He convinced him to come home. How could I...?" Then panic crossed her face. "And Will, he's here for the awards ceremony. He'll see everything!" Rhea shook her head vehemently. "No, no way. I'm sorry."

Maggie felt her elation fade. "But before, you said—"

"I know what I said," Rhea cut her off with a pleading look. Her hands trembled as she lowered her empty glass onto a nearby table. "But after everything yesterday... I can't be part of it."

"It's not right, Rhea," Maggie said, feeling a flush of anger as her voice grew louder. Several people nearby turned to look. "You know it's not. And we have a chance to fix that."

"Shh," Rhea warned, looking around. She pulled Maggie

toward a quiet corner. "Look, I know it's not right," she said tersely. "But—"

"I don't think you do know," Maggie interjected hotly. She raised the USB drive in the air. "What's happening—what we have proof of—is systemic fraud. And it doesn't only affect Brooks and your family and the other families who are part of it. It also affects all the ones who aren't. It's not a zero-sum game, Rhea. What Will and the other kids got, others didn't. Kids who actually earned it. Kids who need it in a way that someone like Will never will." She practically spat the last words.

Rhea closed her eyes for a long moment. When she opened them, her voice was heavy with emotion. "For as long as I can remember I've felt like an imposter in my own life," she said in a low voice. "Like, it was all so perfect it couldn't actually belong to me, especially after what I did. A happy marriage, a beautiful house, two amazing kids, plus the ability to give them things I could only dream of at their age. They've been skiing in Andorra, for God's sake! I didn't even know Andorra was a country, when I was their age." She let out a sound between a laugh and a strangled sob and blinked back tears, leaving dark, wet feathers of mascara streaking her upper cheeks. Then her face turned grim. "And I was right," she said. "I didn't deserve any of it. I mean, I abandoned my child." Her voice broke and she looked up at Maggie, her eyes twin pools of tortured guilt. "What kind of mother does that?"

Slowly, Maggie's face softened. "The kind of mother who knows she's not ready to be one," she said. She took a step toward her friend, placing her hand on Rhea's shoulder. "Rhea, you're a good mom. And all those years ago you made the best choice you could at the time." She paused. "You know what I'd say if you were my patient?"

Rhea blinked, listening.

"I'd tell you that at some point, you're going to have to forgive yourself." They stood in silence for a beat, then Maggie grabbed a napkin off a nearby table. "Here. You look like a well-dressed raccoon."

Rhea laughed through her tears and dabbed at her cheeks.

Maggie held up the USB drive once more. "This doesn't have anything to do with your choices," she said. "These are your husband's choices. And it's going to come out sooner or later."

Rhea gave her eyes a final wipe and gritted her teeth. "God-damn it, Brooks," she swore under her breath.

"Rhea," Maggie said, her voice soft but firm. "We have to do this. For everyone it impacts, but also for you, me, and Anna, and everything we've been through to get here."

Rhea closed her eyes again as if she could wish herself away to somewhere, anywhere else. She reopened her eyes. "Fine. OK. We'll do it. For the three of us." She looked around, her face grim. "But let me warn Brooks so he can get Will out of here."

Maggie nodded and reached out for Rhea's hand. Rhea clasped it briefly with a determined smile, then walked away.

FIFTY-NINE

Rhea made her way back across the ballroom to where she'd last seen Brooks, walking as fast as her high heels and long dress would let her.

"Hey, so what was that all about?" Tamara appeared out of nowhere and Rhea stumbled, twisting her ankle. "I mean, Maggie Reed?" Tamara continued, oblivious to Rhea's grimace of pain. "Since when are you guys so friendly?" She narrowed her eyes.

"We're on the gala committee together, remember?" Rhea said, bending over to rub her ankle as she scanned for Brooks.

"I guess that explains why she's here." Tamara sniffed. "I wouldn't exactly have pegged her as a 'major donor.'"

The sharp retort on Rhea's lips died as the emails Anna had shown them flashed through her mind. Initially fixated only on Will's name, now Rhea remembered another one from the list: Beau Gibbs, Tamara's son.

Rhea looked at Tamara in her long, shimmery dress and perfect blond waves cascading over her shoulders. She thought about all the time they'd spent together, at book club, couples' dinners, and even the occasional joint family vacation. And still

Tamara didn't know anything about Rhea beyond how many times a week she went to Pilates and that she preferred white wine to red. Nor did Rhea want her to. Despite their years of friendship, Rhea realized she felt no connection to Tamara. Especially now that she had Maggie and Anna, who after only three months knew her better than anyone—perhaps even Brooks. Only three months and she already didn't know what she'd do without them.

Standing there with Tamara now, Rhea knew they were finished. "I have to go," she said. Without waiting for Tamara to respond, she hurried away.

Ignoring the pain in her ankle, Rhea wove through the crowd as she continued to search for Brooks. Moving faster than her heavy dress wanted her to, she collided with a chair, nearly losing her balance again. Grasping for support, her hand found someone's shoulder.

Farrah yelped in surprise as Rhea grabbed her.

"Oof, sorry." Rhea steadied herself and released her grip on Farrah, who looked down at the dark, wet spot on the front of her green dress where her drink had spilled, her distress evident. "Oh honey," Rhea exclaimed. "I'm so sorry. Here, let me help." She grabbed a napkin off a table and began to blot Farrah's dress. "What were you drinking?"

"A Coke," Farrah said in a small voice.

Rhea nodded and tried to smile. "Well, it's a good thing you're wearing a dark color. Once it dries no one will notice."

Farrah looked at Rhea as she blotted, recognition sweeping over her face. "You're Zane's mom, right?"

Rhea straightened up. "Yes, why?" She'd been so worried about Will these past few weeks—but had something happened with Zane, too?

Farrah bit her lip. "My mom gave me this to give to you or Dr. Reed." She opened the clasp of her small sequined wristlet and produced a piece of paper folded up so small it looked like some kind of complicated origami.

Rhea looked at Farrah quizzically as she took the note from her and opened it. At first glance it appeared to be a grocery store receipt, but when she turned it over something was scrawled on the back.

I'm counting on you.

Rhea scrunched the paper in her fist. "Did you read this?" she asked Farrah.

The girl blushed. "Um, yeah." Then her expression turned to one of worry. "Is my mom OK?" she asked, a slight tremor in her voice.

Rhea frowned. "What do you mean, honey?"

"She hasn't been... I don't know... herself. Like, she was supposed to come tonight but she didn't." Farrah shifted in her ballet flats. "I feel like maybe something's not OK." Her bottom lip quivered.

Rhea felt a pang of worry. "I had no idea," she murmured. She put her hand on Farrah's shoulder. "Thank you for telling me. I promise I'll check on her later, OK?"

Farrah's face softened in relief. "Thanks." She bit her lip and her face tensed again. "But can you not tell my dad I said anything?"

Rhea nodded. "Of course." The worried feeling in her chest expanded. Then, spying Brooks on the far side of the room, she squeezed Farrah's shoulder. "There's something I have to do, but I won't forget my promise, OK?"

Farrah nodded as Rhea stepped away. Brooks's back was to her as he waved his drink in the air, speaking animatedly to someone. As she drew closer, Rhea saw it was Jerry. Her stomach flipped but she put on her best smile as she hobbled over to Brooks's side, Anna's note still balled up in her fist.

"There you are." Brooks slipped his hand around her waist.

"Rhea." Jerry smiled broadly. In his tuxedo with his self-congratulatory smile he looked like a puffed-up penguin. He leaned in to kiss her cheek as if they were old friends.

She stepped back, smelling the liquor on him. Of course he was celebrating. This was supposed to be his night. *Act natural*, she instructed herself as she clutched Brooks's elbow. "We should find our table, honey," she suggested, her voice hitting a high, bright note.

"I think we have a couple of minutes," Brooks said, checking his watch. Rhea felt a pang looking at him. He looked so dashing in his bow tie and tuxedo jacket, his shoulders broad and strong. Could she really go through with this?

She dug her fingers into his arm and leaned close to his ear, still smiling at Jerry. "I need to talk to you," she muttered.

Brooks nodded and flashed an apologetic smile at Jerry. "It seems I'm needed elsewhere."

"Of course." Jerry beamed. "I should take my place, anyway, I think we're about to get started."

Rhea watched Jerry stride toward the podium in front of the room as she dragged Brooks away and summoned her courage. This was bigger than her. "You need to leave," she said in a low voice once they were in the shadows at the edge of the ballroom.

He squinted. "Leave—like now?"

The lights flickered and everyone began to take their seats. The chair of the board of trustees, a tall man with a full head of silver hair that shone under the spotlight like a lighthouse beacon, stepped to the podium and tapped the microphone.

"Good evening, everyone," he said. "As you take your seats I wanted to thank you for joining us on this auspicious occasion: celebrating one hundred years of Civitas pride." There was a smattering of applause as people settled in at their tables.

"But everything's about to start," Brooks protested, looking confused. He offered Rhea his arm. "We should sit."

"We can't," Rhea said, looking around in desperation. "You need to find Will and get out of here. Now."

Brooks's frown of confusion deepened. "Sweetheart, what's—"

"... the honor of welcoming our esteemed headmaster, the man who has successfully guided Civitas into a new era..." continued the chair.

"Please. It's happening," Rhea pleaded, clutching his arm. "I didn't know—I didn't think—please. Go." She pushed him toward the exit.

"What's happening—" Brooks's question was drowned out by loud applause. Rhea watched Jerry move forward to shake hands with the silver-haired man, who clapped him on the back and whispered something in his ear. The two men shared a hearty laugh.

"Thank you, thank you," Jerry said, stepping to the podium and waving his hands to quell the applause.

"The Civitas Fund." Rhea strained to make herself heard. "Other people know, Brooks." His muscles tensed under her grip.

"What do you mean? Who knows?"

"... such an honor to serve a headmaster of this esteemed institution..." Jerry continued.

"People," she said, giving him another push. "And they're going public. Here. Tonight." She turned to scan the room. Where was Will?

The color drained from Brooks's face and he turned his head sharply toward the crowd. "But how—who?"

"And now for a video that offers a brief history of the last hundred years at Civita," Jerry announced. The three large screens around the room illuminated with an image of the Civitas crest and its inscription. *Scientia, labore, integritas.*

But as he stepped away from the podium, Maggie stepped toward it. "Actually, before the video I wanted to say a few words," she said, waving to the crowd. A murmur went through the room as people consulted their programs for Maggie's name, which was not there. Rhea watched Jerry try to step back up to the podium but Maggie turned, blocking his way. Rather than cause a scene, he was forced to stand there and smile as if it was all planned.

"Knowledge. Hard work. Integrity," Maggie read from the screen. "Admirable traits, to be sure." Only Rhea noticed the tremor in her voice. Next to Maggie, Jerry's posture was rigid and tight, like a slingshot stretched back. "But unfortunately," Maggie continued, "those traits are not present in a small group of Civitas parents, nor many of the faculty you know and trust with the education of your children."

The image on the screen changed from the Civitas crest to a photo of an email from Jerry. The subject was *Re: Civitas Fund*.

Rhea spotted Will at a nearby table with his fellow award winners and tears pricked her eyes. Her son looked so handsome in his dark suit and tie. Every day he was less like an awkward teenager and more like a man. She turned to Brooks, nodding in Will's direction. "Go," she instructed. "Now."

Brooks nodded, utter panic on his face. He turned to go, then stopped. "Wait, you're not coming?"

Rhea shook her head. "One of us needs to see what happens."

Brooks's face was twisted in shame. He gave Rhea a desperate look. "I'm so sorry," he whispered. Rhea gave a small nod, then watched as Brooks strode toward Will, exchanged a quiet word, then guided him toward the exit.

Behind Maggie, the screen flipped over to a list of the families and teachers involved. Jerry was now next to her, trying to edge her away from the podium with his body, his face a shade of reddish purple. The murmur from the crowd had turned into a loud, frenetic buzz, and Maggie bent closer to the microphone. "—these documents demonstrate a long record of bribery and fraud within Civitas, orchestrated by—"

"Enough!" Unable to reclaim the podium, Jerry pushed it away from Maggie. It toppled slowly, hitting the floor with a thunderous bang amplified by the attached microphone. "Security!" he shouted. "Do we have security?"

Maggie cupped her hands and shouted into the chaotic ballroom, "The documents are posted on the Civitas parents Facebook group! See for yourself!" As the hotel security guard moved toward her, she hurried toward the door Rhea held open.

They paused in the hallway, Maggie's face flushed, her bun coming loose as hair trailed down her shoulders. "I'm sweating," she gasped. "Oh my God am I sweating."

"How did you get all that on the screens?" Rhea asked. She felt like she'd stepped off a carnival ride: exhilarated but also like she might throw up.

"I showed the guy operating the laptop my gala committee badge," Maggie said, wiping her brow.

Down the hall, another door from the ballroom opened and the security guard scanned the hall, his eyes stopping on Maggie. "Ma'am," he said, striding toward her.

"Time to go," Rhea said, grabbing Maggie's hand.

"Ma'am!" the security guard called, breaking into a run. He pulled even with them just as they reached the exit to the hotel lobby and slammed his palm against the door to keep them from opening it.

Rhea whirled to face him. "What do you think you're doing?" she hissed. "Do you know how fast I can have you fired for detaining me against my will?"

He took a step back and put his hands up. "Fine, but she stays." He pointed to Maggie.

Rhea rolled her eyes. "We both know you don't have any actual authority here." Then she grabbed Maggie's hand and pulled her through the door.

Once they were through the lobby and outside, Maggie looked at Rhea. "Wow," she said. "You can be a real bitch."

Rhea smiled. "Lucky for you." She looked around. "Crap, I'm pretty sure Brooks took our car," she said.

Maggie looked around, then pulled out her phone. "OK," she said. "Uber it is. Which somehow feels very anticlimactic."

"I can't believe you just did that," Rhea said. She pressed her hand to her forehead, trying to process what had happened.

"You and me both," Maggie said with a slightly crazed laugh. "I might throw up. And I could really use a drink." She pressed her hands to her cheeks and opened her mouth in a silent scream. Then she looked at Rhea. "Wait, is Brooks...?"

Rhea sighed and shook her head. "I don't know."

Maggie consulted her phone. "Murad is one minute away in his Volkswagen Passat," she said. "So I guess we need to decide where we're going."

At that moment Rhea realized she was still holding Anna's note.

SIXTY

Anna watched the clock, her palms itching with a mix of anticipation and dread. The gala would be in full swing by now. Had it happened? Did everyone know the truth? She pictured Jerry's furious face, the shade of purple he turned when angry. Then her stomach dropped thinking of Farrah. Where was she during all of this? Anna hoped she hadn't been front and center to witness everything, under the scrutinizing eyes of everyone. "I'm sorry, sweetheart," she murmured. "I'll make it up to you for the rest of your life if I have to."

The sound of a car engine in the driveway sent a chill down her spine. She hadn't considered that Jerry would come back. Then it dawned on her that of course he wouldn't be handcuffed and hauled away immediately. Fraud wasn't murder, after all. Legal proceedings would take time—weeks, even months—before any charges were filed. She cursed herself; as a lawyer, she should have anticipated this. Of course he'd come home; there was nowhere else for him to go.

And he would be furious.

She scanned the living room like a caged animal seeking a place to hide. Then she stopped. No. No more hiding. No more cowering. Tonight the first domino had tipped, and she was the next one. With everything at Civitas out in the open, she'd go to the police and get a restraining order and he wouldn't dare violate it now that he was under a microscope. She was leaving. Tonight.

Anna tensed at the sound of footsteps on the porch, expecting Jerry's key in the lock. Instead, the doorbell rang. Startled, she hesitated, wondering if Farrah had somehow returned alone. Cautiously she approached the foyer as the doorbell rang again. Outside, she heard laughter, followed by familiar voices. Peering through the curtain, she spotted Maggie and Rhea, still in their gala attire.

Maggie caught sight of the movement of the curtain. "Anna!" she called, and stepped over to rap excitedly on the window. "Open up! Oh my God, we did it. We actually did it!"

Anna moved to the door, then stopped. She touched the alarm keypad on the wall and the screen sprang to life, a glaring red X reminding her of what would happen if she opened the door. Then, taking a sharp breath in through her nose, she turned the lock and threw the door open.

Immediately the alarm began a high-pitched squeal. "Front door open, front door open," a robotic voice said above the din.

"What the fuck?" Maggie yelled, cupping her hands over her ears as she stumbled over the threshold, wearing a black dress and heels.

Rhea was behind her, her hands also over her ears. "Can you turn it off?" she yelled, nodding at the screen.

"I don't know the code!" Anna yelled. But at that precise moment the alarm fell quiet and her voice echoed through the hallway.

Maggie lowered her hands from her ears. "Oh, thank God."

Rhea made a tsking noise. "How do you not know the code to your own alarm?"

Anna shook her head. "Jerry changed it."

Rhea looked confused. "And didn't tell you the new code?"

Shame flooded Anna, nearly silencing her as it had so many times before. But this time she fought her way to the surface of it and made herself speak. "I'm not supposed to go anywhere," she said.

Rhea's eyes widened. "*What?*"

Maggie stepped forward. "Anna, what happened to your cheek?" She pointed to the cut on Anna's cheek that was now scabbed over and had a faint, yellow bruise around it.

Anna opened her mouth to speak but she couldn't get the words around the tight knot of humiliation in her throat.

"Oh my God," Rhea breathed. "Anna, why didn't you say something?"

"I couldn't," she finally managed. Then she looked from Maggie to Rhea. "Is it... did you...?"

Maggie nodded and Anna felt the tears come. "Oh my God, oh my God, oh my God," she heard someone saying, then realized it was her. Her knees buckled and Maggie caught her from one side before she fell, and then Rhea from the other.

"Jesus, Anna," Maggie said once they'd helped her to the living room and deposited her on the couch. Her eyes traveled over Anna's stained sweatpants and limp, unwashed ponytail. "You look like shit."

"When was the last time you left the house?" Rhea asked, shooting Maggie a concerned glance.

Anna pondered this through the tears that had begun streaming down her face. "I'm not sure," she said, thinking of how the days had begun to blur together.

"How long, Anna?" Rhea insisted.

Again the wave of shame rose up, and Anna fought to keep it at bay. "Does it matter?" She looked up at Rhea, feeling a bittersweet mix of hope and defeat. Jerry's secret was out there, but now so was hers.

"Fuck yes, it matters," Maggie said, balling her hands into fists. Then she squared her shoulders. "Let's go."

Rhea nodded firmly, looking resplendent and powerful in her dark pink dress. "I'll get your things. Where's your bedroom?" Anna pointed, and Rhea disappeared down the hall.

"I'm getting another Uber," Maggie said, whipping out her phone.

"Did you see Farrah?" Anna asked, gripping the edge of the couch. Everything was happening so fast. She felt dizzy from a mix of relief that they were there and the panicked need to find her daughter. What if Jerry made good on his word and took Farrah away? "Is she OK? Where did she go? Is she with Jerry?"

"I didn't see her," Maggie said, her eyes flicking up from her screen where she was punching in Anna's address. "We, uh, made a pretty quick exit." She lowered her phone. "Five minutes," she called toward Rhea in the bedroom.

"Can I call her?" Anna reached for Maggie's phone.

"Of course," Maggie said, holding it out.

Anna dialed Farrah's number, which rang and went to voicemail. "It's me, sweetie," Anna said, trying to keep her voice from shaking. "Call me on this number as soon as you get this and let me know where you are, OK? I'll come get you. Love you."

Rhea hurried back into the room with a canvas shopping tote over her shoulder. "I grabbed a few clothes," she said. "Do you have your phone and wallet?"

Anna felt her back pocket out of habit, then remembered. Again shame gnawed at her. "Jerry took them," she said. The worry on Rhea's face deepened and she and Maggie shared a look.

"Our Uber will be here in two minutes," Maggie said.

"Let's wait outside." Rhea motioned toward the door.

"Wait for what?"

Anna's head snapped around in terror as Jerry loomed in

the hall, his eyes ablaze with icy fury. His tuxedo jacket was unbuttoned, his bow tie askew. Rhea swiftly moved to shield Anna. "Hey, Jerry," she said, flashing a forced smile. "We thought we'd take Anna out for a drink. In case you need some... space."

"Mm." He nodded calmly, then quick as a cobra strike he lashed out and punched the framed family photo on the wall. Glass shattered, sending Rhea jumping back with yelp. "I'm not a goddamn idiot," he growled. Anna felt fear grip her chest like a vise.

Ignoring his torn, bleeding knuckles, Jerry pointed to Maggie. "What the fuck is she doing here?" he slurred.

Maggie raised her palms in front of her. "Let's all take a minute," she said.

"Take a minute?" Jerry's voice was pure venom as he stepped further into the room. "You want me to take a minute? You lying cunt." He seized Anna's water glass from the coffee table and hurled it to the floor.

"That's enough," Rhea declared, unlocking her phone. "I'm calling the police."

"I'd advise against it," Jerry warned. With two swift strides, he reached the bookshelf beside the TV. Stretching to the top shelf, beyond Anna's reach, he retrieved something hidden behind the books. Anna gasped as she glimpsed the glint of black metal in his hand as Jerry cocked the pistol.

Jerry laughed and turned to her. "Changes things a bit, doesn't it?" He pointed the pistol at Rhea. "Put down the phone."

The phone slipped from Rhea's fingers and clattered on the floor. Then he swiveled toward Maggie, shaking his head. "I really didn't want things to come to this," he said. "But you forced me."

"Jerry, please," Anna whispered, her voice pleading as she stared at the gun aimed at her friend. *This is my fault*, she thought. *I shouldn't have dragged anyone else into this. Shouldn't have taken those files. Shouldn't have joined that stupid committee to begin with.*

"So here's what we'll do," Jerry said to Maggie. "First, you'll delete the photos you posted to the Facebook group."

Maggie raised an eyebrow. "You do realize they don't go away because I delete them, right?" she asked. "I mean, people have definitely screen-shotted them by now."

Jerry ignored her. "Second," he continued, "you'll post a message admitting you faked this whole thing after we had a dispute about your daughter. Then you'll withdraw Pen from Civitas and I'll magnanimously agree not to sue you for defamation."

"Yeah, no," Maggie said, crossing her arms. "Not going to happen."

A lightning bolt of fury shot across Jerry's face. "Just do it," Anna muttered in Maggie's direction. "Please. You don't know what he's—"

"Dad?"

Anna turned at the same time Jerry did, swinging the gun around with him. Farrah stood in the doorway, a long puffer jacket over her short green dress. Her eyes were wide and her face had drained of color.

"Farrah," Jerry said, startled. "I told you to stay in the—" His words cut off as he stumbled over the coffee table. He pitched backward and there was a dull thud as his head hit the end table.

The acrid scent of gunpowder filled Anna's nostrils a split second before the gun went off, like a whip being cracked next to her ear. Someone screamed, then everything was drowned out by a high-pitched ringing sound.

SIXTY-ONE

Dan picked up on the first ring. "Where the hell are you?" His voice was laced with worry.

Maggie laughed weakly. "So, funny story, I'm at the police station."

"What?" His voice rose. "Are you OK?"

"I'm fine," Maggie assured him. She shifted in the unforgiving plastic chair that sat in the drafty hallway. "I have to answer some questions, is all."

"Questions? Maggie, what's going on?" Dan's voice was frantic.

Maggie slipped off one of her high heels and massaged her throbbing toes. This was why she normally wore flats. "It's a lot to explain over the phone," she said. All at once tears flooded her eyes. *Delayed trauma reaction*, her therapist brain explained. "Do you think you could—"

"I'm already on my way," Dan said, and she heard the ding of the seat-belt indicator in his car.

She heard Dan before she saw him. "Sir, you can't—"

"I need to see her *now*," he said, rounding the corner. "Oh thank God," he said, catching sight of Maggie and rushing toward her. He wrapped his arms around her.

A stocky officer glared at him from the end of the hall, her arms crossed. "She'll be finished up soon, sir," she said. "Can I kindly ask you to wait—"

"I'll wait here," Dan said, his arms still tight around her.

"Please?" Maggie said, looking over his shoulder at the officer. "I mean, I had a gun pointed at me earlier, and—"

"*What?*" Dan drew back and looked at her in horror. "Are you all right?" He began scanning her body for a wound.

"Fine," said the officer with a begrudging sigh, and disappeared back around the corner.

"I'm OK," Maggie said with a quivering smile. Then she collapsed into his chest, biting back sobs.

"Shh." Dan stabilized her and lowered both of them into the chairs. "I'm here."

Once Maggie's breathing steadied, she told him everything: Farrah giving her the files. Anna's captivity. How oddly small the pistol had looked in Jerry's hands as he pointed it at her. The fear and confusion in Farrah's eyes when she walked in. The metallic tang of gunpowder on Maggie's tongue after the gun went off. Farrah's scream as the blood stain bloomed on Anna's shirt. Jerry's limp body on the floor. Rhea's voice through the haze, instructing her to call 911 as she yanked the shawl from her shoulders and pressed it to Anna's body to staunch the blood.

Dan kept his arm around her shoulder as she spoke, his grip tightening with each new revelation. When she finished, his face was ashen. "Maggie, you could have been—" His voice caught and she squeezed his leg.

"But I wasn't."

"And Anna?"

Maggie shook her head, her voice catching. "I don't know,"

she said. "She was conscious when they put her in the ambulance, but I don't know."

He buried his face in his free hand. "Oh my God. What if—oh my God," he said, his breathing shallow.

"Hey," Maggie said, giving his knee a squeeze. "Hey, I'm OK." Dan lowered his arm and looked over at her, his face wet with tears. "And anyway," Maggie continued with a shaky laugh, "aren't you supposed to be comforting me?"

Dan pulled her into a fierce embrace. They stayed like that, locked together, until a door opened at the end of the hall. Two police officers walked out, followed by Rhea. There were smudges of dark eye makeup under her red, puffy eyes and an orange fleece blanket hung around her shoulders, clashing with the dark pink of her rumpled dress. Maggie disentangled herself from Dan and stood as Rhea approached. The women reached for each other at the same time. The musky scent of Rhea's perfume mixed with the smell of stale coffee that permeated the hallway.

"Ma'am?" the older, taller officer said, addressing Rhea. "Ma'am, if you could please keep moving." His thick salt-and-pepper mustache stretched at the corners as he gave an apologetic smile. "We haven't questioned Mrs. Reed yet."

"Dr. Reed." The words echoed through the hallway as Rhea and Maggie said them in unison.

"Dr. Reed," the officer corrected himself.

"I understand." Rhea nodded. She squeezed Maggie's hand and followed the younger officer down the hall.

Dan stood and addressed the remaining officer. "Should she have a lawyer?" he asked.

"That's always her right, sir." The officer gave a serious nod. "But it's not necessary as she's only being questioned as a witness." He shook his head. "And it's pretty clear what happened."

The young officer returned to the hallway and Maggie turned to Dan. "I'll be fine," she said.

He pulled her toward him and kissed her forehead. "I'll be right here," he said, gesturing to the chairs.

Maggie trailed the officers to a small conference room. It smelled faintly of synthetic vanilla, a scent she traced to a white plastic Glade Plug-In in the outlet in the corner. As she sat down across from the officers she wondered who had taken care enough to both notice that the room needed freshening and to purchase and install the Plug-In. Neither of the officers across the table seemed the type.

"Thank you for meeting with us, Dr. Reed," began the older officer. He had a weathered but not unpleasant face, with a sprinkling of deep pockmarks across both cheeks. "Especially in light of the traumatic situation you've been through," he continued.

"We're hoping you can walk us through the evening, starting from when you arrived at the victim's house," the younger one jumped in. His face was round and pale, his skin so smooth Maggie wondered if he'd ever had to shave.

Maggie's stomach lurched at his use of the word "victim." She leaned forward. "Are there any more updates? About Anna?"

The older one shook his head. "She's still stable, as far as I know," he said.

"She's lucky it was only her arm," the younger one offered.

"Excuse me?" Maggie placed her palms on the table and narrowed her eyes. "*Lucky?*"

"Well, yeah, considering the circumstances—" began the young officer.

"Do you have any idea what she's endured with that... *man?*" Maggie shuddered, unable to find a word detestable enough to describe Jerry.

The young officer leaned away from the table. "Look, all I'm saying is—"

"As far as her injury goes, your friend will be fine," interjected the older officer, frowning at his colleague. "As for the other... factors, we're taking the situation very seriously."

Maggie crossed her arms and sat back. "Good."

The older officer offered her an encouraging smile. "Now, I know you must be anxious to get back to your husband outside, so would you mind walking us through the events of the evening? Start at the beginning."

Maggie paused, considering. Because who was to say where the beginning really was? Was it the moment Anna opened the door to let them in earlier that night? Or was it when Maggie had wrested control of the podium from Jerry at the gala? When Anna had taken the documents from Jerry's office? When Maggie had sat in the wine bar, her leg pressed against Isaac's as he revealed the truth about Civitas? Or further back to the first time the three of them had gathered at Maggie's house and found Isaac's resignation letter mixed in with their lists? Or was it even before then, the first time Jerry had laid a hand on Anna? The day Maggie had married her best friend, unaware that one day he'd fall in love with his other best friend? The day Rhea had walked out of the hospital and left Josh behind?

"Dr. Reed?"

Maggie blinked and found the two officers staring at her.

"Are you all right?" the older one asked. "Do you need some water?"

Maggie shook her head. "I'm fine," she said. "So, the beginning..."

SIXTY-TWO

Brooks was pacing the lobby of the police station like a caged lion when Rhea emerged, still in his rumpled tuxedo, the tie undone and trailing around his neck. "Oh thank God," he said when he saw her, sweeping her into his arms.

"Please get me out of here," Rhea whispered. She felt numb, her legs unsteady, her vocal cords barely functioning. In the conference room where she'd been questioned she'd shivered so violently the older officer called for a blanket to be brought in. Realizing it was still around her shoulders now, she shrugged it off, leaving it to lie on the lobby floor like roadkill. She leaned all her weight on Brooks and he half-carried, half-dragged her out to the car. All she wanted was to see her family.

Her family. Her heart skipped as she thought of Josh. She looked at Brooks as he climbed into the driver's seat. "Is Josh...?" She hesitated, unsure she wanted to know.

"He's still there." Brooks smiled gently. "Everyone's there, waiting for you. Let's go home."

As they drove, Rhea recounted what had happened in broken phrases. The gun pointed at Maggie and then at Farrah as Jerry jerked around in surprise. How everything went into slow motion as he tripped and toppled backwards. The crack of the gun and the flash of light, so bright for a split second she'd thought lightning had struck the house. Then Jerry's groan of pain right as his body went limp. The sound of her own dress tearing as she threw herself onto the ground to grab the gun. Anna's shocked, white face as the blood bloomed on her shirt-front. Maggie, trying to make herself heard to the 911 dispatcher over Farrah's screams.

Rhea stared out the car window as she spoke and fingered the angry red blister that had sprung up on her finger where she'd grabbed the hot barrel of the gun. She pressed it now until the pain brought tears to her eyes, just so she would feel something.

Brooks drove with one hand on the steering wheel and kept his other one wrapped around hers. When they pulled into the driveway, Rhea looked over at him, suddenly remembering.

"Wait," she said. "The gala—what happened?" She'd entirely forgotten about the first half of the evening. It felt like a movie she'd seen once, a long time ago.

Brooks's face tightened. "Let's not talk about it now," he said. "You've had a rough night."

"Please," she said. "Tell me."

He shifted in his seat, his face grim. "The pictures of the emails are already everywhere. I came clean with our family lawyer. He's referring me to a friend who specializes in white-collar crime."

White-collar crime? Rhea's head spun. Was that what this was?

"I'm sorry," she said. "God, Brooks, I'm so sorry."

"No." He shook his head. "I am. It was fucking stupid of me. And I deserve whatever comes next."

"You're a good person," she said, her voice breaking under the weight of all of it.

He turned to her, his eyes red and wet. "I'm not," he said. "But I'm going to try to be better."

"Is Will...?" Rhea's voice trailed off.

Brooks brushed away the tear that had snaked down his face. "He's OK. He's going to be OK." Then he unbuckled his seat belt. "Come on, everyone's waiting inside. They've been so worried."

With his arm around her waist he led her to the door. Inside, the boys sat in a row on the couch, as if posed for a photo. Zane jumped up first, hurling himself toward Rhea. "Mommy!" he cried, burying his face in her neck and nearly knocking her off balance with the force of his hug.

"Hi, baby," she said, twisting her fingers into his hair. Will wrapped his arms around both of them, his face streaked with tears. "It's OK, sweetheart," Rhea said. "It's all OK."

"A guy on my team lives across the street from the Armstrongs," Will sniffled. "He saw the ambulance, and the stretchers coming out of the house. I thought—" He choked up.

"Shh," Rhea said. "I'm OK."

"Boys, let your mom sit down, at least," Brooks said.

Will and Zane loosened their embrace only slightly. Rhea lifted her face from kissing Zane's hair and saw Josh nearby, shifting uncomfortably, looking anguished. Had it really been only yesterday that she'd gone to the motel to find him? How had time sped up so drastically?

"Hey," he said, his eyes red.

"Hey." She reached out to take his hand and led him to the couch, along with Will and Zane. Sitting there with some part of her body touching each of her three boys, she finally felt totally safe. Not only for the first time that evening, but possibly for the first time ever.

SIXTY-THREE

SIX MONTHS LATER

Anna worried about the weather forecast all morning as heavy, gray clouds darkened the sky. Now, though, as the doorbell rang, the sun poked through and patches of blue appeared like a promise overhead.

"I'll get it!" Farrah called.

"Oh no you won't!" Anna replied, sprinting ahead, her smocked yellow midi-dress billowing around her. "This is our first party in our new place—I get to answer it!"

They arrived at the front door at the same time, nearly crashing into each other as they yanked it open together, giggling.

"Happy housewarming!" Maggie cried, holding up a bottle of champagne adorned with a giant silver bow. She wore loose white linen pants and a black and white striped T-shirt. Her hair, which had grown longer, was loose and wavy. She grabbed both Anna and Farrah in a tight hug. "Don't worry," she said to Farrah as she released them. "We brought something for you, too." She held out the brown paper shopping bag in her other hand, revealing the three pints of Jenni's ice cream nestled inside.

"Yum, cookie dough!" Farrah grabbed the bag and spun away in her short, flouncy blue dress and coordinating Nike Dunks.

"Hey, manners!" Anna elbowed her.

"Thanks, Dr. Reed!" Farrah called over her shoulder, dashing away to the kitchen.

"Anna, hi," Dan said, following Maggie and kissing Anna on both cheeks. He'd started wearing his hair shorter recently, which brought out his cheekbones, and he sported new Clark Kent glasses. "Wow, the place looks great," he said, looking around.

"I *love* the coffered ceiling," Fernando said, entering and kissing each of her cheeks. He was shorter and stockier than Dan and wore a lavender button-up shirt rolled up over his muscular forearms. "And see how she organized the books in color order," he said, poking Dan in the ribs and pointing to Anna's rainbow of books on the built-in shelves.

Dan rolled his eyes. "We can't agree on how to do ours," he explained to Anna. "I keep telling him you can't find anything by color! Alphabetical is the only way to go."

"And while we argue about it they sit in boxes in the middle of the living room for us to trip over," Fernando complained. The two men exchanged a smile, making it clear that they were anything but unhappy with each other.

Anna caught Maggie's eye, gauging her friend's reaction to the couple's banter. "Welcome to my life," Maggie said, giving Anna a smile that was somewhere between rueful and amused. "Also, I'm going to need a drink."

Anna laughed. "Coming right up." She linked arms with Maggie as they walked to the kitchen.

The townhome was smaller than their previous house, but Anna had filled it with soft rugs in warm, earthy tones and colorful art she'd found at thrift stores, giving it a cozy feel. Anna hadn't wanted a penny from Jerry in the divorce—a good thing since he was flattened by mounting legal fees as he continued to appeal his twin court cases of financial fraud and domestic violence. Anna had wanted to be free of him in every sense of the word, and now that she was working full-time and Farrah was in public school, she was making it work.

"So," Anna said once they were out of earshot of Dan and Fernando. "How's it really going?" She, Rhea, and Maggie had met for dinner the night Dan officially moved out a month ago, but they hadn't had a proper catch-up since then.

Maggie gave a resigned sigh. "As well as it can, I guess. He's still around all the time, and now Fernando, too. Which is good, actually, since he's the only one who understands Pen's calculus homework enough to help her."

Anna plucked two champagne glasses from the counter and pulled a cold bottle from the fridge, unwinding the metal cage from around the cork. "But..." she prompted.

"But it's hard," Maggie admitted, her mouth sagging downward. "And awkward. And now I have to learn how to cook, ugh." She frowned, watching Anna struggle with the cork. "Here, give it." She took the bottle and opened it with a flick of her wrist and a satisfying pop. She poured two glasses, and they clinked them together.

Anna took a sip, enjoying the pleasant fizz of the bubbles as they traveled down her throat. "But Isaac cooks, right?" she said, switching to a topic she knew would get a smile from Maggie.

Maggie blushed. "He does."

"You should have brought him!"

"I thought about it," Maggie admitted. "But we're taking it slow, you know?"

Anna nodded. "Oh, I know." She reached out and squeezed Maggie's shoulder, overwhelmed by gratitude for their friendship. Slowly over the last few months she'd told both Maggie and Rhea all she'd been through with Jerry. They now knew everything about her, and they loved her still. This,

Anna had finally come to see, was how a relationship was supposed to be.

The doorbell rang again, and Farrah thundered toward it. Anna laughed. "I think she's more excited about this party than I am." She ran her finger around the rim of her glass and her voice grew quiet. "You know in twelve years we never once had anyone over to our house?" she said.

Maggie set her glass on the counter and put her hand over Anna's, her eyes brimming with compassion. "I wish I'd known," she said softly.

Anna shook her head. "You couldn't have. I mean, you didn't even know *me* until nine months ago."

Maggie puckered her lips in shock. "Months? How is that possible? God, it feels like years."

Anna raised her eyebrows. "Yeah, well, a lot has happened."

"Mom, your boss is here!" Farrah called.

Anna squeezed Maggie's arm again and headed toward the foyer where Donna stood, holding a bottle of wine and dressed impeccably in crisp cream-colored pants and a hot-pink blouse with large, gold buttons.

"Thank you for coming." Anna smiled.

Donna looked around. "Really I wanted to see your house to make sure I wasn't paying you too much." Then her face softened. "But you know I wouldn't have missed it. Congratulations, Anna. I'm proud of you."

Anna teared up in spite of her earlier pledge to herself not to cry. "Thank you," she said. "For everything."

When Anna had called Donna from her hospital room the morning after everything happened, Donna had blown in like a hurricane thirty minutes later, the paperwork for a restraining order already filled out. She'd sat with Anna through every police interview, and once Anna was ready, she'd gotten a friend to take on her divorce pro bono.

"No waterworks," Donna warned her. "Today is for cele-brating. Now, where can I get a drink?"

"I'll show you," Farrah said, appearing at Anna's elbow and grinning. She was relishing her role as co-host.

People arrived in steady bursts after that: the retired teacher who lived next door and was teaching Farrah to play bridge, several women from the neighborhood book club Anna had joined, a handful of Farrah's friends from her new school, and Sydney from Anna's office along with her boyfriend.

Farrah and her friends circulated trays of mini quiches and bacon-wrapped figs. The crowd spilled out of the small living room onto the patio, which Anna and Farrah had decorated with strings of twinkly white lights and pots of red and pink geraniums. Anna had initially nearly killed the flowers from neglect and then panicked overwatering, but then Farrah had taken over and now their small garden flourished.

With the patio door open, the heady, lemony scent of magnolia from the tree next door wafted in. The gentle tinkling sound of the windchimes outside mixed with the soft jazz playing in the background and the low, lazy buzz of conversa-tion and laughter. Anna leaned against the wall in a corner of the room, a feeling of contentment washing over her.

Despite the smaller house she now lived in, her life felt bigger than it ever had. She had a job where she was respected and valued. Her home was full of friends and laughter. If she wanted to, she could fall into bed that night without cleaning up; the only consequence in the morning would be a messy house. She could laze on the couch with a magazine without looking over her shoulder, and let the laundry pile up. Farrah could behave like a teenager, stomping and yelling (which she did) and Anna didn't have to shush her out of fear. They could eat ice cream for dinner and leftover pizza for breakfast. There were no eggshells to walk on, no tripwires to avoid, no other shoe that would inevitably drop.

The doorbell sounded, rousing Anna from her reflection, and she made her way across the room.

"I'm so sorry we're late," Rhea exclaimed, hugging her. Her face was free of makeup and dark tendrils of hair snaked down from her messy bun. In her simple white sneakers and navy T-shirt dress she looked years younger than she ever had when leading a Civitas PA meeting. "Will's game went into overtime."

"I thought she was going to get us kicked out for yelling at the ref," Brooks said, raising his eyebrows at Anna.

Rhea shot him a look. "It was a bad call!"

"Whatever you say, honey," he said, patting her shoulder. His hair had grown shaggy since Anna had last seen him, and salt-and-pepper stubble graced his chin. He looked relaxed in jeans, a gray T-shirt, and All Birds, more like a West Coast venture capitalist than the ex-CEO of a pseudo-government cybersecurity firm.

Things hadn't been easy for Brooks—and by extension, Rhea—in the aftermath of what the press was calling the "Civitas Coverup." Brooks had pled guilty to multiple counts of mail and wire fraud for his role. He'd stepped down as CEO of Ironwall and his court date was set for that summer. As a lawyer, Anna knew the best he could hope for was a hefty fine and minimal jail time in one of the nicer private prisons. But, Rhea assured her, they were prepared for the worst, and were ready to have it behind them.

Brooks's final act as CEO had been to make sure Josh had a job at Ironwall—a real one, not an internship, and that it came with tuition reimbursement while Josh took night classes toward his college degree. Then he and Rhea had pulled the kids from Civitas, as had nearly half the parents there, and moved to a small town an hour outside of Atlanta, where Will was currently dominating the high school basketball team and Zane had been cast in the lead role of the middle school's production of *Finding Nemo*.

Brooks wandered off to circulate, and Maggie came over with a glass of champagne for Rhea. "So," she asked, "how's country life?"

Rhea scrunched up her mouth. "Actually," she said, "I don't hate it. I mean, yeah, I miss Whole Foods and good sushi—and you guys, obviously—but it's not without its charms." She took a sip of champagne. "Will's on the high school's float in the Memorial Day parade next weekend. Apparently the whole town turns out for it."

"Very Norman Rockwell," Anna observed.

Rhea laughed. "Yeah, I guess. Like, I know the whole simpler life thing is kind of a cliché, but I'm digging it. The kids aren't in a million activities, Brooks is home every night, and I refuse to join the PTA so my life is basically drama-free."

"Other than being married to a future felon," Maggie said cheerfully.

Rhea snorted. "Yeah, there's that. But apparently everything has a silver lining—Will's guidance counselor is convinced he'll have a good shot at an Ivy if he writes his essay about it."

Maggie choked on her champagne.

"They're probably not wrong," Anna said. "I mean, I'd read that."

"How's work?" Maggie asked, recovering. A few weeks ago, Rhea had accepted a job as a part-time editor for the local paper, finally putting her college English degree to work.

Rhea shrugged. "Good. Last week I got to write five hundred words about a rabbit infestation that's destroying people's lawns." She raised her eyebrows. "Turns out it's a *very* divisive topic. Pulitzer material for sure."

Anna laughed. "I can't wait to read it."

"Do you think you'll move back to the city?" Maggie asked. "After the trial, and... everything?"

Rhea made a face. "I don't know. Honestly, we're doing pretty well there. Josh comes out on the weekends sometimes, which is nice, but he's got his own apartment in Midtown." She sighed. "And also a girlfriend, who I want to hate on principle, but really she's very sweet."

"You sound happy," Anna observed, smiling.

"Oddly, I think I am," Rhea said. "Like, who would've thought?" She looked at Anna. "What about you? How are you? Any updates on... him?" She grimaced.

Anna shook her head. "Jerry isn't allowed to contact me. Technically he has supervised visits with Farrah, but she's decided not to see him." She shifted and glanced around, feeling a flash of her old nervousness, as if talking about Jerry might conjure him in the flesh. Then she straightened up and tried to smile. "Anyway, I'm fine. It's over now. He's out of our lives."

Maggie and Rhea exchanged a look. "Anna," Maggie said softly. "It's us, remember? You can cut the 'I'm fine' bullshit."

"But I *am*—" Anna began, then stopped. Her hand had begun to tremble, the champagne sloshing over the side of her glass. Setting it on the counter, she wiped her hand on her dress and gave a shaky laugh. "It's infuriating," she said slowly, looking up at her friends, "how much I still think about him. The bad times, sure—" She winced and shook her head to rid herself of the painful memories exploding in her head like fireworks. "But also the good ones." She closed her eyes, unable to put into words the conflicting swirl of emotions inside her. Jerry had done unforgivable things. Yet, she'd loved him, once. And that was what she was most ashamed of. That she'd stayed so long, not out of fear, but out of love. Even after that love had faded to a faint whisper, Anna had still held out hope. And that hope had nearly killed her.

She opened her eyes and looked at Maggie and Rhea, wishing she could say all of this to them—and saw on their faces that she didn't need to. They understood.

"Of course you think about him," Maggie said, reaching for

Anna's hand. "He's part of your story. But he's not the whole story."

"Far from it," Rhea said firmly. She gestured at the party. "Look at you. Look at all this. You're just getting started."

Anna blinked rapidly. "I promised myself I wouldn't cry today," she said.

"It's your damn party, you can cry if you want to," Maggie observed, and all three women broke into laughter.

"To us," Rhea said, picking up Anna's glass and holding it out to her. "Still standing."

"Still standing," Maggie repeated.

Anna took a deep breath, then smiled and raised her glass. "Still standing."

A LETTER FROM THE AUTHOR

I want to say a huge thank you for reading *Things We Never Say*. I hope you were as hooked on reading about Anna, Maggie, and Rhea as I was on writing about them. If you'd like to join other readers in hearing all about my new releases and getting access to bonus content, you can sign up for my Storm newsletter:

www.stormpublishing.co/caitlin-weaver

You can also sign up for my personal newsletter—I promise I'll never send you nonsense.

www.caitlinrweaver.com/contact

If you enjoyed this book and could spare a few moments to leave a review, that would be hugely appreciated. Even a short review can make all the difference in encouraging someone else to discover my books for the first time. Thank you so much!

A writer's job is to put their characters into impossible and uncomfortable situations. In *Things We Never Say*, this was most acutely the case with the character of Anna. Sadly, she is not alone. According to the National Coalition Against Domestic Violence, in the U.S. nearly twenty people are abused by an intimate partner every minute. Someone you know is likely one of them.

Intimate partner violence is a widespread yet often invisible truth for so many women, and I did not enter lightly into writing about it. I hope I managed to convey how isolating and dangerous it can be. If you are experiencing abuse, there are people and organizations who can help. I urge you to seek them out.

At the core of this book is a story about the transformative power of female friendship. It's a theme that resonates profoundly with me because it mirrors my own life. I would not be here without the myriad women who have cheered for me, laughed with me, and held my hand when I needed a good cry. I'm eternally grateful for their presence, love, and friendship.

I also recognize that making friends as an adult is hard! We can be reluctant to make ourselves vulnerable enough to forge a true connection with someone—but if we let that fear get the better of us, we risk missing out on potentially life-changing relationships. Just ask Anna, Maggie, and Rhea.

Thank you again for being part of this amazing journey and I hope you'll stay in touch—I have so many more stories and ideas to entertain you with!

Caitlin Weaver

www.caitlinrweaver.com/contact
www.threads.net/@caitlinrweaver

facebook.com/CaitlinRWeaver
x.com/caitlinrweaver
instagram.com/caitlinrweaver

ACKNOWLEDGMENTS

First, a huge thank you to the whole Storm Publishing team for all their support and for a truly stellar publishing experience. Particularly to my brilliant editor, Vicky Blunden, who believed in this book when it was only an idea, and helped me shape it into something I'm proud of.

Thank you also to my early readers and critique partners, who offered wise and honest feedback that strengthened this book immeasurably: Amanda Vink, Jen Craven, Kerry Chaput, Layne Beckner Grime, Ojus Patel, and Renee Ryan.

I'm grateful also to two organizations in which I've found wonderful connections and resources, the Women's Fiction Writers Association and the Toronto Area Women Authors.

To my parents, thank you for always being proud of me (and for always being willing to talk about my books!)

Thank you, Marcus, for putting up with my ridiculous, self-imposed writing deadlines, for keeping me grounded, for celebrating with me, and for helping me care for our two delightful but exhausting small people.

To my small people, Elijah and Sam, I love you both more than chocolate milk and donuts. Thank you for being proud of me even before you could read a word of anything I'd written.

A huge thank you to *you*, dear reader! With so many books in the world you chose mine, and for that I am very grateful.

Finally, at the heart of this novel is a story of the power of female friendship. So, it feels only right to close by expressing my gratitude to the many amazing women I'm fortunate enough to call my friends. The world we live in is wild and wonderful, but also brutal at times. I could never survive it without my friends, nor would I want to, because they make the hard times bearable and the good times that much better. I'm so grateful to have a collection of kind, compassionate, whip-smart, and gut-achingly funny women in my corner. You know who you are. I love you.